Indebted

THE PREMONITION SERIES

VOLUME 3

AMY A. BARTOL

Also By Amy A. Bartol

Inescapable: The Premonition Series Volume 1
Intuition: The Premonition Series Volume 2

For Molly, my childhood friend and partner in trying to be
And also for Max and Jack, my reasons to be

Contents

Evie

Jade Dragon Mountain

He can't hide from me. Not that he is ever trying to, but still, it's impossible. I know where he is at all times. I'm attuned to his voice, his scent…the beat of his heart. It's my favorite pastime these days—stalking Reed. It's a game that I play without knowing that I'm playing it half the time. I hunt him…and he lets me.

As I move through the stone-walled courtyard, my bare feet make almost no sound while I traverse the stone bridge that crosses a tranquil plunge pool in the middle of the Zen garden. A galaxy of stars reflects in the water beneath me, but they can't hold my attention. Reed is ahead of me, in the bedroom of the Naxi-inspired pagoda that we have been sharing. He is poring over maps of the surrounding terrain. Reed studies these maps frequently, learning everything he can about Lijiang and the Jade Dragon Mountain that has been our base of operations since we arrived in China last week. He has been very busy—too busy.

My eyes shift to the banyan trees in the courtyard that nestles just outside the wide doorway of the pagoda. Illuminated red-paper lanterns are strung within its weeping branches. The light from the lanterns turns my pale skin pink as I creep behind the twisted trunk. I scan the slate porch from my leafy position. The doors are open, allowing the breeze to pass freely through the room on either side. Reed hasn't looked up from his seat at the desk, but that doesn't mean that he doesn't know I'm here. I can't tell if he has sensed that I'm stalking him; he never gives anything away.

I study him for a moment. His dark brown hair has gotten longer than how he had been wearing it in Crestwood. But, I like it; it looks very sexy. His body is curved at sensual angles, making me want to touch him, to feel the raw power beneath his skin. His wings are in, so he looks completely human, well, as human as Reed can look. Since he is absolutely ethereal, I can't see him as anything but angelic now.

When I look up at the arcing, gray tiled roof of the pagoda, I try to see if there is another way in—a sneakier way because I want to take him by surprise—jolt him out of his tactical plotting. He has been singularly focused since our arrival: amassing an angelic army, one strong enough to match Brennus' army.

I shiver at the thought of Brennus. With a little luck, Brennus and his army of Gancanagh are half a world away. Reed is going to great lengths to protect me from Brennus. He has literally gone to the other end of the Earth to accomplish it, bringing me to China, to the secluded base of an enormous snow-capped mountain. Reed and Zephyr have been working on little else other than keeping me safe from the Gancanagh leader who wants to make me his queen…his undead lover. I cannot allow that to happen. If he gets me back and bites me, there is little chance that I will not succumb to his venom and become one of them. Now that I'm reunited with Reed, I'm desperate to remain with him, no matter what.

A deep, primal growl, coming from the room ahead of me, makes me freeze where I am. I glance back towards the room and every hair on my arms rises. Another low, rumbling growl drifts to me on the gentle breeze that stirs wisps of my auburn hair around my face. The sound is terrifying in its intensity, and every instinct within me urges me to run from it as my eyes connect with the animal making it. Fierce green irises peer at me from the enormous, sleek cat crouching before me near the doorway to the pagoda. A shiver of pure fear shakes me as I involuntarily take a step back from the massive, black killer.

"Nice kitty…" I whisper to it, taking another shaky step backward and feeling the rough bark of the tree at my back, impeding my retreat. "Reed!" I whisper urgently as I cast a glance into the room, but he is no longer seated at the desk. My eyes fly back to the aggressive animal in front of me that is stalking me like I'm a luscious morsel. The panther's muscles tense, looking as if it will pounce on me at any moment. I look wildly around for an exit strategy while several killing scenarios pulse in my mind, but I would rather try to run than try to engage it.

"Stay!" I command the panther, watching its tail swish as it deepens its crouch. It's not listening to me—it looks like it's enjoying itself immensely, the way its tail is swishing back and forth like it's toying with a mouse or something. Hide, I think when the hackles rise on its sleek, black pelt.

"Reed!" I squeak, watching the cat bound up and lunge in my direction. I squeeze my eyes closed, holding my breath and pressing deeper into the tree, waiting to feel its sharp teeth sink into my skin.

"Evie!" Reed says from directly in front of me. I open my eyes to find that Reed is no more than inches from my face, looking at me with panic in his eyes. His powerful, charcoal-gray wings are arcing out around him, shielding us. His hand reaches out, cupping my cheek.

I try to answer him, but I find that my entire body has gone rigid, so much so that I cannot even move my mouth to speak his name. Reed braces his hands on my shoulders, running his hands up and down me as if he cannot see me. "Evie?" he says again, but this time he is leaning into me, inhaling the air near my face. I try again to speak, but I feel stiff.

It takes several seconds for some of the rigidity in my limbs to ease, allowing me to inhale a breath as I look up into the face that I love above all others. "Big cat!" I utter as I attempt to pull away from the tree at my back only to find that I am entangled in vines that are holding me to the trunk. Looking at my arms, they have taken on the rough texture of the mossy bark of the tree. When I raise my hand to my eyes, my fingers appear twig-like as I wave them in fascination and horror. "What the—" I inhale a sharp breath, my eyes move to Reed who is observing me now with a mixture of pleasure and awe on his face.

"You can relax, Evie, it's not permanent," Reed says to reassure me. "You are evolving. It appears, you can change your shape now," he says, smiling and raising one of his brows.

"But—I'm a tree," I whisper to him, feeling appalled by my current shape. I have taken on the mossy exterior of the banyan tree that I'm near.

"Yes, but you are not really a tree—you are more like a chameleon," he says as he leans his face closer to my ear, brushing his cheek to mine. I feel the suppleness of his skin against the course roughness of my current bark-like exterior, which causes a small measure of my fear to melt away.

"Buns said that when this shapeshifting thing evolved I would be able to turn into butterflies or something, like she can." I respond, remembering how Buns had shapeshifted before my eyes into a swarm of butterflies to demonstrate her angelic ability to me. I'm beginning to feel disappointed over my current predicament of looking like some sort of woodland sprite. I was really hoping to be more like my friends, the angels, when I evolve, not less like them. I'm already too different from them, being only half angel and the rest of me human that this is just one more thing that will separate me from being seen as one of them.

"This is so much better than that, don't you see? he asks me, grinning.

"No, from this angle, it kind of sucks, Reed." I reply, stepping forward as my knees become less rigid, enough to bend them as I pull away from the tree that I had become a part of only moments ago. Reed wraps his arms around me, steadying me by pulling me tight against him.

"No, what you can do is so much better. We have to change into something animate, like butterflies or a panther, but you can change your shape to reflect your surroundings…camouflaging yourself. It's a huge asset—" Reed says with excitement until I cut him off.

"That was *you!*" I accuse him as my skin begins to take on its normal hue and I start to change back to my original form. "You changed into a panther!"

A chuckle escapes Reed then as he hugs me tighter. "I thought for sure you knew it was me, but you didn't, did you?" he asks.

"I probably should've known. Your eyes were the exact same color as the cat's eyes. I've always thought that you move just like a cat," I say, gazing up into his perfect face that is mere inches from my own. "Is that the only shape you can take or will I be running from a bear next time?"

"Oh, I can take many, many forms, but I cannot do what you can do—my forms have to be animate. I have to change into an animal, but you—do you think you can do other forms?" he asks with excitement. "Do you think that it has to be just a solid form—can you be liquid…air?"

"I don't know." I reply honestly.

"What were you thinking right before you changed?" he asks. "Were you thinking 'tree?'"

"No…I was thinking 'hide,'" I reply.

"Of course!" Reed exclaims. "I have someone I want you to meet. His name is Wook and he is a Virtue angel, like Phaedrus, who has lived near the Naxi for several centuries. He has studied the Tibetan monks and the Naxi mystics and has seen some of their abilities. Perhaps, he can instruct you to hone your human capabilities. I will not be much help to you in that, as I have little insight into the human side of your nature."

"You think this is a human trait?" I ask Reed with a skeptical look, "Because I can't think of any human that I know of who can change herself into a tree."

Reed's eyebrow arches in a cunning way. "I don't know, maybe it's a hybrid trait. No angel I know of can do what you just did. It is very unique," he says, and awe is back in his voice again.

"I don't even know if I can do it again, Reed," I reply, feeling strange about what just happened. *This evolution into a stronger being is really disturbing. It takes the awkwardness of puberty to a whole new level,* I think. "And maybe we shouldn't tell anybody about it."

"Why not?" Reed asks, frowning now while scanning my face.

"Because it's unnatural and…freakish," I reply as casually as I can, but I'm a little too stiff just yet to pull off the casual shrug.

"Evie, you don't understand, this is 'mad cool' to use your words. It makes you even more dangerous!" Reed breathes and I can see he is really charged up about this. Searching his face for signs of disgust, I can find none. He is truly happy that I can now turn into something else. He must be worried that he will not be able to defend me. He must see this as one more evasion technique.

"You think a tree is great? Just wait until I can turn into an avalanche and come pouring down the mountain," I smile as my arms creep around his neck, pulling his face closer to mine.

"Yes...that would be excellent," he exhales near my ear, causing shivers to run through me.

"So you don't think this is sketchy?" I ask, feeling relief that he is not repulsed by me.

"I don't question your existence anymore. I'm just grateful you are here, in any form," he says, picking me up off of my feet and carrying me back into the bedroom.

The bedroom is sparse by the standards of western culture. It contains only a rather large bed and a writing desk. The silk clad bed is centered in the room on a low wooden platform. Folding doors open up the entire room to the outdoors so that the room is exposed to the gardens and courtyard. High stone walls that allow for privacy from the other pagodas cluster around our own to shield the entire pagoda.

"Isn't it your job to question my existence?" I ask him teasingly.

"No, my only job was to annihilate fallen angels and since you are not one of them, you do not fall under my job description," he says, nuzzling my neck and placing me in the middle of the bed. Following me down, he brushes the hair back from my forehead with his strong fingers while gazing into my eyes. "But now that we are bound to one another, I have a new job description."

"You do? What's your new job?" I ask, fascinated by the sensual turn of his mouth. I trace his lips with the tip of my finger that has now returned to normal.

"To love Evie..." Reed says, holding each of my fingers to his lips, kissing them one by one, "to protect my brave girl from any evil that would dare to speak her name..." he continues, tracing a line from the palm of my hand to my wrist. "To make her enemies bow at her feet..." he murmurs before his lips find mine. I recognize his words as those that Buns had translated for me after Reed said his binding vow to me in his Angelic language. He had promised to protect me in the descriptive detail that only a Power angel can convey. It is a little overwhelming to hear the words, even when it may become necessary for him to actually do all of the things he is saying in order to protect me.

"Reed," I whisper against his lips, "that's kind of scary—"

"Thank you," he replies smugly just before deepening the kiss as he completely misinterprets my words as a compliment. At the moment, I'm in no mood to correct the mistake. Kissing him back, I reach my hand up to gently stroke his wing. A soft groan escapes Reed at my touch. *I love that.*

Slowly, Reed's hands move over my body and the feel of his hands on my bare skin, although exquisite, is shocking because I just realize that I'm not wearing anything. I squeak in surprise, causing Reed to pull back a little so that he can look into my eyes again in question.

"My clothes?" I ask.

"Trees don't wear clothes," he replies. "That very pretty little sundress you were wearing is now shredded at the base of the tree outside."

"Oh…and where are your clothes?" I ask as a smile forms in the corners of my mouth, allowing my eyes to rove over his perfect form.

"Panthers don't wear clothes either," he shrugs.

"How…convenient," I sigh, wrapping my arms around his neck again and pulling him back down to me.

Just then, Reed's cell phone rings annoyingly on the desk behind us. I tense, holding Reed tighter to me. "You are absolutely forbidden to answer that phone," I whisper against his lips.

"What phone, love?" he says as his head dips lower, tracing my collarbone with his lips, causing shivers to course through me as desire ignites within me. I relax as the phone stops ringing and my hands slip to his hair, threading through it and feeling the softness of it.

I trace the line down his neck to the place just above his heart, the place where my wings have been symbolically branded into his skin. I'm still fascinated by the way in which it appeared, after the binding ceremony that linked Reed's life to mine was performed. I can't hide the smile of satisfaction that this mark on him makes me feel. It literally screams the word "mine." Reed is mine and no one can take him away from me now. Our fates are connected and I know that I should feel guilty for tying him to me like this. My fate can turn on a dime because most angels, when they first see me, believe that I must be evil, since no angel before me has ever possessed a soul. But, in this moment, I can't feel anything but happy that we are here together.

"What are you thinking right now?" Reed asks, searching my face.

"Umm, right now?" I ask, trying to stall because I just got caught reveling in the fact that he's mine. "I was just thinking about how happy I am, about this," I say, feeling myself blush as I trace the shape of my wings that are imprinted on his chest.

"This makes you happy?" he asks and when I nod he speaks to me in Angel as he tenderly kisses the symbol of his wings etched into my skin just above my heart.

"What did you say?" I whisper because I haven't learned to speak his language yet. It still sounds like music to me, like a hypnotic lullaby.

"Me, too," he replies, smiling broadly.

"That sounded a bit more than 'me, too,'" I counter, but Reed's smile only broadens. "And I wasn't just thinking that, I was also wondering what I can call you." At his look of confusion, I go on, "I mean, you're not my 'husband' because you're much, much, more than that…" I trail off, waiting for him to say the word for what we are to each other, now that we both swore a vow to be united for eternity.

He responds immediately in Angel and I smile because I should've known that it wouldn't be English. It sounds like he said *aspire*, but in a way that is so beautiful that it makes tears form in my eyes. My voice is thick when I ask, "Translation?"

Groaning, Reed's brow creases in a frown. He is struggling with the limitations of the human language, so I wait patiently for him to answer me. "It means… 'beloved above all others'…

'most revered, venerated'…but it's more than that. It means 'essential to me' and 'a part of me.'"

I can't help the tears that slide from my eyes. "*Aspire*," I whisper to him as my hand cups his cheek. His eyes close briefly, savoring the contact.

Feeling Reed tense against me, his eyes snap open as he begins scowling right before he says, "We are busy right now, Zephyr. Come back later." Quickly, Reed covers me with a silk sheet.

"I cannot. This is important," Zephyr replies from somewhere outside of our room. From the distance, it sounds like he is standing near the stone bridge that traverses the jade-tiled pool in the courtyard. "You should answer your phone."

"He was kind of in the middle of something, Zee. He still is—how important is it?" I ask, trying to hide the irritation in my voice.

"Very," Zephyr replies and at the sternness of his voice, dread seeps through my senses. It causes my arms to tighten on Reed, pulling him nearer to me.

"What's wrong?" I ask, hearing panic in my own voice.

A growl comes from Reed then as he leans his forehead to mine. "Evie, it's okay, whatever it is, I'll take care of it," Reed says soothingly, trying to calm me down. But I have seen too much lately to be reassured by his words.

"Is it Dominion?" I ask Zephyr with my heartbeat drumming rapidly in my chest. I look over at Reed, seeing that he is already dressed. Startled by the fact that I hadn't even seen him move, I sit up in the large bed, pulling the sheet up with me and wrapping it securely around me. Zephyr steps into our room then, keeping his eyes averted from me as he speaks directly to Reed, but he is using their Angelic language that I can't understand. My panic increases. Zephyr never does that. He never speaks in anything but English when I'm around because he knows I can't understand them. Something is wrong—something big— something he doesn't want me to know about.

"What's going on, Zee? What's happening?" I ask them, looking between their two faces as they debate something important. If it has to do with Dominion, it can't be good for me.

The military headquarters that acts as the high court for Power angels put me on trial for my life only days ago, which wouldn't have been so bad if they hadn't also told me at the time that the only right I possess, in their eyes, is the right to pray for death.

The next thought has all of the blood draining out of my face as I whisper, "Brennus—"

"No, it is not Dominion or the Gancanagh," Zephyr says rapidly, trying to reassure me, but still, his face looks grim.

There is only one other thing that can be severe enough to warrant a look like that from Zephyr and my brain can't even move past the name that it keeps repeating over and over like a prayer. *Russell.* Something inside my heart recoils painfully.

"Where are Brownie and Russell?" I ask them, watching their faces closely. They both have blank expressions, like they are deliberately trying to hide something from me.

"They are still in the Ukraine," Zephyr replies in a calm, soothing voice. "They are being very cautious and they are moving slowly. Many, many kingdoms have risen and fallen in that part of the world. Many beings still like to call it home," Zephyr explains with patience.

I exhale a breath that I didn't know I was holding as his words register with me. I know I won't be able to completely relax until they are both safely with us. I still have no idea yet what I will tell Russell about Reed and me. I made Buns and Zephyr promise that they wouldn't breathe a word of the binding vows to either Brownie or Russell. I have to be the one to tell Russell and it has to be face to face. No matter what I say to him, he's going to have a hard time understanding why his soul mate has chosen to bind her life to someone else, after all of the lifetimes we have shared together. I don't think I'm going to be able to explain it to him, my need for Reed. I don't even understand it. All I know is I tried to live without Reed and it was impossible. I was dying inside every day.

"Maybe we should go to them. We can pick them up and bring them back here," I say, because I'm extremely worried about them. Brownie is a Reaper angel, and although she's immensely stronger than a human, she does not possess the brute strength of a Power angel. Russell is part Seraphim angel and part human, like me. His strength will soon rival that of Reed and Zephyr, and all other Power angels, but he has not fully evolved yet, so he is at a disadvantage should he run into a fallen angel…or Brennus.

"Zee and Buns are going to go to the Ukraine. They are leaving within the hour," Reed says softly and I bounce out of the big bed and head to the bathroom wrapped in a sheet. After I retrieve some clothing on the way, it only takes me seconds to change before I am back in the room, searching for a bag to pack some of my clothes.

When I look up, I see Zephyr and Reed studying me. "How long will it take us to get there?" I ask, trying to gauge what I will need to take for the trip. Buns has done some shopping for us, but Zephyr has been attempting to lock her down. He has been trying to explain to her that she is a target for the Gancanagh, too, since she is my friend, but she doesn't want to listen to him. She has never really had to take any of this into consideration before because she is a divine Reaper angel. Since her job is to negotiate for human souls, she has essentially been immune to the fighting taking place between divine Power angels and the Fallen. As for other beings, they too, leave her alone because of her divine status. But the Gancanagh have vowed to get me back. They have even gone so far as to attack Dominion's compound while I was there to "rescue me." It would be nothing to them to use Buns to get to me and I can't have that.

"You are safer here for now, love," Reed says and he uses his sexy voice when he says it.

My eyes narrow because I'm onto his attempts to soothe me, I say, "I want to go, too. I can help, if there's trouble."

"No, you cannot, not right now, Evie," Zephyr replies in a low tone, like he is talking to a child. "You are too emotional right now."

"I can handle whatever comes, Zee, I promise. I'll be fine, trust me." I reply, not looking at him and continuing to pack my clothes into the bag.

"Evie, listen to me," Zephyr insists as he moves nearer to me in order to make me look at him. "I can see that you believe that, but I can prove to you, right now, that you are unable to separate yourself from your emotions."

"Zee, I'm fine—really. Let's go," I insist, crossing my arms in front of me in defiance.

"Brennus has Russell," Zephyr says quietly.

Panic hits me and I struggle to take the next breath. My heart twists and pounds in my chest as my hands shoot out to grasp Zephyr's forearm so I won't fall down. Flashes of Russell's smile, his face, the way he looks at me when I enter the room come to my mind in an instant. "How?" I breathe, searching his face. "We have to go now! I have to talk to Brennus—he will listen to me—"

"Shh...Evie, it's okay. The Gancanagh don't have Russell," Zephyr says with a soft tone, putting his warm hand over mine to comfort me. "I said that to emphasize my point. Right now, you will do anything, agree to anything, in order to keep the ones you love safe. *We* can't have *that*."

"That was mean, Zee," I accuse him with a grimace as my hand trembles underneath his. Reed hovers near me and I can tell by the look on his face that he wants to jump in and comfort me, but he is trying really hard to hold himself back from doing it.

"I am sorry you think so," Zephyr replies with an even tone; his amazing blue eyes reflect his regret. "I have decided that I need to take a different approach with you from now on."

"Oh yeah, have you decided on the scare-me-half-to-death approach?" I ask with a salty tone in my voice as I look at him.

"No. My approach will be to emphasize what is best for you. I will be your mentor and the first thing that you will learn is that we will protect you from now on, not the other way around," Zephyr says. "The word is out about you, Evie, and it is trickling down like rain to even the lowest level of demons. Many will come for you and they will die. We are organized and well equipped to deal with them, but you must listen to us and believe that we have your best interests in mind.

"I already know that, Zee," I reply rapidly. "But, you have to understand that I have *your* best interest in mind as well."

Some of the sternness leaves his face then as he glances over at Reed and then he looks back to me again. "Evie, you are a Seraph and it is in your nature to guard and protect, but we are ancient warriors while you are still very young and have had little training. You have been born on the front line of a battle that you are still ill prepared to fight. I will train you so that, one day, you may fight at my side. I promise that I will teach you all that I know so you will become very powerful, like me."

Hearing the sheer arrogance of his last words makes a small smile curl in the corners of my mouth. I move forward and put my arms around his waist, hugging him tight. "It's hard for me to remember you're scary old, Zee, because you look as young as me."

"I *am* scary old and you will listen to me from now on," Zephyr replies as he picks me up off of my feet and gives me a bone-crushing hug.

"I'll hang on your every word if you let me come with you to get Brownie and Russell," I whisper to him because it's hard to talk when all of the air is being squeezed from me. "You can explain all of the strategy that you have planned to protect me."

"Nice try," Zephyr replies, setting me back on my feet, "but there is little chance that I will take you to the Ukraine with us. You are staying here with Reed. I am sure you will find something to do while we are gone."

"How come Buns gets to go and I don't?" I ask Zephyr as I pull away from him.

"Reed will have his hands full watching one wild card. He does not need another unpredictable female to pin down," Zephyr replies.

"Are you sure that's the reason, Zee, or is it that you can't be away from Buns?" I ask, watching him close.

"Is it my fault that neither of you respects authority?" Zephyr counters gruffly, but I can see that he is worried about Buns and unwilling to let her out of his sight for too long. Since we have been here, it is rare to find one without the other. Zephyr guards Buns close. Several plots take shape in my mind as I consider ways to make Zephyr take me with him to get Russell.

Seeming to read my mind, Zephyr says, "Reed is staying here alone. What if he needs your help?"

"Zee!" I exhale as if he drenched me in icy water. He knows me well enough to know that I can't seem to tear myself away from Reed for very long. I'm constantly monitoring him at all times. A part of my brain is always tracking him. Reed explained that it's instinctual for Seraphim to protect what they consider theirs. I don't think that I can stop doing it, even if I wanted to. I reach out involuntarily to Reed, hugging him to me. His arms immediately wrap around me, encompassing me in a feeling of security.

Zephyr grunts in satisfaction. He knows he has just outmaneuvered me and so do I. "We are leaving soon, Reed. I want to go over some things with you before we go."

"I will meet you in your rooms in a minute," Reed says to Zephyr over my shoulder, snuggling me closer to him. Zephyr nods and is gone in a fraction of a second.

"It's going to be okay," Reed whispers against my hair.

I'm quiet because I know better. My dreams have made it horrifyingly clear to me that something big is coming. It's so big and terrifying that I have trouble remembering what I dream when I awake. My conscious mind keeps trying to blot it out, denying what the future holds in store for me. A word keeps filtering through my mind: *kazic...kazic...mer.* "Do you know the word 'kazic?'" I ask Reed as my cheek leans against his shoulder.

Reed stiffens and replies, "It means 'to destroy.' Where did you hear that word?" he asks me quietly.

I ignore his question. "What does 'mer' mean?"

"It means, 'the great,'" Reed responds instantly. "What is this about?"

"I don't know," I reply, giving him a smile as he pulls back to look at me. His eyes narrow, telling me he is not buying my attempt to cover the fact that his answers have freaked me out.

"Again, where did you hear those words?" Reed asks with persistence. He wants to interrogate me about it and I really don't have many answers for him.

"I think I may have dreamt them," I reply, resting my cheek back on his shoulder.

"What else did you dream?" Reed asks in a low tone, his hands running up and down my back gently.

"I can't remember," I say.

"Try," Reed replies, brushing his lips against my hair.

I tip my face up to meet his. "I will, I promise," I breathe against his lips as I kiss him. Reed's phone rings again on the desk.

Leaning his forehead to mine, Reed gazes into my eyes, "That is Zee. Let me speak to him and I will be right back, and then it will be just you and me…alone."

The thought of being alone with Reed without the potential of being interrupted is a delicious one. "Okay," I agree in an instant, causing a grin to appear on Reed's face. He kisses me one more time and then he is gone from sight.

Left alone in the room, I look around for something to do. There is a television in the next room, but Chinese T.V. is really weird and I can't understand much of it because I can't speak their language either. The commercials are bizarre, too. There is always some sort of huge, stuffed animal mascot bouncing around on the screen holding the product and looking jovial. It reminds me of Yo Gabba Gabba!

Spotting Reed's new laptop on the desk, I open it up and log on to the Internet. I love this computer; it's uber fast. Surfing the Internet for a while, I check the Facebook website under Leander Duncan. Russell has been using his site that I had set up for him to correspond with his family and me. He has post-ed pictures of Brownie and him as they have been traveling through Europe in the last week. He has written about what he has seen. I especially like the picture of them traveling through the rural vineyards in France. He looks stoked.

I post a note on his wall, telling him that I miss him and I'll see him soon. I do miss him. He is my best friend, but I don't know how he will feel about me after I tell him what I've done. I try not to think about it and move on to other web-sites. I really want to talk to someone about how I should tell Russell about what happened between Reed and me while I was at Dominion's chateau. I need some advice. I wish that I could ask Uncle Jim what I should do. The thought of my uncle sends waves of sorrow through me because I miss him, too. There has to be someone I can talk to about this.

Molly, I think as my adolescent friend pops into my mind. Summer is almost over and she will be going back to Notre Dame soon for her sophomore year. I haven't spoken to her since I left Crestwood with Russell. I was afraid to contact her, because if I let her know where I was going, Reed could have persuaded her into revealing it to him. His uncanny ability to use his voice to persuade humans would've rendered Molly unable to refuse to answer any question that he asked her. If she had any clue where I was all summer, he could've found out instantly and been there to take me back to his home.

I couldn't allow that to happen at the time. I was sure that the only way to protect Reed from being seen as a traitor to his own kind, the divine angels, was to leave him so that when Dominion caught up to me, he wouldn't be executed for helping me. I didn't know that Dominion would arrest Reed and Zephyr anyway and torture them to find out what they knew about me. I also didn't know that while Reed was being tortured, the Gancanagh, the undead vampire-like species that wants me to give up my soul to become one of them, was targeting me. *Maybe it's better if I try to avoid telling Molly how I had spent my "summer vacation,"* I think, cringing at the lies I'll have to come up with to protect her from all of this.

I know that Molly has probably emailed me a zillion messages, but I haven't checked them because I had been afraid that Reed could have been able to find me if I logged onto my email. Now, with all of Brennus' resources and the fact that he has ransacked both Reed's house and my storage unit to collect all of my possessions, I think it's pretty safe to assume he is monitoring things like my email. *Creepy vampire*, I think as Brennus' face looms in my mind.

He may be monitoring my email, but that doesn't mean I can't send Molly one from a different account. With that in mind, I create a new account under a fake name and write her a quick message, telling her that I'm alive and that I need to talk to her. Sending the message, I contemplate what I can tell her when she writes me back. Maybe I can say that I had an opportunity to travel that was just too good to turn down. While thinking about different excuses, an email alert window pops up on my screen. *Molly must be online*, I think excitedly. I look at the message line, it reads: "I miss you."

Quickly, I open up the message, but it's blank. It has an attachment to it so I click on the attachment and I wait briefly while a video feed sets up. Curious, I watch as a dark, hazy room comes into focus. Loud, bangin' music is playing in the background of the video as the camera pans past several colorful looking individuals. It looks like this is some kind of nightclub filled with scenesters. The camera is moving down a dreary, graffiti enshrined hallway. Panning around, there are several emos standing near the wall watching a band that is in the back of the club on the stage. The camera moves again to the bar where people are milling around trying to get the attention of the bartender.

Slipping in and out of focus several times, the cameraperson uses the lens to scan the crowd near the band that has just started playing a whiny cover song. The thumping of the amps and flashes from a strobe light make the video chaotic as I try to see what this is all about. The camera is slowly coming back into focus and is zeroing in on one particular individual who is milling around with a group of friends. I recognize Molly immediately. She is sipping her drink coyly, holding it close to her as she laughs at something someone leaning near to her is saying. I can't see her companion well because he has his back to the camera.

I reach out and my hand trembles as I touch the screen where Molly's image appears. She looks exactly the same, like nothing has changed with her. Seeing her smile again at whatever the person next to her says, she doesn't even move when the tall man reaches over and gently touches her cheek, caressing his fingers down it. The look on Molly's face slowly changes; her flirty smile seems to sag. My throat tightens and I find it hard to take the next breath.

The man turns then, looking at the camera behind him. Walking towards it with the stealthy grace of a supernatural predator, his eyes never waver from it. His face is exactly the same as the image I have of him in my mind. His eyes have an iridescent shine in their watery-green depths, piercing with intensity. His ebony hair is artfully falling over his arching eyebrows and the planes of his face are just as beautiful as they ever were—as exquisite and youthful as they had been on the day that Aodh, his Gancanagh sire, had changed him from a faerie into a parasitic creature. Nearing the camera, he poises before the lens, like he is looking directly at me. "*Mo chroí...*" Brennus breathes. Hearing Brennus call me "my heart," I instantly feel the burning infection of his venom within my blood flare up in response to his voice.

CHAPTER 2

Missing Pieces

I feel all of the scars in me that Brennus has left behind as he continues to speak to me in his video message. "I missed ye at da chateau—'tis sorry I am for da mistake I made dere. I should have come ta ye meself, na sent da fellas," Brennus says with regret, not looking away from the camera. "Finn tought we should be cautious. He said I may need ta send an ambassador ta ye—he tinks I may have hurt ye a wee bit too much when I tried to change ye. I tink he is right about dat, but I should have come ta ye meself, nonetheless—if nuting else den ta make ye see whah ye mean ta me."

"I'm jus a shadow on the floor wi' out ye, Genevieve," Brennus murmurs and his words are just barely discernable over the music in the background of the club. "I have lost all sense of purpose, save one, and dat's ta find ye. Ta be so close ta ye and ta lose ye—'tis almost more dan I can endure." Brennus pauses then and the lack of light from the camera hides the true pallor of his skin. He almost looks normal, except for the fact that he is unearthly beautiful. In the haze of the club, no one would ever know that he is an undead faerie. He looks like a supermodel and no human could detect the sweet, cloying smell that the Gancanagh emit from their toxic skin. He is the perfect lure for any young female: the ultimate killer.

Brennus runs his hand through his dark hair and holds it to the back of his neck as a pained expression crosses his face. "I know ye will na believe dis, but I plan on doing tings differently dis time. I will na try ta change ye. Ye can decide when ye're ready ta become one of us," he says and I scoff at the computer, not believing him for a second. I can still feel the pain from the bites he gave me. The gnawing hunger registers in my mind along with the echoing agony of it. "I jus need ye near me, for now. I can make anyting happen when ye're back wi' me. Ye can come ta us now, or we can find ye. 'Tis yer choice, but ye may na like whah happens if ye make me come ta bring ye back home. I love ye, *mo chroí*, ye're moin…but ye already know dat, do ye na," he says the last part like it was not at all in question and a part of me believes him. I don't know why I do—maybe it's Stockholm syndrome, but I feel like one of his possessions, just waiting to be collected.

"I have been giving our situation some tought," Brennus continues as he casually glances over his shoulder at where Molly is standing. She looks dopey, like she just took something, but I know that she hasn't. It's Brennus' touch that is making her act that way. His toxic skin contains a highly potent drug that is now rendering Molly his slave. She will do anything he wants now that he has touched her—everything. Peering back into the camera, Brennus says, "I do na want ye ta feel alone when ye come home ta us, so I found a friend for ye. We will turn her, and den ye can have her wi' ye for eternity. Ye see…I plan ta give ye everyting ye want…anyting yer heart desires will be yers. Tell me where ye are, and I will bring ye home—'tis time, Genevieve. 'Tis yer destiny." The screen goes black then for just a moment until the email window engages again. As I stare at the blank email I feel as if I have gone into shock.

I've been lying to myself. No, it's more like pretending that this wouldn't happen, that somehow it would be prevented. I thought if I just keep things simple, just keep the few people that I love close to me, that I would be able to protect them. But, Brennus has eternity on his side. He can pick them off one at a time, until there will be no one left to protect. Will I then beg him to kill me, to stop the pain from the loss of everyone I love?

I don't know when this video was taken. Am I too late to save Molly? I wonder as panic seeps into my mind. A rational voice in my head tells me that the answer is yes. I was too late the second he touched her. Molly will crave him now and she will be his stalker if he doesn't either turn her or drain her blood and kill her. She will be like a junkie looking for more of the toxin in his skin, unless she could somehow be cured, but I don't even know if that's possible for a human. I survived the venom of the Gancanagh bite because Russell had fed me venison blood, which ebbed my craving to drink Brennus' blood, but his skin does not affect me. Brennus can touch me and I'm not susceptible to him like other beings are susceptible—like humans and angels.

Brennus isn't going to stop. He will come for me, but I already knew that. This is a game and it's to the death, his or mine. This ends when Brennus ceases to be or when I become his undead Gancanagh queen. The only question is, how many of my friends will he kill before this ends? Maybe my defensive position is the wrong tactic to take with him. Maybe I should find him right now and destroy him, before he gets anyone else. The Gancanagh don't respect anything but strength. Maybe I need to show them that it's not in their best interest to pursue my loved ones or me. With that in mind, I begin formulating a response after I click on the reply button to compose an email.

```
Brennus-


You seem to have forgotten that I'm not
like the others; your charms don't work
on me. My soul is not for sale and I
will never surrender it. If you truly
want to give me what my heart desires,
then do not change Molly. If it is in
your power, then I want you to let her
go. It will NOT make me happy to have
her as my Gancanagh BFF. What WILL make
me happy is for you to go away and never
bother me again. If you do not, I will
make you leave me alone and you may not
like what happens when I show you just
how temporary you can be. If you refuse
```

to hear me and you choose to come for
me, I will see it as a declaration of
war and I will not hesitate to kill you.
Don't make me do that. You are not my
destiny. I'm your enemy.

SO COMPLETELY NOT YOURS,

Evie

P.S. I want my stuff back you creepy
stalker.

Without contemplating the consequences of my actions, I click the send button and mail the reply to Molly's account. Gazing at the screen, my throat tightens. Tears cloud my vision as what this means hits me. Molly is probably dead by now. *Not dead, she's undead,* I think as flashes of the desolate cells beneath Brennus' lair come to my mind. They won't be in Houghton anymore so he couldn't have locked Molly in one of those cells like he did to me. Dominion knows about the copper mine that the Gancanagh had inhabited, so they probably left the area. They couldn't stay in the mine anyway, since Russell's grenades blew it up when he rescued me from the Gancanagh.

Remembering Russell walking into the mine to save me, forces the tears from my eyes. *He was magnificent,* I think as I wipe my tears with the back of my hand. He faced Brennus for me and wouldn't let me surrender to him. I owe him my life and I have left him out there to fend for himself without me. Just like I left Molly out there alone. Crushing sadness grips me as something in my chest squeezes tight. I am too new to all of this: naive and stupid, but I can't claim ignorance. I know what Brennus is capable of and I had refused to listen to that voice in my head that was telling me that he's coming.

Staring ahead of me, the email alert window flashes onto the screen again. Seeing the brightly illuminated pop-up, the hair on my forearms rises as a chill passes through me. Dragging the cursor to the inbox, I depress the button near the keyboard.

One message is in my inbox. It's from Molly's account again, but there is no tag in the subject line. They are actively monitoring Molly's email. It's not just a programmed response, I reason. Brennus has been waiting for me to contact her. Suddenly, I feel like a butterfly caught in a spider's web. I open the email.

My Dearest Heart,

Had I not known before that you are perfect for me, then your most exquisitely executed note would have solidified it for me. I hope that you do not mind, but I showed it to the fellas and they are all most eager now to get their queen back. You may have to put up with a wee bit of chaffing when you come home because the fellas may not be able to help themselves; you are just too tempting.

I am sorry to disappoint you, mo chroí, but we have already turned your friend Molly days ago. It took no time at all because she was most willing to be Gancanagh. She is very content, but she is a little irritated with you for not telling her what you really are. I explained to her that you were probably trying to protect her. She did not realize 'tis what Seraphim do.

As for me being temporary, I can assure you that I am permanent and I am your destiny. You forget that I have tasted you. I know all of your deepest desires. The needs that you hide deep inside of you, I know them all. You want a family above all else. I will provide that

family for you. You want other things
as well, things that you don't speak of
to anyone. Ever. I will find your sire
for you, I promise. I have been making
inquiries, looking for your daddy. If
he is here, we will find him.

I do not fear you. I fear for you. You
have aligned yourself with the wrong
side. You cannot trust the angels. They
will turn on you. If there is even an
inkling that you could be seen as evil,
it will be over for you. We are ever
ready to protect you.

It is you who is refusing to hear me. I
am finished asking you, Genevieve, now
I am telling you. Come to me before I
have to come to you. I am not your enemy. I love you, and in time, you will
love me too.

So Completely Yours,

Brennus

P.S. All of your belongings are await-
ing your return, my beautiful angel.

Rage is overcoming me as thoughts of Molly's death
enter my mind. It's just like the anger I feel when I think
of what Alfred did to my uncle. Alfred viciously murdered
Uncle Jim and I couldn't stop him. I keep the secret of
that anger locked away because it makes me feel as if the
lining of my stomach is rubbing together when I allow it
to rise up in me. My fingers are shaking as they fly over the
keys of the laptop, responding with all the hatred I feel in
this moment.

Dear Walking Corpse,

I will never forgive you for Molly.
Send me your dead and I will bury them
deep for you. I'm done making sense to
you and I'm ready to face you. Come and
die.

Hate you,

Evie

I have only minutes to wait until the email alert window crops back up, delivering Brennus' response.

Dear Darkest Night,

I'm already dead, but looking forward
to seeing you...in China. Be there soon.

Love You,

Brennus

I pick up the laptop and throw it across the room. It hits the far wall and showers in pieces to the floor. I push back from the desk and drive my fists right through its thick, ancient wood. It shatters and splinters into a pile at my feet. Looking around, all I can see is Molly's face as it sagged after being touched by Brennus—I didn't think to protect her. Of course she was a target. Brennus has all of my pictures—Molly is probably in half of all of those pictures.

The room starts spinning around me as my fists come up to my eyes to try to blot out the images of what her death must have been like. It would've been gruesome. They would have fed on her blood before one of them allowed her to feed on him. I wonder which one of them turned her. Was it Brennus or Finn...it could've been any of them...maybe Declan or

Lachlan. I'll find out which one it was and kill him slowly… painfully. Several killing scenarios pulse in my head as it's spinning like someone stuffed me in a blender and hit puree.

Dizziness makes me sway on my feet. Bringing my hands away from my eyes, I feel as if I should be moving—I need to go to Molly—help her—it's too late to help her. I need to go to Brownie and Russell. They need to be warned that Brennus is on his way to China now—he traced my email. He at least knows where the POP, point of presence, which I used to send the email is located. He will find me. *If he gets close enough, he'll probably be able to smell me,* I think as nausea rolls through me. I need to warn Zephyr, Buns and Phaedrus—if he touches them, they will be Brennus' slaves too.

Reed, I think as the room sways again. I feel like I'm spinning in infinity. Unable to control the whirling, I crouch down on one knee, resting my head on my other knee. My hands go to the floor as I attempt to steady myself.

I have to warn Reed…Russell…Zee, I think. The most unnatural feeling of lightness pulses through me like a shockwave while something lifts out of me. Looking up, my stomach twists as an image of myself becomes visible to me. It hovers near me like a luminous ghost for a few brief seconds. Blinking at the perfect representation of myself, I watch as my mirror image turns from where it is standing just in front of me. With a grim expression on her face, the glowing impression of me rockets itself forward so quickly that I can barely track it as it exits the room. I grit my teeth as another shockwave erupts within me. A second holographic image projects out of me like an ascending soul and immediately bolts from the room. When the third luminous "me" bursts from my body like a physical echo and leaves the room, I lose most of the dizziness that was overwhelming me. I stand on shaky legs and try to make sense of what I just experienced. As I stumble to the bed, I lean against the frame, willing myself not to fall onto it.

I take deep breaths and raise a shaky hand to my forehead, but I pause when a movement near the door distracts me. Reed is staring at me from the entrance to our room. His face is blank, but there is pain in his eyes. He moves forward, engulfing me in his arms. He is not wearing his shirt and his charcoal-gray wings are arcing out menacingly. I inhale his sexy, masculine scent as he presses me to his chest.

"You're alive," he breathes into my ear as his arms hold me like I'm a fragile flower. A clatter sounds behind me as he drops whatever weapon he had been holding. It sounds like some kind of sword as it hits the ground with a heavy metallic clang.

"What?" I choke, pushing against him so I can see his face again.

"I saw you. You passed right through me—there was such pain—sorrow when you went through me and then you just disappeared," Reed says in a hushed and urgent tone, holding me to him and refusing to let me go.

"When did you see me?" I ask, giving up trying to see his face. Instead, I hug him back.

"Seconds ago—I thought…" he trails off as his voice thickens.

"You thought I was dead?" I ask and he just tightens his grip on me until I wheeze and then he eases his embrace so that I can breath again, but he still doesn't let me go.

"How did you do that—send out a piece of you—your emotion to me?" Reed asks.

"I—my emotion?" I ask in confusion.

"At first, I thought I was seeing your soul when it approached me, but when it ran into me, right through me—I didn't know what it was because it didn't feel like a soul. It was raw emotion—panic and agony—but the scent…I could smell you, it left your scent on my clothes," he says and pulls me back from him so that I can finally see his eyes. "How did you do that?"

I shake my head numbly. "I…don't know," I say, seeing his beautiful face, his eyes searching mine. "I wanted to warn you—it's Molly—they turned Molly and now they're coming here," I say in a rush. "I didn't protect her and now they have her—they picked her up at a club—he said he turned her already—they made her a monster and I let them…" My voice breaks and I bury my face in his chest.

"Brennus?" Reed asks in a dark tone, resting his cheek against the top of my head. "How did he contact you?"

I manage to nod again, but it takes me a few moments before I can say, "I emailed Molly to tell her I'm alive and I found out she's not." Tears leak from my eyes to run down my cheeks. "Brennus made her a Gancanagh. He knows we're in China. He's coming. I'm sorry, I blew our cover."

"Shh…" Reed just holds me for a few minutes and then he asks in a quiet tone. "Is that how you felt when you learned Molly was changed…sorrow, pain?"

"Uh huh," I nod.

"Your human emotions are…excruciating," Reed utters in a soft tone. "I had no idea you feel that much. When the image of you hit me with such raw emotion, I could think of nothing but finding you."

"You don't feel that…deeply?" I ask as I sniff to hold back more tears.

"I do, but I didn't know that you do too," he replies. "It was almost unbearable when I thought you may be gone." I squeeze my eyes closed and hug him tighter.

"It was not intentional, I didn't even know I was doing it. I was thinking that I needed to tell you what just happened and then, suddenly, images of me were spinning out of me," I try to explain.

"Is that your version of a beam of light? Like the one in the Seven-Eleven? Only you send an image of yourself as light to warn us of what is coming?" Reed asks in a serious tone.

I grow still in his arms. *Is that what I just did? Did I send them out of me?* I wonder, feeling overwhelmed by all that is happening to me. "I don't know, Reed. I wish I came with an owner's manual or something."

Stroking my hair, Reed says, "That is a book I would enjoy reading, Evie. Our timeline just moved up. We have been planning for the Gancanagh since we arrived here. We will have the superior position. Every angle has been analyzed. They will come and they will die." I close my eyes because fear makes it hard for me to hear what he is telling me. "This changes things, though, I need to call Zephyr—ask him to return here. We have to bring in our reinforcements now. We will tell Dominion where we are, they have been demanding to send a team to protect you—"

"What?" I ask as my eyes widen in surprise.

Reed's expression darkens. "Bodyguards. Dominion has been demanding that you have them to protect you," he says and he sounds a little sour, like the thought of someone else defending me is making him ill.

"Do you trust them?" I ask as Brennus' words echo in my mind.

"No," he replies. "There will be some who will give their lives to protect you, but there will be others who will have another purpose."

"What other purpose?" I ask.

He avoids looking at me when he replies, "I can think of several. They think of you as a weapon. You are the perfect lure to draw out evil. They would like to use you whenever and wherever they see fit to entrap the Fallen. I'm in the way of that because I will not allow Dominion access to you. I believe that some will want you to return to Dominion, with or without your consent."

"Oh," I say. Dominion wants me back and there will be a few of them with orders to seize the moment and make that happen. "So, my bodyguards could turn into my jailers, if given the right set of circumstances?"

"Yes," Reed replies as if he is proud of me for understanding what he is telling me. "We have not allowed them close to you for that reason, but we may need them now that our timeline has been bumped up."

I nod, "What about Brownie and Russell?" I ask, pulling away from Reed. Pacing the floor in front of him, I say, "They shouldn't come back here, not with Brennus coming. He'll kill Russell, after what Russell did to Ultan and Driscoll." Brennus will torture Russell if he finds him because Russell killed several Gancanagh when he rescued me. Well that, and the fact that Russell is my soul mate, which seems to really bother Brennus.

"We can protect them when they arrive here," Reed replies confidently, but paranoia is setting in now. I feel weak and vulnerable.

"Let's go now, Reed. Let's leave here, just you and me. We can lead Brennus away from here," I reason. "That way, he will be forced to follow us and we can lose him—I know we can." *Then, at least Zephyr, Buns, Brownie, and Russell will be safe,* I tell myself.

"No," Reed replies. "This is the best position for us. We will fight here, and you will be safe, and so will Russell. We will protect him," he says, reading my mind.

"I want to believe that, Reed, you have no idea how much I want to believe that, but I've seen what they can do. They walked right into my room at Dominion's chateau, without any of the Powers knowing that they were there. Brennus is obsessed. He is like a spoiled child who has never been denied a toy before and he can't stand it," I explain, wringing my hands.

"You are not a toy," he barks and I flinch.

"No, I'm not a toy," I agree, as I stop pacing to look at him.

A small sound from the wooden gate that connects our pagoda to the others registers in my mind right before Zephyr's tall frame materializes just inches in front of me. He reaches out to me, grasping my upper arms and pulling me off of my feet to dangle before him. His brown wings are stretching out, blotting out everything behind him but the menacing looking hilt to a broad sword that is strapped to his back.

"You are alive," he states between panting breaths as his eyes rove over every inch of me, assessing me and looking for anything out of place.

"Yeah," I nod in a soft tone, smiling sheepishly while gazing into Zee's ice-blue eyes. "You get my message?" I add, and then I bite my lower lip as his eyes narrow.

"Explain," he barks, but Reed steps between us, pulling me gently from Zephyr's grasp.

"Evie has a new ability that we didn't expect. She can send out clones of herself," Reed says, standing between Zephyr and me. "If your message was anything like mine, then…"

"Is that what you are calling it? A message? It felt more like emotional terrorism to me," Zephyr replies, piercing me with his stare.

"Sorry, that's what I was feeling when it happened," I reply, feeling ill remembering Molly's face. I brief Zephyr on what just happened. Zephyr grills me about every detail of the email exchange between Brennus and me. I watch the corners of his mouth lift a little when he asks me to tell him again about addressing Brennus as a "walking corpse."

Zephyr grunts when I finish. Looking at Reed, he says, "Buns should be here any minute. I didn't wait for her after Evie's clone ran into me. Buns tried to tell me that it was definitely not Evie's soul, but you felt it too, didn't you?" Zephyr asks Reed and he nods. "I have never felt that way. I did not enjoy it."

"Sorry, Zee, I was freaked," I say, looking down at my feet.

Using his finger, Zephyr lifts my chin up so he can see my eyes. "Yes, and now I finally know what 'freaked' means," Zephyr replies. "You have more courage than I thought."

"Sweetie!" Buns calls out right before she lands outside the doorway of our room. Her golden butterfly wings float behind her with effortless grace as she strides into the room. Coming to me, she embraces me, squeezing me briefly. "That's a killa new trick you came up with," she says.

"Thanks, Buns," I reply, seeing that she is trying to make me feel like less of a freak than I feel right now. "It just happened, I wasn't even trying."

"Well, it's a very stellar party trick. You can clone yourself and then we can make everyone guess which one is the real Evie," Buns says, smiling into my eyes with her cornflower-blue ones as she brushes a stray hair back from my face. "Can you do it again now? Can you send one to me?"

"I don't know," I waver, biting my lower lip and looking uncertainly at Reed who is watching me. He nods to me in encouragement.

"Try," Reed says.

Nodding slowly, I close my eyes, breathing in deeply. Now that Brennus is coming, this may be my last chance to tell each of them what they mean to me. My heart speeds up as I allow thoughts of Brennus to create in me a sense of urgency, like I had felt when this first happened. Thinking of Buns, of the love

I have for her, I begin to feel like I'm spinning, caught in a centrifuge. Opening my eyes, I sway again. Trying to keep my balance, I find it's impossible and I have to go down on one knee again so I won't fall down. A tremor jolts through me, causing a sense of lightness to expand within my body. Light is pushing its way out of me as my form is separating from itself. Seeing my likeness in front of me, it turns and rockets towards Buns, running right into her and disappearing in an instant.

I have no time to gauge her reaction to it because another shockwave hits me, causing another image of me to spill out. This one runs towards Zee, disappearing into him. Concentrating now on all the love and desire that I have for Reed, a pulsing heat, like fire, erupts within me as the light from me grows more intense. A brightly lit image of me bursts forth from my body and it turns immediately towards Reed. Losing the dizziness that drove me to my knee, I watch as my clone bolts to Reed, enveloping him in its fiery light before it vanishes within him. He closes his eyes as his perfect face transforms from a concerned expression to one of bliss. Slowly, he opens his eyes again and the deepest desire smolders within their dark green depths.

"Sweetie, I was wrong…that's not a party trick," Buns says as she staggers to the bed to sit on it. "That's—I can smell you!" she remarks as her eyes widen and she pulls her honey-color hair to her nose, breathing in. She speaks to me in her musical language before she smiles and says, "That was like seeing love through another's eyes. I will not forget it."

"Dominion," Zephyr says, not taking his eyes off of me. He has an awed expression on his face that I have seen only one other time and that was right before I managed to cut his arm with my dagger while sparring with him.

"We need to get them here now," Reed finishes for him, but he's not looking at Zee, he's looking at me with that same expression of bliss still plastered to his face. "I will make the arrangements while you make the arrangements to get Brownie and Russell here sooner."

"I cannot leave here now. They will have to make their way alone. I have not explained Russell to Dominion as yet. We can protect him once he is here, but I do not trust them to deliver him here if I were to tell them about him. It is too great a risk that they will keep him if I ask them to protect him," Zephyr finishes.

Fear causes my palms to sweat as I see what I have done. I have ruined all of their carefully made plans. The plans to bring Brennus to them according to their own timeline and the plans to secure the safety of Russell and Brownie are now being scrapped because I messed up again. "No, Zee, you have to get them!" I say adamantly.

"They'll be fine. Brownie is a Reaper and she kicks ass. She'll be able to handle it," Buns says with assurance, but I see the look she gives Zephyr over my shoulder. She is looking for him to reassure her.

As I observe Zephyr, something in his demeanor makes me feel cold. He is uncertain about them, that's why he was going to get them. "Please, go get them, Zee," I whisper in a hollow tone.

"He can't, Evie. He has to stay with us now," Reed says firmly. "We will have to rely on Brownie and Russell to make it here without help." I want to argue with him, but I can see by the set of his jaw that he is not going to change his mind. He is firmly entrenched in the "protect Evie" mode and he will not deviate from that mission, no matter what I say.

Clenching my hands into fists, I want to break something. I keep thinking that this is all my fault. Grasping my phone, I walk from the room to out beneath the endless expanse of darkened sky in the courtyard. I dial Russell's number, but it goes straight to voicemail. When his brief message prompts me to leave a message, I say, "It's me. Call me when you get this." Hanging up, I start to wonder if I affect Russell just as Brennus affects me. I wonder if the sound of my voice rips open all of the scars I have left behind in him.

CHAPTER 3

The Army

Trying to sit quietly and clear my mind as Phaedrus is instructing me to do, it is proving to be nearly impossible. I have thousands of thoughts going on in my mind and there are new layers of thought expanding almost daily. *How am I supposed to channel that into one stream of consciousness?* I wonder. Several "what if" scenarios are currently at work, viciously torturing me. Most of those scenarios have something to do with either Russell or Brennus, and in the worst scenarios, they involve both of them.

"This is not working," Phaedrus sighs next to me. Opening my eyes I turn my head, looking at him sitting next to me. His legs are crossed, like mine, and his back is ramrod straight, exhibiting a perfect meditative pose. He is staring at me with his pitch black eyes. If I didn't know that he is a Virtue angel, I would be creeped out by his eyes because there is no color differential between his pupils, irises and sclera—they are all black—making him look wicked. But I do know him, and I know that he is the farthest thing from evil. He is sent on missions of mercy to perform miracles, and at this moment, I'm very grateful that he is choosing to spend his time with me. We have been at this for hours now and I want to tell him it's time to take a break, but I don't want to let him down.

"Sorry," I say, exhaling a breath that I have been holding.

"You are not letting go," Phaedrus points out. "You are also not breathing."

"Breathe more," I remind myself, closing my eyes again.

"Yes, focus on what you want to accomplish–peace, seren-ity– if you can maintain those things and transcend rational thought for a moment–you can explore your newest ability," he says in a coaxing voice.

"Everyone is always telling me I have to be more rational, Phaedrus. Now you're saying I have to transcend rational thought. You guys are proving to be consistently inconsistent," I sigh.

"You are doing fine, Evie. Relax…think of a favorite poem… or music…do you know any songs that are rhythmic?" he asks.

"Let me think…" I trail off, trying to think of any appropri-ate songs, one that I can focus on. The only one that's coming to mind at the moment is *Ninety-nine Bottles of Beer On The Wall.*

"I don't believe I know that one," Phaedrus says, reading my mind in his uncanny way.

Annoyed that he can read my mind so easily, I begin singing it loudly in my head. *Ninety-nine bottles of beer on the wall, ninety-nine bottles of beer, take one down, pass it around, ninety-eight bottles of beer on the wall…*

"Urr, delightful…" Phaedrus mutters, "I was hoping you knew some Bach, maybe Handel or Wagner—my eyes will never get heavy with this lullaby."

Smiling at his sarcasm, I continue to sing the rousing lyr-ics in my head as I hum the music aloud. On the 12th or 13th cycle through the song, I begin to feel calmer. A few more times through and a feeling of detachment filters through me and I lose the need to sing.

Slowly, I control the spinning that I feel, not allowing the sensation to overcome me, but channeling it. The energy is building within me, ramping up to the shockwave that I know is about to tear through me. Focusing as the tremor of light erupts from me, I keep my eyes closed while my clone juts out. Instead of being an empty shape full of emotion, I'm trying to control the image of me, maintain a consciousness within her, a connection to her. Murky images of our surroundings are flit-tering in my mind. It's like having my eyes open under water; I can see shapes and contours, but they are not crisp or very clear.

"Can you direct her?" Phaedrus asks.

I don't reply, but concentrate on the desire that I have to get up right now and look for Reed. Immediately, my clone moves towards the doorway that leads to the courtyard. The sunlight is bright outside, causing the shapes that I can see through her eyes to become clearer. Groups of angels are standing at intervals around the perimeter of the courtyard. The angels began arriving last night. Most of them are Powers that aren't part of Dominion's division of rank. They are the elite assassins that Reed and Zephyr know personally.

Moving across the garden, I have trouble discerning which of the angels is my angel. I can't see facial features too clearly and colors are bleeding together. As my clone passes several figures, I move her closer to them and peer into their faces, searching for the one that is perfection. Needless to say, the ghostly image of me is not going unnoticed. In fact, all movement around her has ceased as well as all of the conversation, not that I would understand them anyway because they aren't speaking English. Inhaling deeply, I smell Reed's familiar scent dimly through the muted senses of my counterpart.

Following the meager scent of Reed, I direct my image forward over the carefully raked stone paths to the center of the garden where a small stream winds effortlessly around an ancient tree. Leaning against the tree, a hazy figure of an angel regards my clone silently. Sniffing the air around him, I push nearer, listening for any sound he might make. Drawing close, I bring my ghostly lips inches from his ear. Concentrating very hard, I move those lips and manage to just whisper, "Boo."

Reed's arms try to wrap around me, but as he does so, my clone dissipates into him like fog, and my consciousness immediately shifts back to my body still sitting dormant next to Phaedrus. Inhaling a sharp breath, I open my eyes and look at Phaedrus who grins back at me with his black, shiny eyes.

"Well done!" he says, extending a hand as he rises to his feet. I take his hand and let him help me up off the floor.

Blushing a little at his praise and enthusiasm, I reply, "Thank you for your help, Phaedrus."

"Not at all. Do you want to try again?" he asks.

"Not right now, maybe later," I reply, feeling exhausted from the effort to control my new ability. But, as I say this, something in Phaedrus' look makes me ask, "Is something wrong?"

"No, it's just that I'm not sure how much longer I will be here to help you," Phaedrus replies with a puzzled expression on his face.

My eyebrows pull together. "You're leaving?" I ask in a sad tone, squeezing his hand tighter. I had hoped that Phaedrus would want to stay with us. He has become part of our circle quite quickly, more quickly than anyone else could, since we are all so tight now.

"I don't know," Phaedrus says in a frustrated tone. "I am getting really strange signals. I am not sure what I am supposed to be doing and it is very irritating because that has never happened to me before."

"What do you mean?" I ask, letting go of his hand and seeing his brow knit.

"You know how I told you that I see images in my head, pictures of a target that I'm to help?" When I nod, he continues. "Well, I get these pictures and then I set out to find my target. The closer I get to the target, the warmer it gets. Conversely, the farther away the colder I feel."

"Right, like you said before, it's like a game of 'hot and cold' for you," I reply.

"That is correct. I am getting images of a new target that needs my help," he says.

"Oh," I say with disappointment. I was hoping that I would remain his target to aid. Since he is an angel of mercy, a Virtue angel, who is sent to execute miracles for his targets, I like having him around.

"Yes, but here is the disturbing part of all of this. The further I get from you, the colder I feel," he says in confusion.

"You mean, you can't set out to find the person that you are seeing in your head because I keep drawing you back to me?' I ask.

"Yes. I have several theories as to why this is happening, but I have come up with no definitive answer yet," he admits.

My mind furiously attacks the puzzle that Phaedrus just presented to me. I could be in greater danger than the other target, and therefore, in greater need of Phaedrus' help. Or, I could just be a draw for him by my very nature, blocking out the other target. My mind shifts again as I think that maybe I'm meant to go with Phaedrus on his next mission. Maybe he can't leave me because I'm supposed to help him—go with him.

"I had not thought of that, Evie," Phaedrus murmurs, reading all of my thoughts as if I had been speaking them aloud. "I have never had a partner before, it would be unusual for that to be the case."

"Who is your target?" I ask him out of curiosity.

"I don't have names, just faces," Phaedrus says, sounding frustrated. "It is all very strange. I don't know how I am to find them if I cannot follow my senses to them."

"Them? There is more than one target?" I ask.

"Yes," he replies, deep in thought. I was just about to ask him more questions regarding his pending mission when I hear a growl coming from outside. A part of my mind is constantly monitoring what is going on around me. Even though I can't understand any of the conversations taking place outside in the courtyard, I listen anyway. *I know that growl,* I think as I bolt to the door to find Reed. It only takes me seconds to see him where my clone had just left him by the tree, but he is no longer alone. Scores of Powers are surrounding him, causing me to stiffen. They arrived so silently, I hadn't even heard them coming.

My wings force their way out of my back as I realize Reed is alone amid Powers from Dominion. Plucking one of the wicked-sharp swords off the wall near the door, I turn and stride out into the courtyard, calling over my shoulder to Phaedrus, "Get Zee." As I approach the mob of angels by the tree, all eyes turn to focus on me. I scan the crowd, seeing several faces that I recognize from my stay at the chateau. Foremost among them is Preben, the Power who was in charge of me after I arrived there. I recognize his silver hair and light brown wings that are so similar to Zephyr's wings in coloring.

Seeing Preben makes me lose some of the fear I have associated with these angels. He had tried to help me when I was at the chateau, even when he thought that I might be evil. I slow my pace and attempt to reign in my aggressive emotions that urge me to attack them for the threat they represent to Reed. My instincts to protect him are almost overwhelming me, making it difficult to assess the situation clearly. Adopting a casual mien, I stretch my hand out to Reed as I near him. He instantly takes my hand in his.

"Your bodyguards have arrived, love," Reed says in a casual tone, but I can feel that he is tense. He reaches down, taking the sword from my other hand and holds it non-threateningly at his side.

Trying to play along with his relaxed air, I reply, "They can't all be my bodyguards."

"You are very important to us," Preben says, smiling at me easily as I regard him with skepticism. He is so tall; I almost have to take a step back from him. Remembering how he helped me by translating for me what the war council was saying during my trial and how he allowed Reed and me to be together later, some of the animosity I'm feeling dissipates and I smile back at him.

"Hmmm," I reply, quirking my eyebrow at him, "You mean I can stop praying for death now?"

Preben's smile deepens. "I have my doubts that you ever began, Seraph," Preben replies in a mildly mocking way that makes me smile a little more, too.

Assessing all of the members of his unit that are standing behind him, forty or more, I ask, "So many angels just to guard me? You must think I can't defend myself at all."

"You are very young. How can you possibly stand against ancient evil like the Gancanagh?" he asks me rhetorically.

"They don't want to kill me, Preben. They want me for their queen. I think my odds are better than everyone else's as far as they are concerned. They will want to keep me alive so that they can turn me later, but I doubt they will feel the same way about you when they come," I say with honesty, looking at the other angels amassed around us who are listening to our every word. "Are you sure this is something you want to get involved in?"

The entire group erupts in laughter, like I had just made a joke. Looking at Reed to see if he will explain to me why everyone is laughing, I see that he's watching me carefully, not giving away anything that he is thinking. I'll have to learn to be more like him; he doesn't show his weaknesses to everyone, whereas I wear them on my sleeve.

Preben gives a sharp nod. "I am quite sure that I want to be involved," Preben replies. "We were just discussing your protection. I will choose who will be your personal guard, and then the others will be assigned other duties in your army."

"Hmmm," I reply, regarding this new bit of information. "I'm sorry to disappoint you, but this is not my army. It's Reed's army. If you join it, you are joining him. As for who will be my bodyguards, I leave that to Reed. He is in charge here."

Preben's eyes narrow. He is used to calling the shots. Dominion has given him authority over all of these angels, but his rank doesn't translate to us because Reed now outranks everyone here. My Seraphim wings etched on his chest, just above his heart, makes him essentially Seraphim. He ranks above all of the Powers and is now at the top of the chain of command. I didn't know I was giving him an upgrade when I agreed to bind with him, but I'm glad that there was at least one perk for him in being stuck with me for eternity.

"That is semantics, Seraph," Preben states. "Since you are bound to him, you are one, so I fight for you. It is your army, as it is his army. Unless he ceases to exist, then it is just your army."

A menacing growl escapes from me. What Preben said just now feels like a threat to me and the growl that it elicited is purely instinctual. It's my first insight into the risks that Reed has undertaken in binding with me. *What lengths will Dominion go to in order to get me back?* Any talk of Reed ceasing to exist I take very seriously.

Reed tightens his grip on my hand a little, but he doesn't say anything. I think that it's his way of telling me to play it cool. I squeeze his hand back before letting it go. "Preben, it's good to see you again," I say a little icily, extending my hand to him to shake. He looks at it for a second, not sure of what to do. He takes it hesitantly, watching Reed over my shoulder the entire time. I shake his hand, but when I try to let it go, he doesn't relinquish it right away.

Preben leans closer to me, saying in a low voice, "I am not your enemy."

"You wouldn't be the first to tell me that and be wrong. We will see, won't we, Preben?" I reply, pulling my hand gently from his. To everyone else, I say, "Thank you all for coming. If there is anything that you need, please ask and we will try to accommodate you."

"We need intel," Preben says right away. "We have been briefed with the information that has been gathered on the lair in Houghton and other nests that have been uncovered, but you have more personal information. I have listened to your statements to the war council. We need to go over all of it with you again."

"I will arrange it," Reed says with authority. "We will provide you with the information that we have uncovered and you can ask all of your questions. We can do this after you and I speak about Evie's personal guard. Zee, you in?"

"Lez go," Zephyr replies, materializing from nearby and sounding a lot like someone from my generation is supposed to sound. He has been hanging around Buns and it's starting to rub off. I can almost imagine that he's really nineteen or twenty years old, instead of a few billion, give or take. "You won't be needing this while we parley," Zee says, wrapping one arm around Preben's shoulder and plucking the sword from the sheath strapped to his back. Tossing it to Reed nonchalantly, he continues to talk to Preben in a friendly tone. "All of you can follow me to the conference area," he says to the Dominion angels. Then he turns back to Preben. "You play golf?" he asks, steering him towards the largest Naxi pagoda that is central to the cluster of pagodas.

Taking my hand once again, Reed says, "Walk with me." We stroll casually away from the other angels. Reed doesn't speak until we are halfway across the courtyard. Then, he says to me in a low tone, "Stay by my side until I tell you differently."

I nod my head once in assent. My heartbeat picks up then, hammering at the walls of my chest, while all of the reasons he doesn't want me out of his sight dance in my mind. Stopping suddenly, Reed pulls me into his arms. When his lips touch mine, all of those thoughts cease. I press my hands to his chest, leaning into him as I kiss him back, tugging his lower lip between mine. My heartbeat races faster as his hand skims over my wing, trailing downward hypnotically. "Don't be afraid," Reed whispers close to my ear, "Trust me."

I close my eyes, and I focus on slowing down the beat of my heart. He must have heard it and wanted to give the angels another reason for it to be beating so fast. "I trust you," I breathe back, resting my head against his shoulder. I let him go and we continue towards our pagoda. "I just don't know who is fronting and who is real."

"You let me worry about that, love," Reed replies with ease.

"How bad did I just mess up back there?" I ask in a serious tone. He shrugs lightly. "That bad, huh?" I cringe.

"I would not call it messing up. I would just say you gave them some information that I don't mind them knowing," he replies, bringing my hand to his lips and kissing it.

Stopping in my tracks, I face him and ask, "What did I just tell them?

Brushing my hair from my face he says, "Well, you walked into the middle of the meeting brandishing a weapon when you thought that I was alone with them, letting them know you don't trust them and are willing to fight them if necessary," he explains, tucking my hair behind my ear.

"Oh," I say, feeling a blush creeping into my cheeks. I cross my arms in front of me.

"Then you positioned yourself between me and their leader, like a lioness protecting her cub, letting them know that you value me above your own safety. You demonstrated that the way to get to you is through me," Reed says.

I stiffen, biting my bottom lip in panic. "So, I put you in more danger instead of protecting you?" I ask, dropping my arms and pacing a little in front of him while looking at the angels behind me.

"Yes, thank you," Reed says, smiling and enjoying the fact that he is now the center of any plot they conceive. "They will attack me to gain your cooperation."

"WHAT?" I yell, not caring who hears me, my heart is now ramping up to tear through the walls of my chest.

Pulling me behind a large tree that shields us from the angels, Reed kisses me deeply. My arms wrap around his neck as I press my body into his. His lips move over mine as his hand threads through my hair at the base of my head, angling my face to his. Running my hands from his neck to his chest, I hear Reed growl low as he reluctantly breaks off our kiss. Drawing back from me, he says, "They would have seen me as a target anyway, Evie. You are mine and they know that I will never let you go. They already knew that I am the key to your compliance because you risked your life to save mine at Dominion. You just solidified the fact that nothing has changed."

"You're enjoying this, aren't you?" I accuse him, running my hands over the solid muscles in his back.

"Yes," he smiles, nuzzling my neck. "They'll have to go through me if they ever hope to get to you and that is a very satisfying thought."

"I'll never be able to sleep with them here," I mutter, thinking of all of the ways they could possibly come for Reed. There are so many of them; I can't possibly protect him.

"Yes, you will. I will make sure you are sufficiently distracted so that there will be no time to dwell on them." My mind immediately contemplates several effective distractions that I wouldn't mind him employing. Reed's eyes soften with affection. "Let's go, I need to speak to Preben about your guards," he says, pulling me forward again.

"Can you tell him I don't need any guards? Those guys creep me out. They're always looking at me like I'm the latest technology and they would like to take me apart to see how I work," I say honestly, remembering how they acted toward me after the trial at Dominion's chateau.

"They'll get used to you," he replies. "You're very alluring. We may have to rotate them often so that they maintain objectivity."

"What do you mean by that?" I ask in suspicion.

"You have a way of turning us to your favor. You wrap us around your little finger. It's your special gift, but one that is not always an asset when it comes to your safety," he replies.

"I would think that you would *want* them to listen to me," I reply, picking some imaginary lint off of my sleeve with a pout.

"No, what I want is to protect you, and unfortunately, that means protecting you from yourself," he says, watching me close.

"Protecting me from myself? That's ridiculous! What am I going to do to me?" I ask rashly.

"Throw yourself in front of the enemy to protect everyone else," he replies in an instant.

"I have more game than that," I mumble, looking at him grudgingly. At Reed's skeptical look, I drop the subject, walking away towards the pagoda. Reed's arms snake around me, pulling me back to his chest.

"You are the most amazing eighteen-year-old I have ever encountered. You have the cognitive abilities of someone thousands of years old, but you have no thought for yourself. It is as if self-preservation is secondary," he explains quickly.

"That's not true at all, Reed. It's just that I know what I cannot survive without so the risk of dying isn't as grave as the risk of losing what I love," I reply, turning in his arms to look at him.

"Then I will protect what you love so that you will survive," he says and I know that he is thinking of Russell.

And I will protect you, I tell myself, but I don't say it out loud because he is always so adamant that he doesn't need protection.

I want to argue with him about the bodyguards, but this isn't the place to do that. We are out in the open where we can be overheard by just about everyone. Finally, I begin to relax a little as I weigh the benefits of having these angels around when Brennus arrives. "Evie, what are you thinking?" Reed asks.

"I was thinking that whoever you pick to guard me couldn't be as sketchy as my last bodyguards. Although, I don't really know if you can call them bodyguards because they were mostly there to prevent me from leaving. At least the angels won't stink like Declan, Lachlan, Faolan and Eion," I say, remembering the sweet, sticky scent of my Gancanagh entourage. Their smell was so potent to me before I was bitten that it burned my nose. The scary part was that, after I was bitten, their scent began to smell pleasant to me. *I wonder how they will smell to me when I see them again,* I think.

"Do you realize that this is the first you have spoken of your captivity with the Gancanagh since we've been here?" Reed asks in a gentle tone. He hugs me to him, pressing his lips against my temple when he sees the color drain from my face. He was careful not to say Brennus' name, but I know what he meant.

"Really…huh?" I murmur, trying to act nonchalant, but I'm shaking so I'm probably not fooling him.

"Really," he says, stroking my hair, making tears well up in my eyes. "You haven't said any more about what you went through."

"Well, I already told you what happened, so there is not a lot left to say," I reply in a low tone because my throat feels tight, like someone is squeezing it.

"You didn't tell me everything. You told me most of it, but there are details that you omitted…" he says, trailing off to see if I'll say anything more about being Brennus' favorite slave. "You gave me a general understanding of the events. You gave me the facts. You didn't tell me the details or how you felt when certain things were happening to you."

"I don't want to talk about it anymore," I reply, giving him a ghost of a smile, as my mind races with images of the piles of dead women stacked upon each other, waiting to be incinerated in the ornately carved fireplaces. "I don't want to waste any of my time with you talking about him."

"Why?" he asks me gently, "I want to know."

"Well, I don't want to tell you," I reply, feeling hollow.

"Preben and the others are going to ask you questions about the Gancanagh," he points out and I stiffen. "They will want to go over all of the facts again and they will want you to tell them everything—every conversation you had while you were there—every conversation that you overheard—how they operate—who is the second in command—who is next in line after him…"

"I can't," I whisper, feeling frozen and thinking of Finn. I never mentioned Brennus' brother and second in command to anyone. Finn helped me when no one else would and I haven't forgotten that.

"Why not?" he probes.

"I already told them everything they need to know," I mumble, trying to avoid his eyes.

"Evie," Reed says, making me look at him, "why can't you talk to me about this?"

"What about Russell?" I say, not looking at him.

"We will have to tell them about Russell now," he says. "He should be here soon so there will be no hiding him. But, that is not the reason you won't talk about the Gancanagh to me."

When I won't look his way, he puts his fingers under my chin, turning my face towards him. He looks grave, like I'm hurting him by not talking to him about this. Pulling my chin from his hand I blurt out, "Because it's disloyal."

"Disloyal?" Reed repeats the word like he doesn't know what it means.

"An act of betrayal," I admit, biting my lip as I see confusion in his eyes.

"Whom will you be betraying?" he asks in a low tone.

I twist my hands. "The family…"

"They are not your family," he counters.

"I know," I reply lamely. "He thinks they are my family."

"What do you think?" Reed asks, cocking his head to the side and reading every detail of my body language.

"I think I'm going to pay for my sedition when he gets me back," I say the words like I can't help myself, like I can't keep them in even if I wanted to.

"Sedition?" he asks, "that means to rebel against a government…"

"Or a king," I reply with a sad tone. "Brennus is the king."

"Their king, but not yours," Reed replies, "and he is not getting you back."

"You're right, he's not getting me back," I agree, swallowing my tears and squaring my shoulders, but my throat feels raw anyway, like I've been crying for hours.

I can see that Reed wants to interrogate me regarding all the secrets I'm still holding back from him. I want to tell him—need to—but I can't. Guilt and shame won't let me. He doesn't know that a part of me, a very small part, loves Brennus and is grateful to him. Brennus destroyed Alfred for me. He had Alfred viciously torn apart like an animal on the floor of my prison. He made Alfred suffer—scream in agony, just like Alfred made my Uncle Jim scream in agony. I can still feel within me some of the darkness I felt after Brennus bit me, but I can't tell Reed that either—too much honesty can be unkind.

"When you are ready to tell me everything that happened, I am ready to listen," Reed says. "I know that he has gotten inside your head. He made you suffer, and then he gave you something very powerful. He avenged your Uncle Jim. That doesn't excuse him for what he did to you—for torturing you."

When I don't speak Reed sighs and says, "We need to speak to Preben now. Are you up for it?"

I nod and take his hand, following him quietly into the central pagoda. We walk down a narrow hallway to a dining room that is equipped with several low, black wooden tables. Large mat-like cushions are arranged around the tables and several of the maps that Reed and Zephyr have been studying are draped over them, covering much of their long expanses. Zephyr is listening to Preben describe a few of the holdings in Houghton and Marquette owned by the Gancanagh. Preben has brought with him a few of his lieutenants, but the majority of the angels are not present.

Joining them at a table, I listen, discovering that Dominion uncovered some small apartments owned by several Gancanagh. The apartments are fronts so that the fellas could appear to be normal students attending the technical school. Their apartments didn't lead to much. Dominion did manage to locate a cargo ship used to import the women that the Gancanagh fed upon.

Hearing this makes my stomach ache. *They have to be stopped, no matter what,* I tell myself, thinking of all the women they have harmed. Molly's face enters my mind. *She's one of them now. Will they kill her, too, along with the others?*

"Can a Gancanagh be saved?" I ask abruptly, interrupting Preben's intel.

Preben doesn't look irritated by my interruption. He has been watching me since I entered the room, as if he is speaking to me instead of to Zephyr and Reed. He pauses, his silvery-blond eyebrows drawing together in question. "Do you mean, can they ever be restored to their previous state, before they were changed?" Preben asks. When I nod, he answers, "No."

"What if they changed their behavior? Would that make them less objectionable?" I probe again, not looking at anyone in particular.

"I'm sorry, I don't understand," Preben replies.

"I was just wondering, what if a Gancanagh chose not to feed on humans, but got her blood from a different source, animal blood or donated human blood—like from a blood bank or something?" I ask. "If she changed her nature, would you still hunt her?"

"Yes," Preben replies without taking a breath.

I close my eyes. "Why?"

"Because they are evil," Preben answers without hesitation.

My nose wrinkles. "I'm sketchy on the whole good evil thing, Preben. I thought that deeds are good or evil, but that beings have the ability to choose their own paths, so they have the ability to be good as well as evil," I say, feeling hostile.

"There is inherent evil, Seraph," Preben replies. "Evil by its very nature. They have no use for anything they can't abuse. They destroy all that they touch."

"That sounds very black and white to me, Power," I reply. "It must be nice to have been created to the right ascendancy."

"It is," he states, "very nice, wouldn't you agree? You are Seraphim and you have a soul. I would say your ascendancy is nearly absolute."

"If I am so powerful, then why do I need bodyguards from Dominion?" I counter.

"Your existence has its drawbacks," he replies and he has the audacity to smile at me. "You are at a serious disadvantage right now. You don't possess our strength yet. You have no knowledge of Paradise except for human hearsay. You cannot speak our language. I can say anything I want to right in front of you and you won't know if I'm ordering dinner or plotting your death. When you speak of evil, I can see that you don't really know what you are talking about. Don't get me wrong, I know you have seen evil deeds, murder, mayhem, but true evil like what dwells in Sheol? I don't think so or you wouldn't be debating the Gancanagh with me. You would be focusing on how we can eradicate them."

"Did you just call me weak and ignorant?" I ask Preben in a calm voice, feeling a blush creeping into my cheeks.

"No, not weak and I would never call you ignorant. I called you young and half human with a pure heart. You came to us. Remember? You asked for our help," he says.

"You had something I wanted," I reply, looking at Reed.

"Yes, but something has changed. You were willing to tell us about the Gancanagh before, but now you ask if they can be saved," he probes.

"They've taken a friend of mine—a human friend. They changed her. I want to know what can be done to save her," I say, dropping my animosity in order to gain the information I need to save Molly.

"If your friend gave up her soul, we cannot save her," he replies without even pausing, like she asked for what happened to her.

"No, she didn't give up her soul, they took it. She was drugged by their touch, unable to make a fair decision," I retort.

"Did you just say 'fair?'" he asks, raising his eyebrows. "You don't expect the Gancanagh to be fair, do you? They are evil killers who never do anything without it being entirely to their advantage. There is no fairness in them. I would have thought you would have learned that during your time with them. Did they ask you if you wanted to be Gancanagh?" he asks me pointedly. I look down, shaking my head. "No, they tried to force you into becoming one of them. The fact that you aren't one of them speaks volumes for you—it is probably why you are alive now. No one could successfully argue that you are evil after seeing what you endured at their hands and still managed to hold on to your soul. Your friend was given a choice…"

"You mean she could have chosen death, that was her only other option," I say quietly.

"Yes, but in death, she would have been given Paradise. We cannot understand why she would not choose it," Preben replies.

"No, you can't, can you?" I say in a bitter tone. "You have no idea what it is to be human—to doubt—to not have seen all that you have seen. It's easy to judge us from your lofty heights, angel. It's a little harder to see through the bolt hole."

"Right, love, I think you should go see what Buns is up to," Reed says, stepping in front of me quickly. "I will fill Preben in on what we know." I look into Reed's eyes to see concern in their green depths. He is worried about me. He wants to protect me from all of this, but that is impossible since I'm at the center of it.

I feel brittle, like I'm made of glass and all of my cracks are beginning to show. I nod slowly to Reed because I would like nothing more than to get away from all of this and just sit and talk with Buns for a while. "Okay," I exhale the word. Pausing, I look at Preben and say, "I am grateful that you have come to help me." Preben nods to me once in acknowledgment of my words. He looks like he wants to say something else, but he holds back.

I turn back to Reed as he says, "I'll walk you over to Buns and then I'll come and get you when we are finished here."

"Sure," I reply, taking his hand that he offers me.

Reed looks past me over my shoulder and his brows draw together. In an instant, he pulls me behind him, trying to shield me from what he is seeing. Peering over his shoulder, I see Russell moving towards us at the speed of a bullet. I brace myself for impact as Russell runs into Reed, but Reed doesn't fall down because Russell passes right through him like a ghost. Russell's image hits me full force and I absorb his ghostly light into me as he evaporates from sight. Then, pain like I have never felt before tears through me and I scream in agony.

Russell

CHAPTER 4

Torture

"Tell me where she is…where is my Alya?" he asks, pullin' a sharp pointed implement from among the many he has already used.

"Not Alya, her name is Red—never yers…" I whisper, closin' my eyes and thinkin' of Evie's beautiful face.

The perfect curve of her neck—the way it sweeps cunningly to her shoulders. The incredible scent of her hair—I can still smell her on me.

Thump, bright light. Searin' pain.

Groan.

Her bare shoulders—the delicate line of her clavicle under her supple skin.

Crunch, dizzyin' nausea.

Heave.

Her eyes…gray and blue with small flecks of violet near the center of the irises.

Slice. Dark spots.

Shakin'.

The sensual contours of her silhouette, the shape of a goddess, as I run my hands over the silk of her skin. The way her body rises to meet mine.

Rip. Choke.

Driftin'…floatin'…fallin'

Red…I love ya…I'm gonna go home now…

Blackness.

Evie

CHAPTER 5

Echoes

As my eyes flutter open, I feel ice-cold and nauseous. I gaze at the ceiling from my position stretched out on top of one of the low tables in the gathering room. In the next instant, I lean over the side of the table and heave repeatedly. Reed, sitting at my side, holds my hair back from my face as I retch. After a few minutes, I moan and lay back on the table, closing my eyes. Most of the angels in the room are conversing, all speaking at once, except for Reed and me who are silent. I cannot speak because all of the fortress walls that I have been trying to build around me are tumbling down as my entire body shakes. It's as if I have experienced the most gruesome torture first hand and not just an impression of it carried on the wind by my soul mate's spirit.

"Russell," I whisper and all of the voices around me cease. Pushing myself up on my elbows, I manage to sit up a little before Reed gently pushes me back down.

"Evie, wait," Reed says.

"I can't. I have to…go'" I reply, sitting up again.

"What did Russell send you?" Reed asks.

"You didn't feel it?" I ask him as the terror of what I just experienced comes back to me full force, crushing me with echoes of pain and leaving the taste of desperation in my mouth. Reed shakes his head, so I say, "Someone is torturing him. He needs help…"

"He was asking for help?" Reed asks, trying to piece together what I'm saying.

"No…he was…" I stop, covering my mouth. I struggle to get to my feet, but Reed isn't letting me get up.

"What?" he asks me with a grim look.

"He was trying to warn me…they know about me…he can't hide me from them…too much pain…"

Reed's hands grip my shoulders. "Who are they? The Gancanagh?" Reed asks in an urgent tone.

"No…I don't know…no…" I choke. *This is not really happening,* my mind tries to reason with my heart, but my heart knows better. *Balance,* the thought flitters through my mind like an accusation, *you chose Reed…you can't have both. Here is the flip side to your happiness…choke on it.*

"Evie, focus…" Reed is saying, holding my chin in his hand and looking into my eyes. "What else did you feel? Is Brownie still with him?"

"I don't know…" I say. "This isn't Brennus' style—I don't think. He would be much more poetic, much less…brutal." I grasp my head to block out images of flesh being shredded from Russell.

Reed's eyebrows come together in a scowl. "Did he tell you anything else?" Reed asks me in a grave tone.

Breathing heavy, I push against Reed's chest so that I can run. I have to leave now. Russell needs me; he can't withstand what's happening to him. If I don't find him, he will be lying under different stars—his soul will leave. "He said 'goodbye,'" I choke. "How do I find him, Reed? I have to find him," I beg, putting my forehead against Reed's chest as his arms pull me to him.

"Zee, find out their last known position. Track the cells. Try to get in touch with Brownie. When you target the area, find out whom we have there to investigate. Take Preben and Phaedrus with you, keep them updated on whatever you discover," Reed says, while scooping me up in his arms, carrying me to the door. "You four, follow me," Reed orders the Powers who are standing just outside the room. Nodding they fall in behind us.

"Wait, we can start towards the Ukraine, to wherever they were last and Zee can call us and let us know where they are, while we're on the way. We can keep in touch," I say, trying to use logic to overcome the panic that is making it hard for me to breathe.

"No," Reed replies in a firm tone, continuing to carry me in the direction of our room.

"No?" I ask because he can't be serious. My best friend is being tortured. There is no way I'm staying here while that is happening.

"We will find Russell. I will send angels to look for him. We will get Dominion involved because we have no choice. They are the logical choice. Powers are created to track and annihilate the Fallen."

"Dominion will keep him if they find him. They will use him like they want to use me," I say, grasping his arm.

"I think he will prefer Dominion over the Fallen," Reed says with grim conviction.

"You think that the Fallen have him?" I ask, feeling fear stab me.

"It would make sense. Someone is torturing him, but they haven't killed him. They want answers—about a being that is exactly like him that they have been looking for, a female—that was his warning to you. He can't keep you from them, he will have to tell them about you because of the pain," he replies with regret. "Every type of demon is looking for you—the Gancanagh haven't been discreet in their inquiries. The fallen Seraphim already knew about you—they had Alfred watching you, but he failed to report back. They have begun their search for you in earnest."

"And now someone has Russell, but you think what they really want is me?" I ask, feeling sick.

"I'm sure they won't kill him until they get you," he says. "The fact that they don't have you yet is what will keep him alive."

"Why do they want me?" I ask weakly.

"Evie, there are so many, many reason to want you, I don't know where to begin," he says as we arrive at our pagoda. He lays me gently on the huge bed, saying, "You will need to stay here for now while I take care of some things. I will send Buns to keep you company." He doesn't wait for my reaction, but turns towards the door again.

"*What!* No, Reed, I have to…" I say, scrambling off the bed to follow him back out.

Reed turns back around abruptly. "You have to stay here, Evie. If you leave and stumble into whoever took Russell, then he is dead. Do you understand? You are the key to keeping him alive. They need him to get to you."

Zephyr enters our pagoda just then with Buns slung over his shoulder.

Buns is saying something in Angel that sounds really lovely, but by the look on her face, I can tell she is really telling him off. Zephyr seems to be ignoring her and waiting for her to stop speaking.

When Buns pauses, Zephyr asks her, "What will you do if I put you down?"

"I'm going to look for Brownie and Russell, Zee—this is so shady—you can't stop me! I know tons of Reapers who can kick Fallen ass. If one of those evil half-wits is torturing them, then I'm in," Buns says flailing her feet, trying to get free. Zephyr looks like he can hold her all day with his one hand. She is not moving him an inch.

"You are not designed to fight Fallen, Buns," Zephyr says in a patient tone. "And neither are your friends."

"Ha! Like you guys are the only ones able to go toe-to-toe with them," Buns says with sarcasm. "Just because we're Reapers doesn't mean we can't fight this war alongside you. It just means we have to be a little craftier than Powers. They've got my family, Zee."

"You are going to tear them apart, are you?" Zephyr asks with skepticism.

"*No!* I'm going to light 'em up," Buns retorts, "*after* I get Brownie and Russell out of wherever they are. I can find them. I have contacts. *Reaper contacts!*" she says significantly.

"Good. Find them. That will be very helpful. You can work the phones, get your people involved, but you are staying here and your people are not to engage the enemy. They are to report their findings to us. Do you understand?" he asks Buns in a grave tone.

"What are my other options?" Buns asks coolly.

"I can sit here with you and babysit you, if you like, but that won't help find Brownie or Russell," Zephyr says and I watch Buns scowl.

"Fine, Zee!" she retorts with heat. Zephyr relents then and puts Buns down and she immediately crosses her arms in front of her, tapping her foot as she scowls at his face. "When I find them, I'm going to go and get them," she says in anger.

"And, I will go with you," he replies with calm.

I put my hands to my eyes to cover them in frustration. I inhale a breath and smell Russell on my hands. Pulling my hands back from my face, I lift the sleeve of my shirt to my nose and inhale again. His scent is covering me, like I have been pressed up against him and it fills me with a longing that I have come to know as the yearning of my soul. Buns sees me and says softly to Zee, "I'll work the phone, you get to your contacts. We have to get them back."

"It's definitely not the Gancanagh that has him," I murmur, looking up and seeing all of their eyes on me. "Smell me. I'm not sticky sweet, like someone who has been with the Gancanagh. There is something about this smell that is different from how Russell smells. It's Russell, but it's something else…something…" I trail off because I have no idea just what I'm smelling. It's not Sheol because I know what the Fallen smell like: rotten and grotesque. This is something else. It smells like— a gas main smells—like natural gas or sort of like the hallway smelled near the boiler room at my old high school when the janitors left the door open.

Reed comes close to me again, inhaling the scent from my hair. Stepping back from me, his face pales. He speaks rapidly to Zephyr in Angel and Buns gasps as she drops the phone that she had clasped in her hands. Instantly, she is hugging me, inhaling deeply. When she lets go of me, her eyes fill with tears. Without a word, she turns towards the door and begins to leave. Zephyr steps in front of her quickly, catching her in his arms before she can make it out the door.

She speaks brokenly to him in Angel as Zephyr sweeps her off of her feet, murmuring to her in her ear. Their reaction to what I just said scares me more than anything else I have experienced today. It's as if they have just gotten the worst news of their lives.

"Who do we know?" Zephyr asks Reed, his deep voice resonating in the quiet room. "I haven't…I have little experience with them. You?"

"Some," Reed says faintly. "We will need magic, powerful, ancient…some humans possessed the knowledge—the Bedouins, we would need someone with knowledge of the…" he breaks into Angel, apparently because it does not translate to English. "Or, possibly an Undine…"

"You want to bring a wraith into this?" Zephyr asks as his frown turns grim.

"Undines have a natural defense against Ifrits—it makes sense," Reed replies with equal grimness.

"What's an Ifrit?" I ask them, honing in on their conversation. My question is met with silence, and then blatantly ignored.

"Do you have anyone in mind? Have you had any dealings with Undines recently?" Zephyr asks.

I want to ask what an Undine is, but I'm holding back because they are working the problem out and I don't want to interrupt their thought process.

"Yes," Reed admits with reluctance. Zephyr's eyes widen, but he doesn't say anything. When I look at Reed, he looks a little flushed, like he is blushing. "Sort of—define your idea of recent…"

Seeing Buns's phone on the floor, I pick it up, bringing it to her. She doesn't take it from me when I try to hand it to her. "Aren't you going to call your contacts, Buns," I ask in a soft voice, watching her face as she rests her cheek against Zephyr's chest. She shakes her head no, looking like she is in shock.

"She can't involve the Reapers," Reed says in a gentle tone, taking Buns's phone from my hand and setting it on the desk.

"Why not?" I ask.

"It's not safe for them," he replies.

"Safe?" I say, like it's a foreign word that has no meaning to me. My head is spinning. *Buns was talking about kicking Fallen ass only minutes ago, now it's not safe for Reapers.*

"That leaves finding them difficult," Zephyr continues. "We have to be careful regarding who goes. They will have to work in teams—take precautions—have alternative methods to employ if they get pinned down. Dominion should be advised—with such a threat in the area, no one is safe."

No one is safe? I hear the words from one of the most powerful creatures in the universe and beyond.

"What in the *Hell* is an *Ifrit?*" I demand, seething. "I have been led to believe that angels are the most powerful beings around, but you act like theses Ifrits are invincible."

Reed, looking tense, says, "They are not invincible, Evie, but they are endowed with powers that make it hard for us to kill them. Their skin is virtually impenetrable, so force and strength doesn't mean much. There was a purpose for that. They are angel hunters—angel assassins. They were created to annihilate the Fallen and they were highly effective. But they grew…disgruntled and stopped hunting just Fallen. They saw all angels as a threat—inferior to them."

"Why?' I whisper, feeling like I'm drowning.

"Who can say? Maybe they don't like competition. They have a weakness though," he says.

"What kills them?" I ask.

"Magic," Reed replies with absolute seriousness. I want to laugh and pretend he didn't just say "magic." The very word "magic" makes me want to roll my eyes. "It's probably only one Ifrit, the princes don't usually work together—they are not social creatures," he continues, not seeing the complete unreality of the situation.

"Princes?" I repeat, latching on to the word.

"The princes are the only Ifrits left. The most powerful had set themselves up as a monarchy—royalty. With help, we managed to wipe out most Ifrits, but the royals just won't die. They have pacts with the Fallen now, they work together when it's convenient for the Ifrits."

"The enemy of my enemy is my friend," I whisper to myself.

"Yes," Reed agrees. "The Fallen could have gotten the Ifrits involved to search for you, but that takes things to a different level."

"Why?" I ask.

"That would mean that the Fallen are more afraid of what you are capable of doing than what the Ifrits are capable of doing," Reed says, watching my reaction.

"Or they are better buddies than you know," I reply, hoping we are both wrong.

Reed blinks slowly, surprised that I'm keeping up with him. I am, but just barely. I have had to brush off the chill that is creeping all through me, like someone is walking on my grave, and an equal feeling that I'm really insane and haven't taken my meds today.

"Or, they just *want* Evie," Buns says in a soft tone. "She is part human...remember? Maybe they heard of her and want to see her for themselves."

Reed's face turns livid and I think for a second that he might smash something. "I didn't need that visual, Buns," Reed mutters through his teeth.

"Sorry, sweetie," she says, "but aren't human women their thing? I mean, they find angels appalling, but they would probably be psyched to run across someone like Evie. She is human with the endurance of an angel. For a dying race, that would be significant."

Reed does freak then, he barks out orders in his Angelic language to the angels just outside our room. They are the ones he had ordered to follow us earlier. Then he turns to me, grasping my upper arms. "Promise me that you will stay here," he says in a tone that he hasn't used with me in a long time. It's his icy tone.

I nod shakily. He leans down and quickly brushes his lips to mine, and then he turns and leaves the room without any other explanation.

I walk to the bed in confusion. "Did you just tell Reed that an Ifrit wants to make me his baby-mama?" I ask Buns, sitting rigidly on the corner of the bed.

"Uh huh," Buns replies, letting go of Zephyr and coming to sit next to me on the bed. Taking my hand, she leans her head on my shoulder. "They love human women. They fall in love with their souls…but they usually end up killing what they love because, well, they are freaking monsters and human women are frail. But, that's not the case with you, is it?"

"What…there aren't any female Ifrits?" I ask her.

"Nope," she says.

"So they fall in love with human women?" I ask.

"Yep, they got it goin' on," she says without a hint of humor.

Goose bumps rise on my arms. "What do they look like?" I ask.

"Whatever they want," she says in a low tone, "they shape-shift, but I'm told they have a few…traits."

"Traits?" I ask, trying to sound calm so she will continue to tell me what I need to know.

"They mostly like to be human looking. Since they're attracted to women, they want to look pleasing to them," she says and I don't know if that makes me feel better or worse. "They have wings, too, but not like ours or yours."

"What are they like?" I ask, puzzled.

"They aren't separate limbs, like ours. Their wings sprout from their arms. Like pterodactyls would be the best description," she says. "Or bats."

"Sexy," I say, feeling appalled. "So they can fly?"

"Uh huh, that makes them dangerous, because they're hard to escape."

"So they're fast," I say, listening intently. "What else?"

"They have an ability to manipulate fire," she says.

"Manipulate it, how?" I ask.

"Oh, well, they can roll around in it…pick it up…throw it… eat it…become it," she says, not smiling.

"Hah," I whimper, and then swallow hard. "Okay, that's a little scary."

Buns shivers in agreement. "Sweetie, if it wants you, it won't want to hurt you," she murmurs.

"That's a big if, Buns," I reply. "The first thing we need to do is find out where they are."

"I tried calling Brownie, she's not answering her phone. Neither is Russell," Buns says and we are both silent for a moment.

"What if I ask Russell where he is?" I ask in a thoughtful tone.

Buns's brow wrinkles. "He's not answering his phone," Buns says.

"I'm not going to call him," I reply, standing up.

Zephyr growls and says, "Let's discuss this further. You want to send him one of your clones?"

"Yeah," I nod.

"If he is with the Ifrit, then you run the risk of exposing the fact that you do, indeed, exist," Zephyr reasons.

"Okay," I say with a shrug.

Zephyr's eyes narrow dangerously. "Okay?" he asks, shaking his head like he didn't hear me.

"Yeah, maybe the freak will stop torturing Russell if he sees me. I'll tell Russell to come clean, to tell him about me," I say, pacing the floor. "I only wish that I could send one that I can control, but I don't know how I'll find him that way. When I let them burst out of me, they seem to know where they are going."

"We do not know if it will be able to follow the trail of your clone straight to you," Zephyr says, using logic. "We need to have a back up plan in place in the event it comes for you. You must wait…"

"No way, Zee," I shoot back. "You didn't feel the torture. If there is a way to stop it, I have to try."

"What if it kills us all?" Zephyr asks me in a quiet tone.

"Can one Ifrit kill all of the angels we have here?" I ask, freaking out at the thought of one creature being that powerful.

"I honestly don't know," Zephyr replies. "We should discuss this with Reed. He has the most experience with Ifrits. I do recall him telling me once that he led missions against them in the past."

"But it's Brownie and Russell we're talking about here, Zee," I say pleadingly. "The time that we're killing here might be killing them."

"Or, we are keeping them alive because the Ifrit doesn't know where we are yet," Zephyr counters. "I will go talk to Reed if you promise not to succumb to your emotions."

"Okay," I say when I see Buns nod in agreement with Zephyr.

CHAPTER 6

Undines And Ifrits

"So, we are in agreement?" Phaedrus asks, searching the faces of everyone around the table. I watch as Zephyr, Buns, and Preben all give their assent. Turning my head to look at Reed, I see that he is sitting stonily, staring at me. He hates this plan. He also completely hates my new ability right now. He made the argument that we don't know if the Ifrit can track my clone back to me if I release one and send it to Russell.

A plan B is being put into place to counter the risks. The Undines have been sent for and should be arriving soon. I thought that nothing would surprise me after hearing about Ifrits, but it turns out that I was wrong. I'm in complete shock when I learn that water sprites are coming to perform their magic to defend us against the Ifrit, should it become necessary.

"Evie will send her messenger to Russell. I will try to track it. If I can follow it, then I will report back their location. If I'm unable to keep up with it, there is still a chance I can find where it's going. If I can track it like all of my other targets, its heat may lead me to Russell," Phaedrus says.

Reed remains silent, not agreeing to our plan. I sigh because I know all of his reasons. He thinks that I'm not able to see the big picture. He thinks that I still look at all of the scary creatures that I'm learning about as myths. He's wrong. I'm learning that "myth" doesn't mean what I thought it did. It really means, "based on truth" and the truth is terrifying.

"It's all right, Reed," I say in a gentle tone. "I know what the princes are…and I know what I am. I was created to do this, or else I wouldn't have been given this ability—this gift."

"*No*, you don't know the princes, Evie," Reed states, putting both his hands on the table and leaning across it to glare at me.

Meeting him halfway, I say in a placating voice, "Well then, this will be my baptism by fire."

That is the exact wrong thing to say. Before I know what's happening, Reed picks me up and flies with me out the door. He flies straight up into the dusky twilight at a speed that I couldn't have matched if I were running. He takes me up high enough that there is not even a whisper of sound but our breathing.

Reed murmurs in my ear, "I don't possess magic. I cannot protect you from the Ifrits. I'm not made to withstand them." He says it like he is admitting to the worst crime imaginable.

"Reed," I whisper back, hugging him close to me as we hover in the air. "We have to trust that this is meant, because I can't leave them there. You can't either."

We begin to lose altitude as he leans his forehead against mine. "I can't lose you again," he says.

"I will always find my way back to you, no matter what. I love you…just promise me you'll never let me go," I say, looking in his eyes.

"Never. I will never let you go," he agrees as we begin to slowly descend. "I'm fighting my own war here. I don't want to tell you this, but I know you haven't even considered the possibility that we might not be able to save them."

"Don't say that," I hush him, feeling ill.

"There may not be a compromise," he says, searching my face for signs of understanding.

I shake my head, "I can't just let them die."

"You may not have a choice," he says quickly. "Bargaining with the enemy is never a good idea. We need to defeat them, but I cannot see a clear way to do that without the loss of the hostages."

"We'll find them and a plan will present itself. We have Phaedrus. He can work miracles," I say, grasping at any argument that will keep fear from crushing me. I see uncertainty in his eyes.

"You can send Russell the message, but you're not going to them," Reed says in a way that makes me think that arguing isn't going to help.

I try anyway. "But if Phaedrus finds them, then—"

"Then, a rescue attempt will be mounted, but you won't be involved," he says with finality.

"What if I can help?" I retort.

"You can't," Reed states without a hint of doubt.

"You don't know that," I counter.

"I will not risk you beyond the messenger. You may send it, but that will be the extent of your involvement," he replies.

"Reed, you're being unreasonable," I say.

"No, I'm protecting you," he says stiffly. I can see that he is completely serious about this.

"You can't keep me in the dark—they're my family. I need to know what's happening to them. Will you tell me if you find them?" I ask. I want to know how far he plans to go to protect me.

"I don't know," he answers.

My eyes narrow, "I don't want that kind of protection," I respond.

"I'm not interested in what you want right now. I'm only focused on what you need,'" he says in a calm voice.

"What makes you an expert on what I need?" I ask him heatedly.

He points to the symbol of my wings that are branded on his chest, "This makes me the expert and the authority on what you need."

I pull my shirt back so that he can see his wings branded on my chest and ask angrily, "Then, what does this make me?"

"Mine," he replies. I begin to shake my head and feel him tighten his grasp on me. "You are mine and you will listen to me," he says as my feet touch back down on the ground in the courtyard outside of the main pagoda. "Do you think that it's a coincidence that I am as old as I am? That I have lived this long?" he asks. "I know what we are facing. I've faced it before."

Pulling away from him, I turn and begin walking back towards the conference room. As Reed walks next to me, his jaw sets as he reaches out and takes my hand in his. Looking at his profile, I stop walking and say, "In case you haven't noticed, I have a brain. I can think for myself."

"Yes, I know," he says. "That is precisely the reason I don't want you involved in this."

"WHAT?" I shout.

"You are too unpredictable. You'll do something rash," he says positively, like there is no doubt that I will go off like a loose cannon.

"That sounds much better to me than doing *nothing!*" I retort.

"I have no doubt that you see it that way," he replies, giving me his severest frown.

We're on the threshold of the pagoda and I'm sure that everyone inside can hear everything that we are saying now so I just glare at Reed. Before I can think of a reply, a voice sounds from inside the pagoda.

"REED!" The musical-twinkling voice says, just as a lithe, beautiful woman runs out of the pagoda ahead of us and launches herself into Reed's arms. Reed lets go of my hand as she wraps her arms around his neck, clinging to his body seductively. Her long, blond hair trails down her back like waves of gold. "I am very angry with you, Reed. Why weren't you here to greet me when I arrived?" she asks as her lovely mouth pushes out in a pretty pout while she trails her fingertip slowly down his chest.

Before I can check my reaction, a low growl emanates from me as jealousy at seeing this woman pressed to Reed overwhelms me. Hearing my warning, her face snaps in my direction. Her sapphire eyes narrow in anger as her glare rakes me up and down. She raises her hand in my direction and I notice that her fingers are webbed. High-pitched sounds flow from her mouth as the wind picks up around me blowing my hair.

Looking in the direction of the wind, I'm just in time to see the water from the tranquil plunge pool in the courtyard rise up out of its tiled reservoir. The water hovers in the air, like a massive wave for a moment, before it flows towards me. I'm unable to react as the water pours around me, engulfing me within its icy depths. The water swiftly pulls me back with it as it recedes, returning to the pool at an incredible velocity. Sick and dizzy, as if I have fallen from a towering height, the current tows me down and I fight hard to regain the surface. My panicked brain becomes frantic when I'm able to kick back up to the surface of the water only to find a thick sheet of ice covering it.

Swirling in the eddy beneath the frozen water, I pound my fists against the ice trapping me. Reed and Preben appear on the other side, trying desperately to break the ice between us. Pressing my hands against the magical barrier that won't allow Reed to penetrate it, I watch as he grimly turns from me, shouting something in the other direction that I hear only as muffled noise.

My hair waves in my face as I scratch my fingernails into the surface of the ice. It's cold but there is also a quivering energy coursing beneath my hands as I touch it. Closing my eyes, the palms of my hands begin heating up; they burn like they did when I had healed Russell all those months ago.

As I open my eyes again, the lack of oxygen makes my lungs ache while my hands glow like they're being lit from within me. In seconds, I push through the surface of the ice, evaporating it to steamy vapor that rises from the pool. Gasping for air, Reed pulls me out of the water, clutching me in his arms while whispering soothing Angelic words in my ear.

I try hard to breathe evenly as I see the blond harpy scowling at me from where I had been standing before I was swept away by the water. Rage builds in me and I struggle in Reed's arms to get away from him so I can cut her heart out, if she has one. "You can't kill her, not if you want to save Russell," Reed says in my ear. "That's Safira. She's one of the Undine who has come to help us defeat the Ifrit.

"She just tried to kill me," I retort, glaring at the beautiful creature who sneers back at me with equal loathing.

"Well, love, you did growl at her," Reed says neutrally.

I stop struggling to look at the traitor's face in front of me. My eyes narrow to slits. "Are you serious?" I ask him incredulously.

"She was just about to let you out of the water, right before you broke through it. She was startled by you and she over-reacted," Reed explains, defending Safira.

"So you're saying this is all just a misunderstanding?" I ask with *faux* sweetness.

"Yes," Reed says with a look of relief until I narrow my eyes and growl at him. Buns steps between us then; she pulls me away from Reed, wrapping her arms around me.

"Are you okay?" she asks, leading me away in the direction of her pagoda. I look back over my shoulder to see that Safira is now amid several ethereal-looking young women, all of which are now glaring in my direction.

"No, that witch just tried to drown me!" I say with disgust, pulling at my wet clothing.

"I know, we all saw it," she says. "You really scared her. You should've seen her eyes when you broke through her spell. Her jaw dropped open and she called for back up from her sisters. I think she was afraid you were going to come after her," Buns finishes, grinning at me like she's proud of me.

"The thought did cross my mind," I reply, trying to get a grip on myself. I feel edgy, like I want to smash something and my heart is still pounding from my struggle in the pool.

"Maybe we should keep you two separated, I mean, you're just getting used to being bound to Reed—you don't need the pressure of having a Reed groupie around, especially with…" she stops talking because I'm no longer moving with her to her room.

"Excuse me?" I ask Buns softly.

"I was just saying maybe we should keep you two apart," she says.

"No, no…the other part," I say, winding my finger in a circle.

"Oh…the Reed groupie part?" she asks with a sheepish look.

"Yes, that part," I reply stiffly.

"Zephyr is going to kill me…it's ancient history and I mean *ancient*," she says quickly. "This all happened thousands of years ago—before I even got here."

"You mean Reed and Safira…" I trail off.

"No, not for him, but for her it was like love at first sight. They worked together in a unit that targeted Ifrits, back in the day. Here's the thing about Undines, when they fall in love with someone, they don't care if the feeling is mutual or not—they pursue the object of their affection with a single-mindedness that is very close to stalker, if you know what I mean," Buns explains. When she sees my face, she adds quickly, "But we need her. She and her girls can bury an Ifrit with their magic."

"How?" I ask.

"They're wraiths—elementals that can manipulate water. Water trumps fire," Buns says, leading me again towards her room. "And you can see how effectively they can wield it. We need her. Brownie and Russell need her, so you're going to be nice to her—kiss her butt if you have to. We can't afford to lose them and they are *extremely* touchy."

"Are you telling me I should just let her put her hands all over Reed and not do anything about it?" I ask Buns, struggling with the new circumstances of this arrangement.

"I'm saying let him handle it. He'll keep her off of him because he only wants you. Just be cool because if you don't, Russell is dead," Buns says, putting it in no uncertain terms.

"Oh," I say, paling at the thought of losing Russell and Brownie. Buns leads me into her room and hands me a towel. I dry myself off while she walks to her closet. I pull the wet clothes from me and slip on a very sexy little Asian dress Buns hands me. The silk fabric clings to me just like my wet clothes had.

As I look up at her skeptically, Buns shrugs, "I said you can't kill her, I didn't say that you can't be hot while you play it cool."

"I don't care how I look right now," I reply, running my hand down the deep red silk of the dress. "I just have to get back to Phaedrus, so I can send my clone and he can track it."

"Here," Buns says as she winds my hair into a bun and shoves two black sticks in it to secure it from unraveling.

"Thanks," I say, walking towards the door. As I step outside, I see Reed leaning against one of the posts of the porch. He falls in step next to me as I walk past him towards the conference area.

"Buns told you?" he asks, scanning my face with a grim expression.

"Told me what?" I counter, my jaw clenched as I quicken my pace.

"The only reason that Safira is here is to help us fight the Ifrit," he says in a low tone.

"Does she know that?" I ask him, not slowing down.

"What do you mean?" he asks.

"Does she know that it's the *only* reason you asked her here or does she think it's because you wanted to see her again?" I ask.

"That is not why she attacked you, Evie," Reed says. "She thought you were evil when she saw you."

Stopping in my tracks, I bring my hands to my eyes, rubbing them in frustration. "And that's okay with you?"

"No, it's not. I had to fight the intense urge I had so I wouldn't kill her. Believe me, many brutal ways to kill her crossed my mind when I couldn't break through the ice and get to you. She has no idea just how close she was to being dead," he says in a quiet tone, pulling my hands away from my eyes so that he can look into them. "But, if I killed her, we would have almost no chance of saving Russell. Do not think for one second that I enjoy having her around. It took me years to convince her to love someone else. Do you have any idea how persistent an Undine can be?" he asks in frustration.

Seeing how miserable he is, makes me feel awful for being jealous about Safira. "If the Undines are anything like the Gancanagh, you have my sympathy," I murmur, wrapping my arms around his neck and hugging him.

His hands slide down my sides, caressing me as the silk dress slips beneath his fingers. "There is no one for me but you," he says as he leans nearer and kisses me.

"I'll try to keep that in mind the next time she throws herself at you," I reply, melting against him.

"Please do," he whispers just before his lips tease mine again.

"Hey, does your persuasion work on Undines?" I ask, pulling back a little to look in his eyes.

"No," he replies, smiling at my disappointment.

"She can't make you—I mean her magic can't…" I trail off, wrinkling my brow as I trace my fingertip over his chest.

"Nothing she has tried has worked on me yet," Reed says, grinning.

"Good," I reply with relief at the thought of Safira being unable to make Reed fall in love with her by using magic. I hug him quickly and then pull back out of his embrace. Taking Reed's hand, I begin walking again towards the conference area. "You should've warned her about me, before she came here."

"They were all told of you, it's just that seeing you is so…" he trails off.

"Horrifying?" I ask, trying to hide the sinking feeling I have inside at their reaction to me.

"Not horrifying…it's just that you are so dangerous and so beautiful that your presence offers almost no room for rational thought," he says. "But there is nothing I would change about you. You are perfection."

I roll my eyes at him like he's insane. I'm about to tell him all of the things that I would like to change about myself, given the opportunity, when Zephyr shows up on the path ahead.

"Problem," Zephyr says, looking at Reed.

"Undines?" Reed replies.

"Yes, they refuse to help defend Evie or Russell. They will fight the Ifrit for us, but they will not intervene if it comes for the 'half-breeds,'" he says seriously.

"Why?" Reed asks in a low tone, looking at me to judge how I'm taking being called a half-breed. I try to remain neutral, but what I really want to do is scoff.

"They say that they don't want to anger God," he replies and Reed scoffs, which makes me want to throw my arms around him and kiss him again. "Do we proceed with our plan?" Zephyr asks Reed.

"Yes," I say before Reed can answer.

Reed closes his eyes briefly before he opens them again and turns to me. "Love, if we don't have a guarantee that they will help if an Ifrit should find you, then we cannot move forward with our plan.

"We can. They said they wouldn't help me, but if an Ifrit comes they will defend all of you. That's good enough for me," I say.

"It's not good enough for me," Reed replies sternly.

I turn to Zephyr, "Will they go in to save Brownie, since she isn't a half-breed?"

"Yes," Zephyr replies.

"Fine, then we're mostly covered. We just have to make sure that when they go in, they plan to kill the Ifrit. It can't just be a snatch and grab of Brownie. If they kill the Ifrit, then they save Russell, too, even if it is inadvertent." I reason.

"That will be the strategy that we will be pushing for. We do not want the Ifrit to survive for any reason," Zephyr affirms, his blue eyes watching me as I nod.

"Then there is no problem," I say, seeing that Reed is having a huge problem with it already.

"You can't just shrug off this new wrinkle. The parameters of the mission have changed. There are new variables now," he says.

"We don't have time for a strategy lesson. We need to locate the Ifrit. I'm the only link we have at this point to finding them. No one is safe until we kill it, you said so yourself," I say rationally, watching his face go blank so that I can't read what he's thinking. "I have protection—an entire compound of angels—"

"If I tell you no, Evie, what will you do?" Reed asks, cocking his head to the side, waiting for my response.

I look down, not wanting him to see my eyes. I don't want him to read what I will do. My mind has already come up with several plans to find Russell and Brownie, none of which will make Reed happy. "This is the best compromise, you should take it," I say in a soft tone and then I hear two sets of growls, one from Reed, the other from Zephyr.

Reed speaks softly to Zephyr in Angel. Zephyr counters and my head snaps up because I'm now being shut out of the conversation. Growling at them, I begin walking again, but Reed scoops me up, changing direction and heading towards our room. "Reed, what are you doing?" I ask.

"I'm going to negotiate with the Undines. You're going to stay here until I'm finished," he says, dumping me on my bed and turning towards the door. Reed speaks to Zephyr who has followed us. Together, they begin to walk out of the room. Getting off the bed, I start to follow them, but two of Preben's men step in front of me at the threshold to the courtyard. One is Elan and the other is named Sorin.

"Excuse me," I say to Sorin, trying to get around him, but he won't move.

"*Reed!*" I call out behind the wall of Power angels, seeing him walking away and talking to Zephyr.

"I will be back shortly. Try not to irritate your guards," he says smoothly.

"That's not fair!" I call to him, but he doesn't answer me as he disappears from my sight. Completely infuriated, I pull the doors closed, shutting out the angels who are grinning at me like I'm some sort of sideshow freak.

Pacing the floor, I feel like I'm about to jump out of my skin. *They're making this so difficult when it's really so simple,* I think to myself. It's Russell. There is nothing that anyone is going to say that will convince me not to give him any help that I can. Now that I know the others will be protected, I really don't need their permission. With this new clarity, a calm settles over me. I sit down on the bed and concentrate on what I want to do.

Controlling the spinning that makes it seem as if the entire room is being picked up and shaken, I allow a clone of me to push steadily from my body. I direct my clone to pass through the closed doors of my room. The darkness outside makes it difficult to tell exactly where I'm going so I focus on the red hanging lanterns strung in the trees ahead of her. The familiar faces of the angels guarding me outside enter my consciousness. Elan tries to stop my image, but she passes right through him. Sorin enters my room; I can feel him near me, but I'm keeping my eyes closed so that I can concentrate on navigating my clone.

As my image walks in silence towards the conference room, I hear the heated debate ahead as Reed's beautiful voice speaks in Angel. I follow the sound of it, knowing that Phaedrus must be somewhere nearby. Entering the room, there are several intakes of breath, mainly coming from the side of the table where the Undines are seated. Ignoring them, I continue moving my clone beyond each one on my way to the end of the table.

Nearing Phaedrus, I almost make it to him when Reed steps right in front of me, trying to block my way. My clone passes right through him like a dream, approaching Phaedrus to whisper to him, "You have five seconds. Be ready."

Phaedrus rises out of his chair, exhaling in relief. He has been in torment over knowing that his targets, Russell and Brownie, need his help and not being able to find them on his own.

Even through my clone's dim senses, I know that the entire room has heard me because they erupt in chaos. I don't pay any attention. I know that this may be the last thing that Russell will hear from me. Adrenaline flashes into my system at that thought. With my heartbeat drumming in my ears, I reach deep within myself, pushing every ounce of love and devotion that I feel for Russell out of me and into my clone. As I do it, my senses within her heighten until the room around her begins to glow from the light she emits. Then, like a bolt of lightening, she streams out of the room in a flash, and I lose the connection to her.

I find myself back in my room, seated on my bed. I quickly reach deep within myself again, tapping into all the rage and anger that I feel for the creature who has taken my soul mate. The room spins again as I formulate my message to the Ifrit. My messenger bolts from the room with my last thought: *Mercy for them or there will be no mercy for you.*

CHAPTER 7

Water And Fire

Feeling like the room is still spinning, I reach my hand up to my face, wiping my nose. A smear of blood transfers to my hand, letting me know that my nose is bleeding. Dabbing at it with the back of my hand, I walk towards the bathroom to get a tissue. Before I make it halfway there, Reed is standing in front of me looking like an avenging angel who has come to smite me for my sins. His charcoal-gray wings are arching out so that I can't see around him and he is glowering at me as his hands are clenched in fists at his sides.

Knowing I'm in serious trouble with Reed and possibly every other angel in China, I back away from him while holding out my hands in front of me. I'm disturbed to realize that my hands are shaking a little. "You can't be mad at me because *you* shut *me* out first!" I say, trying to go on the offensive, while looking for a better defensive position within the room, but there is no place to hide in here.

"There were two," Reed says with deathly calm as he holds up two fingers, matching me step-for-step, not letting me gain any distance from him. "I assume the first clone that Phaedrus followed was intended for Russell. Please tell me that the second one was sent to Brownie."

My nervousness increases, knowing that he is not going to like the truth. "I had to make sure it knows that I exist so that it stops trying to wring the information from Russell and Brownie," I say as an explanation to his question.

"Genevieve," Reed says icily and I pale. "What did you say to the Ifrit?" he asks, struggling for control.

"Well…I don't want to tell you that part," I say in honesty.

"Why not?" he snaps back.

"Because it might make you mad," I reply shakily.

"I'm already angry," he snarls.

"True, but you're not going to like this," I warn him. When I hear him growl I quickly say, "I told it, 'Mercy for them or there will be no mercy for you.'"

Slowly, his wings retract as his face loses its scowl. He cocks his head to the side asking, "You said that to the Ifrit?" I nod, watching him shake his head tiredly. "The Ifrit will come for you now. He won't be able to resist such an enticing challenge issued from such an incredibly beautiful being." He turns then, striding towards the door.

Moving faster than him, I manage to get in front of him before he leaves the room. "Wait! Where are you going?" I ask, panicking because he looks grim.

"I have to negotiate with the Undines. They have to see reason and protect you from the Ifrit, now that you have provoked it," he says in a stern tone.

"You have to do that right now?" I ask him, wringing my hands. "Can I come with you?" I ask him hopefully. I don't want to stay here alone. What I just did is now beginning to register in my mind and fear is making my hands tremble.

"No," Reed answers evenly, "get some sleep. You look exhausted." He steps around me then, telling the angels who have been guarding me not to let me out of my room.

"Reed! You'll tell me if you hear from Phaedrus?" I call from the doorway of our room. He ignores me and continues walking. I turn away from him, feeling miserable. I have managed to anger everyone that is here to help me, but I can't pretend that I would do anything differently because I wouldn't. Walking listlessly to the bed, I lay down on it, pulling Reed's pillow to me and hugging it for comfort. Shivering with dread, I close my eyes, feeling the need for sleep burning me. I begin to drift off and I try to fight it. I want to stay awake in case they hear from Phaedrus. If he loses the clone, I plan to send another one that may pass him, allowing him to pick up the trail again. Jerking my eyes open once or twice, I soon lose the battle against fatigue, falling asleep.

Warm air filters in the open windows, stirring the hair that has fallen in wisps from the sticks holding it in a knot at my nape. *"I cannot give you his soul, Alya, but I can give you his heart. I will cut it out for you…"* a voice whispers to me like a caress, making my heart pound in my chest and panic grip me. *"That is the only mercy that you will have from me…unless, you give me what I desire."*

"What do you want?" I ask sluggishly, feeling weighed down and listless. *"You give me Russell and Brownie, and I'll give you what you want."*

"You are wise, Alya," he says with a raspy resonance. *"We may both get what we want, in the end. Tell me where you are now."*

"China…I'm in China. Where are you now? I'll come to you…" I insist.

Drops of water raining on my face and body cause my eyes to flutter open right before the drops become a deluge, soaking me. "Wake up!" a twinkling voice says from near me as rain continues to fall on my head.

Dripping wet I open my eyes to see Safira standing over me with her arms crossed in front of her. "What do you think you're doing?" she asks me, tapping her foot and frowning at me from the dry side of the bed. She looks like some kind of beautiful mermaid who has been transformed to walk on terra firma. I think I can even see something on her neck that looks like gills just behind her ears.

Shivering from being doused with cold water, I clench my teeth and reply, "I was sleeping! Do you mind?"

"Don't lie to me! I can smell magic all over this room. You were *speaking* to the *Ifrit!*" she accuses, flicking her hand and dispelling the rain like she is turning off a tap.

"I was…" I pause, thinking about what just happened—the whispering voice—the smell of molten heat in the room. "How did it find me?" I ask her with a shudder.

"*You* gave it a connection to you when you sent it your spirit or image or whatever you are calling it" she replies, pointing her webbed fingers at me. "Were you bargaining with it?" she asks as her skin sparkles a little, like she is covered with a light coating of crystallized brine.

Rubbing my eyes, I sit up in the bed. I duck my head and admit, "Yeah, I think I was bargaining with it."

"I *knew* it! I *knew* you were an evil creature," she says, running her hand through her golden hair that sways like it's floating in a current. "I told them that you would betray us, but no one would listen to me after they heard the message you sent to the Ifrit. Threatening it with no mercy has won over all of the Powers; they will follow you into the abyss if you asked it of them. But, the first chance you get, you bargain with it," she sneers at me, exposing her wickedly sharp, pointed teeth.

"Do you know what 'Alya' means?" I ask her, ignoring her rant and trying to remember every word the Ifrit spoke.

"Why? Did he say it? It's a name...old...Arabic, it means 'heaven,'" she replies, and my heart skips a beat.

"Listen to me," I say, sitting up with supernatural speed and reaching for her. I grasp her upper arms before she can evade me, startling her with my strength and speed. Staring into her sapphire eyes, I continue, "If that thing comes here, I want you to do something for me," I say quietly, watching her eyes narrow. "I know that you care about Reed. I want you to make sure that nothing happens to him. I don't care how you do it—freeze him in a block of ice until the Ifrit is gone if you have to, just do it, okay?" I ask in desperation.

"You *are* evil!" she says, struggling to pull away from me. "He is a Power. No one protects a Power. They will slay you if you try."

"But, you love him..." I counter, trying to understand why she wouldn't want to save Reed.

"Yes, and I have loved him longer than you, long enough to know that he will never love me or forgive me if I try to protect him from danger," she retorts. "You do not know him at all, do you?" she accuses me. "Have you seen him fight? I doubt the Ifrit has a chance against him even with all of its magic. I'm much less worried about Reed fighting an Ifrit than I am at seeing him with you!"

"Why?" I ask her in shock.

"Because he will die for you," she glowers at me, causing me to feel the ferocious, stabbing fear that the image of Reed being hurt elicits.

"That's exactly what I'm trying *really* hard to prevent," I glower back. "So you find a way to help Reed because if something happens to him I'll find you."

"Are you threatening me?" she ask incredulously, blinking, and I notice a second set of eyelid-like film that covers her eyes momentarily before it retracts back beneath her normal eyelid.

"Yes!" I retort, going nose to nose with her.

Elan and Sorin step into the room then, grinning like they've been enjoying themselves. "I think that Preben will replace us if we do not step in now, although, my money is on the Seraph," Elan says to Sorin, as they casually flank us while we continue to glare at each other.

Safira's head snaps up at the insult and Elan is quick to sidestep the spout of water that she hurls at him. "Marlowe, Kendall—you must be losing your appeal. I wasn't finished speaking to the half-breed," Safira says insultingly.

Sorin's chin motions towards the door. "Don't blame them, they were highly entertaining, but it just didn't compare to what was going on in here," Sorin replies, watching the two lovely Undines who show themselves just outside the doorway to my room, looking vicious with their bared, sharp teeth. "And do not even consider freezing me in a block of ice or I will slay you," he continues with a cheeky grin.

"Is nothing private around here?" I ask them with irritation in my voice, letting go of Safira's arms and stepping back from her.

Elan's bright-white smile flashes at me, showing his perfect teeth. "You were hardly being discreet. You were shouting at each other," he says.

"Urr, you are all in love with this half-breed," Safira accuses them, storming towards the door. "Trouble will follow her wherever she goes. She is a tsunami and you are dancing around in a small boat."

"Yes, she is very dangerous—what could be wrong with that?" Sorin asks Elan with a perplexed expression, and then he sidesteps a funnel of water that comes spinning at him through the doorway as the Undines leave. It crashes into the far wall, causing a large puddle to splash onto the floor. It looks like monsoon season has begun early.

Still dripping wet from being rained on, I turn to my bodyguards, saying, "Do either of you know any magic that will clean up this water?"

"Towels," Sorin replies, running his hand through his sunny-blond hair.

"That's weak," I say, exhaling as I walk to the bathroom and gather a few towels to clean up the mess in the bedroom. I am surprised when Elan and Sorin both help me mop up the water. When we finish, I drape the wet towels and sheets over the porch railings and then go back in alone to clean myself up.

Stepping into the bathroom, I eye the bathtub, thinking how nice it would be to soak in it for a while. Then, thoughts of being trapped in it by Safira surface in my mind. I ignore the tub and turn on the shower. I don't know if I can really call it a shower though, it's more like a very large, marble-tiled glass enclosure with several large shower jets positioned around it. Stripping off the red silk dress, I pull the sticks from my hair, allowing it to spill down my back.

Once in the shower, I close my eyes as the warm water runs over my face and hair. Bowing my head, the water runs down my back and wings as I concentrate on the conversation I had with the Ifrit in my dream. *He had been about to tell me where he is. He had shown me something…a grassy field with a cluster of little wooden windmills with thatched roofs. They are not the type that I had seen in pictures of Holland, but much smaller, set on small pedestals of fieldstones with Queen Anne's lace growing around them. They are more like grain mills because there are lines attached to the sails so that they can be turned by hand if necessary. I had drifted past the windmills that had turned silently in perpetual motion and by a low, earthy house with whitewashed walls and a thatched roof. Beyond the modest white house there was…*I shudder.

"Are you cold?" Reed asks from behind me and I jump, spinning around just as his arms embrace me, pulling me to him.

Water spills onto his chest and neck, running in rivets over his bare skin. He reaches over and bumps the hot water nozzle a little, making the water steamy. I must have been really concentrating because I hadn't even felt the butterflies in my stomach that should've warned me of Reed's presence.

"Reed, what are you doing?" I ask.

"I'm checking on you," he replies in a gentle tone, his sexy voice touching me like a caress.

"Ah. And how do you find me?" I ask. He was angry with me when he left earlier, but he doesn't appear to be angry now. A slow smile is creeping to the corners of his mouth.

"This part of you, right here…" he says, leaning forward as his mouth nears my shoulder, "I find to be very lonely." He brushes his lips over the curve of my shoulder. "That's better," he breathes, while I exhale deeply, inching closer to him as my knees become weak. Lifting his lips from my shoulder, he brings them to the sensitive curve of my neck, saying, "And here, this spot, looks neglected, too."

"It does?" I ask, feeling unsteady. I slip my arms around his neck.

"Yes," he replies as his cheek grazes my sensitive skin, causing a shiver to escape me.

"What about this part, right here?" I ask him, touching my lips with my fingertips.

He responds by pressing his mouth to mine gently, savoring the feeling of the initial contact. When he pulls back to look into my eyes, I see the smoldering heat within his. "What happens to bad people when they die?" I whisper, feeling his lips tracing a path downward.

"Why?" he breathes against my skin.

"Because, what I want to do to you right now is very, vey, bad…" I trail off as he brushes his fingers lightly over my wings.

"This is not bad," he smiles at me, his green eyes deepening in the soft lighting of the shower. "This is right. You are mine and we are one."

"Ohh…that's good…" I say as my eyes close briefly, savoring the feeling of his hands. "That's very, very, good…" I sigh.

His hands weave through mine as he presses me back to the wet, marble-tiled wall. "*My* angel..." I hear him say against my skin. Neither of us speak again for quite some time.

◦◦

Reed holds my languid body to his, turning off the water and wrapping me in a huge towel before he carries me back into the bedroom. He finds the extra sheets I left there. Spreading them out, he quickly makes the bed while I watch him.

"So, you're not mad at me anymore?" I ask, leaning my head against the high back of the chair.

"No, I'm not angry with you at this particular moment," Reed smiles at me and my heart skips a beat. "The Undines have agreed to protect you," he explains.

"Really?" I ask, because I'm shocked to find that they will help after my conversation with Safira. "Your negotiations were successful?"

"Yes, Liv, their leader, agrees with us. She gave them all the order to defend you," he replies.

"Liv? Which one was that?" I ask.

"Light blue hair, violet eyes..." he says, describing Liv for me.

"Hmm...blue hair, really? I must've missed her in the crowd. I guess I was focused on the one clinging to you," I reply, watching the towel that Reed has wrapped around his narrow hips slip a little lower.

He nods, seeming to read my mind, he moves over to the chair, picking me up again and kissing me. He carries me to the bed, following me down onto it. Snuggling me to his side, he combs his fingers hypnotically through my hair. My eyes feel heavy and I'm struggling to stay awake because I have so many questions to ask him. "Reed, we need to talk," I say as he pulls the covers tighter to me.

"Shh, Evie, it's the middle of the night. You have to rest," Reed replies.

"I need to know if you've heard anything from Phaedrus yet," I say. Reed's smile fades. "What have you heard?" I ask, pushing up to a sitting position.

Reed exhales heavily, saying, "I'm not going to tell you anything now."

"Do you know something?" I ask.

"Sleep," he says cajolingly. He holds me in his arms, spooning me as we lay together in bed.

"I can't sleep. I have information I have to tell you," I reply in a calm voice.

"Elan told me about Safira coming in here," he says with a frown in his tone. "I'm sorry. I'll make sure she doesn't get near you again."

"She is the least of my worries," I exhale. "I spoke to him… to this Ifrit…" Reed's hand, which has been gently stoking my side, stills. "He called me Alya…it means—"

"Heaven," Reed interrupts.

"Yeah," I murmer as a shiver rushes through me.

"How did he contact you?" Reed asks in a low tone.

"He spoke to me in my dream. He wants me to come to him," I admit.

Reed's body becomes rigid against mine. "What did he say?" he asks.

As I tell Reed everything that the Ifrit had said to me, as well as my responses to him, he doesn't interrupt. The more I explain, however, the tighter his arms around me become. When I describe the windmills and the little whitewashed house that was shown to me, I turn to look in Reed's green eyes.

"I think the Ifrit was leading me beyond the little house," I say, trying to remember the building, "to a little rustic church. The building is in three sections. The middle section is the tallest and two smaller sections flank it. Each section is made from vertically placed rough, tree trunks. A bronze-toned roof covers all three sections with the highest roofline in the center section and lower rooflines on each side. In each section, there is a tall spire with an oblong, bronze cap set upon it. Each cap holds a bronze cross above it. The tallest spire is in the center and it is flanked on either side by shorter versions of the same."

Reed's voice is gentle as he says, "That sounds like a fairly detailed description, given that it was in the distance, beyond the white house."

"It seems familiar to me. Like déjà vu…like I've been there already," I reply, meeting his eyes.

"In a premonition," he says, not at all like a question.

"Yeah…I think so. I can't remember it, though. I think it's too…ugly," I admit, trying to pull off a casual shrug. "So, have you heard from Phaedrus?" I ask.

I wait for Reed to answer me, but he remains silent.

"Reed," I sigh, "I told you everything. Now it's your turn."

"No, it's not. I'm prepared to protect you, even if that means protecting you from yourself," Reed says firmly, meeting my eyes.

"What does that *even* mean?" I frown in exasperation.

"It means that you're no longer involved in this mission. I'm not going to allow you to martyr yourself," he replies firmly.

"Martyr myself? You're being unreasonable. I can help Brownie and Russell," I say in a pleading tone.

"At what expense, Evie? At the risk of your life?" he asks as his eyebrows draw together. "You've already agreed to go to the Ifrit, which is unacceptable," he replies, finally losing some of his cool.

"We're not even sure what this Irfit wants from me," I say in what I hope is a reasonable tone.

"It is an Ifrit, Evie," Reed says in a way that makes the hair on my arms rise. "He will not ask you what you are willing to give. He will take whatever he wants."

"But—" I begin.

Reed interrupts me. "I'm not going to let you trade your life for theirs," he says with finality.

"I will survive this," I say with conviction I don't really feel, "I have to protect Russell. He's my family."

"And you are my family," Reed replies. "I will do everything I can to get him back for you. Trust me."

"I can help," I say, wringing my hands.

Reed groans. "Evie, you are not in this alone."

I'm just about to tell him all the ways I can help find Russell when I hear the sound of crying coming from somewhere outside. It isn't just one cry; it is like weeping from a crowd of women. "What's that?" I ask Reed.

"I don't know. Stay here. Don't leave this room," he orders, and then he moves supernaturally fast and is gone in a fraction of a second.

I get up quickly from bed and put on a pair of jeans and a top from my closet. Going to the door of my room, I look out into the courtyard to see every angel that we have here amassing. They are flying around the high walls that run the perimeter of the compound. I hear wailing coming from outside the walls, like a mass of people all crying and shouting at once. Turning to see Sorin and Elan standing on the porch outside my door, I ask, "What is that?"

Sorin looks grim when he says, "Humans."

"What?" I ask, searching his face for an answer.

"It is thousands of humans. They are all throwing themselves at the gates, trying to get in." Elan replies as we watch the gates rattle from being pressed from without.

"Why?" I ask in shock.

"They said they want their queen," Sorin replies.

I close my eyes and ask, "Who is their queen?"

"You are their queen," Elan answers me, watching me flinch even though I already knew the answer to my own question.

CHAPTER 8

The Stone Forest

As I inch closer to Elan on the porch that overlooks the courtyard outside my room, I listen to the crowds of people outside our compound. They are clawing the gates and walls demanding to get in to see me. "The Gancanagh have been busy." Elan observes. "They have managed to enthrall many of the locals here. They must have been here for several days because their victims look like they have had a substantial amount of toxin administered to them. Some look like they haven't eaten or slept in a while. They have orders to come and fetch you."

"Show me," I whisper, turning to Sorin because he seems to like me more than Elan does.

"We have orders to keep you in your room," Sorin replies apologetically.

I frown, "Then fly me to the roof of my room. I have to see what's going on outside," I say with exasperation. Sorin considers this compromise for a second before taking me in his arms and flying me quickly to the pitched rooftop of the pagoda. Elan follows us up, unwilling to let us go alone. Hovering in the air, my view stretches for several miles outside of the compound. The roads and outlying areas, as far as I can see, are filled with people…or maybe a more accurate description for them would be enthralled junkies.

I feel myself paling. "There are so many of them," I say, my heart breaking for all of Brennus' victims. Even in the darkness of the night sky, their numbers look frightening, like a legion of zombies, throwing themselves at the walls of our sanctuary in despair. Their clothing is shredded and in disarray. I can't understand what any of them is saying because they're speaking a Chinese dialect, but I feel like I have to try to do something to help them. "I have to talk to them. Maybe I can make them go away."

"No," Sorin replies, "you can't help them. Most of them will die. They will refuse to eat unless told to do so by the Gancanagh—they will perish. It is fortunate they have not been turned fully; they still retain their souls. None of the Gancanagh has shared their blood with them. They are collateral damage—weapons."

I see the worn-out faces of the victims. Their cries are torturing me. Brennus had said that if I made him come for me, I wouldn't like his methods of getting me back. He is building his empire of violence that I can feel in the collective sorrow of the crowd. "Are the Gancanagh out there?" I ask Sorin with calm that I don't feel. I feel like cowering and pleading for them to hide me from Brennus, while there is another part of me that is burning to see him again.

"We haven't seen them. This is their first wave—perhaps a distraction from what they are really planning. That is why you are not to leave your room. The humans are a great distraction for us. We are unwilling to harm them, even though we know there is little hope for them until they die," Sorin says. "The Gancanagh have limited our options. His humans are drawing attention to our position, so we'll need to leave our sanctuary or eliminate the humans."

"Could you take them somewhere else?" I ask.

"Brennus will only make more," Elan says.

"We must take you somewhere else, Evie," Sorin adds. "Then we can go on the offensive. We have already called for more Powers. We have to take out their army."

"Unless I surrender," I say to myself. "Brennus is knocking at the door. Soon, he will be kicking it in."

Elan and Sorin both growl at me before Sorin flies me to my room, setting me down gently. "You will stay here," Sorin says in tone of authority, crossing his arms over his chest.

Elan looks equally determined to make me stay in my room. In seconds, Reed and Zephyr materialize beside Elan and Sorin, startling me. They're dressed in black body armor that covers all of their skin. Hoods are attached to their collars so that they can be pulled over their faces, protecting them from the touch of the Gancanagh. Their wings are exposed in the back, but since their feathers aren't susceptible to the toxic skin of the Gancanagh, it will not affect them if they're touched.

"Reed, I have to talk to Brennus. Maybe I can reason with him. Why does he have to come now? I have to find Russell and Brownie. Can we slip out and leave for the Ukraine now? Has Phaedrus called?" I ask in a stream of words.

Reed frowns. "One thing at a time, Evie. Brennus has pushed himself to the top of the list," Reed says with a grim twist of his lips. "You're not speaking to Brennus. You're staying here."

"Where is Buns, we can't leave her alone," I say, panicking because I don't know where my friend is at the moment.

"She has already left," Zephyr says in a soft tone. "She went with half the Undines and Preben to meet the other Dominion Powers."

My eyes widen, "Meet them? Meet them where?" I ask, feeling completely locked out of what they have been planning.

"The Ukraine—Pirogovo, it is south of Kiev, Evie. They are meeting Phaedrus—collecting more intel on the Ifrit," Reed replies with military precision.

"Were you going to tell me?" I ask them, and seeing their blank faces, I know that the answer to my question is "no." "Do you know where Brownie and Russell are?" I ask when no one speaks.

Reed frowns at me. "Stay in the room, love. Don't leave it for any reason. I'm going to go with Zee—we will be back for you. We will move you soon, then we will answer all of your questions," Reed says, pulling me into his arms. Realizing that he is going out there without me, I cling to him tight, all of my anger at being shut out of their intel forgotten.

"Let me go with you, Reed," I plead, not wanting him out of my sight with Brennus so near.

"I won't be gone long. We are looking for the best way to get you out of here undetected. Once we have worked that out, we will be back," he says, hugging me tight and then letting me go. Nodding to Zephyr, they leave in a fraction of a second.

Taking up positions outside my room, Elan and Sorin don the same kind of body armor that Reed and Zephyr had on. Soon after, the crying outside the walls of the compound dies down and is replaced by an eerie silence. Goose bumps rise on my arms as I look at the alert faces of the angels guarding me.

The tense silence stretches on until it is replaced by a strange, hissing sound from somewhere off in the distance, beyond the protective stone walls. Deep growls sound from my bodyguards. Elan sniffs the air and scowls. "What is it?" I ask, my heartbeat drumming painfully in my chest when screams of agony float to us on the air.

"Flame-throwers," Elan answers.

"What?" I choke.

"They are burning them," he says.

"What?" I ask in a weak tone.

"The Gancanagh are burning the humans, attempting to draw us out," Sorin says stiffly. "It is impossible for us to watch them torture humans. We will engage them."

More hissing of flame-throwers sounds as billows of smoke drift over the walls of our fortress.

A driving wind starts stirring the leaves and the red hanging lanterns in the trees around us, pushing my hair away from my face. Thick, dark clouds collect above us like an ominous omen of impending doom. As I gaze up at the darkening sky, rain falls in hard, pelting drops.

"The Undines are bringing the rain, trying to help," Elan explains, while we watch the storm clouds.

Shivering from the soaking rain and the horror around me, I jump when Reed speaks to me, "The rain will also be good cover when we fly you out of here." I gasp, feeling his arms go around me, gathering me to him. Then he whispers something to me—something in Angel.

"What did you say?" I whisper back, relieved that he's here.

"I said, 'I love you, my *aspire*,'" he replies, squeezing me to him. "Are you ready to go?" he asks and I nod immediately, wanting to leave as quickly as possible. Zephyr moves to one side of us as Elan and Sorin take similar positions around us.

We are just about to make our leap into the air, when the flickering of several sets of helicopter blades sound from somewhere within the black clouds above us. Dark, shooting images begin to rain out of the night, plummeting towards us at a frightening velocity. Hitting the ground, the first Gancanagh soldier pauses on one knee momentarily before he stands up, completely unharmed from having hurled out of the sky. He bares his sharp fangs as his hands move quickly to his back holster, drawing from it a wicked automatic rifle and indiscriminately spraying bullets all around the compound.

Pulling me behind him, Reed shouts a warning to the angels nearest the gunman. The army of angels immediately engages the Gancanagh as they continue to fall from the sky. Some of the angels have taken flight, plucking their enemies out of their freefall and grappling with them, tearing them apart and dropping them to the ground in pieces.

Hundreds of Gancanagh continue to fall from the sky like locusts, but they are only one wave of this assault. The stream that winds throughout the compound soon begins coughing up more Gancanagh who rush out of it, dispersing like rats from a flooded sewer.

"Evie, stay behind me," Reed says in an intense tone as he grasps me by my upper arms, staring into my wide eyes. I manage to nod to him. He drops his hands from me and pulls a long sword from a sheath strapped to his back. Everything takes on a surreal tone after that. I try hard to stay with Reed, who is moving like a graceful assassin, slicing through evil, undead corpses as they approach us, trying to get at me. The Gancanagh have the sheer numbers on our encampment, but the angels are ferocious, tearing the limbs off of their enemies. Their strategy seems to be to maim the Gancanagh and then move on, leaving the wounded undead to stagger around until they can be completely destroyed.

Reed is a machine when it comes to killing Gancanagh; it's almost like the Gancanagh are moving in slow motion next to him. He is so much faster than any of them. Even when they rush at him *en masse*, he easily finds the weakness in their attack and cuts them all down. I don't even think he really needs his body armor because not one of them gets close enough to touch him. It would be impressive if it weren't so utterly terrifying.

Looking around me, I see that Zephyr is creating his own mayhem, slashing and carving up our enemies as they approach us. Zee is also shielding some of the Undines who are spraying the Gancanagh nearest us with jets of water that far surpass the power of a fire hose. Safira is near us now, too. She is concentrating on driving the water up from the stream and sweeping hordes of Gancanagh back into it, freezing the water so they can't get back out.

As I watch Safira work, I look beyond her, to the stream and the Gancanagh who are near it. A petite figure just emerges from the water where it is not yet frozen. I can't see very well through the rain, but this Gancanagh doesn't resemble the other massively strong looking soldiers. This figure is feminine and well...girlish. She slips in the mud, staggering forward towards our position. She falls down and crawls away from the others, looking around her in desperation. "Evie! Where are you? Help me!" Molly's voice calls to me in anguish.

"Molly," I whisper, the shock of seeing her here is overwhelming me. A tall Gancanagh moves up just behind Molly then, pulling her roughly to her feet by her upper arm. Molly struggles to get away from the soldier holding her, but she stops when he backhands her across the face, letting her fall back down to the ground.

Reacting out of instinct, I dart away from the protected area behind Reed and run as fast as I can towards Molly. Hearing Reed calling my name, I can't stop. I have to try to help the person that has been like a sister to me for most of my life. Intending to kill whoever it is that just hit Molly, I pluck an automatic weapon out of the hands of a Gancanagh soldier as I speed by him. Drawing the weapon up to my shoulder, I begin spraying bullets at the Gancanagh who hit Molly.

The bullets from my rifle aren't reacting like they should. Instead of hitting my target, the bullets careen around my target, refusing to kill him. Nearing them, I see Molly cowering on the ground, her face turned away from me. Through the haze of the rain, recognition and dread hits me at once. Brennus stands only a few feet from me, hovering over Molly.

"Ahh, *mo chroí*," Brennus breathes, like he is immensely relieved to see me here. "Ye look grand."

I don't answer him, but instead I lift the rifle in my hands, shooting the gun until the trigger clicks, indicating that I have emptied the magazine. At nearly point blank range, I should've hit him easily, but the bullets swerve around him, like they are intentionally avoiding him.

"Dat gun is enchanted, Genevieve," Brennus says in an easy tone, like he's amused by my reaction to him still standing. "Ye don't tink I would come in here and be banjaxed by me own arsenal. Dat is na me style atall." Turning to Molly on the ground, he offers his hand to her, saying, "Tanks me wee lass."

Molly takes the hand that he offers her, popping up off the ground with a soft giggle as she turns her face to me, smiling. "Eaves, you're so gullible," Molly says teasingly, her beautiful smile marred now by her sharp, snake-like fangs. "I swear, you should've seen the look on your face when I called for help. You looked so sad! Cheer up! We're going to have such an awesome time from now on."

My heart squeezes tight, looking at the beautiful monster in front of me that used to be my friend. Her hair is much longer than I remember her wearing it, but it's the same chestnut brown. Her skin, always pale like mine, is now nearly milk white and flawless.

She had played me to get me away from Reed. I begin edging away from them, but I have to stop as my back comes up against a solid wall of ice that blocks my way back to Reed. I turn, pressing my hands to the thick wall, trying to push through it. The rain has suddenly stopped falling as I use all of my strength to try to crush the frigid fortress surrounding me.

"Safira is an old…acquaintance of moin," Brennus says, indicating the barrier cutting me off from all of the angels. "I told her ta take yer advice when da time came—freeze da *ain-geals* in a block of ice 'til we have gone. She wants ta save dem from ye. She tinks ye're evil," he says conspiratorially and then he shrugs. "I might have helped wi' dat a wee bit. I told her dat ye're really me spy. 'Twas all very simple after dat."

Turning back to face him and adopting a defensive posture, I say, "You're going to have to kill me here because I'm not going with you."

"I did miss ye so, *mo chroí*. Ye're such a challenge. I canna leave ye here for da Ifrit ta claim. Dey are such nasty craiturs. So we will be going home now…" he says, opening his hand to me. Bringing his hand up, he blows some dust that is in his palm and it floats around me like sparkling glitter, coving my wet skin and sticking to me. Trying to wipe it off, I begin to sway on my feet as black spots swirl in my vision.

"Don't do this, Brennus, please…" I plead weakly, losing all of my strength so that I can't fight back.

"Alfred was right about one ting. Ye are very beautiful when ye beg, Genevieve," Brennus says, catching me in his cold embrace before I fall to the ground. "Soon, ye will never need ta beg me for anyting. I'll give ye everyting."

As I look into his light green eyes, I mutter, "Don't want you…"

∽

My eyes flutter open, focusing on an enormous, carved Buddha head. It's lying next to the crumbling body of the statue, having toppled to the ground beside it. Everything is hazy as I float in the half conscious realm between sleep and wakefulness. The statue head looks as if it's asleep on a pillow of vines and it occurs to me that I must still be in China, or maybe Tibet.

When I lift my head, the room around me shivers and whirls so I lay it back down on the bed, cursing a little. I close my eyes, but that makes me feel dizzier, so I open them once again, trying to focus them on something. The doorway is across the room from the bed, leading directly outside. Its opening is so large that it spans almost the entire wall of the room and is flanked on either side by folding doors that can be moved into place to close the room off from the outside world.

I scan the world outside this room and discover a wide, sweeping terrace of stone, crumbling with age. Lush forest with dense trees forms the landscape and the strangest looking stones I've ever seen surround the terrace. The stones resemble enormous trees. It's as if some sort of ash covered the trees at some point thousands of years ago, petrifying them and turning them to stone.

As I move my head on the pillow, I see that this room is very much like the one I shared with Reed. Exposed wood beams arch above my head like the bowed bottom of a ship.

"How is yer *ceann*?" Brennus asks quietly from somewhere nearby.

As my heartbeat kicks up and the organ in question lodges somewhere in my throat, Brennus whispers something softly to me in Gaelic—something that sounds soothing while the bed moves under his weight. He reaches out and gently strokes my wing that responds to his touch by fluttering lightly.

"*Póg mo thóin*, Brennus," I reply stiffly, using the Gaelic Russell taught me to tell him to "kiss my ass." "I don't know about my *ceann*, but my head is aching you evil a-hole. Do you have any idea how much this hurts?" I ask as I hold my head in my hands, feeling it throbbing in pain. Then, I reach back and slap his hand away from my wing as a deep, rumbling laugh issues next to me for my brash response.

"Yer *ceann* is yer head, *mo shíorghrá*," Brennus replies with a grin in his voice. "'Tis sorry I am dat yer head hurts ye. I forget jus how delicate ye are yet. I must've made me spell a wee bit too strong—ye have been out for hours—much longer dan I intended."

"Yeah, well, a little less faerie dust next time, hmm?" I reply with sarcasm, still holding my head. As I try to sit up in the bed, I have to pause because the sheet begins to slip and lets me know that I'm completely naked in the bed. "*Brennus!* Where are my clothes?" I ask, clutching the sheet to me as I turn to him and glare into his eyes.

"Yer clothes were wet, so I took dem off ye," Brennus says with a warm smile, leaning his back against the pillows next to me and crossing his arms behind his neck innocently. "Whah's wrong? I've seen ye in da altogether before, remember?"

"I *hate* waking up *naked* next to *you!*" I spit out, glaring at him again.

Brennus' eyes narrow, "Be careful, Genevieve, as bad as I like ye right now, I need ta remember 'tis worse wi'out ye," he says in a deadly calm voice.

I sigh in exasperation. "What does that mean?" I ask him, matching his tone and frowning at him.

"It means, I'm bloody angry wi' ye. I saw da mark on yer chest," he says accusingly, as he clenches his teeth like a jealous lover, referring to Reed's wings branded on my heart. "I nearly went mad when I did, too. Finn had ta point out dat 'twas me own fault, na being strong enough ta have kept ye in da first place. I know 'tis me fault. I drove ye back into his arms, did I na?" he asks me rhetorically. "I will na be dat weak again, I promise ye."

"You being weak had nothing to do with me binding to—"

Brennus cuts me off. "Do na say his name ta me," he warns me with a growl.

"All right," I agree, seeing the seething anger in Brennus' eyes as he sits breathing heavily next to me. "We won't talk about him. When did you contact Safira?" I ask in a quiet tone, feeling goose bumps rising on my arms and knowing I have to be careful of what I say and do until I find a way out of here. An angry Brennus is very dangerous for me and...painful.

"We were watching da compound. We saw da Undine arrive. I realized dat I knew some of dem, but I didn't know whah dey were dere for 'til I spoke to Safira. Ye should've told me of da Ifrit. Da *aingeals* canna protect ye from it like we can," Brennus replies, gaining control of his anger.

"I don't want your protection," I reply, trying to remain calm.

"Arrgh, so now ye will be taking on da Ifrit? He is a persistent wee buggar. I have had ta block his magic no less dan a score of times from reaching ye while ye have been asleep" Brennus informs me.

"You can block the Ifrit's magic?" I ask him in an urgent tone, looking at him.

"I can," Brennus responds with a sharp nod.

"How?" I ask, almost afraid to breathe.

"'Tis na difficult," he replies with a shrug. "I am very powerful."

I stare at him and I don't dispute his statement. He is powerful. His men walked into Dominion and then they blew it apart. He found out where I was and just did it again. Although, Safira all but handed me to them when she froze the angels in a block of ice and me behind the wall of it, but still—extremely powerful to have orchestrated all of it.

"How did you know Safira would help you?" I ask.

"I did na know. Need teaches da plan. I needed someone on da inside, so I explored all of me options," he replies. "Da plan developed when I found dat she needed an ally for whah she wanted and whah she wanted was ye gone, ye see?" he asks, giving me a strategy lesson.

I nod. "Why did you let Russell and me leave the caves in Houghton, if you have this kind of magic?" I ask him suspiciously, not understanding why he couldn't stop us then.

"'Twas too great a risk, trying someting in dat situation," he says in a soft tone. "He was willing ta kill ye wi' dat grenade and I could see he wasna afraid ta die. Den, dere was da fact dat I had jus had a significant amount of yer blood, which is like drinking da sweetest poison," he says with a rueful shake of his head.

"I taste bad?" I ask, not understanding because he seemed to have a different opinion when he was tasting me.

"No, ye are like tasting heaven. I jus did na like whah it did ta me," he says with a frown.

"What did it do to you?" I ask with morbid curiosity.

"It muddled me—made me feel happy and…well, drunk," he says, his green eyes scanning my face like he's memorizing every detail of it. "I could na even kill da fellas when dey failed at da *aingeal* hive."

"You mean when they took a swim in the St. Lawrence without me at the chateau?" I ask, trying hard not to smile, remembering the look on Declan's face when Reed threw him in the water.

"I do," he says, watching the corners of my mouth twitch and it's doing something to the corners of his eyes—they soften like he is amused, too. His coal-black hair is lying elegantly on his brow. *Why is it that there's the look of an angel on this demon,* I ask myself, looking away as I feel that darkness within me pull towards him. It's frightening to find that I still feel an attraction to him, like I felt when I surrendered to him—kissing him before Russell saved me.

I clear my throat and ask with *faux* casualness, "You can kill Ifrits?" I try to avoid looking at him, running my fingers over the silk sheet. My heartbeat is increasing as I wait for him to answer me.

"I will sort the Ifrit out for ye," Brennus says like a caress, running his finger lightly up my arm. It feels like he's running an ice cube over me, but it's not repulsive, like it used to be. It's sensual and it's making me crave something that I have no trouble defining now. "Ye do na need ta fear it," he says in a sultry voice.

My mind races, *I know that he will kill it when it comes for me, but that might be too late to save Russell and Brownie.*

"What now?" I ask him abruptly, as I begin to fidget in anxiety. I need to know what he is planning. He promised not to try to change me if I came back to him, but I didn't come back to him. I made him come and get me.

"Dat depends on ye, *mo chroí*," Brennus replies, watching me with hooded eyes.

"It does?" I ask, trying to beat down the fear that is rising in me now that the shock of being back in Brennus' lair has worn off.

"It does. I mean to keep ye dis time, Genevieve," he says resolutely. "Ye must see dat ye are far safer here wi' me and da fellas dan wi' da *aingeals*. Dey cannot protect ye. Dey had ta call da Undines, one of which wants ye dead," Brennus says. He looks hostile when he adds, "Ye put yerself in the hands of yer enemies instead of yer family."

"You want me dead," I accuse him, afraid that he has a point.

"No, I wanted ye undead—dere's a difference. Now, I do na know whah I want," he says in a soft tone.

"What?" I ask in confusion.

"Ye heard me," he snaps back. "I like ye fine da way ye are now. Whah if I change ye inta one of us and ye…"

My eyes widen in surprise. "What are you afraid will happen if you make me Gancanagh?" I ask, seeing him frown as his finger skims over the contour of my cheek.

"I jus do na want ye ta be different, dat's all," he replies.

"I might lose some of that danger that you are all in love with. Is that it?" I ask, seeing that I'm right as he drops his finger from my cheek, staring into my eyes. "Don't worry," I whisper, "if you promise to keep your fangs off of me, I promise to become even more dangerous." I watch his eyes go softer still in the corners. *He wants that—he wants to see just how powerful I will become when I evolve to my full potential,* I think, seeing him look at me like I'm the 'in' toy of the moment.

"We have ta come ta an agreement, *mo chroí*," Brennus says with authority. "I know dat ye do na trust me atall. Finn says ye have reason na ta trust me and I know he is right. I should never have tried our methods on ye. I treated ye like a faerie instead of da *aingeal* dat ye are. 'Tis sorry I am dat I hurt ye like dat. Locking ye away in da cell was da wrong ting ta do ta ye, I admit dat."

My jaw drops open. This ancient, evil creature that has been taking whatever he wants for as long as he's been around, which is a significant amount of time, just apologized for hurting me. "Brennus, have you ever apologized for anything in your life?" I ask him in shock.

"I have na. Did I do it rightly?" he asks with a quirk of his eyebrow, looking concerned and sincere.

I nod, too shocked to answer him. This is not what I expected from him at all. I expected to have been bitten the moment it was safe for him to do so and then I expected to writhe in pain until he shared his blood with me, making me his undead slave. I have no strategy for dealing with an apology from him instead of an assault. "What do you want from me, Brennus?" I blurt out, too stunned to be anything but direct.

"Dere are so many tings I want from ye," he says and his voice is like silk. "But, ta get ta dose tings, we must build some trust between us. I can na trust dat ye willna run off da moment da opportunity of escape presents itself. Dat is why we are still in China. I can na take ye ta me home until I have assurances from ye dat ye will na escape or bring a horde of *aingeals* down on us ta fetch ye. If I change ye, I will be assured dat ye will stay wi' me—ye would be bound ta me as yer *máistir*. But, I do na want ye as me *sclábhaí*. I want ye ta be me queen. I want ye ta choose me."

"What does *sclábhaí* and *máistir* mean?" I ask with my heartbeat pounding in my chest.

"Slave and master," Brennus replies.

He doesn't want me to be his slave. He wants me to be more, I think, feeling weak.

Brennus continues, "Whah I need ta know is whah ye need from me so dat we can make a bargain."

"I've been told that it's shady to bargain with evil," I reply in a quiet tone.

Brennus snorts derisively. "I've no doubt dat ye have. I also have no doubt dat whoever told ye dat tought ye were evil at one point or de other." I cannot dispute that. All the angels thought I was evil at one point, except for Buns and Brownie— they never questioned me. Preben's words come to me then— he had said that the Gancanagh don't do anything that is not strictly to their advantage.

"You must already know what I want so why don't you tell me what you have planned, Brennus. I know that you wouldn't leave anything to chance. You must think you know how to keep me here," I say, calling him on his strategy.

A deep, rumbling laugh of pure pleasure erupts from Brennus as he looks at me with a sensual darkness in his eyes. "Ye are so clever, *mo chroí*. I will na be able ta compete wi' a mind like yers in a few tousand years. I will have ta work hard ta win ye over before long," he smiles, and I try not to pull away from him as he reaches over and gently toys with a lock of my hair. "I want us ta come ta an agreement. I will save yer *aingeals* from da Ifrit for ye and in exchange, ye will agree ta live wi' me," Brennus says softly.

"We already have a plan in place for that, Brennus," I say, bluffing, because I have no idea if Reed and Zephyr have worked out a plan to save Russell and Brownie.

"I banjaxed dat plan," Brennus says casually. "Yer plans involved da Undines. Now dat I've turned Safira against da *aingeals*, da other Undines will na save yer *aingeals* from the Ifrit. Dey tend ta stick together, ye see? Yer *aingeals* will now die wi'out our help."

"I need my clothes, Brennus," I say quickly, pushing my hand through my hair in agitation.

"Ye do na need yer clothes," he says as his eyes rove over my body, making me feel like he can see right through the sheet covering me.

"Yes, I do. I need them so that I can get out of this bed and pace. I need to think and I can't do that sitting here," I explain in frustration.

"Whah do ye need ta tink about? 'Tis simple. I give ye whah ye want and ye give me whah I want," he says, smiling.

"Please give me my clothes," I say again.

Brennus exhales a heavy breath, saying, "Very well." He flicks his hand and my clothing appears on my lap in a neat, little pile. Surprise registers on my face, making his smile deepen. "I'll teach ye how ta do dat soon," Brennus promises.

Shivering at the power he wields so easily, I shrug quickly into my jeans and shirt, feeling relief at having them back. After tying my shoes, I get up off the bed and begin to pace the room, going to the doors that open to a forest outside. I feel like a caged animal with the doors of its pen wide open. I want to run, but I'm afraid of what will happen if I do. Putting my hand on one of the folded doors, I say over my shoulder, "Your plan only saves two of my angels. There is one that will go to any length to get me back." Reed will not stop until he gets me back.

"He is welcome ta try," Brennus says with deadly calm, "I am counting on it. I need ta remove him from yer heart and dat can only happen if he is dead."

In my mind I'm screaming in anguish, but I try to remain outwardly calm, only my hands tremble. "I just thought of another option, Brennus."

"I see no other option open ta ye. I save yer friends and ye agree ta stay wi' me as me queen or I bite ye and ye stay wi' us as me slave while I let yer friends rot," he says plainly.

"Or, I could show you how much I love my angel. Then, I can leave here and save Brownie and Russell by sorting out the Ifrit myself," I say, not looking at him, but at the world outside the door. I can sense that there are several Gancanagh hovering around the room just outside of it and many more within the forest of stone surrounding us.

"Dat sounds like an improbable plan, *mo chroí*," he says in a calm tone as he gets up from the bed and walks towards me. He comes up close behind me and his sweet scent floats to me, no longer unpleasant to detect. I feel the cold radiating off of his body, but it feels like it's pulling me towards him now. "How do ye plan ta do all of dat –particularly the part where ye show me how much ye love yer *aingeal?*" he asks, while my body betrays me as it responds to his nearness.

"That is the easiest part of my plan, *mo sclábhaí,*" I whisper to him, calling him my slave, while turning to face him. He is so close, just a whisper away from me, as I channel the love that I feel for Reed into one perfect word. The room begins to spin as my clone juts out of me. Brennus takes a step back from me in surprise. He doesn't have time to evade my clone that runs into him, delivering my emotion with it. A look of bliss crosses his face for a brief moment, before he hears the message that accompanied it: *Reed.*

A jealous look of black rage transforms Brennus' face just as I bolt out of the archway of the pagoda and down the crumbling stone steps outside. Feeling the fellas converging in on me to halt my escape, I pause for only a moment and bend down on one knee. Several of my clones explode out of me, fifteen or more, going in every direction. Shooting back up, I continue to run forward, escaping into the woods along with all of the echoing images of me.

Confusion reigns around me as the fellas split up trying to follow several of the clones that they believe to be the real me. I don't have time to celebrate that victory because several of the Gancanagh fail to be thrown off their pursuit of me. Declan and Goban emerge off to my left side, so I veer sharply to avoid them. Declan chases me and he is faster than I expect. Hearing him growl behind me, he calls, "Genevieve, ye are still a bleedin' hallion!" Something whistles by my head, striking the tree in front of me and exploding in a shower of fire, igniting the ground around me. Declan is using his magic to pitch flaming death at me. *Freaking faeries*, I think, dodging more sparks.

As fire ricochets off the rocks around me, I speed up the path ahead while it narrows and twists upward towards some kind of summit. There is a wall of rock on either side of me, so I can't deviate from the direction that I'm headed. I'm pulling away from Declan, but I still hear him trash talking me, "Tick, tick, tick…BOOM!" he exclaims as a loud blast falls behind me, rocking the ground I have just vacated and leaving the bitter taste of fear in my mouth. He is not playing with me. He is probably still a little salty about getting tossed off the balcony at the chateau the last time we met.

"Give up, Genevieve. Dis path goes nowhere but up!" Declan calls from farther behind me. "Dere's nowhere left ta run…" he says, and I hear laughter in his voice, hitting me like an anvil from above, crushing my spirit when I see that he's not lying. The path ends at a peak where an observation gazebo was erected a long, long time ago.

As I reach the peak, I twist and turn, but there is nowhere left to run. I back away from the path and into the gazebo. My eyes focus on Declan as he makes it to the crest of the peak. I stop moving as my back soon comes up against the railing of the gazebo. Pivoting, I glance over my shoulder. I see a sheer drop of several hundred feet to the rocky terrain below.

Declan approaches me cautiously with Goban directly behind him and another Gancanagh that I have not yet met behind him. The fangs of the unknown Gancanagh jet forward in his mouth with a *click* as they engage. He attempts to walk past Declan to me, but Declan's hand shoots out, holding him back from entering the gazebo. "Dat one would be sweet to taste, Keefe, but bitter to pay for. She belongs ta Brennus—no one touches her except ta stop her from leavin'." The look of yearning is in Keefe's eyes as he stares at me like a deranged psychopath, making every hair on my body stand on end.

"Oy, Genevieve, where are ye goin'?" Declan asks, as he raises his eyebrow that always seems to be asking the questions. Declan looks older than Brennus. He must have been middle-aged when he became undead, but he is still attractive in a hot-older-man kind of way.

"Who, me? Oh, you know, hot date with an Ifrit—can't be late or he'll kill my friends, so if you don't mind, I'll just—" I start to say.

Declan frowns, "An Ifrit, is it now?" he says with his dramatic accent. "Dat's like talkin' trash ta da rubbish, goin' ta speak ta an Ifrit, dat is. Did no one ever tell ye dat da devil ye know is always better dan da devil ye don't?"

"Brennus is the devil I know in this scenario, I assume?" I ask, pressing against the rail of the gazebo.

"He is," he says as he takes a step to enter the gazebo, forcing me to climb up on the railing overlooking the valley far below.

"Then you stay with this devil and I'll wish you all the best," I reply, trying to stretch out my wings as far as they will go.

"Dere is another sayin' where we come from, Genevieve," Declan says, watching me hold on to the post and look again over my shoulder.

"Oh yeah, what's that?" I ask Declan, trying to gather the courage I need to jump.

"He who has da boots does na mind where he places his foot," he replies. "If ye make Brennus chase ye now, he is gonna have dat boot pressed ta yer neck."

"They have a saying where I come from, too, Declan," I say, turning to look at him.

"Oh yeah, whah's dat, Genevieve?" he asks in all seriousness as he inches closer to me.

I hold up both of my middle fingers to him as I step off the railing of the gazebo and begin to fall.

CHAPTER 9

The Unholy Church

As I fall through the air, I have the extreme misfortune to still be facing up as Declan launches himself off the edge of the gazebo where I just jumped. He looks less than happy too; his face is a mask of determination as he rockets towards me. He appears extremely bitter as he exposes his dagger-sharp fangs in a sneer. Maybe he is mad that I flipped him off as I jumped from the railing, or maybe he's angry at me for making him come after me on a several hundred feet drop. Whatever the case, he's salty.

I turn over in midair, stretching my wings out as far as they can go, but that slows me down. With Declan moving like a streamlined missile, he is going to be able to grab me within seconds, and then we will fall together to the rapidly approaching ground. Judging by the fact that several Gancanagh plunged out of the sky back at our compound, they must have some way of cushioning their fall. I have a feeling that Declan is going to make it very uncomfortable for me once we hit the ground.

Panic seizes me as I glance over my shoulder, seeing Declan reaching out to grasp my ankle. Kicking my foot, I try to evade his hands, hoping that he will fall past me. Declan is practically an expert at freefalling, by all outward appearances. It's probably because he's a faerie and he used to have wings before he became a Gancanagh. His wings were destroyed when he was transformed into an evil, undead creature, but he doesn't seem to need them at the moment. He is grinning at me now because he knows he doesn't need them either.

Feeling my wings catch an updraft and flutter in the current, the movement triggers something—some deep-seated instinct in me. I concentrate on that movement, how it feels—where it originated. With effort, I move my left wing up and it pitches me sharply to the right.

Declan hasn't anticipated that I would move, so he shoots past me, just missing me by inches. Concentrating harder, I move my wings rhythmically, up and down. The most amazing thing happens: I stop falling and flutter up. Looking down, I watch Declan continue to fall to the ground; his grim expression would almost be comical if he wasn't so scary. But, because I am who I am, I give him a little wave as he plummets away from me.

I continue to move my wings and it takes me a second to realize I'm flying. I mean, *really flying*, not gliding, like I did with Russell in the woods of Houghton. I'm slow though, not moving very far or very fast, but I am definitely moving. I try to veer away from the rough cliff wall, so that if Goban or Keefe decide to jump off the gazebo and pursue me, they won't be able to land on me.

When I am far enough away, I turn and look back at the gazebo. Several Gancanagh are watching me from the railing now and one of them is the unmistakable figure of Brennus. Fear threads through me as Brennus extends his hand to me, indicating that I should return to him. I feel a pull to return to him, like he is my master. Fighting that feeling, I turn away instead and begin to head in the opposite direction, wondering how far I can fly as I try to figure out where I am.

Flying is much harder than running—totally harder. It's nothing like being held in Reed's arms as he soars through the sky with confidence. This is like being a kite and being torn in the direction that the wind seems to want to take me. I have to fight against wind currents to continue in a fairly straight trajectory. Beginning to tire almost immediately, my head still aches from the faerie dust Brennus used on me and I'm exhausted from the struggle of evading Declan and his firebombs. I need to rest and regroup—find a phone—call Reed.

Reed must be out of his mind with worry; I cringe as I descend towards the ground. The dense woods beneath me cause me to panic because I have no idea how to land on even ground, let alone in the woods, but I have to land or I'm going to drop out of the sky.

I pull my wings in hard as I near the trees and I manage to fly between the branches most of the way down. When they get thicker at the bottom, however, I crash into a pine bough and fall about twenty feet to the ground. Feeling the wind get completely knocked out of me, I lay there for a few moments trying to get the air back into my lungs. I'm tempted to just lie here forever. My body aches and I need to rest, but I pull myself up off the ground and stumble forward. I have to find a town so that I can find out where I am.

I lean up against a rock, breathing heavy. Stumbling forward, I walk past a few extremely large trees and then I still as someone says, "Evie."

Poising to run, I stop when recognition dawns on me. "Phaedrus!" I exhale in a rush. "How did you find me?" I ask, turning and stumbling towards him. I fall against his chest and he catches me and hugs me to him. As I peer into his black eyes, he smiles back at me, brushing pine needles from me.

"I have a knack for finding my targets when they need me. Rough landing?" he asks, holding me up as I lean against him unsteadily.

"A bit," I reply, feeling the super soft feathers of his wings brush my cheek like silk as I rest it on his shoulder. He rubs my arms, trying to warm me up because the shock of what just happened is now setting in.

"We had better start moving, Evie," Phaedrus says, sniffing the air. "I can smell them." Seeing the alarm in my eyes, he adds, "They are not close, but they have been through here recently. It makes me nervous."

Phaedrus grasps my hand, leading me away from where I had landed. Pulling a protein bar from his pocket, he smiles as he hands it to me. Tears come to my eyes as I say, "How did you know?"

He shrugs, "You looked hungry in my head."

Ripping open the packaging I all but stuff the entire protein bar in my mouth, chewing rapidly. After I manage to swallow it, I ask, "When did you start seeing me in your head?"

"Last night," he replies. "I saw you taken by the Gancanagh. I was already on my way back to the compound because I had seen some things in my head that made me worry about you. I have been in contact with Reed and Zephyr. They are planning on attacking the Gancanagh to get you back, once they find out where they are. I didn't know that you had escaped until I just saw it in my head. They don't know," he says.

"Where are they now?" I ask in panic.

"They are still back at the compound. They killed most of the Gancanagh that remained behind after Brennus took you. They didn't know where he went with you, so they have been interrogating Gancanagh survivors to try to find out."

"What about Brownie and Russell? Did you find them?" I ask.

A pained expression crosses his lips. "We think we know where they are. We had a plan, but now—I will tell you about it when we meet up with Reed and Zephyr," Phaedrus says, cryptically. "I need to get us out of the mountains so we can find a tower that gets cell phone reception. We are blacked out, so it is just us for now."

I slow my pace, pulling against his hand and stopping him. "What happened? Did the Undines really back out?" I ask. "Because of what Safira did?"

He glances back at me before he gently pulls me forward again. "It's more complicated than that, Evie," he says, picking his way between dense trees and over jagged rock.

"I'm sure it is, why don't you tell me about it?" I say, following him.

"Reed nearly killed Safira. If it weren't for Zephyr, she would be…" he trails off. "As it is, I hear that most of the Gancanagh did not survive because of him. Zephyr had to ban Reed from interrogating the prisoners because he lost perspective and was just carving them up one-by-one."

"Oh," I murmur, knowing that I have to get back to him so that he will know that I'm okay. "So he is flipping out a little." Phaedrus gives me a sidelong look to indicate that I have understated the situation.

"He will be better once he sees you. I doubt he will let you go anywhere after that, so enjoy the scenery while it lasts," Phaedrus says, half-joking, trying to lighten the grim topic.

I still, letting go of Phaedrus' hand. *No, Reed will never let me out of his sight or near anything remotely dangerous, not after this. He'll keep me in the dark about Brownie and Russell. They're dead now, without the help of the Undines; they stand almost no chance at all. That's why Phaedrus left them to find me—he can help me, he can't help them.*

"Slight change of plans, Phaedrus," I murmur, knowing that he is not going to like what I have to say. "We can't go back to the compound, or meet up with Reed." I add, almost choking on my words.

"No?" Phaedrus says with confusion.

"You're going back to help Brownie and Russell, aren't you?" I ask in a low tone.

His expression turns grim. "I have to, it's what I do," he says.

"Well, me too," I reply.

Phaedrus' eyebrows pull together. "No. I was sent here to protect you," he states firmly.

"Are you sure about that?" I ask. "Why do you think that you couldn't find them before? You needed my help because I'm supposed to go with you. It's the only way to save them."

"You are not a Virtue, you are a Seraph. You cannot perform miracles," he says with a stubborn edge in his tone.

"No, that's why you'll be there. Just look at me as back up, a bargaining chip," I say reasonably.

Phaedrus' expression grows darker. "I don't bargain with evil, they never hold to their end," he replies, like I'm a naïve child.

"They will if you give them everything that they want—at least I think they will," I say, biting my lip in indecision. "It'll be worth the price, if we save Russell and Brownie."

"What if you are the price?" he asks.

"I'm evolving new tricks every day. I bet that soon there won't be any cage that can hold me," I say in all seriousness. "If

I can survive, then I can get away. You have seen what I can do and there are other things that I can do that you haven't seen yet."

"Other things? Like what?" he asks, narrowing his eyes at me.

"You have to turn around," I say to Phaedrus.

His black eyes widen. "I have to—"

"Just do it," I sigh.

When Phaedrus' back is to me, I remove my clothes. I move a few paces to a moss-covered boulder nearby, and then I press myself against it. Closing my eyes, I imagine Brennus walking towards me from the trees nearby, causing overwhelming fear to course through me. In the back of my mind I whisper the word *hide*. "Okay, turn around—" Instantly, rigidity overtakes my limbs while my body resembles the gray mass of stone speckled with moss and bracken.

"You are a nymph, a sprite…" he exhales in shock, while his hand traces my silhouette. It takes a couple moments for me to lose some of the rigidity so that I can answer him.

"A chameleon is how Reed described me. I'm evolving to survive. Let me help you, it's my mission," I plead.

Phaedrus turns his back on me again as I begin to change into my original form. Quickly, I collect my clothes and put them back on. When I'm done, I walk to face Phaedrus in order to gauge his reaction.

He stares at me for a few moments before he puts his hand through his hair in agitation. "Here is what I am willing to do. I will take you to Buns and Preben. We will contact Reed and Zephyr from there, but I am not taking you with me. Too much can happen."

I nod grimly to his new plan. It gets me most of the way there. I can find them on my own when we get close. If I have to slip away to accomplish that, I'll do it. Something tells me that my enemy, the Ifrit, will find me. Brennus said he had to block the Ifrit's magic from getting to me. There will be no blocking it now. He will find me and I will save my friends. I try hard to block my thoughts from Phaedrus, because if he listens to what I'm thinking, then he will never let me come with him.

෬෨

As Phaedrus and I travel through China, we are mostly on foot but sometimes we fly, and not on a comfortable airline either, but with our wings. I thought it would be mad cool when I finally gained the ability to fly, but it's hard work and it makes every muscle in my back, neck, and shoulders ache. I can only fly for an hour or so at a time before I need to stop and rest. Phaedrus is encouraging, trying to show me ways to streamline my technique. I'm grateful that he is here, not only for the advice, but because he had to catch me a couple of times early on when my wings just gave out on me and sent me plummeting towards the ground.

Phaedrus has access to money, too, which helps tremendously. We are able to rent a car. I like to say we "rented it," because we left them money to purchase a new one before we took it out of the rental garage near an airport in Russia. We were considering trying to fly, but I have no papers and the risks are too high that we will be spotted by an "unfriendly," which can be anything from Gancanagh, to Fallen, or even an unenlightened divine angel.

We only stop in small towns on the way, where I buy us food, gas, and a change of clothes. Well, I don't buy Phaedrus clothes because he explains that he has "special clothes" not bought off the rack. His clothes look the same to me, but it's definitely not from around here because humans can't see it. Humans can't see Phaedrus either. He's a Virtue, so I have to do all the negotiating for whatever we need. I rely on him to translate whatever anyone is saying to me because there is quite a language barrier for me in this part of the world. Phaedrus does most of the driving while I sleep. I haven't been this tired since the last time I fled from the Gancanagh and it's beginning to show.

Every time Phaedrus' phone rings, he just looks at the display and then puts it back in his pocket. We both know that it's one of our inner circle trying to get an update from him to see if he knows where I am. We haven't talked about it, but it's kind of an unspoken agreement that it's better for them to think that Brennus has me. We both know that our chances of some kind of survival seem better with Brennus, so we decide not to tell the other angels the truth about going to confront the Ifrit.

Phaedrus keeps watching me with a pained expression on his face, like he is reconsidering his decision to bring me along with him. Hiding my thoughts from him is becoming almost impossible because I can hardly keep my eyes open, let alone stop my mind from wandering where it will. Maybe he is having trouble reading me because I'm so scattered or maybe it's easier to read me because I am, I don't know.

Unfortunately, Phaedrus is not my only companion on this trip. Not long after we leave Russia, the Ifrit invades my mind while I'm sleeping. His raspy voice comes to me when I'm in the twilight between sleep and wakefulness. He keeps asking me to show him where I am, but I've been able to stop him from seeing our location. He is frustrated. He oscillates between threats and the seductive promises of pleasure beyond my wildest dreams. At this point, the wildest pleasure I can think of is sleeping for a couple of days straight in a soft bed—with Reed.

It is growing dark by the time we leave Kiev where we had stopped to use the bathroom and to get something to eat; Phaedrus and I drive south, out of the city. "We're close now," I say in a low tone. The city lights are gone and the scenery has become more of a rural landscape. Enormous fields stretch out near the road, dotted with the kind of small windmills that I recognize from visions the Ifrit has been sending me.

"Yes, we are very close now," Phaedrus agrees.

"You know that I have to go to him," I say, looking out the window at the scenery speeding by me.

Phaedrus is silent for a while. Then he says, "I know that is your plan. You have been saying that since we left China—over and over and over. I know all of your reasons—all of your arguments. It's your conversations with the Ifrit that are the most painful to me." He looks directly at me and I cringe.

I close my eyes, knowing that I haven't spoken any of this out loud. It's all been playing in my mind. He was listening to my thoughts the entire time. "I'm sorry. I didn't know that you were listening," I reply with a sad expression. I wet my lips, knowing that I have to convince him to let me do this alone.

The Ifrit wants me, not him. He will crush Phaedrus. I can't have that. I will already be negotiating to save two members of my family. I don't want to add to it. "I have to go alone," I say, looking at him.

"This is all wrong," Phaedrus says, gripping the steering wheel tight and clenching his teeth. "I don't understand it at all. I feel…"

"What?" I ask in surprise that he looks so frustrated and angry—bleak. He is usually so calm, like nothing can rattle him.

"The closer we get to the Ifrit, the colder I feel," he says, looking at me with fear and dread. It takes a second for me to understand what he is saying. When he nears a target, he feels heat—it gets warmer for him. The fact that he is getting colder means he is moving away from his true target.

"I'm not your target anymore," I murmur, looking at him to see fear on his face. "Russell and Brownie aren't either. This is not your mission."

"No, you are not my mission any longer and I feel as if I am delivering you to your execution," Phaedrus admits, not looking at me. "I know I'm supposed to let you go, I just cannot. Let me take you to Preben. He will have a plan—he can help."

"No, he can't help," I say quickly. "The Ifrit wants me. You have been listening to it speak to me. You know that if I bring Preben, the Ifrit will kill him. I have to go alone."

"Maybe Preben will keep you from going there altogether," Phaedrus says soberly, trying to find a way to keep me away from the Ifrit.

"Then they're dead," I say, feeling bleak, too.

"Maybe they already are, have you considered that?" he asks.

"*No!*" I retort angrily. "Do you have a new target?" I ask, fighting not to show him the dread I feel.

"Yes," he says with reluctance.

"Do I know your target?" I ask, and see him nod grimly. "Who?" I whisper.

"Reed," he says and I close my eyes.

"Stop the car," I rasp, my head is spinning and I feel nauseous. I press my forehead against the cool pane of the glass, waiting for the car to slow down. When Phaedrus pulls to the side of the road, I say, "I'll get out here. You have to go to him."

I open the door and climb out of the car, hugging my arms to me as a cold breeze hits me, pushing my hair back from my face. Phaedrus opens his door, too, following me as I begin walking on the side of the road. "Evie," he says in fear.

"Where is he?" I ask, turning to him, feeling panicked. We both know that I'm asking about Reed.

"He's near where I found you. He and Zephyr located the Gancanagh nest where Brennus had taken you, but no one is there now. He is distraught, but in no real danger that I can see," he says.

"If he's not in danger, then why are you being sent to him?" I ask in confusion.

"Sometime Virtues are sent not just to help with miracles— sometimes we are sent to console others," he says and his words bring tears to my eyes.

"I see," I say, trying to hold back my tears. "Thank you for all of your help, Phaedrus. I couldn't have done this without you and I have to do this—alone. I love you. Take care of Reed— make sure he knows I love him, too."

"Wait!" Phaedrus says in desperation, rushing to my side. He strips off his jacket, wrapping it around my shoulders as he pulls me to him, hugging me.

"It will be okay, Phaedrus," I whisper. "I'm tougher than I look."

"No, you are not," he says in a low tone.

"How far is it, do you think?" I ask.

"A mile, maybe a little more. There is a church—I believe they are in there," he says against my hair.

"Keep him away, if you can," I say. He knows that I mean for him to keep Reed away from the Ifrit, and possibly me, too, if that monster decides to keep me and not kill me. "If I can get away, I'll let you know."

He nods. I pull away from him and turn to walk down the rural road that leads to the church. I don't look back when I hear the car door close. He doesn't start the engine for a long time, but watches me walk away, out of the pool of his headlights and into the darkening night. Finally, the engine whines as Phaedrus wheels the car around, heading in the direction of his new target.

I hang my head in sorrow for just a moment when I know I am truly alone. I feel like I'm going to my execution, just as he had said. Then I move forward again. I hop a fence of fieldstone and cross a field dotted with Queen Anne's lace. Goose bumps rise on my arms as I pass the cluster of windmills that I have seen in a dream. The scent is sweet in the field though, not the scent of heat, like it had been when it was forced upon me in visions. I gaze down the hill, beyond the small, whitewashed house that I knew would be there. The church looms dark and grim with its rough-hewn, timber façade, capped by tall, oblong spires reaching to the sky. Black, ominous clouds have collected above the roofline, as if Heaven is showing me the way.

Russell

CHAPTER 10

Survival

"Russell...Russ..." Brownie's quiverin' voice cuts through the hazy darkness. I try to open my eyes, but only one will cooperate with me. The other one is swollen shut.

"Yeah?" I croak, liftin' my head an inch or two off the dirt floor. The corners of my mouth are achin' where crusts of blood have dried and cracked.

"I...just wanted to make sure," she whispers. I hear the clankin' of the thick, metal chains that bind her to the wall movin' as she shifts somewhere across the room from me.

My body is shakin' so bad that I'm surprised she had to check to make sure that I'm alive. It doesn't really hurt that bad right now. My head hurts, but that's the only part I can really feel at the moment. He broke a couple of my vertebrae high up on my back. I can't feel my arms or anythin' below them at the moment 'til my spine heals, but when it does, I'm gonna be in a world of hurt. He cut pieces off of me and stood right in front of me, eatin' them. When he first did that, I couldn't stop screamin', horrified by what he was doin'. Now, I know that I can regenerate tissue, bone, flesh...so I try just to block out his image as he stands over me, hammerin' my bones.

But, the longer this stretches on, the more I'm gettin' to welcome the pain. The pain isn't the worst of this, although, it's pretty freakin' bad. The worst part is the fear...wonderin' what that freak is gonna do next and when. Waitin' for it to come is almost worse than it comin' and when he comes and he doesn't take me, but takes Brownie instead, I can hardly deal with that fear...and when he brings her back all broken and torn, I just 'bout go insane. I figure I get another chance—maybe a shot at the Paradise that everyone keeps talkin' 'bout, 'cuz of my soul. That's not the case for Brownie. If it kills her, she's just dead.

It's hard to even think now. I have no concept of how long we've been here. There's no light wherever we are—some kind of cellar of a church. I know it's a church 'cuz he drags us up past the pews to the altar surrounded by religious idols. He tortures Brownie and me on that altar and all I can see is the archin' spires of the ceilin' high above my head while I'm lyin' there in a pool of my own puke and guts.

The Ifrit keeps tryin' to turn my head inside out, to see what I'm made of, to gauge what I am. It seems confused by me and extremely pissed off. The only thing I know for sure is that it wants her. It wants Evie with a need and an urgency that I can taste, and I don't know how much longer I'm gonna be able to keep it from her.

"I'm so sorry, Russell," Brownie whispers to me across the room. "I never saw him coming...I should've seen him coming." I can just make out her platinum blond hair. In the absence of light in the basement, it looks white. She's sittin' on the floor with her back against the wall and her long, sleek legs are pulled up to her chest.

"S'kay," I manage to whisper back, "I think he's startin' to like me. He didn't burn me this time." I hear Brownie exhale and I know she's cryin' again. "Ahh, Brownie..." I say softly, "this ain't yer fault. I know what I am. Somethin' was gonna get me sooner or later. I'm just sorry it got ya, too. I thought it was gonna be the Gancanagh or one of the Fallen or one from yer team—Dominion maybe."

"No. We should've been okay. We were almost there, just a day or two more," she says, and I can tell she's beatin' herself up again 'bout it. "You know, Russell, this is like being kidnapped by an urban legend. I've heard about Ifrits, everybody has, but they're so rare—almost extinct—I never thought I'd ever see one," she whispers, soundin' dazed.

"I don't think this was random, Brownie," I say softly, "I think he was huntin' Evie—found us instead."

"Yeah, I think you're right," she replies.

"Are ya any closer?" I ask her, tryin' to be cryptic. Brownie and me had been tryin' to get the steel cuffs off of our limbs before the Ifrit came and got me the last time. She thought that maybe she was loosenin' hers the last time I checked.

"No. They're enchanted...dark magic—I feel them moving over my skin. It's making my flesh crawl," she says.

I know exactly what she means. I feel it, too, when I have the chains on me. They are alive, like serpents wrappin' 'round me instead of metal. It's just another layer of scary in this hellhole. The Ifrit didn't bother to chain me back up when he dragged me back in here this time. He knows I won't be able to move for a while, after what he just did to me. The metal rattles again and I lift my head enough to see Brownie's butterfly wings movin' rapidly, elevatin' her from the ground as she tries with all her strength to pull the chains from the wall, but they aren't givin' an inch.

She gives up after a few minutes and drops with a heavy *thud* back onto the floor. "Have you...gotten anymore messages?" Brownie asks in a tentative way, while panting from the exertion.

"Naw," I murmur, spittin' blood out of my mouth while touchin' the new molar tooth pushin' up through my gum with my tongue. It's replacin' the one that was just yanked out. "I hope Red doesn't send anymore," I add, feelin' a portion of my spine heal with a *pop*. I feel my arms now and that really, really, sucks. Tentatively, I try wigglin' my smashed fingers, but I wince as I realize that my knuckles are still shattered on my left hand, so I just move my right one. "Ya wouldn't happen to have some aspirin over there, would ya?" I ask, tryin' to lighten the mood.

"Yeah. I've been holding out on you. I've got some of that Swiss chocolate that you love so much, too. Heal faster and I'll give you some," Brownie says with *faux* lightness in her tone.

"That was good chocolate..." I say, rememberin' how I was gonna bring some to Red, but that was the first thing we ate down here when we woke up chained to the wall. "Ya know what I've been cravin' though?" I ask Brownie.

"No," she responds.

"Grits, the way my mom makes 'em—with milk instead of water and she smothers them in butter...real butter—not that fake crap—margarine or whatever—with salt. My sister, Melanie, she likes them with maple syrup on them. She really likes sweet stuff, but Scarlett and me, we like them just with butter and salt," I say, thinkin' of my family.

"I remember...I like them when the egg yoke runs into them on my plate," she says with a catch in her voice.

"Yeah, that's good, too," I agree quietly. A tear slides down the side of my nose. I clench my teeth 'cuz I can't cry now. I can't move my hands to wipe the tears away, but my throat is achin' with the need to bawl like a little girl. I'm so hungry that one minute I think I can eat anythin'...anythin', but then the next second I'm so nauseous that I don't think I'll ever be able to eat again.

"Why's this happenin', Brownie?" I ask, feelin' completely broken and weak, like I'm gonna start cryin' at any second and I know that if I do, I might never stop.

"I don't know...you're older than me, I think—I'm sure. I was hoping you might know why," she says in a low tone.

"I'm older than ya?" I ask, lookin' in her direction, hearin' the skepticism in my own tone. She's thousands of years old by her own estimation.

"Oh, there's no question, Russell," she replies, her wings flutterin' as she tries to find a comfortable position on the floor. "Your soul is older than Moses, to use a cliché...and I mean, *way* older."

"How do ya know that?" I ask her in suspicion. "Have we met before now? Before this?"

"I don't think so," she answers slowly. "I'm sure I would remember you. You're quite a character. You would stick out."

"Ya mean ya never reaped me—my soul?" I ask, still feelin' weird 'bout her bein' a Reaper and knowin' all 'bout Paradise. She won't tell me nothin' though. I've tried to squeeze her for information, but all she keeps sayin' is how she's not tellin' me, so that if I ever have my soul leave my body, she can negotiate for it with no worries. She wants to make sure that I get into Paradise.

"No…and I don't think I met you in Paradise either," she says. "No, you're older than me for sure and very…elite. Let me ask you this. How many names have you had?"

"Shoot, Brownie," I say, exhalin'. "There are so many I couldn't begin to recall them all."

"Okay, now, think back farther. Can you remember a time when you had no name? A time when there was no time—before there *were* names?" she asks. The hair on my arms rises up like wires.

My heart pounds hard in my chest, so hard I think it will burst as I see glimpses of things that I have never seen before with these eyes—Russell's eyes—things I want back, things I have no names for—dark, ebony wings. "What…where?" I ask her, feelin' stunned. I lose the track to that memory in an instant, like somethin' turned out the light on it.

"Your soul is scary old, Russell," she says with a smile in her tone for the first time since we have been here. We are both quiet for a while as I think of all the things I do remember.

Anger builds in me, makin' my throat feel tight and painful. "Naw, I don't know why we're here, but what I really can't figure out is why they would leave us lyin' on the floor down here," I say in a soft tone.

"I doubt they know where we are, Russell, and even if they did, they don't have magic to kill it. They would have to get help," Brownie whispers.

"Brownie, I'm not talkin' 'bout Reed and Zee. They have to take care of Buns and Evie. Naw, I'm talkin' 'bout *them*," I say, grittin' my teeth, usin' my index finger to point up.

"Oh," she says in a sad tone. "I don't know why we're here, in this place, with these circumstances. But, have you ever played with dominos, you know, when you were a kid in one of the many, many, lifetimes that you've had?" she asks me seriously.

"Yeah, in fact, I've played with them in *this* lifetime," I reply. Then I grunt, feeling another *pop*, and then searin' pain, as my spine heals some more. I can feel that there are several ribs still mendin' after being crushed by the Ifrit's bare hands.

"Are you okay?" Brownie asks with panic in her voice.

Sweat is tricklin' down the side of my face as I fight through the pain. "Yeah—dominoes," I pant, wantin' somethin' to think 'bout other than the agony in my chest.

"Okay," she whispers, her voice shaky, "when you set up lines of dominoes, you have to place them just right, so that when you knock the first one down, it will fall and hit the next one in the line," she explains in a rush.

"Yeah," I manage to say, so that she knows I'm still listenin' to her.

"You can't get to the end, the last domino, without lining everything up just right," she says. "You know?"

"Yeah," I say, gettin' what she's sayin'. "You think this is leadin' to somethin' else?" I ask. "Somethin' bigger?"

"I know it is. This is huge, Russell," she whispers, lookin' over her shoulder to make sure the Ifrit isn't standin' behind her. Seein' nothin', she continues on urgently, "I never expected to be in on a mission like this—with someone like you—well, I never imagined someone like you either. I'm just a Reaper, we are never asked to do work like this—this is the realm of the Seraphim and work of souls that gather in *His* presence."

"Ya should talk to yer union rep then, 'cuz I think yer due for some overtime pay," I reply sourly.

"No, you don't understand. This is an honor for me—a great responsibility to help you with your mission. I'm just scared, but I know my role is important—more important than anything I have ever done to this point and I…" she is choked off by the intensity of her emotion.

"Are ya sure I'm older than ya? 'Cuz I feel like I don't know nothin' compared to ya," I mutter, feelin' grateful to have her here and guilty for feelin' that way.

"Russ, you're like super old," she says, and I can hear her eyes rolling in the tone of her voice. "You are as old as George Hamilton is tan."

"Ahh, Brownie, that's disgustin'. Yer freakin' me out now," I say, wrinklin' my nose at her, but feelin' a little relieved, knowin' that thing upstairs hasn't beaten the smart-ass out of her yet.

"Don't start trippin', Russ, it's awe inspiring to be so old. I bet Reapers don't even come for you when you die. I bet it's the Thrones or the Cherubim that collect a soul like yours," she says, and I can tell she's been thinkin' 'bout that a lot, by the reverent way she had said it.

"Yeah, well, if they come for me, I hope they know I'm fixin' to get karmic all over that Ifrit. If they're gonna leave us down here, then they better let me get some kind of apocalyptic revenge," I reply, tryin' to shrug off the fact that Brownie thinks I'm some kind of sainted soul. I'm just me—pissed off and wantin' retribution. "I don't wanna die before I get a chance to kick his ass."

"Can't say I'm surprised—you are part Seraphim and they need to get serious payout when their line is crossed," Brownie says. "You guys don't play nice and if you were fully evolved, I would have serious doubts about the Ifrit's chances. I don't want to die either. There is something I want and I haven't had a chance to find it yet," Brownie says, pullin' her knees to her chest and restin' her chin on them.

"Wut?" I ask, listenin' to the sound of her gentle breathin'.

"It's nothing," she shrugs, givin' me a sad smile.

"Brownie, in all this time I've known ya, ya never once said ya wanted anythin'—'cept maybe to kill the Kappas. Ya can't leave me hangin' like this," I reply.

"Promise you won't laugh," she says, not lookin' up.

"I'm pretty sure that there's no chance of me laughin' anytime soon," I respond.

She grunts softly in acknowledgment of the truth of my statement. "Sorry, you're right," she agrees.

"What do ya want?" I ask her again.

"To be in love," she says, like she's admittin' to a crime.

"Why?" I ask, thinkin' 'bout how much it sucks to be in love with someone else, especially if they don't love ya back. Or, even if they do, they don't love ya the way ya want them to love ya—the way ya love them.

"Because I've seen what love can do—make you do things that you'd probably never do otherwise. It makes you stronger," she says with a humble tone.

"Naw, ya got it wrong. It makes ya weak—vulnerable. It makes fools of us all," I contradict her.

"Bullshit," she rejects my answer. "It gives you the strength to be great. I watched you prepare to go down in that hole and save Evie from the Gancanagh. Don't tell me that you could've done that without love."

As I remember that nightmare, it makes a shiver of dread pass through me. Brennus is still out there. He still wants Red. Zephyr told me that he attacked them at the chateau. Brownie and I had managed to stay a few steps ahead of the cold, stinky bastards, but that wasn't easy. We had spotted a couple of them near Kiev, right before we ran into the Ifrit—the angel killer.

"Brownie, just make sure that when you do fall in love, that there's a chance that whoever it is will love ya back," I advise.

"Why would that matter?" she asks me.

"It sucks if they don't," I reply, feelin' the cool ground under my cheek, not lookin' at her.

"It sounds like a gift just to be in love," she says in a naïve way. "To find someone who you think is perfect, even when they aren't."

"What if the person ya love doesn't love ya back, Brownie?" I ask. "And all that ya say to that person is nothin' to them? And wherever they are, they don't think twice 'bout ya?"

"I know we're not talking from experience, Russell, because I know that she loves you," Brownie replies. "And you are lucky that you can love the way that you do. Try living without the ability to love…or at least to love with the intensity that you do. I know that kind of emotion must be exquisite. I have only just started to love like that and it's amazing. The way I love you guys—you're my family. I would do anything to protect that and *that* is a gift."

She falls silent then, and I hang my head in sorrow, thinkin' 'bout all that has happened. Liftin' my head, I reach forward, pullin' myself an inch or two towards Brownie where she is chained to the wall. I can feel one of my fingers bendin' the wrong way, but I ignore it.

"What are you doing?" Brownie asks, soundin' worried.

"I'm comin' over there," I reply, gruntin' as pain is makin' me sweat while I'm fightin' for air.

"But, what about our psychotic friend? He doesn't like it when we move," she whispers with fear in her voice.

"What's he gonna do? Beat me?" I ask her sarcastically. "Brownie, he didn't chain me…he forgot."

"You gotta get out of here, Russell! Can you walk?" she asks, hope surgin' in her voice.

"Not yet," I reply, not bein' able to feel anythin' below my waist.

"It will kill you," Brownie whispers. "You need to head towards the stairs," she says, tryin' to redirect me in the other direction.

"I don't think he plans to kill me—not yet anyway. It wants Red and it's not gonna kill me 'til he gets her," I say, continuin' towards her.

"Russell, let me tell you something about evil," Brownie says, crawlin' as close to me as her chains will allow. "Evil doesn't know when to stop. It feeds on itself, until there is nothing left. He may want her, but he is out of control—powerful as he is, he still needs to be cautious because he is alone. But, he is not being cautious. Ever since Evie sent her spirit to him, he has been out of his mind. I don't know what she said to him, but his urgency to have her has increased exponentially."

"She didn't have to say nothin'," I reply, pullin' forward again and gainin' another couple of inches. "He just had to see her and…" I squeeze my eyes shut against the pain. "I'm gonna come help ya pull on yer chains. If we can get them out of the wall, then you can get me outta here."

"You are going to have to explain later how you do that thing you and Evie can do," she says, watchin' me struggle towards her. "How did you send out a twin of yourself?"

"I don't know how it works. I just figured I could do it if she could, and after her twin came to me that first time, it was like she had turned on the light switch and I could just do it, too," I whisper a hasty explanation.

"It's so amazing when you do it, Russell," Brownie says with admiration. I know she's tryin' to keep my mind off the pain I'm in. "It's like someone pulled you through a mirror or some-thing. The one that you sent to me was…timely. I felt like I wasn't going to make it. You helped me," she says. I had sent Brownie a message while she was with the Ifrit, tellin' her that Red sent me another message: Red is tryin' to find us.

"Well, it feels like someone stuffed me in a keg and kicked it down a hill when I do it," I explain. A groan of pain escapes from me.

"Are you okay?" she asks with anguish in her tone.

"Naw, I'm hurtin'" I reply honestly, tryin' not to let my voice crack, but it sounds thick to my ears.

"All right, get your ass over here then and let's do this," she whispers, stretchin' her arm out to me as far as it will reach. "Come on, boy, time's a wastin'," she says in the perfect imitation of my mom, givin' me the incentive I need to fight. I pull myself across the floor. When I drag myself the last inch, Brownie grasps my fingertips with her own, pullin' me almost effortlessly into her arms. As she wraps them 'round my shoulders, she holds me to her, restin' her cheek against my hair. "You are such a bad ass, Russell. Good job! How do we do this?" she asks, strokin' my wing lightly as it trembles under her fingertips.

As I take deep breaths, I say, "My dad always says that the best way outta somethin' is to go through it. I think that we're never gonna get the metal of yer manacles to give, but that wall looks like it wants to let ya go."

"Okay," Brownie says, turnin' me towards the wall and bracin' her feet against it. I wrap a length of the chain 'round my wrist and forearm, while leanin' my back into her. "Say when," she mouths near my ear.

"On three," I whisper near her ear, "One, two, three…" We pull the chain in unison as hard as we can. The wall strains and cracks under the intense pressure that we put on it, givin' a little and makin' my heart beat like it did when I first kissed Alice Peterson in the seventh grade. Watchin' the cracks spider up the wall, I feel Brownie squeeze me as her hope translates to me.

"Again?" she asks urgently.

"Hell freakin' yeah!" I whisper back. Bracin' myself against her we pull several more times, managin' to get the chain to pull through the several feet of mortar, steel, and stone. The last pull ends with half the wall givin' way and slidin' to the floor 'round us. I cough at the fountain of dust that the wall kicks up, and then I put my finger to my mouth as Brownie begins to say somethin'. My heart is poundin' in my chest again, 'cuz the wall crashin' down was loud enough to wake the dead. Listenin', I don't hear anythin' from above. Maybe the monster stepped out for a while. I don't think he stays upstairs, but comes here from somewhere else when he wants to hurt us.

I pull Brownie's legs out from under the debris that fell on us, and then we both grin at each other when her legs are unearthed. They are still shackled together, but her chain isn't attached to the wall anymore.

"How did you do that?" Brownie asks me in awe.

"Well, I have to give ya a chance to fall in love—so you can be miserable, just like the rest of us," I reply, tryin' to move my legs. I succeed in movin' my left one, but I have to stop when I realize that both my knees are still smashed into pulp. I can't walk yet. I can't even stand up.

"All right you wise-ass redneck, let's go," she says, gettin' to her knees, and then up to her feet. She reaches down and scoops me up in her arms, like I'm a little girl or somethin'.

"You been workin' out, Brownie?" I ask her near her ear. "You know, strong women can be a turn off, but right now, it couldn't *be* any sexier."

"Shut up, Marx! You talk too much," she whispers back as her copper butterfly wings beat with the effort to lift us both off the floor. She angles us towards the steps.

We pause at the narrow stone staircase that spirals up. We both glance at each other in apprehension. The only way out is up, but that terrifyin' monster is most likely up there some-where, probably pullin' the tail off a puppy or somethin'. "Wut do we do?" I whisper to her.

"Pray," she whispers back, graspin' the long length of her chain that had been attached to the wall.

"I'm way ahead of ya on that," I admit.

She hands me her chain to hold, so it won't drag near the ground. The chain is attached to the chain between the manacle cuffs on her ankles. I have no idea how we are gonna get them off of her, but since she is still able to use her wings, we can figure that out later. Slowly, she begins to fly up the stairwell carryin' me. She loses her balance and crashes into the wall. Brownie has to squeeze me tighter so she won't drop me. "Sorry, but you're completely huge—you freakin' giant," she mutters. I think she is dizzy and hurt, but she is tryin' to hide it from me 'cuz that's the way she is—an ass kicker, just like Red.

"S'kay," I say, tryin' not to wince. "It just felt like ya stuffed me in yer pocket."

"That sounds painful," she whispers back as she continues up the stairs.

"Not arguin' with that," I whisper low, managin' a grim smile. Some of the tension leaves Brownie's face for just a second.

The air is gettin' hotter, muggier as we near the top. It could just be that we're leavin' the cellar or it could be that we are gettin' nearer to the furnace man. Sniffin' the air, I can't tell. This place smells like him, like the smell of a gas stove just before ya light it. When we almost get to the last step, Brownie stops and sets me down on a step, proppin' me against the wall so I won't go tumblin' back down the stairs. She puts her finger to her lips, then she points to herself, and then she points to the threshold of the stairs. I nod and she hobbles over the top of me to go up. I hand her the chain as quietly as I can. As she inches upward, I reach out and squeeze her hand gently, wishin' she didn't have to be the one goin' up there alone. She squeezes mine back, and then she slips through the doorway to the church.

I lean my head back against the wall and close my eyes to listen for any sound that will tell me what's happenin' above me. It's quiet. Eerie. Minutes pass and nothin'. Maybe she found a way out and made a run for it—went for help. I hear a rattle of a chain, and then a gaspin' exhale. It is soft, like the sound of air bein' squeezed out…I open my eyes and struggle to pull myself up the last few steps of the stairwell.

I claw my way to the landin', pullin' my useless legs behind me, and I make it to the top of the stairs. When I look up, I see Brownie suspended in midair with that long, evil chain wrapped tightly 'round her, crushin' the air out of her lungs. She is floatin' aloft in the center of the church, pale and broken, her head fallin' back as she struggles to take a breath that's bein' denied her by the bindin' chain squeezin' her like a python. He must be usin' his magic on her 'cuz there is nothin' holdin' her up but air.

"NO!" I shout, tryin' hard to stand, but I can't, I can't reach her and I'm suffocatin' 'cuz I can't get enough air in me to breathe either.

The slimy Ifrit bastard appears above me then, his golden-brown eyes reflectin' the fire within him like they're mirrorin' a campfire—flickerin' and dancin' like flames. "Russsell," he lisps, while graspin' me by the back of my neck and pullin' me up to a mere inch from his face.

"Let her down, yer killin' her," I growl through my teeth, clawin' at his hands with my own and tryin' to get him to let go of me.

"I really despise it when you speak, Russell. You never tell me what I want to hear," his slithering voice intones, puttin' his finger on my throat and speakin' his ugly Ifrit language. I open my mouth to tell him to go to Hell, but my voice no longer works. He turned it off. "That's better," he sighs.

Furious, I drive my head forward, battering' my forehead against his. He sneers at me with breath that feels like a blowtorch against my skin, frying' the small hairs and causin' the smell of burnin' flesh to curl up to my nose. I scream, but no noise comes from me. I writhe as the achin' patch of skin begins to bubble up.

The Ifrit straightens up and pulls me by the back of my wing up the aisle of the church towards the altar. Brownie is still levitatin' in the middle of the room, her face growin' paler—her lips turnin' blue.

The Ifrit tosses me up on the altar. I try not to look at him as he moves in front of me. "Russselll, I was coming to tell you that she is nearly here, my Alya. Did I tell you what that name means? It means Heaven. Appropriate, no? You do know what that means, Russselll?" he asks me with a smug smile. "I no longer need either of you," he says, grinning happily. His black hair and tanned skin make him look like he should be on the cover of some magazine, not freakin' carvin' me up in the middle of a church. If I ever picture the devil again, he is gonna look just like this monster. Sickened by him, I turn away to look at the statues of the saints that have witnessed most of the unholy atrocities that have occurred here in the past few days.

A sanguine smile crosses his lips. "How shall I kill you, Russselll?" he asks with his gravelly voice hissin' my name. "It has to be slow, though, because you refused to cooperate with me, so I have to make it as painful as possible. You seem to enjoy burning so much—should we start there?" he asks.

I choke on anguish as I turn my face away from him. Behind the Ifrit, my eyes alight on the most beautiful statue I have ever seen. Its marble-white face is perfection—the face of love. It steals my breath away as the stone comes to life in the next instant, sheddin' its rocky exterior for the crimson feathers of an' angel as the wings of the statue lash out 'round it. The angelic statue loses more of its pale veneer, takin' on the soft glow of angelic skin as it soundlessly grasps the golden staff that holds a crucifix attached to the end of it. Usin' the staff like a sword, Evie's marbled arm thrusts the golden crucifix right through the back of the Ifrit, so that it comes out the front of it, impaling him.

Evie's teeth gnash together in a twisted sneer. "Let's start your death here, shall we?" Evie asks between her teeth, twistin' the staff and yankin' it back out of the Ifrit, leavin' a gapin' hole in his chest as molten hot blood pours out of him.

Evie

CHAPTER 11

The Bargain

The Ifrit's blood melts the metal crucifix right off the pole it is affixed to as I pull it out of its chest and through his back. Molten blood spews from his mouth, spraying the ground in front of him with a sizzling smolder. Using what is left of the melted pole like a bat, I swing it as hard as I can at the Ifrit's head, connecting with it and knocking him away from Russell's prone body on the altar. I have no idea if I can kill this wicked thing, but I have to try. He can't live, not after what I just witnessed. He dies or we all die. There is no other option open to us; I can see that now. There will be no negotiations.

I must have stunned him, because Brownie drops from where she hovered and crashes to the ground. I hear her begin to take gasping breaths as I look around for another weapon, because mine is still melting. I collect my clothes as my alabaster-stone skin begins to take on its original form and I shrug into them.

I pick up one of the nearby statues and use it as a club, beating the inert body of the Ifrit as he lies on the ground by the altar. Rage is fueling me, I can't seem to stop smashing him even when I can see he is shifting, taking another form. The Ifrit is growing.

With a desperate look, I scream, "GOD! WHAT KILLS YOU?' I watch as the Ifrit becomes a formless blob, expanding with every second, so much so that I have to take several steps back from it.

"Red—RUN" Russell shouts to me from where I have left him.

"HOW DO I KILL IT, RUSSELL?" I shout to him in a desperate plea.

"YA DON'T! YA RUN!" he shouts back in equal desperation.

The Ifrit's blood on the floor has ignited a fire; it is spreading to the altar. I have to drop the statue because it is not even hurting the Ifrit anymore. I run back to the altar. When I pull Russell into my arms, I feel how broken and beaten he is as he hangs loosely in my grasp. Rage causes tears to brighten my eyes.

"Run!" Russell demands as his head lolls back.

"Shut up if you can't be constructive, Russell," I retort in anger, dragging him to where Brownie is lying listless on the floor.

I glance back at the altar; the Ifrit is shifting, taking on the shape of a man again, but huge: a giant who is filling the apse like it is shrinking to dollhouse size.

"Can either of you move?" I ask them in an urgent voice. Brownie groans, twisting, she tries to sit up, but her ribs are clearly broken, making her gasp and writhe.

"Naw, my legs don't work," Russell says, staring at me like I'm going to disappear any second. I lean over and kiss him hard on the mouth, so he knows I'm real. After I pull back, I see tears gather in his eyes that match mine.

"I'm going to drag you back to the corner," I explain, grasping them both, one in each hand. "This is going to suck," I warn them, and then I pull them as fast as I can to the far corner of the church, away from the apse and the altar. Brownie passes out, but Russell remains conscious. "Hold on to her," I order him, putting Brownie into Russell's arms.

Russell grits his teeth. "Ya have to leave, Red. Ya can't kill it—ya can't save us. It's enough that ya tried—that ya came for us," he says in a taut voice.

I grit my teeth, too. "Don't tell me what I can't do," I retort. "You don't happen to still have any of those grenades handy, do you?" I ask, knowing he doesn't. He shakes his head. "Damn!"

I say under my breath. "Okay, maybe I'll have to reason with it after all."

"NO!" Russell shouts at me in anger, but I take flight then, soaring up so that I'm at eye level with the enormous Ifrit. The Ifrit smiles at me and I watch in fascination as his golden eyes have the appearance of being on fire, like flames are lighting them from within.

"You said that we could both get what we wanted if I came to you. I'm here and I want you to allow my friends to leave," I say as my wings beat steadily to keep me in the air.

"YOU HAVE A SOUL!" The Ifrit's voice erupts in a roar as the walls of the church reverberate with the echo of his voice.

I quake inwardly. "Yep, and I'm a Scorpio, who enjoys holding hands and taking long walks on the beach," I reply with my jaw clenched in a sullen expression. "Let's talk."

A deep rumbling laugh comes from the giant monster, his breath reeking from him in scorching vapors, making me veer away from him to save my flesh from melting. Then he looks at me again and his demeanor completely changes. His eyes narrow and he sneers, "YOU ARE SERAPHIM, THE WORST KIND OF REFUSE! I HAD HOPED THAT YOU WOULD APPEAR MORE WOMANLY."

"I can look human, in fact, I am half human," I reply in an even tone. Flying back down to the ground, I land on my feet, retracting my wings into my back so that I no longer look like an angel.

He stares at me for a few moments and I stand as still as possible, feeling rigid with fear with my heart pounding in my ears. He steps nearer to me, shaking the foundation of the church with his massive tread. My fear increases because he can stomp on me and squash me like a bug. Reaching his hand down, he picks me up in his fist and brings me up to his eye level again.

"What do you want from me?" I ask as he studies me.

Gently, he reaches back down and sets me on my feet. He begins to change then, shrinking in size and shifting into several grotesque shapes before resuming the same male appearance as before, but in human size. He looks just as he did when he stood over Russell at the altar and I want to smash his face in again.

"I want what I have been denied for eternity," he says in a silky tone, reaching out to touch my hair and then the skin of my face, feeling the texture of me.

"Don't tell me you want a soul, because I kind of still need mine," I say, trying to head him off.

His lips twitch. "No, I do not wish to possess your soul. I like it in you," he smiles at me tenderly. He looks almost charming. If I didn't witness his evil only moments ago, his beauty might have fooled me. He is dark, with sultry, olive skin. His hair is really long and straight—tribal. His chest is bare and covered with hair, but it's not unattractive, just very masculine. He's wearing a pair of loose fitting pants that are pajama-like. They make him look exotic.

"What is it that you want then? I would like to be clear, so that there are no misunderstandings between us," I ask him.

His eyes soften. "I want you and what you can give me," he says, smiling. "I have tried for centuries to acquire offspring. I want true immortality—to pass on my traits to another. I want a child," he says with reverence.

Buns was right! He does want to breed, I think to myself, feeling ill.

"Why me?" I ask, attempting to hide my revulsion.

"I believe you can give me what I want. It would be a shame to kill you without even trying. You are so wonderfully human— a true beauty. If I hadn't seen your wings, I might not have realized right away that you are an angel, too." Quickly and without warning, he slaps me hard across my face, making my head snap back, but I don't fall down. Holding my hand to my throbbing cheek, I look back at him, growling low. He smiles in delight at me. "You see, you are not as fragile as a human. That could've snapped a human woman's neck, but not yours. I can be rough with you."

Russell growls low and deep from the corner where I have left him with Brownie. I pray that he keeps his mouth shut and doesn't draw attention to himself. "You like it rough, huh?" I ask, straightening back up.

He shrugs. "I have never been allowed to be rough. When I take a woman to my bed, I have to be very, very careful. But, when she becomes pregnant, I know that it is over for her. The child within her will kill her eventually and they both will die," he says with a sultry smile. "But, perhaps, you will not. No, you are strong, healthy—durable."

"You're a flatterer," I respond with sarcasm.

His eyebrows come together in menace. "You mock me?" he asks.

"Sorry," I hold up my hand, wanting to bite my tongue. He is an insane demon, I have to remember that, or I'm dead. "So what do we do now? I know what you want—you know what I want. Let's let Russell and Brownie go, then we can talk."

"They have offended me. I cannot let them go now," says the Ifrit in a stern tone. "They endeavored to escape me. I cannot tolerate such defiance."

My heart beats painfully, "What is your name?" I ask him, trying to head him off.

"I am Valentine," he says. Several sarcastic remarks come to mind, but I do bite my tongue this time.

"Valentine, there is no deal if you kill my friends. I will not agree to anything," I state, trying to make him see reason.

His expression is one of puzzlement. "You will have no choice," he replies.

"There is always a choice," I counter.

He grasps my wrist and his hand heats up to burn my skin. Searing pain shoots up my arm as he leans near my face, saying, "No, you do what I say or I kill you."

Gritting my teeth, I reply, "Exactly—you will have to kill me."

His eyebrows become one. "No, I will have to break you," he says with an evil grin.

"I will kill you if you try," I promise, leaning into his face, ignoring the pain in my wrist.

In an instant, he picks me up and throws me away from him across the church where I hit the far wall, crashing to the floor. I lie there, stunned. "You think that because you are a Seraph, the top of the chain, that you are a threat to ME?" he shouts. "I kill Seraphim for sport," he intones, beating his chest with his fist to indicate himself.

I groan, using the wall to help me to stand because he is coming for me and I have to evade him. I get to my feet, but he catches me before I can sprout my wings and fly from him. As he holds me by the collar of my shirt, he lifts me off my feet, so that we are eye to eye with each other. With a wicked smile, he says, "I am going to kill your friends now and you are going to watch. Then, I am going to see just how much pain you can take while we work on getting me a child. You want fire and brimstone, Alya? I will give it to you."

"No," I choke in desperation, kicking at him, but it is not doing a thing to hurt him.

"Dat is me *aingeal* dat ye're breakin', Valentine," Brennus says from the mouth of the church where he's standing with Finn, Declan and a score or more of the fellas.

Valentine lowers me to my feet with a startled look on his face, but he doesn't let go of my collar. His face is changing though. There is fear in his eyes as he watches the Gancanagh enter the church.

"Brennus," I whisper. My eyes widen in surprise to find that I feel relief in seeing him here—it's more than relief and I know that is an absurd feeling to have.

Brennus walks casually into the church, looking around at the blood and destruction. A small fire still smolders near the altar. Blood is everywhere from days of torture and things are smashed and broken, especially Russell, Brownie, and me.

Brennus' face is turning paler as he looks back at Valentine and me. "Do ye need more tellin'? Whah did ye na understand, Ifrit? She is moin," Brennus says through clenched teeth, raising goose bumps on my arms because he is truly enraged and scary. His fangs are engaged and he is scowling at Valentine like he will pounce on him at any moment.

Letting go of me, Valentine moves back from me and I almost fall down from the shock of being released so quickly. "I did not know," Valentine says in a humble way, bowing his head to Brennus.

Brennus raises his arm, holding out his hand to me. I don't hesitate, but stumble towards it, like a lifeline. Grasping his hand, he pulls me to him, hugging me to his cold chest and I feel relief and dread. He presses his cheek to the top of my head, saying, "Dis is na how ta sort out an Ifrit, *mo chroí*. Ye need magic. Did ye try ta wound it?" he asks.

I nod. He gives a small laugh. "I tought I smelled his blood. Ye are me heart, 'tis true," he says with a grudging pride in his voice. "Come, we will go home now."

"Wait!" I say, pulling away from his chest so that I can see his face. He looks less angry than he did when he was looking at Valentine.

"Whah?" he asks me gravely.

"What about my friends? I can't leave them here with the Ifrit—Valentine. He wants to kill them!" I explain with panic in my voice. Brennus looks over at Russell who still holds an unconscious Brownie in his arms. Brennus' eyes narrow when he sees him.

"Oh look, 'tis da other," Brennus says, gazing at Russell with recognition on his face. I begin to really panic then, feeling ill as my face flushes with heat and my heart pounds wildly.

Russell tries to give him a smart-ass grin, but it turns into a grimace. "I didn't ever think I would say this, but I'm glad to see ya stinky devils," Russell says listlessly. "Y'all think ya could put me outta my misery before ya leave? Valentine and I don't get on, if ya know what I mean."

"Whah, no grenades?" Brennus asks Russell.

"Fresh out," Russell replies with a slow shake of his head.

Valentine moves then, facing us. "They are my kill," he says with malice. My legs go numb with fear.

Brennus' eyebrow arches. "Dey are whahever I say dey are, Ifrit," Brennus growls back at him. "I will deal wi' ye in a minute." Brennus waves his hand, freezing the Ifrit. In shock, I see that the Ifrit is completely still, but its eyes are moving, dancing like fire. Lonan and Goban approach Russell, flashing their fangs at him. They remember him. Russell killed Ultan and Driscoll, their buddies.

"Brennus!" I say in desperation, watching the fellas hiss at Russell. "Please!"

"Please whah, Genevieve?" he asks in a quiet tone, watching me.

My mouth goes dry as my eyes shift from Russell to Brennus. "What do you want?" I ask with urgency.

He blinks, like he didn't expect me to say that. A slow smile forms in the corners of his sultry lips, making him look almost angelic in his beauty. "I want Persephone," comes his slow reply.

"Excuse me?" I murmur, not understanding him.

"I want da goddess dat I saw in da portrait, da one dat Alfred gave ta me. It made me want ye, crave ye. Dat's whah I want," he says, speaking of the portrait that Mr. MacKinnon had painted of me as the goddess Persephone. "If ye make me bite ye now, ye will die and become one of us, a Gancanagh. Ye will stop evolving, stop growing in power. I do na want dat. I want ye ta be as powerful as ye will be. But, I can na hold ye—ye are wily. If I do na turn ye and make ye me *sclábhaí*, me slave, ye could jus run off. I'm willing ta change ye ta keep ye. Ye are moin and I want ye. But, I want da goddess more."

"What do you propose," I ask him hurriedly, still watching as Lonan hovers over Russell.

"A bargain," he says with a silky voice. "Ye agree ta live with me and I save yer friends for ye."

"For how long?" I ask, feeling the crushing weight of his words. I hardly lasted a week living with Brennus the last time. If I agree to this, then it will be war between Brennus and Reed. Reed will never stop trying to get me back.

"Forever," he says without taking a breath and I pale.

"You said you want Persephone, the goddess. She only lived with Hades for six months out of the year," I retort, remembering the story. All of the fellas laugh, like I've made a joke. I glance at Brennus to see that he is trying not to smile, too.

"Ye're so quick, *mo chroí*, it makes me wonder how old ye really are," Brennus says.

"I'm eighteen," I reply and they all laugh harder.

"Of course ye are," Brennus replies, shaking his head. "Six months of each year?" he asks, like he's thinking about it, and then a slow smile graces his lips. "Dat sounds interesting. But I'm a jealous craitur. I want ta know dat ye will be loyal ta me and only me when we are together."

"How will you know that?" I ask him.

"Ye have ta promise na ta talk ta yer *aingeal* when ye are wi' me," he says. I know he means Reed without his having to say his name. My heart drops. *Can I even do that? I've never gone that long without Reed before. The longest I lasted was a little longer than half of that.* I must not have answered him fast enough because he asks, "Faolan, ye like *aingeals*, right? How about taking da beautiful, little blond one?"

"NO!" I shout, glaring at Brennus, and then at Faolan as he moves closer to Brownie. "Okay!" I agree.

"Dis is fun, me sweet," he says, grinning at me. "Whah else do I want?" he asks, rubbing his chin. He stills and his face becomes deathly serious as he scowls. "Ah, I know. I want ye ta bind yer life ta mine," he says, frowning at me.

"What?" I say, feeling dizzy. I'm already bound to Reed; I can't bind to him, too. "I can't I'm—"

"No, ye are right, one at a time only—still, we can be connected, ye and me," he says.

"Connected how?" I ask, not really wanting him to explain.

"Yer life and mine will intertwine. If one is cut, da other one bleeds, too," he enlightens me.

My shoulders round as I cross my arms in front of me. "You can do that?" I ask him feebly.

"I can," he says. "Yer *aingeal* can na kill me when ye're wi' me, or he will kill ye as well. I will give him a sporting chance. He will have the opportunity to kill me when ye live wi' him, but dan he will be forever hunting me, and na spending time wi' ye. Dat will be so dull for ye, will it na?" he asks me.

"I can't do that, Brennus," I say pleadingly.

"Dat's da deal breaker, den?" he murmurs as if to himself. Then, he shrugs. "Ah, well, it sounded fun. Okay, let's go fellas, da *aingeals* stay here wi' da Ifrit."

Finn moves to my side as my knees begin to give out on me. He catches me to him, holding me up as he says in a grim tone, "Genevieve, tink about dis for a second. He will let the Ifrit kill yer soul mate and yer friend and den we'll take ye from here where ye'll be bitten and turned. Whah he really wants is yer compliance. Do ye na see dat? Brenn can kill Russell himself right now, but 'twould make ye hate him more. Be reasonable or yer soul mate will die and ye will still be ours wi' no chance of any other future."

"Why is he doing this?" I ask in a daze.

"He wants to win yer love, like Hades won Persephone's love. He made her love him; even when she did na want ta love him. Give him dat chance, ye canna do much worse dan da alternative ta his bargain," Finn says with a grim twist of his beautiful mouth.

When I see that the alternative to my agreeing to this arrangement leaves Russell and Brownie to the torture of Valentine and his vast knowledge of pain, I reply in a weak tone, "Brennus, I agree to your terms."

A slow smile graces his lips once again. "Dat is very reasonable of ye," he murmurs, taking me out of Finn's arms gently and pulling me to his side. "Finn, say da words, so it shall be."

"Wait," I interrupt before Finn starts the magic that will create the contract. "I have one stipulation."

"Whah?" Brennus asks with curiosity.

"NO ONE BITES ME!" I shout to all of the Gancanagh standing around. "I'm bitten and the contract is broken!"

"Was it dat bad, den?" Brennus asks with concern.

I nod, unable to look in his eyes.

"Right, lads, ye heard her, anyone who bites her and breaks me contract will wish dey were never turned because da torture will go on forever—eternity," Brennus promises all who listen. "Now, are ye willing ta agree ta dis contract?" he ask me.

"Yes," I say with a curt nod. "When I agree, you will then kill the Ifrit and let my friends live. They can't die or become undead or be touched or harmed or…" I trail off, trying to cover every angle that may lead to a loophole.

"Is dat all?" Brennus laughs. "Ye really do na trust me, do ye?"

"No, I really don't trust you," I agree.

Brennus' eyes soften with affection. "Ah, well, we will change dat," he says in an easy tone. Finn moves in front of us then. Brennus nods to him and Finn begins speaking words that I can't understand. The room is filling with energy, I feel like I can reach out and touch it—taste it in the air. Brennus translates the terms of the contract as we had just laid them out while Finn speaks them in another language.

"Are they telling the truth, Russell?" I call softly to Russell.

"I think so. I don't know some of their words, but it mostly sounds right," he says in a feeble tone.

"Hang in there, Russell, it's almost over," I say to him and hear him laugh humorlessly.

"Yeah, Red, for me it is, but not for ya," he replies bitterly, holding Brownie closer to him.

"Ye have ta repeat after me, Genevieve," Finn interrupts us. He waits until I look at him before he speaks something in his language. I try very hard to repeat phonetically what he says. When I'm done, he produces a knife. *Of course*, I think, looking at Finn and Brennus with a frown.

"Can't we just shake on it?" I ask Finn testily.

He smiles broadly at me, shaking his head no. "'Tis not binding dat way."

I exhale, and ask, "What do you need?"

"A finger will do," he smiles and his iridescent-green eyes sparkle.

I produce my finger. Piercing it with his knife he gathers a drop of my blood. Brennus extends his finger, too, allowing Finn to pierce it. Brennus' blood mixes with mine on the blade. The blood smokes and sizzles as it runs together, but otherwise it is uneventful.

"What did I say, just now?" I ask Finn as we both watch the blood slowly dissipating off the blade in a plume of smoke.

"Ye said, 'Let treachery return ta da betrayer,'" he quotes, watching me.

"Uhh," I exhale as I realize I forgot to ask about the terms of the contract. "Brennus, what happens if I break the contract?" I ask him with fear overwhelming me. "What will happen to me?"

"Ye can na break it," he says in a gentle, reassuring way. "'Tis me contract. Ye're bound ta it. Here, try ta walk away from me now, like ye are leaving and ye will never come back."

"Seriously?" I ask.

"Seriously," he replies, suppressing a smile. I turn from him with tentative steps and walk towards the church door, my heart pounds in my chest as I have an urge to run as fast as I can and get away from here forever. My feet begin to drag and grow heavy. Soon, I find it almost impossible to take another step.

"Oh," I say dejectedly.

"Do na look so sad. Ye wound me," he says with a new lightness about him, smiling as I face him.

"What happens to you if you break the contract, Brennus?" I ask.

"Ye go free," he says. "But, since I would have to bite ye to break it, I guess I would jus have ta make ye a Gancanagh and bind ye ta me dat way." I ball my hands into fists seeing his logic. If he bites me, I'll probably end up begging him for his blood to ease my pain. It would be really hard to resist him and try to escape, even with the contract null and void.

"Can you let me out of our contract, if you want to?" I ask.

"I can rescind it at any time," he states firmly. "Do na hope for it. 'Twill na happen."

"You will have to let me go in six months, Brennus. Remember?" I ask.

"I have ta give ye da option. It doesn't mean ye can na choose ta live wi' me after dat," he corrects me.

"Same thing," I say.

"If ye say so, but we can discuss it in six months, can we na?" he asks rhetorically. "Now, how would ye like ta see da Ifrit die?" he asks with a cool, calculating stare. My heart twists and Brennus' eyes soften when he sees my expression change from sadness to one of vengeance. I want Valentine dead. Valentine tortured my soul mate and made me lose my love. I want him to die slow, in the most painful manner I can think of, and the realization of how badly I want that makes me feel cold inside.

"Russell," I whisper, taking a few steps to him so I see him better. "How?" I ask, deferring to him.

Russell's face hardens as he loses some of the sorrow and a light enters his eyes. "I like what they did to Alfred. It was poetic."

My eyes shift to Brennus'. He nods and says, "Do na try ta bite da Ifrit, lads, 'twill burn yer insides out. Jus tear him apart and den do da spell, we do na want him ta reassemble and come after da other again. It might break da contract."

Immediately, Declan, Lachlan, Faolan, and Eion fall on the immobile Ifrit, tearing his limbs off while they melt Valentine to nothing with their magic. The rest of the Gancanagh watch in silence as they enjoy the gruesome scene. I can't watch it all. Instead, I watch Russell's face as he receives justice for what was done to him. Russell's eyes shift to mine when it is finished and I see overwhelming sorrow in them.

I silently mouth the words, "I love you" to him and he mouths it back to me.

"'Tis time dat we went," Brennus says to me, extending his hand for me to take. I don't hesitate, but take his hand in mine, knowing that I can do nothing else.

"Thank you," I murmur.

Brennus' eyes widen a little. "Ye are da most confusing craitur I have ever encountered, *mo chroí*," he says, smiling down at me and leading me to the door. He stops when we get there, turning to Russell, he says, "She saved ye dis time. Da next time we meet, however, ye may na be so fortunate. Do ye need more tellin', boy?"

"I think we understand each other, Brennus," Russell replies with utter sadness.

"Goodbye, Russell," I say, and then I turn with Brennus and walk from the church.

CHAPTER 12

The Fellas

We arrive at Brennus' home and I see the house itself is amazing—but it's not really a "house." It's a true medieval castle built on the northern cliffs of Ireland. I'm not exactly sure where I am, but we are very near the sea because I can hear it coming through the car window. When we first enter the ornate, iron gates of the estate, I think it has to be some kind of golf course because the grounds are expansive, tailored and pristine. But, that is nothing compared with the noble façade of the stronghold that it surrounds. The castle has much of the old stone of the original fortress, but there are places where it has been re-built with new stone and lighting.

We pull through a medieval portico and park before imposing wooden doors. As I step out of the sleek car that had carried a silent Brennus and me from the private airport, I feel intimidated by the sheer size and scale of this place. Brennus takes my hand in his cold one and I do not pull away from him as he helps me out of the car. Walking with Brennus towards the enormous doors, I see man-sized, stone gargoyles with vicious fangs on either side of the entranceway. I shiver at the sight of them and I wonder if these gargoyles represent the distant relatives of my new family.

In the formal reception area, the huge stone fireplace of the old hall still remains, but the ceiling had tumbled in ages ago. Now, wrought iron columns stretch up to the glass ceilings so that when I look up, I can see all of the ivy-covered towers of the castle above me. Tapestries and carved, wooden furniture mix with beautiful, modern items, such as a grand piano, in a way that makes it seem that they belong together—have always belonged together. If the circumstances of my arrival at this place were different, I would've wanted to see everything, but instead, I ask to be taken to whatever room they have planned for me.

Brennus assess me coolly, not saying a word. He nods his head and Faolan and Lachlan materialize in front of me, indicating that I should follow them. The rest of the place is just a blur because I am led down several winding hallways and up elaborate staircases to arrive at one of the tower's posh suite of rooms.

෧෨

I have been in this elegant room for several days now. As I lie in the enormous bed and listen to the footsteps coming down the hallway to my room, they have such a purposeful stride, that I know they are coming for me. I pull one of the exquisite pillows up over my head with a groan just before my door is thrown open from without. The footsteps stride through my sitting room suite and into my bedroom where they stop at the end of my bed. One heavy foot taps for a couple of seconds before a muffled voice says, "Genevieve, are ye gettin' up in dis century?" Ignoring the voice, I pull the blanket up over the pillow and snuggle further into the comfortable mattress of this enormous bed.

"I tink dat was 'no,' Brenn," Finn's voice lilts.

"She's acting like a waster! Ye're acting like a waster, Genevieve, and 'tis going ta end," Brennus says, and I can feel the anger and frustration in his voice.

"That's *dark* and *scary*, Brennus," I reply, my voice dripping with sarcasm from under the blanket. "What's a waster, Finn?" I ask.

"A human junkie," Finn responds helpfully.

"Well, you would know, I guess, Brennus, since you *make* them that way on a daily basis," I reply, feeling harassed.

"Do ye intend ta stay in here alone da entire time ye're here?" Brennus asks me angrily.

"Our agreement says that I have to live with you. I never said I'd TALK to you. ANY of YOU!"

"*Sin é, ye rua aingeal,*" Brennus mutters before the bed levitates off the floor and begins to shake. In seconds, I am dumped on the carpet while my bed still hovers over my head in midair.

As I sit on the floor in just an oversized t-shirt that I had scavenged from a wardrobe in one of the other rooms, I give Brennus one of my severest scowls. "What did *he* just say, Finn?" I ask, gritting my teeth.

"He said, 'Dat's it, ye red-haired *aingeal,*'" Finn translates helpfully, trying hard to suppress the smile forming in the corners of his mouth. My eyes lock on the light green ones of Brennus as he crosses his arms over his chest, glaring back at me nefariously, while scanning every inch of my legs exposed by the hitched up t-shirt.

"Where did ye get dat ting ye're wearing?" Brennus asks with his eyebrow arching.

"Whah, dis?" I ask with an innocent widening of my eyes while using his accent to mock him. "I borrowed it from one of the fellas. I have been wondering what, *Dún do chlab* means," I say, looking at them to see they are both trying hard not to smile now as they read the words printed across the front of the shirt.

"It means 'shut yer gob,'" Brennus says as the corners of his eyes soften. He holds out his hand to help me to my feet.

I wrinkle my nose and ask, "What's a 'gob?'" Ignoring Brennus' offer of help, I pull my t-shirt down as I rise to my feet unassisted.

"It means 'mouth,' Genevieve," Finn says. "It means 'shut yer mouth.'"

"Then why not just say that?" I mumble in irritation.

"Why would ye want ta wear dat when I have given ye closets full of beautiful tings ta wear?" Brennus asks me in confusion.

"You like them, you wear them, Brennus," I say, crossing my arms over my chest and glaring at them.

"Do na be daft, all da clothes are for wans," he replies, like I'm crazy.

"NO, all the clothes in there are for porn stars," I counter heatedly. "I don't even know what to do with half the stuff in there," pointing my finger adamantly at a wardrobe.

"Arrgh, ye're being silly," Brennus says with a dismissive flick of his wrist.

I storm over to one of the many wardrobes in my room. "Oh yeah? What's this? Or this?" I ask in frustration, pulling lacy bits of things out that I have no idea how to put on, not that I would even want to. I toss them at Brennus who dodges and ducks them.

Brennus' eyebrows pull together in a frown. "Get dressed, I expect ta see ye downstairs today, or else," Brennus says, striding towards the door.

"Or else, what?" I ask as Finn follows Brennus.

Brennus pauses and says over his shoulder, "Have ye na learned yet dat ye do na want ta know?" Without looking back at me, Brennus leaves my room with Finn trailing close behind him.

In frustration, I pace my room, trying to figure out what I should do next. I have to figure out a way to make Brennus break our contract so that I can be free to leave here and find Reed. My heart twists as Reed's face enters my mind. He must be really, really mad at me for agreeing to Brennus' terms. He would have never made a bargain like this. I have to start thinking more like him, he always seems to do the right thing, whereas I make a mess of everything…but my friends are still alive, so I must have done something right.

As I rifle through my closet for something to wear, I hate everything I see. Not because it's all bad, but because it's all very sexy and the last thing I want to do is entice a bunch of killers. No, I plan to repulse them, make them find nothing appealing about me. With that thought in mind, I walk out of my bedroom into the large sitting room that is attached to it. My stomach growls because they stopped sending trays up yesterday in an attempt to starve me out of my room.

I have to go downstairs anyway, just to find some food. I open the door that leads to the hallway a crack. Faolan and Lachlan are milling around at one end of the hall while Eion and Declan are shooting dice at the other end. I don't want an escort on my next mission, so I wait until they all have their backs turned to me. When no one is looking, I dart through the open doorway across the hall from mine. It's one of the fella's bedrooms—one of my personal bodyguards: Declan, Lachlan, Faolan and Eion. I know they all stay on this hallway so they can be close to me, and I'm pretty sure that they are hating their new assignment because I haven't really left my room, forcing them to do nothing all day but wait for me to surface.

I go directly to a wardrobe and rummage through it quickly, finding a green and white striped rugby jersey. I pull it on, but all the trousers are way too big, falling off me the moment I put them on. I have to settle for a pair of boxer shorts and a pair of really long, athletic socks that go up well past my knees. Walking to the window, I open it and look out. There is a stone terrace several stories down from this window.

Our rooms are located in one of the tower sections of the castle. The stone outside the window is covered with ivy that is as thick as jungle vine. Grasping a handful of the vine, I jump from the window and easily pick my way down the wall to the terrace below. I let go of the vine at the bottom and stride by the open glass doors of the terrace, seeing several very chicly attired Gancanagh inside an enormous room. The room is like a comfortable men's club with thick, soft leather chairs and polished side tables. As I pass another set of open, glass doors, I look in and recognize Ninian sitting in a leather chair that is facing the terrace and the grounds without. Ninian is reading a beautiful, leather-bound book.

Walking casually through the doors, I ask, "Which way to the kitchen, Ninian?" When he glances up, his mouth drops open a little. I know I must look shocking to him. He is probably used to all the women around here doing everything they can to look as attractive as possible. I, on the other hand, have not showered since I arrived or even attempted to brush my hair. I know I look frightening and I try to hide the little smirk that is forming in the corners of my mouth. Too shocked to respond, Ninian just points to the door behind him.

"Thanks," I reply. I walk to the door he indicates; it leads to a broad hallway. I call over my shoulder, "Left or right, Ninian?"

When I glance back over my shoulder, I see several Gancanagh milling around where Ninian is seated, watching me with avid curiosity. "Left," Ninian says. I nod and head left.

After walking into several rooms that are clearly not the kitchen, I find what I am looking for at the end of the hallway. It's a huge, medieval-looking kitchen made of stone that has been completely updated with all of the modern amenities of any five-star restaurant. Several women are running the kitchen, doing dishes and cooking what looks and smells to be the chicken soup that I remember so well from my time in the copper mine. My stomach turns over at the aroma. I feel sickened by it and I know that there is no way I will be able to taste that soup without becoming violently ill. *Don't they know how to make anything else?* I wonder, holding my hand over my nose so I won't smell it.

These women are definitely under the thrall of the Gancanagh. I see puncture marks on their necks that indicate they have been a snack for at least one of the fellas. In a daze, a girl about my age speaks to me in an Asian dialect that I don't understand. She seems to be indicating the soup on the stove, offering me some. I shake my head, feeling an overwhelming sorrow for her. *How long has she been here? How long will she last?*

"Do you have anything else," I ask, hoping she might speak English, but she just stares at me, not understanding what I'm asking her. None of the women seem to speak English, so I wander around until I find a huge walk-in pantry. Browsing the shelves, I spot something that I recognize. Pulling a jar of peanut butter down from the shelf, I twist the lid and sniff it. My mouth waters at the familiar, comforting smell. As I walk back out into the kitchen, I find a spoon in one of the drawers. There is a wide table in the kitchen with several stools positioned around it, but the thought of eating in here with "the doomed" is more than I can take.

I leave the kitchen, looking for a quiet place to eat. As I pass a couple of beautifully attired Gancanagh in the hall, they both stop talking and stare at me like I'm an apparition. Their fangs engage with a *click*, causing my heartbeat to kick up. I attempt to remain outwardly calm until I turn down the first hallway that presents itself. Goose bumps flitter up my arms as I stifle the urge to look over my shoulder. I hurry down several more hallways in my search for a place to be alone.

In the middle of another hall, there stand two large, weathered suits of armor flanking an enormous set of double doors. Intrigued by the presence of the ancient armor, I stop to admire the cold, smooth surface of one of the silent warriors. Turning from it, I push a heavy, wooden door aside and enter a very masculine bar that I'm going to name the "Knight's Bar" for all the suits of armor within it lining the walls.

It looks like it may have been the chapel of the castle at one time in the distant past, but it has been converted into a very chic tavern. The walls are lined in dark wood with an intricate Celtic knot carved into the top of each panel. Stained-glass rosette windows adorn every wall, letting in colorful light that draws intricate patterns on the floors and walls. Heavy chandeliers hang from the exposed beams, peaking high above my head and casting soft light down on the tables beneath them. A sleek bar area is built into the side of the room. Wandering behind the bar, there is every kind of alcohol known to man stocked behind it. I let my eyes wander over the labels. Some are in English, but most aren't. It's a menagerie of colorful bottles and liquids that would make any evil scientist cringe in envy.

Selecting a glass from the bar, I fill it with water from the tap and then carry it to one of the polished tables by the bar. Sitting down on a chair, I prop my feet up on the table, while dipping my spoon into the jar. As the peanut butter melts in my mouth I have to fight the tears that spring to my eyes. Memories of homemade lunches packed by Uncle Jim into paper bags with juice boxes and carrots flash in my mind. *How did I get here?* I wonder as I attempt to swallow past the lump in my throat.

I take a sip of water to try to ease my throat and I almost gag on it as Declan, Lachlan, Faolan and Eion stroll into the room. Lachlan and Faolan look relieved as they both slow and go to the bar to lean against it. Declan and Eion, on the other hand, walk with cool, corporate precision to my table. Pulling out chairs across the table from me, they both sit down, glaring at me.

"By all means, have a seat," I remark with sarcasm. "Peanut butter?" I ask, offering my spoon to Declan and then Eion with a quirk of my brow.

Eion looks askance at the peanut butter and growls at me.

"We have ta go o'er a few ground rules, Genevieve," Declan says in a stern tone right before he looks at me closer. "Is dat me shirt?" he asks, appalled.

I shrug, "Could be—where'd you leave it?" I ask.

"'TIS me lucky shirt, Genevieve! Ye blighter! Ye took it from me room—are dose my pants, too?" he accuses me, pointing to the boxers I'm wearing. Dipping my finger in the jar, I pull out a huge glob of peanut butter. I pop it in my mouth, pulling my finger back out, and then I wipe my finger down the front of the shirt in question, watching his brows draw together in a scowl.

"It's not that lucky, Declan. You're still sitting here," I say, picking up my water and taking another sip.

"Ah, ye're disgustin'," he says. "Is dat yer plan, den? Make us toss ye out when ye smell as bad as da rubbish—and ye do smell, lass," he says, wrinkling his nose as if I offend his senses. "It's na going ta happen. He will never let ye go, no matter whah ye smell like."

"Hey, pot, you're black—stinky, rotten flower boy," I mutter, feeling my cheeks redden as he easily sees through my plan.

Eion's fangs shoot forward in his mouth, causing Declan and me to look at him. "I luv it when ye blush," he says, shrugging his shoulders lightly and all the hair on my arms stands up as he gazes at me with longing in his eyes.

Declan rubs his forehead in irritation. "Do us a favor, go and feed and den come back," Declan orders Eion. Eion retracts his fangs and gets up from the table, leaving the room in a fraction of a second. Shaking his head in frustration, Declan turns back to me. "Rules—" Declan begins, but stops when I interrupt him.

I hold up one finger saying, "Rule number one: don't bother me when I'm eating. I don't bother you when you're eating. Let's consider it a mutual respect thing."

"Respect?" he asks, looking at me with widening eyes. "If ye had respect for us, den ye would've told us ye wanted ta leave yer room. Den, we would've come wi' ye and den we would've gotten ye someting better ta eat den dat stuff ye have found for yerself."

"I want to be alone," I say. "Why do you have to follow me around anyway? It's not like I can leave," I point out, frustrated that I can't be alone.

"Dis is na Disneyland, Genevieve," Declan says in a serious tone, watching me across the table.

"You think, Declan?" I shoot back, because he is stating the obvious.

He ignores my sarcasm and says, "Dere are dose here dat could be tempted by ye even tough ye belong ta Brennus."

"I tought ye said I'm disgustin'," I reply, using his accent.

"Disgustin' for ye, which makes ye still very, very, sexy. Have ye no idea den whah ye look like? Whah ye are like? Ye are a legend 'round here. The fellas favorite ting ta do is ta sit 'round and tell all the stories of ye from da caves," he says with a speculative raise of his eyebrow.

"So I'm a fish story? The one that got away...until now," I mutter with a grimace.

"Dere's dat, but dey mostly like ta tell 'bout how ye didn't allow Brennus ta turn ye. Dey all know whah dat means," he says significantly. They all would. Some, if not all of them, have been turned into Gancanagh by the same method of starvation and thirst that Brennus tried on me, but I didn't give in—I was prepared to die. "Course, dey also like da story of how ye killed Keegan," he adds, smiling. "Dey call ye the 'Queen o' Hearts' 'cuz it was off wi' his head."

I feel like he just punched me in the stomach, hearing Keegan's name and knowing how I had killed him. I say quietly, "Keegan was insane. He wouldn't stop."

"He was insane," Declan agrees, "and he would've killed ye, so ye took care of him. No one disputes dat. He died a good death. It jus makes ye dat much more attractive, *aingeal.* So ye need us, because ye are too much of a temptation, for now anyway. If he turns ye, den ye can walk 'round here wi'out us. Maybe ye should ask him ta do dat and den I can be free o' ye."

"But then I'd miss you, Declan," I smile mockingly at him, before eating another scoop of peanut butter.

"Eaves!" Molly calls and my head snaps towards the doorway to see my friend entering the room, walking with a casual swagger that has every eye on her. "There you are! Everyone is looking for you. Brennus is pissed off. You better go tell him you found her, Deck, or he might have a total meltdown. He heard that you were wandering around alone and almost went postal," she says significantly, looking at Faolan and Lachlan who have guilty looks.

"Faolan, tell him where we are," Declan orders and Faolan is out of the room with military precision.

"What are you eating? Peanut butter?" Molly asks me as she comes up to me, and leaning down, she hugs me tight, pressing her icy lips to my cheek. As she pulls back she says, "It smells so disgusting! I used to love peanut butter and now it smells like, ugh, fertilizer or something." She rubs her nose like it stings while Declan snorts in agreement and Lachlan grins.

"Don't laugh, Declan, or the lucky shirt is going to take another hit of stink," I warn him, brandishing the peanut butter near to his shirt.

"Eaves, you look—did you take a shower today?" she asks, trying to be discreet as she plugs her nose.

"I'm so sorry, Molly," I murmur, feeling tears spring to my eyes, as I look at my friend who has been like a sister to me. I can't fix what they've done to her. I can't undo it and the agony of that fact is crushing me. They made her a beautiful, undead monster.

"It's okay, you don't smell that bad," she tries to reassure me when she sees my tears.

"I'm sorry that I made you their target," I explain right away, so that she knows exactly what I'm talking about. My tears are running down my cheeks and I'm unable to do anything about them.

"Oh, that," she says, waving her hand in the air like it's of no consequence. "No worries. I like being Gancanagh—it rocks."

"What?" I ask, not believing what she's saying, as I wipe my tears with the sleeve of Declan's shirt.

"Yeah, it's stellar. They made me a demigod. I can't believe you wouldn't want this," she says, and I can see she's telling the truth. "They made me beautiful—my skin is flawless—look at my hair!" she says, holding it up. It's thicker and longer than it used to be with a beautiful shine to it that makes me want to reach out and touch it.

"You like it?" I ask her, stunned.

"I can have anything I want, whenever I want it, however I want it. I only need to reach out and touch it—take it. The family has been good to me. Since I've been the only female that they have turned in centuries, it's like being invited to join an exclusive boys club," she admits. "I only have to answer to my *máistir*, oh, and Brennus, of course, but I get carte blanche because I'm your 'special friend,' so *sláinte*, Eaves!" she says, hugging me again.

"Who is your *máistir*? Do I know him?" I ask in a quiet tone. My whole body is still, waiting for her to tell me the name of my target.

"Of course you know him. It's Finn," she says his name breathlessly, like she worships him or something. I close my eyes, feeling the knife twist in my heart. I trusted Finn and he killed my friend.

"My life is so perfect now, Eaves," she whispers, seeing the anguish on my face. Her face still holds its innocence even though I know she's truly a killer now. She sinks into the chair next to me and takes both of my warm hands in her icy ones.

"How can it be perfect? You kill people for sport," I ask with regret.

"Yeah, but it's their own fault that they are so tasty," she says, smiling into my eyes. "Sorry, inside joke. If it makes you feel any better, I don't eat what they import here—females aren't my thing, if you know what I mean. I like to find prey that makes demons look like kindergarteners. The really mean ones, because they're the most fun! You know, the men who beat their wives or those wankers who beat up people for no reason other than the fact that they're stronger and they can. They're everywhere, in every pub, on every street, in every neighborhood. There's no shortage of sucky men," she explains to me.

"So you're like a superhero, keeping the streets safe for the normal folk?" I ask her with a skeptical look.

"Not really, I just love watching the horror on their faces when the little girl they were going to destroy turns out to be a freaky monster that can tear them apart," she replies. "The strong ones scream the loudest. Did you know that?" she asks and I shake my head. "The weak expect to be victims, but the strong…they never see it coming."

"Killer karma, Molls?" I ask.

"Irony, Eaves," she replies.

"Ye should see her, Genevieve," Declan says with a proud glance towards Molly. "She's a vicious terror. She likes ta wear gloves so dat she doesna drug her victims when she bites dem— ye would know whah dat is like, wouldn't ye?"

"Yeah, I know what that's like," I admit, losing color at the memory.

"I tell ye true, wans make da most vicious killers. Dat's why we rarely turn females…ye are hard ta control and willful."

"Pain makes everything taste so much sweeter, Deck. It just wouldn't be the same without it," she winks at him and he smiles back like he finds her savage nature precious.

"What about your family?" I ask, trying to change the subject.

Pain enters in her eyes. "What about them? They don't know—they think I'm dead. We made it look like I died in a fire. They will move on and so will I. I'm immortal now. I have Finn and the family to protect me—and now my best friend. My life couldn't get any better than this."

"You have no soul," I say softly with the weight of regret in my voice.

"I don't miss it. There is such power in what we are. Surrender, Eaves. You won't regret it," she says in earnest.

"Can't," I reply, shaking my head and thinking of Reed.

Molly's eyes show fear. "He will break you," she says of Brennus in a low tone to me, leaning towards me.

"He will try," I agree

"I can't protect you," she whispers in my ear.

"I know," I whisper back and I drop her hands to hug her tight. "We're playing for different teams now, Molly," I say, feeling tears collecting in my eyes again.

"We'll draft you—it's just too much fun on our side," Molly says with confidence. Pulling away, her face lights up and she rises from her seat, "Don't be sad, Eaves, check this out—Finn taught me how to do it. I'll teach you," she promises, holding her hand out in front of her.

As Molly concentrates on the palm of her hand, she whispers words that I don't understand, but I feel the air around her changing, like there is now the scent of electricity that wasn't there a moment ago. Instantly, a small, flickering flame bursts into life in the palm of Molly's hand. Looking up, she holds the flame out to me, smiling as it dances and wavers weakly. "I still suck at it, but it's getting better," she smiles, and then she closes her hand, extinguishing the flame.

From behind her, Finn enters the Knight's Bar, clapping his hands, "Dat's very good, Molly, ye learn so quickly, *mo laoch*," Finn says proudly.

Molly's smile broadens while I grow tense. Killing scenarios enter my mind as I get up from my chair. I pull Declan's rugby shirt from me, tossing it to him where he is still seated at the table. Knowing that the t-shirt that I put on underneath is going to tear off me in a second, I hold the front of it to me. When my wings shoot from my back, I manage to tie the tattered ends of the shirt around my neck, and then around my waist, tying it in the back so that the shirt now resembles a backless halter-top.

All of the Gancanagh in the room are watching me with interest as Finn slows his pace to us. Backing up from him, I move to the suit of armor directly behind me. Turning, I pull the battered, war-tested sword from the grasp of the hollow, metal figure and hold it in my hands with a menacing scowl.

"You," I call to Finn, seeing him tense. I back up to the next suit of armor and pull a second sword from its grasp. Tossing the sword to Finn, it falls to the ground with a loud clatter in front of him.

"Genevieve, I canna fight ye," he says in a soft tone, not picking up the sword I threw at him.

"Yes, you can, Finn. Pick it up" I insist, letting my wings arch out boldly as I begin to stalk Finn.

Molly's fangs engage, *click*, when she realizes what I'm doing. Hissing at me, she steps in front of Finn, facing me with a defensive posture that lets me know that I will have to go through her to get to him.

"This is between Finn and me, Molly," I say to her, trying to figure out how I'm going to get to him without hurting Molly.

"He is my *máistir*," Molly replies, not moving an inch away from Finn.

I shift away from them and use all of my speed to run at the wall beside me. My speed helps me defy gravity as I run onto the wall and arc past the point in the room where Molly and Finn are standing. Then, using the wall like a springboard, I rocket off of it and dive to the floor behind Molly and Finn. Finn pivots and shields Molly, while I raise my sword and bring it down, angling it towards his neck. It stops before hitting him as it smashes into an invisible barrier that forms between Finn and me.

Dropping my sword, it feels like I shattered the bones in my arms. I hug my arms to me, growling at Finn through the invisible film between us. As I look around quickly, I reach out and grasp the back of a chair in my numb hands, hurling it at Finn where he stands in front of me. The chair smashes and splinters into pieces as it hits the barrier he has erected around Molly and himself.

"Stop, Evie!" Molly demands while I stalk around their barrier, throwing my shoulder up against it to test it for weaknesses. I need to find a way in so that I can mop the floor with Finn's head.

Circling them, I come back to face Finn. Looking directly into his eyes, I ask, "Why?"

"Because I want her," he replies, "I asked dat she be moin when it was determined dat we would turn her."

"Why you?" I ask and my voice cracks with bitterness at the betrayal I feel. He was my only friend and he destroyed that in an instant.

"Because I had nuting of my own 'til her and I will kill anyting dat tries to take her from me," he retorts with menace.

My eyes narrow as I ask, "Do you love her?"

"She's moin," he replies with lethal precision that makes my eyes widen. That is probably the closest he can come to saying he loves her while we are in front of Declan and Lachlan, who are trying to figure out what they need to do to stop me from killing their second in command.

Cold hands slip around my waist, pulling me back into a solid chest. I don't have to look to know that Brennus is holding me in his arms like a steel cage. Leaning down, he whispers in my ear, "You can na kill me brudder, *mo chroí.*"

"Why not? He killed my friend," I reply heatedly.

"She is content," he replies and I see that he's not lying. Molly loves him, and for now, she is a favored pet…and maybe more than that where Finn is concerned, I think grudgingly. "Finn will be a good guardian ta her. He will teach her everyting he knows, so dat she will thrive. He has affection for her and she has affection for him. Who are ye ta say dat 'tis wrong?" he asks me.

"I'm her sister," I say, feeling tears fill my eyes. I try to choke them off because I don't want to cry in front of any of them. I can't show any more weakness or they will use it against me. "Let me go," I say, but Brennus' hands tighten on me as he pulls me against him, hugging me like he can't let me go.

"'Tis going ta be hard for ye ta adjust here, we know dat. Give it time, *mo chroí.* Ye will see dat we all jus want da best for ye," he says, and I try not to scoff.

"Brennus, you're tearing my heart out and when it's gone you may not like what's left of me," I say softly, pulling hard to get away from him. He lets go of me with reluctance and I point to Finn, "Stay away from me." I begin to walk to the door.

"Where are ye going?" Brennus asks me in stern tone.

"To my room," I reply.

"Good, ye need a shower, but first, we must have a discussion, ye and me. So, have a seat," he orders. I stop, knowing that he'll have his way, one way or the other, so I might as well stay and listen to what he has to say to me. "Declan, Lachlan—wait outside wi' Faolan and Eion. Finn, I'll talk ta ye after," he says, and I stand stiffly as Finn and Molly pass me without a word, like *I* have wounded *them* or something.

When I am alone with Brennus, I sit down at a table and watch as Brennus looks around at the overturned tables and smashed chair.

"Ye know dat Finn could have easily hurt ye?" Brennus asks as his eyes fall on me.

I shrug, "Maybe."

"Na maybe. He could have broken ye in two because he is very powerful," Brennus says. "He would na do it tough, and do ye know why?" he asks me.

"Because you'll kill him if he does," I reply.

"Dere's dat, but wi' Finn, I tink 'tis more dat he loves ye, too," Brennus says in a soft tone. I scoff. "Ye laugh," Brennus' brows draw together in a frown. "Why do ye tink he asked for Molly? He wants someting ta love dat will love him in return, and I tink he has found it. He has na had dat since before he was turned, and after we met ye he began to crave it—to yearn for it." Brennus is watching me for my reaction. "He's tryin' to find da alternative ta fightin' me for ye and I tink he has—I tink he is content wi' Molly."

"He killed her, just like Aodh killed you," I say, watching him for his reaction. "Did you kill Finn so that you could control him like a slave?" I ask, wanting badly to hurt him like he's hurt me.

Brennus stills. *Click*—his fangs thrust forth in his mouth, letting me know that I have offended him deeply. "Ye want ta know whah happened? Ye want ta know how it was for Finn and me?" he asks with deadly calm.

"Yes, I want to know why he's so loyal to you," I reply, feeling every nerve in my body growing tense and alert because I know I'm pushing a very lethal predator—one that can have me begging for mercy in a matter of seconds.

"Finn is me little brudder. Me *true* brudder," Brennus says significantly. "He was da light of our family—always followin' me around. He was the kind of lad dat everyone liked—he could make anyone smile wi' his antics," Brennus says, and his face loses some of its sternness. "He was so different from me. I was the eldest—quiet, responsible—always working hard ta be da best at everyting. Finn jus didna have ta work at anyting...he could jus do whahever he wanted because of his sweetness. He jus drew everyone in and ye felt better for being near him. Do ye know whah I mean?" he asks me and I nod.

"It's the same with Russell. He's just like that, too," I say and see the flash of recognition in Brennus' eyes when I mention Russell's name.

"One day, our village was raided by the Gancanagh and Finn was taken. Me Mam cried for days. She begged me *athair*, dat's me fadder, to send out warriors to try ta fetch the ones dat were taken, ta get Finn back for her. Me fadder was da equivalent ta a king where we come from, but he knew 'twas no use, dat dey were probably dead, drained as food."

"So you went instead?" I ask quietly, knowing the answer.

"I did, 'twas Finn, I had ta try ta get him back," he says, like there was no other option open to him. "I didna stand a chance against Aodh, but I went anyway. I was so scared and filled wi' rage. I know how it feels, *mo chroí*, da rage dat eats at yer insides like a poison because ye know dat ye lost—dat dere's only defeat left ta ye. I was in dat cell, too, but I couldna choose death, like ye did. I couldna leave Finn alone, ta face Aodh alone, ta be his slave. He is na like us, *mo chroí*, he isna strong like dat," he whispers.

He moves to my side, bending down he wipes away the tears that have fallen from my eyes. His face softens as he scans mine. He is looking at me like he has never seen me before, or tears. Maybe no one has mourned his death in a long time, but I feel filled with sorrow over the loss of his life.

"Jus when I tink I know everyting about ye, ye surprise me. Ye can have tears for me, even when I have hurt ye," he says with a gentle voice.

"You're like me, Brennus," I murmur, "sometimes we don't know that it's best to run. Hanging on in desperation seems to be our way."

"Ye're a warrior. Defeat is never ta be tolerated, but 'tis da way, Genevieve. I take someting ye love, like Molly, and it makes it easier ta submit because ye can na leave her here wi'out yer help, wi'out ye ta protect her," he says. "It will be up ta ye ta see dat I do na have ta take anyting else dat ye love, like da other," he adds, and I know he is talking about Russell.

Would he try to turn him, too, just to bind me to him more than I am now? I wonder feebly.

"Ye are too strong. Submission is hard for ye, I know dat. I promise ye, 'tis da last ting ye'll ever have ta submit ta because after dat, I will give ye da world—anyting ye want—everyting, jus choose me, love me."

"Why would you do this to me, if you love me, Brennus?" I ask in desperation, not understanding why he would insist on my becoming Gancanagh if he himself would have chosen death if it had not been for Finn.

He strokes my cheek lovingly as he says, "Because I know more dan ye do. I've lived for a long time, I see whah lies ahead for ye. Ye have more enemies dan ye know. Da *aingeals* who have been protecting ye must know whah ye are facing, even if ye do na. I wanted nuting ta do wi' ye when Alfred first told me of ye, knowing whah ye will face. Wi'out dat portrait, ye would probably still be back in Houghton. It's because I love ye dat ye're here now. I'll protect ye, even if ye do na like it."

"I don't like it. I want to go home," I breathe, placing my hand over his on my cheek and staring into his eyes.

"Ye are home. Accept it," he replies. I lower my eyes from his, dropping my hand.

My shoulders round. "I want to go to my room now," I say in a near whisper.

"Ye can go in a minute. I want to say one more ting ta ye," he says softly, gripping my chin and turning it so I will meet his eyes again. "Ye can na walk around here unaccompanied. Dis is yer home, but 'til everyone gets used ta ye being around, I need ye ta be watched. It's for yer protection, na because I do na trust dat ye will hold ta yer end of our bargain," he says in a gentle tone, watching me for signs of dissent.

The thought strikes me then, like a bolt of lightning—I can't be bitten. That breaks the contract. If they bite me and I survive it, I'm free. Then I cringe, remembering the pain and fierce need for blood after I was bitten the last time. I had been almost completely out of it and would've given in not soon after if not for Russell saving me.

Could I survive it again? If I can, then I can have Reed. That's worth any risk, worth any pain. I must be smiling because Brennus' face stills near mine.

"Whah are ye tinking?" he asks with suspicion.

"Be careful not to get too caught up in my world, Brennus," I warn him in a soft tone, watching his eyes grow darker. As I reach out and touch his face, running my fingertips over the cold planes of his cheek, I add, "I may just end up doing you wrong."

"I will remember dat, ye sweet *aingeal*," he replies, focusing on my mouth.

"See that you do," I reply.

"I want ta spend some time wi' ye, *mo chroí*. Will ye allow me ta show ye around da grounds later on, after ye have cleaned up a bit?" he asks.

My hand stills on his cheek. The Brennus I know gives orders and expects everyone around him to do what they're told. To be asked is quite a change.

"Uhh, sure…why not. I have no idea where I am right now and no way of knowing how to get back to my room. Maybe you can let me in on that secret, too," I say, watching his eyes as I pull my hand away from his face.

"Maybe I could," he replies playfully. "Ye're in da kirk. I should've known dat if ye're looking for an *aingeal*, ye should start in da chapel," he says. Standing, he extends his hand for me to take.

"Well, it was empty, so it looked like a good place to eat in peace." I say, taking his hand and walking with Brennus out the doors.

My personal guards fall in behind us as we pass them, making me feel a little self-conscious. I'm only wearing a backless t-shirt that says 'shut yer gob' and Declan's boxers that I had to fold over at the waistband so they wouldn't fall off of me. My wings are arcing out, too, because I haven't tried putting them back in. I probably can, but they're helping me feel less naked.

Passing fellas I don't know, they all stop and step to the side, allowing us to walk by while they incline their heads. "Why do they all do that?" I ask Brennus, inching closer to him because it's kind of creepy.

"'Tis a sign of respect," Brennus says, knowing what I'm talking about without me having to explain it.

"What am I supposed to do when they do that?" I ask him.

He smiles down at me in amusement. "Nuting, but if one of dem doesna do it, ye tell me and I'll kill him," he says.

"Why?' I scoff, thinking of the fellas in the hallway earlier that flashed their fangs at me.

"Ye are deir queen," he replies.

I roll my eyes. "Oh, that's right," I say with sarcasm, "where is my tiara and I seem to have misplaced that darn scepter."

Brennus' face grows serious. "If 'tis a tiara dat ye want, it will be yers, but dey know whah ye are wi'out it," he replies.

"I don't want a tiara, Brennus," I sigh. "I wouldn't know what I'd do with it. You have seen how I was raised. I know that you have been in the house that I grew up in. They said you took everything that I owned from the storage unit. This is all so…I don't…" I say, before falling silent because this is all so bizarre.

Magical creatures aside, I can't get over the opulence of where I am now. It's like the chateau where everywhere I look there is an amazing work of art or a delicate, silk covered settee and these are just hallways. My room is filled with priceless pieces of furniture and artwork, but I have yet to see anything that used to belong to me in it.

"I understand," Brennus says next to me. I frown up at him. *How can he possibly know how I'm feeling?* "Molly told us many stories of when ye were a wee lass," he adds, placing his hand on the small of my back as we begin to climb a grand stone staircase, ushering me up. "She said dis will be hard for ye in dat ye're na one ta crave a lot of attention or wealth. Dat makes tings harder for me, na easier."

"Why does that make it hard for you?" I ask him curiously.

"Well, making ye me queen makes ye da center of attention, and I am wealthy, so ye probably feel like a stranger in a strange land," he says. I almost stumble because that's exactly how I feel. "And, since I treated ye so poorly da last time ye were wi' me, ye are probably scared too, but ye will na show it because ye have more courage dan ye should."

"Maybe you're not as scary as you think you are," I reply.

He looks at me with a grin. "I am scary, never forget dat," he warns, turning into my room. Only Declan enters the sitting room of my suite with Brennus and me. He checks everything before he nods to Brennus and leaves the room, taking a position with my other guards in the hallway.

Turning to Brennus, I feel awkward with him here. This has been my sanctuary from all of them for the past few days and now he's invading that space. It's his house, but I feel territorial about these rooms.

Twisting my hands nervously, I blurt out, "Where do you sleep?" His eyes grow dark and a small smile softens his lips. I try again, "I mean…where's your room?"

"Dis is me room," he says, watching me grow pale as all the color drains from my face.

"Excuse me?" I ask.

"I have moved most of my tings into dis closet in da suite," he says, walking to one of the enormous walk-in closets and pulling it open, he lets me see his exquisite suits, tailored jackets, shirts and ties, belts and shoes. "I do na require sleep, so giving ye da bed has na been a hardship ta me, unless ye consider dat I miss being in it wi' ye. I tought dat ye needed some time ta get used ta me before we get ta dat."

Feeling my heartbeat kick up and my face flush with color, I turn away from him and the closet, not seeing much of anything.

Brennus walks across the sitting room to the opposite wall from the bedroom. He opens another door, and as he holds it wide, he beckons me into a large, comfortable office area that has a carved desk. Hand-crafted sofas and chairs are arranged in a few seating areas, but there is still plenty of room to roam around.

I walk with measured steps to the windows that have a view to the sea beyond. A wide set of double doors leads to a balcony that has a stone table and luxurious chairs for sitting and enjoying the sun, if it ever comes out in this part of the world.

Mostly it has just been overcast and gray, I think to myself, feeling numb.

When I turn away from the view, my eyes lightly touch everything in the office until they fall on something that makes my pulse beat painfully in my chest. Without a word, I walk to Brennus' desk, picking up the figurine on it that I recognize. My fingers tremble as I run them over the smooth, marble surface—the image of me in my field hockey uniform. It's one of the carvings that Reed created. It used to be in his room in Crestwood.

"'Tis as if he saw ye in da marble and worked 'til he set ye free," Brennus says from just behind me. "It tells me whah I need ta know about him."

I know better than to speak Reed's name to Brennus. He is testing me to see what my reaction will be to all of this. "It says a lot about you, too," I say, putting the statue back down on the desk just where I had found it.

"Whah does it say about me?" he asks as I turn to face him, noticing his beautiful arching eyebrow rise in question.

Reaching out, I play with a button on his shirt, looking up into his eyes to see that they are focused on my fingers. "It says that you are so possessive of me that you will not even let him have a piece of stone, if it represents a piece of me."

A sexy smile forms on his lips while he touches my finger as it rests against his chest. Bringing it to his cold lips, he kisses just the tip of it, watching my reaction to what he is doing.

"Dat is very shrewd, Genevieve. Whah will ye do wi' da information dat ye learn?" he asks, his dark hair falling across his brow as he leans closer to me.

"I'll do with it what you've been doing," I reply, watching his lips near mine. When he is a breath away, I say, "I'll use it to my advantage. You have your plans and I will have mine."

"Da sooner ye stop seeing me as yer enemy, da sooner we can begin ta enjoy one another," he says softly, pressing his cold lips lightly against mine.

I want to be indifferent to his kiss, but that is not the reaction I'm having at all. I feel a mess of emotions all caving in on me. I feel rage and desire—a need to tear him apart coupled with a need to pull him to me. I grip the edge of Brennus' desk so that I won't do either option. I cannot allow myself to hurt him because I'll be hurting myself too—not until I get out of this magical contract.

As he pulls back from me, deep desire enters Brennus' light green eyes. "So strong," he says to himself. "Even wi' me in yer blood, ye can still resist."

"What?" I ask breathlessly.

"I have bitten ye. I'm in yer blood. I know dat ye desire me—'tis whah happens when ye're bitten, and yet, ye fight it," he says, puzzled yet very intrigued.

"You forget, he is in my blood now, too," I say in a soft tone, watching anger transform his face from lovely and sultry to cold and hard. He must not have remembered that I swore a blood oath to Reed. Reed's blood is now mixed with mine, so that he is always with me, no matter where I am.

"I will erase him from everyting, even yer heart," he promises me with deadly calm.

His words steal my breath for a second while images of ways to crush Brennus flash in my mind. The angel in me is raging, wanting to suffocate him, like he is doing to me. He is empty bliss. I will free myself from him and then I will kill him.

I force myself to smile, but I know that it's not reaching my eyes. This is a game and the winner is the one who doesn't lose his cool. "To the victor goes the spoils, Brenn, don't be angry if I'm a sucker for the underdog," I say, pushing him back lightly with my hand so that I can step around him. "I'm going to clean up, then, you can show me the house."

I walk out of the office and across the sitting room into the bedroom. Closing the door, I run to the bathroom. I close that door too, locking it even though I know that he doesn't need to use a key to open the door, he can just break it down. Leaning against the door, I hold my breath, but Brennus is not following me. I still feel the shape of his lips against mine as I put my fingers to my mouth, but that is nothing compared with the empty shape he leaves inside my heart.

CHAPTER 13

The Queen

After taking a quick shower, I walk to the vanity, finding all kinds of perfume bottles that range in different sizes and shapes. I unstop a few, holding them to my nose to smell the scents inside. They range from light, flowery odors to exotic, sexy aromas. I don't put any of them on; I bet that the scent of my blood is heady enough for the fellas without adding anything to it.

Taking my time, I style my hair, sweeping it up away from my neck. A plan has been running through my mind since I left Brennus in his office. I want to see just how much of a temptation I am for him and the fellas. I have to figure out if one of them can be enticed into biting me. If so, I have to prepare myself for that type of scenario, because once I'm bitten, the clock will be ticking for me. I will need to have some access to blood other than Gancanagh blood.

The last time I was bitten, Russell had given me venison blood to drink to curb my bloodlust. The need to consume blood to stop the gnawing ache is overwhelming. If I can get something like venison blood and stash it somewhere that I can get to easily, I may have a chance of escaping before I become a true member of this family.

Running the hairbrush through my hair, I pause as I look at the perfume bottles all lined up elegantly on the vanity. I put the brush down and pick up a glass bottle that is larger than the others. It has French writing on the front of the silver label.

Unstopping it, I dump the contents of it down the drain of the sink, rinsing it out. It won't hold more than a few ounces, but maybe if I fill up several of them with blood, I could put them in strategic places. Maybe if I can get to a couple of them after I have been bitten, I can survive the hallucinations long enough to get away from here. Wine bottles might be more useful. I can fill them with more blood, but the perfume bottle may mask the scent better. I don't want any of the fellas finding bottles of blood lying around. It could tip them to my plans.

My hand trembles as I think of the pain of being bitten. This plan is a huge risk, one I should think about more thoroughly. I had hoped that I could last the six months. Then, when Brennus lets me go back to Reed, as our contract stipulates, I could strategize with Reed and come up with a plan to get out of this contract before I have to go back to Brennus the six months after that. But, I know now that Brennus has absolutely no intention of ever letting me go back to Reed. He allowed for my stipulation to the contract to buy my compliance for a time. The statue in his office told me that Brennus won't let me be with Reed. Not for one second. Never.

If I ever want to see Reed again, it will be up to me to find a way to stay alive and break the contract. It will have to be before the six months are over, too. That is the deadline. Brennus will have to make a decision—figure out another way to keep me or turn me...or make me fall in love with him, as is his current plan.

Good luck, pal, I think with derision.

Time is also a factor for me for another reason. I already ache from not being with Reed. I feel like a huge piece of me is missing. In the night, lying alone in the dark, I have been making bargains with time. That is what I do; I try to go for a few minutes without thinking about Reed, because when I do, my heart feels constricted.

It's worse when I think about what he must think of me for what I have done. I shut him out. Knowing that he wouldn't have let me go to the church that night, I didn't give him the opportunity to stop me. I have made my bargain and left him behind. I hope that he knows that I will find a way to come back to him. I will, but will he let me come back to him after what I've done? I can't think like that or it will bury me. I will have to get away and hope for the best because Reed is my home.

Tying the silk belt on my robe tighter, I walk to the wardrobe in my room and find slinky, little undergarments to put on. It takes me a few minutes to figure out how to put on the lacy, black garter that holds up the matching stockings, but I am finally able to slide the last clasp into place. I locate a sleeveless little black dress that molds to my body and I put on a pair of very high, black heels that must have cost a small fortune, based on the label.

I find a tailored, black trench coat and take it with me as I walk through my rooms to the sitting room. Popping my head into Brennus' office, I find it empty. I walk to the hallway and find Declan and Faolan leaning against the wall, looking bored to tears. They both straighten when they see me; their eyes bulge as they look me up and down like they have never seen me before now.

"Hi," I smile at them both, "I'm looking for Brennus. He said he would show me around the house. Do you know where I can find him?" I ask as they continue to look at me with weird expressions—like they're holding their breaths.

Neither one of them answers me; they just keep staring at me until Faolan exhales. When he does that—*click*—his fangs thrust forward in his mouth.

"Banjax," he mutters in frustration before turning to Declan with an anxious look. "She doesn't even have her wings out either, Deck. Dis is bad."

"'Tis," Declan agrees. "Dis is a security nightmare. We're dead," Declan adds, pinching the bridge of his nose like he has a massive headache. "Have ye fed today?" he asks Faolan.

Faolan gives him a sharp nod. "I did. 'Tis da first ting I do when I know I will be seeing her," he says, running his hand through his hair in frustration.

"We will have ta have a new feedin' schedule. We may each have ta feed a few times a day now. Dat way, 'twill make it easier," Declan says, like he is trying to work out a complex problem.

"Trouble?" I ask them, searching their faces.

"Dere is," Declan says, eyeing me like I still have on his lucky shirt. "Ye are treachery in da flesh, ye hallion."

"ME? What did I do?" I ask incredulously. "I took a shower and I brushed my teeth," I say, smelling myself for any hint of a foul odor.

Declan sighs. "Maybe we can make her put some o' dat peanut butter on, dat helped," Declan says to Faolan.

"Maybe, but we can still see her," Faolan replies grimly.

Putting my hands on my hips, I let my wings shoot out of my back in agitation, while I tap my foot, waiting for an explanation from them. Faolan looks at me again and there is longing in his eyes. He turns to Declan again with concern.

Declan, scowls at me, saying, "Go and feed, Fay. Take Lachlan and Eion wi' ye. We will wait here 'til ye get back. Hurry." When Faolan leaves, he asks, "Was dat absolutely necessary?"

"What?" I ask in confusion.

"Da wings. Ye tryin' ta torture him?" he asks in a severe tone.

"Of course not!" I retort, feeling embarrassed as a blush stains my cheeks. "Should I go and put some perfume on?" I ask, lowering my eyes. "I didn't know that I still stink."

"Ye do na stink. Dat's da problem. Ye smell like whah Paradise must smell like and ye look like da most exquisite sin. Da wolves downstairs will be howlin' for ye and dey are jus stone statues. I have an idea whah da other fellas will do when dey see ye, but it isna good. Most of dem will try ta behave, because dey know dat if dey do na, Brennus will kill dem. But, some may na be able ta control demselves and will have ta be sent away, for now. Faolan is ancient. He has more control den most and ye saw whah jus happened—wi'out da wings. Wi' da wings..." he trails off.

"The fellas like my wings?" I ask.

"We do," he replies grudgingly, like telling me he likes anything about me goes against the grain. "All da lasses where we're from have wings. Although, dey are more like yer Reaper wings, but da feathers are jus as seductive."

"Oh," I say, feeling a twinge of guilt for something I have no control over. "What do you want me to do?" I ask.

He exhales a long breath. "I'd say die, but I do na even know if dat will fix dis. Dey would probably have trouble stayin' away from ye if ye were undead too. We jus have ta be extra vigilant, maybe add a few more seasoned fellas ta yer personal guard."

I wrinkle my nose, "Do you have to do that? Isn't four plenty?" I ask.

"It should be, but ye make me nervous," he says. "I tink I like ye better in me lucky shirt."

I smile brightly at that. "I think I liked wearing your lucky shirt better."

"Hallion," he mutters under his breath, while shakin' his head.

"Do you want to come in and sit down while we wait?" I ask Declan with a *faux*-casual shrug. He looks at me skeptically before stepping inside with me. I walk back into the sitting room and he waits until I sit in a carved chair before he seats himself stiffly on the chair farthest away from me.

Feeling awkward and stiff myself, I wet my lips and then ask, "Have…have you been here long?" His eyebrow arches in question because he doesn't know what I'm asking. I try again, "Have you been a Gancanagh for a long time?"

Narrowing his eyes at me, he says, "I have."

Holding my jacket on my lap, I play with one of the buttons on it as I ask, "Do you like it?"

"Whah?" he asks with suspicion.

"Do you like it…being a Gancanagh?" I ask, wishing I hadn't opened my mouth when I see the sneer on his face.

"Whah kind of question is dat?" he asks, like I'm a complete idiot.

"I'm sorry," I say immediately. "I…Molly said it rocks…I was just wondering what you thought about…you know…being a fella—undead…" I stammer, blushing more because I do sound like an uncouth idiot. "I just thought you would probably have a more enlightened perspective than Molly because you have been around forever—I mean, for a while—I'm sorry…forget I asked…" I say, falling into a painful silence.

The clock on the mantle ticks loudly for a few moments and I almost jump when Declan says, "No one has ever asked me dat question."

"Really?" I mutter.

"Na dat I can recall, no. I am as old as da mist and older by two and ye're da first ta ask me dat," he says, looking surprised.

"Oh. I hope I didn't offend you. I'm usually not as mean as I have been to you. You just seem to find me in my worst moments," I say honestly. I had no idea that I have the ability to shock him, but apparently I can.

"I keep trying ta figure ye out, lass," Declan says, assessing me.

"Oh?" I respond.

"I keep wondering if 'tis courage or if 'tis *naiveté* dat leads ye ta do all the brave and foolish tings dat ye do," he says with sincerity in his tone.

"You will let me know?" I ask with a small smile. When he looks at me in question, I add, "You'll let me know when you figure out if it's courage or *naiveté*, won't you?"

He smiles then, the first real smile I have ever seen from him. "I will," he agrees.

I nod my head and we both fall silent again for a while. "I miss being alive," he says abruptly, like he really didn't know he was saying that out loud. When he sees the question on my face, he explains, "Ye asked me before if I like being undead." I nod my head to him in understanding. "'Twas funny…watchin' ye eat…I felt like I wanted ta join ye, even when it smelled vile."

"Well, I can't blame you, peanut butter is really very good. It just looks disgusting," I smile.

"Being around ye, lass—ye make me remember whah it was like ta be alive. Ye make me remember me family—da one I had before I was turned," he says, looking at me.

"What were they like?" I ask, wondering about Faeries and their world.

"Lively…" he says distantly. "Dey…dey laughed a lot."

"Yeah, my uncle was like that, too. We used to laugh all the time—mostly at things that weren't that funny, but he had this laugh—this great laugh, that when you heard it, you just couldn't stop from laughing, too."

Declan smiles at me again, showing all of his perfect teeth. He says, "Me uncle was like dat, too! I remember—he had a laugh like a goat and when he would get going, dere was ne'er a dry eye in da place 'cuz ye'd laughed so hard ye had tears from it."

I grin as he laughs at his memory.

"Ye ready to hit it, Deck, or are ye gonna be knittin' her a sweater?" Eion asks, entering the room with Lachlan and Faolan in tow.

"I was just warming up to asking Declan to show me how to throw fire bombs, Eion. Thanks for ruining my opening," I say, rising from the chair.

"Ye want ta learn how ta throw elf darts?" Declan asks in surprise, while following me to the door.

"Is that what they're called?" I counter, raising my eyebrow at him as we enter the hall and walk towards the stairs. "Like the ones you were hurling at me in China?"

"'Tis. Scared, were ye?" he asks with a smile on his lips.

"Not really. You missed by a mile. You were shanking them off to the right. You may have to work on your follow through," I tease, and I am gratified to hear them all laugh at my insult.

Eion interrupts then and asks, "Why would ye want ta learn how ta throw elf darts?"

"You have to ask? I just got served by an Ifrit; I need a better arsenal," I answer.

"Ye have us ta protect ye now," Eion replies as we turn the corner, heading down a wide hallway where other fellas stop in mid-sentence, stepping to the side to let us pass.

Walking by them, I hear—*click, click, click*—as fangs engage in their mouths. My entourage and I keep walking like nothing happened, but Faolan and Lachlan glance at each other, doing that male telepathy thing.

I struggle to remain outwardly calm. "I'm willing to learn, if you have something useful to teach me…and elf darts seem… useful," I continue, passing more fellas as we near the hall.

Click, click, click, click as we stride on.

"Genevieve, do ye have any other clothes?" Faolan asks me as we near huge doors at the end of the wide hallway.

"It's all kind of like this. Why?" I ask as we stop at the closed doors.

"Well, when ye walk, yer legs are so—da straps ta yer garters keep showing as yer dress inches up—'tis teasing da fellas is all—'tis so sexy," Faolan stammers.

I blush and Eion whispers to Lachlan, "I luv it when she does dat."

"Maybe that is something you should speak to Brennus about because I already told him I need different clothes and he ignored me," I explain honestly. "Maybe you will get somewhere if you put it under the heading of 'security risk.'"

"She could wear a muumuu and 'twould make no difference," Declan says, shaking his head at me again. "She was jus born da sweetest sin. Eion, tell him we're here."

Eion slips in the door, letting it close so I can't see around it. "What is this?" I ask Declan. "I thought we were meeting Brennus for a tour of the house."

"Ye are, but he wants ta formally introduce ye ta da family first," Declan replies.

"Are they all in there?" I ask, feeling my heartbeat kick up a notch.

"Na even close ta all of us, but da ones dat matter are in dat room," he replies in a gentle tone, probably hearing the beating of my heart.

"A little warning would've been helpful," I breathe, feeling my heart jump to my throat. "What am I supposed to do?"

Declan shrugs. "Nuting. Dey jus want ta see ye. Tink of it as a photo op," Declan replies.

"He is ready for her," Eion says, pulling the door wide.

Declan leans near my ear and whispers, "Stiff upper lip, lass. Do na be afraid. No one will touch ye."

Straightening my posture, I whisper back, "I'm not afraid, Declan. I've had bus drivers that are scarier than you guys."

A deep rumble of laughter issues from Declan at my lie as I move forward into the room. Heavy tapestries line the walls of this medieval hall, depicting faeries in a hunt. I have no idea what they're hunting in the embroidered scenes, since I've never seen reptilian-like, winged creatures like them, but they look vicious. Weapons of all kinds also line the walls and I find it less than comforting that I cannot name half of them.

My eyes find Brennus almost immediately at the far end of the room. He is standing in front of an enormous mahogany table that stretches fifty meters or more, almost the entire length of the room. The other Gancanagh are in front of ornately carved chairs, which line every inch of the table on both sides. They are wearing expensive, tailored suits that fit each one of them impeccably. As I glance back to Brennus, I see that Finn is on his right and the chair on his left stands empty.

My chair, I think, grimly.

Keeping my shoulders back and my chin up, I stroll with my guards past the first few Gancanagh at this end of the table. *Click, click, click, click, click*—the sound of fangs engaging one-by-one resonates in the room as I walk down the line in front of them on my way to the head of the table. I plaster a small smile on my face, trying to make it seem like their reaction to me is no more than I expected, and not in the least bit terrifying. Inside, I'm cringing and hoping that I make it to the end of the room.

My wings flutter a little, causing rapid-fire *click, click, click, click, click* to unfold in an instant. Keeping my eyes on Brennus, his expression is growing darker and darker the closer I get him. By the time I reach the end of the table, his scowl is ferocious.

Not knowing what to do as I near Brennus, I go directly to his side. He doesn't say a word to me, but continues to stare at me. Longing is there, deep in his eyes, making me feel a disturbing pull towards him, in answer to his desire for me. Reaching my hand up slowly to his cheek, I trail my fingers down the planes of his face, like I have seen the Gancanagh do to their victims.

I try to smile. "I think they like me, *mo sclábhaí.* Do you want me to tell them to shut their gobs for you?" I ask, quirking my brow to him.

Some of the fury leaves his face at my teasing. His arm clasps me tight around my waist as he pulls me into him. Lowering his face to mine, he kisses me with no thought of the witnesses in the room—or maybe because of them. Cheers erupt around us while my hands are balled into fists against Brennus' chest by the time he finishes kissing me.

Turning to the crowd of Gancanagh, Brennus announces, "Dis is Genevieve, yer queen."

The crowd all shouts in unison, "*AONTAIGH.*"

"What did they say," I whisper to Brennus, not taking my eyes off the killers in front of me.

"Dey said 'Unite,'" he replies. "'Tis our motto." More cheers echo in the hall, making everything feel off-kilter and surreal, like I'm slowly drowning. "Would ye like ta address dem?" Brennus asks me and I turn to him, feeling stricken.

I glance from Brennus' face to Finn's on the other side of me. His brow wrinkles in concern. I narrow my eyes at him, and then ignore him to face the masses of pale faces ahead of me.

"Sure, why not?" I shrug, clearing my throat. I clasp my hands behind my back so that no one can see them shaking. "Hi, I'm Genevieve. You will have to excuse me if I seemed a little apprehensive when I first came in here. The last time I was in the presence of a gathering of Gancanagh, I had to fight for my life, so shwoo, glad that's not happening again." I say, pretending to wipe the sweat from my forehead. "I just want to say that I've never been a queen before. I don't think that I'll be any good at it. But, I promise not to make any of you eat cake or pay taxes or anything like that. I'm hoping it's more of a figurehead type of position because where I come from, we really don't buy into the whole evil dictatorship thing you've got going on here. We leave that to North Korea. Anyway, thanks for your warm reception. *Sláinte.*"

When I finish, the place is dead silent for a few moments until they all burst out laughing like they will never stop. Brennus pulls me nearer to his side and whispers in my ear, "I may na be able to ever change ye, *mo chroí.* I'm afraid dat if I make ye a true Gancanagh, dey will only follow orders from ye."

"Ah, then my work here is done," I reply, deflecting his flattery.

"Would you like ta see da rest of da house den?" Brennus asks, grinning.

"I would," I respond, using the affirmative that the Gancanagh seem to always use. I think it's their way of never saying "yes" to anything.

"Finn, finish up for me here. I'm going ta take me queen ta see da estate," Brennus orders. Finn inclines his head and Brennus leads me to a set of doors in the back of the room. I'm relieved because I don't want to walk by all of the fellas again.

Moving through a long hallway, I peek at Brennus who watches me with a smile on his face. I clear my throat and say, "I didn't see Molly in there."

"Molly has na earned a spot in dere yet," Brennus replies. "Dat was for da *laoch*. Dat word means 'warrior.' Dey are da warriors who have proven demselves ta me. Molly has much ta learn before she can enter dat room."

"Are you teaching her to fight?" I ask.

"Finn will see ta dat," Brennus replies. "Or, he may na. 'Tis his concern, na mine. She is na me *sclábhaí*. I didna create her." We stop then in front of another set of enormous, wooden doors. The doors are carved with intricate dragon-like figures whose heads jet out ominously from the flat surface of the portal.

Opening the door for me, Brennus ushers me into another long room with vaulted ceilings just like the hall that I had come from, but this one does not contain a long table in it. This one is like an armory where wicked-looking weapons glitter evilly in the slats of light from the narrow openings along one wall.

As I walk further in, my eyes wander over the menagerie of deadly weapons that cover nearly every inch of the stone walls in this hall. Maces, swords, spears, chakrams, daggers, axes, bows, shields, machetes, throwing stars, armor, and other things that I have no names for are on display. Strolling quietly through the room, I pass by scores of armor. It all looks ancient. It's not medieval, like the Knight's Bar armor. No, all this stuff looks otherworldly—inhuman.

I pause in front of a large suit of armor that can be described in no other way but faerie-like. It seems somehow more beautiful than the rest. Making a circle around it, I see that it's long, like a silver tunic that is embellished with intricate gold-tone trim. The entire surface of the metal is etched with Celtic knots and scrolls. There is a golden set of wings affixed on the center of the silver breastplate. Silver chainmail leggings hang from the metal tunic with long, leather boots attached to them. The boots are covered with silver metal, making it look similar to the framework of a stained-glass window. The coolest parts of the armor are the slits in the back of it that were created, I'm guessing, to accommodate wings.

The metal gloves of the armor hold a weapon in its grasp. I reach out with reverence and touch the intricately carved battle-axe that is attached to a long, metal shaft. The shaft of the axe is as long as the javelin that Zee trained me to use, making it nearly as tall as me. It has several notches to position my hands on so that they will not slip down the shaft easily when hefted. The blade of the axe is silver and resembles one of my wings, like the way my feathers lay upon each other and serrate along the edge, but the axe edge is sharp and menacing—lethal.

On impulse, I pick up the battle-axe; the metal in my hand feels different—eerie. It has a vibrating current in it that is like an exquisite hum of an instrument I have never heard before. I rest it against my cheek, feeling the vibration and hearing a sweet melody that sounds like a lullaby.

"Do ye hear someting?" Brennus asks me breathlessly.

"Yeah...it's like music," I reply. I begin to hum along with the beautiful lullaby as it weaves lovely patterns in my ear. Smiling, I glance at Brennus to see that he looks stricken.

"What? What's wrong?" I ask in alarm, pulling the blade away from my face.

"'Tis...I...it has na done dat since..." he falls silent, staring at me.

"Since when?" I prompt him.

"It has na sung since I brought it wi' me ta face Aodh. I tought it died wi' me," he explains in a low voice, reaching out to take the weapon from me. He holds it to his ear and listens intently.

"Can you hear it?" I ask.

He looks so sad that I want to do something to change that. He shakes his head and begins to lower the weapon. I reach out and touch it, grasping the shaft of the weapon in my hand. I press the flat of the axe head gently to his ear. The vibrations ignite in it again as I press my ear to the opposite side of it, hearing the lullaby play again.

"There it is. Do you hear it?" I ask.

"I do," Brennus murmurs. His hand moves to cover mine on the hilt of the axe, squeezing it lightly.

Immediately, my personal guards all jet to different parts of the room, pulling weapons from the walls. Lachlan makes it back to my side first. He stares at Brennus who lowers the axe from between us and inclines his head.

Lachlan turns to me and asks, "Will ye hold dis?" He holds up a spear that is capped with a diamond-shaped double-sided blade. The hilt of the weapon is intricately etched, just like the axe had been.

"Uh, sure," I reply with a confused look to Brennus.

Moving to Lachlan's side, I grasp the shaft of the spear just above his hand, while he raises it to his ear and listens. Lachlan leans down so that I can press my face to the other side of the weapon and hear the humming-sound of a different lullaby.

After a while, Lachlan straightens up and there is pain in his eyes when he says, "I never tought dat I would ever hear dat again."

"What is it?" I ask.

"Home," Lachlan replies sadly.

"Why does it do that?" I ask.

"It wants ye to know dat it will protect ye, dat ye don't have ta be afraid," Lachlan replies, his voice sounding thick with emotion. "It wants ye to know dat it will fight for ye. Dat it chooses ye, too."

Declan interrupts Lachlan by thrusting a ferocious-looking spear non-threateningly between the two of us. "Try dis one," he says gruffly. This spear looks like it has row after row of sharp, spiky fangs jutting out of it.

"Yours?" I ask as my eyebrow arches.

"'Tis," he says, looking lovingly at the brutal weapon.

"Okay," I sigh, gripping the handle of the spear near his hand.

Declan's melody is surprising poignant, like it aches for him. Before the song is over though, Declan lets go of his weapon. He turns swiftly and leaves the room. Holding Declan's spear in my hand, I look at Brennus.

Brennus' eyes soften. "'Tis okay. He will be back in a little while," he says quietly, taking the spear from me and resting it against another suit of armor.

Faolan and Eion have similar reactions to hearing the songs of their weapons again. They both look like someone punched them in the stomach.

"I'm sorry...I didn't know that they would do that if I touched them...I didn't mean to..." I trail off.

"No, dat was a gift dat ye gave ta us," Lachlan replies. "None of us ever tought to hear home again. We jus miss it, dat's all."

"I know how you feel," I say. "The same thing happened to me."

"Whah?" Brennus asks in confusion.

"It's ironic really. It happened in your cell, in the caves in Houghton. When I was dying. My Uncle Jim, whom I considered my 'home,' came and laid down next to me in my cell and held my hand at the end. I never thought I would see him again while I was still alive. I think it was his soul." I say, feeling the poignancy of that moment again. "It's a gift and it's a curse because you can't go back and change the past, no matter how much you want to. You can't keep them. You have to let them go."

Each Gancanagh in the room stares at me with the oddest expressions on his face. They look almost humble and that is something I never thought I would ever see.

"Why did you pick up dis weapon, of all of the tousands in dis room?" Brennus asks, studying the huge battle-axe in his hand.

"Well, it was held by the suit of armor, but I guess it's because it's the one that I wanted," I say. "I like the blade. It looks like my wing, do you see?" I ask, running my finger gently over the edge of the serrated blade.

"I do. Dere are hundreds of suits of armor in dis room," he says. "Whah do ye tink now, knowing dat it belonged ta me?" he asks.

"Coincidence," I reply, not wanting to draw any parallels to Brennus.

Brennus frowns. "Na coincidence. A weapon is personal; it has ta fit ye, it must please ye or ye do na choose it and it will na choose ye," he says in a soft tone. "It has ta be made for ye. I made dis one and now 'tis choosing ye, so now 'tis yers."

"They're all choosing me," I say, indicating all of the weapons I touched that sang for me.

"Dey are," he agrees and something is telling me that he is not speaking of the weapons. "Will ye accept dis gift?" he asks me solemnly.

I think about it for a second, and then I say, "I will accept it, if you promise to teach me how to use it."

The Gancanagh are vicious fighters and I could learn a lot from Brennus, who is their best fighter or he wouldn't be the king. This tribe is ruled by cunning and strength, not by inborn privilege.

"'Twill be me honor ta make ye earn it," he replies with a wicked grin. Desire is clouding his eyes again and I have to look away from him so that I won't respond to it.

Wanting to change the subject, I say, "So this isn't really an armory, like I thought. It's more of an archive—a record of who you all were before you became Gancanagh."

"Dat's right, *mo chroí*. We have other rooms dat contain more effective arms den dese. We create body armor now dat is more practical den dis wi' advanced charms ta protect us," Brennus says, raising his arms to indicate the thousands of weapons and armor that belong to another world. "Come, I want ta show ye a special room we jus created," Brennus says, taking my hand and leading me towards the door.

We exit the room and walk down the corridor turning onto another hallway. We stop in front of another huge set of wooden doors, but these doors are different. These doors have intricately carved angel's wings on them. "Dis, is yer archive," Brennus says as he opens the door.

I am not prepared for what I see. It's a tower room, so it's round with a ceiling that is at least three or four stories above my head. This room leads to tier-like balconies above and there are different spaces arranged on every "floor." A spiral staircase leads to each level, or I can fly up to each one, landing on the platform between each railing. It sort of resembles a cross-section of a hive, in a way, like the way the chateau is arranged, but more open.

The main level is like a reception area. A large, stone fireplace is centered on the far wall and above the fireplace is the portrait that Mr. MacKinnon painted of me as the Goddess Persephone. On the mantel of the fireplace is a small glass box. My steps are slow as I walk forward into the room and move to the mantel.

When I lift the lid of the glass box, I find that it contains a letter opener, cradled on a bed of red velvet. I recognize it instantly as the weapon I had used to try to ward off Brennus at the library in Houghton.

Touching the letter opener lightly, I murmur, "Not as impressive as a battle-axe."

"Ye are wrong, *mo chroí*." Brennus responds immediately. "'Tis more impressive dan da axe. 'Tis an unbelievably brave weapon."

I shut the lid to the box gently and wander slowly around the room. Some of the furniture from my uncle's house is mixed in with very chic furniture to create a lovely place to sit and receive guests. Delicate tables dot the room and on them, next to beautiful vases of fresh flowers, are priceless things that I never thought I would see again. Pictures of my friends, of my Uncle Jim…of my mother…they have all been re-matted and framed so that they are better preserved. I walk numbly to the table in front of me, before picking up a picture of my uncle and me. I think I was in the fourth grade and I had won the spelling contest at school.

"You were a beautiful child," Brennus says from over my shoulder.

"You think so?" I ask, trying to hide the tightness in my voice. "Tell that to some of the boys. They used to call me 'tomato head.'"

Brennus' eyes narrow to a dangerous edge. "Who called you dat?" Brennus asks.

"Mikey…" I begin, and then I stop. "Why?" I ask with suspicion.

"I will kill him," Brennus promises in a soft tone.

"He was nine," I reply.

"Den he has lived many years longer dan he should have," Brennus replies with malice.

"Never mind," I say, placing the picture back on the table and silently moving from table to table, touching the pictures with trembling fingertips.

"Do ye want ta see da rest of yer tower?" Brennus asks me.

"I do," I say, finding it hard to breathe. "I'll meet you up there."

As I expand my wings, I take three strides, and then jump into the air. I fly a little shakily to the second level. I find the railing a lucky addition to the design as it stops me from crashing into one of the bookshelves on the far wall when I come in a little faster than I should on my landing. Clutching the railing, I see that this tier is like a library, with ornately carved bookcases full of leather-bound books and comfortable chairs and sofas where I can read.

"Dat was an interesting landing. Do ye need a couple of pointers?" Brennus asks as he and the fellas make it to the room.

"I think I'm doing quite well for having had little instruction. The first time I flew was in China and well…you were there."

"I was," Brennus agrees. "If I wasn't already dead, dat may have killed me."

"Oh, come on," I reply, rolling my eyes. "I was not *that* bad."

"Dat is debatable," he replies. "I had ta keep reminding meself dat ye are stronger dan ye look. 'Tis why I didna try ta stop ye while ye were in da air. I was afraid ye would na survive it if I did."

"That was kind of you," I remark.

"Na kind, practical. I knew where ye were likely going," he replies smoothly.

"I'm sort of an open book, huh?" I ask.

"I would na say dat," he murmurs thoughtfully. "Ye surprise me too often to ever say dat." I smile as I go to the bookshelf and see many, many volumes of books I haven't read yet, mixed in with books that I have. "Dis room is for me librarian, Lillian."

"I didn't think you liked Lillian. She vomited all over the bleedin' beemer," I say.

"'Twas Finn's beemer," Brennus replies with a grin.

We head up to the third floor and I opt to take the stairs this time. This level is a chic office area complete with several computers and a seating area with a theatre size screen. DVD's that I have long since lost interest in line the shelves, relics from my life with Uncle Jim. I let my fingers roam over the selection, pulling one from the shelf, I read the front aloud, "Hackers."

"Whah is dat?" Lachlan asks.

"Is it instruction on killing?" Faolan asks, and I burst out laughing.

"Uh, no," I reply. "I'll host a movie night and we can watch it. I'll make popcorn."

"Whah's popcorn?" Faolan inquires as we walk up the stairs to the next level.

When I make it to the landing, I pause because it is almost like walking into my bedroom at my Uncle Jim's house. Everything is there: my bed, my dressers, and my posters of the bands that I like. They even have my prom dress hanging in the closet. Molly must have been instrumental in recreating this room because everything is placed pretty much where I had it before I left for college.

"Whah's dis ting, Genevieve?" Eion asks, picking up a little troll with purple hair from a shelf.

"That's a troll," I mutter numbly.

"No, 'tis na," he replies, sniffing it.

"Uh, yes it is," I reply.

He raises his eyebrow at me and says, "Dis is na a troll. Trolls are huge and dey smell like arse and dey have razor-sharp teeth dat 'twill gut ye if ye get too close to dem. Dis is a little naked, plastic ting dat's na da least bit scary."

"Oh," I reply, stumped.

I walk over to the bed and pick up my pillow. Bringing it to my nose I can just make out the smell of home that still lingers faintly on it. In an instant I begin sobbing and I don't think that I'm ever going to stop.

"I'm sorry! 'Tis a troll, I swear 'tis a troll," Eion says in a rush.

I sit down on the edge of the bed with the pillow grasped tight to my chest. "Lads, wait downstairs," Brennus orders.

When they are gone, he sits down on the bed next to me, pulling my head to his chest. I cry for a long time while Brennus strokes my hair. He doesn't say anything like I would have expected a human to say. He doesn't promise me that I will be okay or that things will be better soon—not in words anyway. But, even if he didn't say any of those things, sharing my pain with him—letting him see me vulnerable and him accepting it—makes me feel better somehow.

When I stop crying, he wipes my tears away and says, "Dis is yer room. Ye can come here whenever ye desire, but, when ye sleep, I want ye up in me room. Da fellas and I can protect ye better up dere. It makes it easier for dem to work in shifts and I can work in me office and still be near ye. Do ye understand whah I'm saying?" he asks me.

"Yes. You like me in your bed," I say sullenly, looking at his wickedly handsome face as he smiles at me.

"Dat's exactly right," he agrees. "Ye must be hungry. Let's go feed ye."

Russell

CHAPTER 14

Angel And Soul Mate

I take the shot and point to the shot glass that I slam back down on the bar. "Another," I say, watchin' the barmaid look at me skeptically.

"Why don't ya pace yourself, honey? You look like a nice kid. And ya have sucha purdy face. I don't want to see nothin' bad happen to ya," she says with a pityin' look.

"Then, don't look," I mutter, waitin' as she pours another shot of Johnny Walker Red.

As I set the glass back down on the bar, I see a movement out of the corner of my eye. Looking over at the barstool next to me, Reed is sittin' there like he materialized out of thin air. I stiffen, but I don't say anythin'.

What's there to say anyhow? She's gone, for now anyway, we let him get her. I let him get her.

"It's noon, Russell," Reed says, not lookin' at me, but across the bar.

"Thanks Big Ben, why don't ya head back to parliament, where ya belong. Run along now—there's a good chap," I reply, sippin' the beer I had ordered earlier.

"Wow, you're purdy, too," the barmaid preens as she drops a napkin in front of Reed. "Ya got I.D, Mr. GQ?" she asks him.

"Ma'am, he's older than dirt," I say honestly, but she ignores me.

"Nothing for me, thank you," Reed says with a polite frown. "I came to collect my friend," he says, indicatin' me.

"Ahh, that's nice," she says, smilin' at him. "Did someone break his heart?" she asks Reed, like I'm not even sittin' here.

"Something like that," he murmurs and I snort.

"He stole my girl," I say to the barmaid, and she looks at us both and takes a step back, not sure that she wants to be involved in this conversation.

"You think that's what happened?" Reed asks me in his quiet, contemplative way, watchin' the woman walk down the bar to assist a couple that just sat down at the other end.

"Yeah," I reply grimly, takin' another sip of my beer.

"I don't think that's what happened, Russell," he says.

"Oh, ya don't? What do ya think happened then?" I ask, not really carin' what he thinks.

"I think you tore her heart out and her soul too," he says in a low tone as he turns to look at me. "It's the only thing that makes sense to me."

"What are ya talkin' 'bout?" I ask him, growin' still.

"I would be interested to know about what happened in your last lifetime...the one just before this one. Did you leave that life early? Die young?" he asks. "Did you leave her behind?"

"I'm not sure. Why?" I counter as my eyes narrow.

"Because she still won't let you go. She loves you even when the angel part of her keeps telling her not to—begging her not to and I keep wondering why that is. It's like the angel side of her knows something that the human side of her refuses to admit. The only thing I can come up with is that you must have betrayed her somehow. You never intended to stay here—in this lifetime. She pulled you back. She changed your destiny—made you stay with her."

"There's no way I'd betray her," I scoff at his reasonin'. "And I wanted to stay, or I wouldn't be here. I had a choice—I asked to stay. I remember beggin' for it as I was dyin'. I had to stay to help her."

He faces forward again, pickin' up my empty shot glass and studyin' it. "I keep wondering why anyone would pick a mission like this one. To be born the only half-breed with a soul." When I look at Reed he says, "Oh, yeah, she chose this. Although this is an honor, it's more like a suicide mission and one that not many souls would volunteer for because there are so many ways to lose yourself—lose your soul to Sheol, it's the probable outcome. So I have to wonder why she would agree to do it. Was it that she is just that good?" he asks me rhetorically, "Or, was it because she no longer cared what happened to her? And if that is the case, why didn't she care what happens to her? And no matter how I look at it, I keep coming back to you," he says, turnin' the shot glass over and puttin' it down in front of me.

"You think I know the answer?" I ask him angrily.

"No, I know you don't. But someone does. I'm just waiting for that someone to show up," he says, lookin' at me.

"Good luck with that," I reply, hopin' he'll leave soon.

"No, she won't let you go," he murmurs, almost to himself. "It's like she still needs you even when you don't need her anymore," he says in a flat tone.

"What do you know 'bout what I need?" I ask him furiously.

"Do you know what she did when she found out that the Ifrit had you?" he asks me rhetorically. "She allowed an Undine named Safira to humiliate her in order to not offend Safira so that she would help her save you. She lied to me, she lied to Zee, she went against every precaution that we set up to protect her, and then she made a deal with the Gancanagh so that they would save you from the Ifrit."

"I never asked her to do any of that," I mutter, feelin' like he's chokin' me.

"No, you didn't have to, she would do it again in a heartbeat, too," he says without a hint of doubt.

"How do ya know that it wasn't me that chose this mission?" I ask.

"For one, she was born to it, and for another, she never sat around in a bar at noon while her soul mate needed her help," he replies. "You are here out of obligation…maybe some guilt, too. Why don't you just let her go, if you aren't going to help her?"

I point my finger at him. "This is all bullshit, Reed! Yer total bullshit! Ya know ya stole her from me and this is yer way of tryin' to get rid of me," I accuse. His speculation is makin' me want to hurt him more than I normally do.

"How is it possible to steal a soul mate? Have you asked your-self that? It's impossible, and yet, she loves me with a fierceness I've never—could never fathom existed. She chose me. I don't know why, but I'm grateful and I love her and I will do anything for her...even talk to you—if it will save her."

"I'm gonna get her back, Reed," I promise in a soft tone, lookin' him in the eyes, so he knows I'm not playin'.

Reed's eyes narrow dangerously. "She is bound to me, she swore an oath to me. She's my..." and he says some word in Angel that I don't know.

"She has sworn many, many, oaths to me in more lifetimes than ya can count and she's my soul mate and I will have her back," I assure him.

"Then, help us so that there will be something left in her to win back, Russell!" he says with a fierce scowl. Reed is seriously pissed off that I'm gonna try to get her back, but he had to know that I'll try even before he walked into the bar. He must be convinced that she won't be comin' back if we don't figure out a way to save her.

My heart sinks further. "Is he torturin' her?" I ask, goin' white. I have nightmares 'bout what might be happenin' to her.

"Brennus is extremely intelligent, Russell," he says. "He already tried torture. He knows she's too strong to succumb to that."

"Then, she'll survive this. He can't bite her, it's the stipula-tion that breaks the contract," I say, and I watch as Reed turns and stares at me like I'm an idiot.

"Once she's one of them, he wouldn't need the contract to keep her with him, would he? She would be his slave and he her master and her soul will be forfeit to Sheol. No, but that is plan B. If Brennus cannot win her, he will bite her. She knows that, I think–she is so clever," Reed says as a small smile comes to his lips. "So, she will play along for a while, but he is not a patient demon. He is used to getting his way and we cannot underestimate how dedicated he will be to his plan. He wants to win her and he knows more about pleasure than you and I put together…all forms of pleasure."

I think 'bout that for a second and feel my face flush hot with anger.

Reed glances at me and says, "Exactly," and his face mirrors my coloring.

"So what do we do?" I ask.

"Our first priority is to find them. They are experts at cloaking themselves. The Gancanagh use their magic well and it's ancient magic. They have learned techniques to help them fly below the radar, like importing their food supply, perhaps even raising their own 'stock' and disposing of the evidence," Reed says. "But they cannot block you, I don't believe. You and Evie are connected. You are 'the other,' as Brennus so aptly calls you."

"You need me to find her for ya? And then what?" I ask. "You go there and try to take her away, yer gonna make it worse for her. She can't leave and if ya get caught, he'll kill ya, or worse. What else will Red have to give up to save ya, too?" I ask solemnly. "None of y'all can kill him! Not with her tied to him. He intertwined his life with hers, so if ya cut him, she bleeds." I explain, and I feel almost crazy with the pain of knowin' I am the one that did that to her.

A look of frustration crosses Reed's face. "I'm not going to try to take her from him, not physically anyway. I have to try to help her so that he doesn't break her, so that he doesn't get her soul," Reed admits, like he is ashamed of not havin' a better plan at the moment.

"How're ya gonna do that?" I ask.

"*We* are going to do it. It's going to take both of *us*," he says, turning to look in my eyes and I see what it's takin' him to say that, the pain that I have refused to see until now. "I'm not just worried about him breaking her. He is strong—powerful," Reed admits grudgingly before he goes on. "But, when the evil community realizes that he has her, he is going to need every ounce of his power to keep her."

"Whaddaya mean? Ya mean that there are worse things out there that can get her if ya don't find her?" I ask. I can't begin to estimate how very, very, pissed off that is makin' me. I already know that there are crueler things than the Gancanagh...I know it first hand. "So yer saying, ya might have to help that demon hold on to her?" I ask.

"Let's pray we can figure out an alternative to that—but if it comes to that, then yes, that is what I will do. There is evil that you have not seen yet. Things that make the Ifrits look benign," Reed says with a worried frown.

I shudder and begin to quietly shake like I've been doin' since I left the church. "Why didn't none of y'all tell us that? Ya know, before?" I ask.

"Could you have conceived of what I was saying until now?" Reed counters in a soft tone.

I slowly shake my head. "Naw. Nothin' could've prepared me for Valentine." I say, feelin' sick. "I'll help ya, Reed. It's Red. There's no question that I'll help only..." I trail off, takin' my tremblin' hands from the bar and hidin' them under it. They are shakin' so bad that I want to order another shot to see if it will stop them for a few hours.

"Russell, it's been a long time since I endured the kind of torture that you just experienced and when it happened to me, I was much older than you—at least your body, anyway," he says without a hint of humor. "It is gruesome and it won't get better for a while. Even when your body heals within days, the memory of what happened will linger. Everything will make you feel tense—noise, silence, certain scents, the emotions of others..." he trails off before he says, "Brownie is going to be someone you will be tied to for a long time. She shared your pain. You will need to be near her at times, and at other times, it will be almost impossible to look at her face."

"How long does that last?" I ask quietly, not sure I want to have this conversation with him, but not able to stop myself from havin' it.

"As long as it lasts," he says, and his answer makes my throat feel tight. "I have learned something in the length of time that I have been here. This is temporary. Everything changes, whether you will it to or not. What you feel now will eventually fade and you will cease to remember it, until you need the information that you learned from it to survive, then it will be there for you. At the times that I have felt out of control, like you do now, I found that one thing always makes me feel more in control, more focused."

"What's that?" I ask.

"Work," he says. "Do you feel like working?"

"What do you have in mind?" I ask, feelin' like I know what he's sayin' without him havin' to say it. Maybe he and Zee will let me stalk some Fallen with them.

"Well, I thought that I had taken care of all the Gancanagh who have been following me before I came in, but I think there are a few of them outside waiting for me to come back out. You want in?" he asks, and I freeze.

"The Gancanagh have been followin' you?" I ask, stunned.

"Yes. I am their public enemy number one," he smiles at me, like he is delighted with the distinction. "Brennus is persistent. He wants me to cease to be. He has been sending me only his most seasoned killers. Zephyr is very jealous. Don't tell him that I let you help me, or he will sulk."

Evie

CHAPTER 15

Forgiving Magic

Hearing Brennus chuckle next to me, I don't look up from the book I'm reading as I say smugly, "I told you that you'd like it."

"Ye did," Brennus replies, turning the page in the book I gave him. "I must admit dat dis Poe human has a way about him. I enjoy da inventive ways he tortures. He employs da fear of pain much more dan I do—I jus go wi' da pain—'tis usually very effective."

"Is it, *The Pit And The Pendulum*?" I ask, lowering my book to look at him next to me on the sofa in my library room.

"'Tis," Brennus smiles nefariously.

"I didn't give you that book to read so that you could learn new forms of torture. It wasn't supposed to be instructional, you know?" I say with a sigh.

"Like I would need instruction on torture," Brennus says with a laugh. I shiver a little because truer words were never spoken. "Dere are many forms of torture. Did ye know dat? Dere is sensual torture as well…" he says, lifting my hand and kissing my palm, sending a shiver of pleasure through my body this time.

"I'm sure there are, Brennus," I say, trying to tug my hand away from his lips. "That's not something I want to learn from you."

His eyes darken with desire. "But, I am da best teacher," he says with hubris, undaunted by my rejection of his affection.

"Maybe you can answer a question for me then," I say, trying to distract him from kissing me again. He lets go of my hand and waits for me to ask my question. "Do you know why I'm broken?"

"Whah?" Brennus asks with concern, while scrutinizing me with his eyes to see if there is some physical deformity to be repaired.

"I could do things before that I can't do now," I admit, biting my lip.

"Whah can ye na do now?" he asks me with concern in his green eyes.

"I'm no longer having any nightmares...premonitions," I say, not sure if he knows that I have been seeing the bad things before they happen.

"Ye are safe now, *mo chroí*. Nuting is going ta harm ye now, so ye would na have nightmares, would ye?" he asks in his rhetorical way.

I hadn't thought of that. Could it be true? Could being with Brennus make me safe, so that I no longer dream of a scary future? I wonder. I had thought it was because Paradise has deserted me because I willingly entered into an evil contract.

"I...I can't send out any of my...clones either," I say, blushing. "I tried to send them to my friends, to let them know that I'm all right, but nothing happened."

"Dat, I believe, is part of our contract," Brennus replies. "In yer mind, ye know dat even if ye are na sending a message ta *him*, yer friends will relay da message ta *him*, so ye would den be 'communicating wi' him' which ye can na do."

"Oh," I reply. "That makes sense because I can't even send an email. I tried to write to my friend, Buns, but I couldn't send it. It was so frustrating, because I wrote it all, but every time I tried to click on 'send,' I would click on 'cancel' instead."

"I tink ye are na broken. I tink dat 'tis jus dat ye can na communicate wi' dem. Ye should try sending one of yer clones ta Molly or ta me," he says casually, like he is not angry that I tried to talk to my friends.

"I tried to call Buns, too. I couldn't even dial her number to call her," I say.

"Ye are too intelligent, *mo chroí*," he smiles. "Ye can na fool yerself into tinking 'tis na jus like speaking ta him. Ye're da one dat sets da parameters of da contract—yer mind sees all da possibilities and den it compares dem ta da contract. Ye are much too honorable for yer own good. Dis contract works so well on ye because ye are na evil," he says, shaking his head with an ironic grin creeping to the corners of his mouth.

"Well, that completely bites, Brennus," I say in frustration.

He laughs hard at my comment, "Dat's funny."

"So, in theory, if I could lie to myself effectively, then I could do anything I wanted?" I ask him. "Even leave here."

"In theory, ye could. I would na have entered into dis type of contract wi', say, an Ifrit, because dey are evil and dey can convince demselves dat up is down and down is up if dey wanted ta. Evil will believe deir own lies, ye see?" he asks.

"Yes," I say grudgingly. "I hate magic."

"Ah, come now, dere are a lot of very nice spells, too," Brennus says in a gentle tone, putting his arm around my shoulder and hugging me. "Would ye like ta see one?" he asks.

"No." I say in a salty tone.

"Ye will like dis one, I promise," Brennus says.

Standing up, he offers me his hand. I take it with reluctance as I stand as well, watching him close his eyes and concentrate. His lips move, but I hear nothing of what he says. I feel the energy in the room begin to collect and sizzle, like static electricity. It all seems to be rushing towards Brennus, like he's pulling it to him. Then, like he flipped a switch, the energy explodes outward in a rush.

I feel the sizzling pop of energy pass through me like a shockwave while the room around me begins to change. Ferns and vines grow up from the floor and the walls. Wild flowers sprout out of long grass, covering the carpets. A waterfall tumbles down the spiral staircase in a rush, while lush trees grow from the first floor and continue past us on the second floor on their way towards the ceiling. Humming birds of pure light fly by me to feast on the flowers near the bookcase. Fireflies drift around, glowing magically in my room.

I would have sat back down in awe, but Brennus catches me by the elbow, saying, "Do na sit on da bunny, *mo chroí.*"

Turning, I find a yellow rabbit made of light on the sofa where I had been sitting. As I straighten up, Brennus smiles at me in amusement.

"Hey, do ye mind?" Eion calls from downstairs, "We are playin' cards down here."

"Shut your gob, Eion," I call back, while admiring the magical rainforest that Brennus has created.

An instant later, a black-winged, shadowy creature that has the physical characteristics of a man, but with a long, spiky tail and ferocious claws leaps to a branch of the tree near me. It climbs up a little higher, leaning towards me, like it will pounce on me at any second. Sinister, yellow eyes bore into mine, causing me to go into a defensive crouch as I growl at it. My heart pounds in my chest while killing scenarios pulse in my head. Trying to read its intentions, I take another step back, pulling Brennus' elbow back, too, so that he doesn't get too near to it.

Brennus scowls next to me and flicks his wrist. The frightening creature melts away in seconds while Brennus calls downstairs sternly, "Dat's na funny, Eion."

"Me apologies," Eion calls back as a rainbow shoots up to the ceiling, an apparent attempt from Eion at making amends.

"Well, that was…interesting," I say, straightening up. I try to slow the beating of my heart to an acceptable level. "Do those creatures exist?" I ask, gesturing towards where the scary thing had been standing.

"They did, but I have na seen a *nevarache* in a very long time," he replies, looking concerned.

"That's good," I murmur, raising a shaky hand to my forehead.

"Ye know dat ye are safe here. I was standing right next ta ye and I would never let anyting harm ye," Brennus says in a gentle tone, reaching out to stroke my arm.

"You already have," I say, backing away from him. "You have hurt me before…so bad that it would have been kinder to let me die. You locked me in a cell—I was so alone—when I had barely recovered from it, you made me fight Keegan—then you bit me and it ached and I wouldn't stop bleeding while my whole world turned to fire and melted around me."

Brennus looks ill. "Ye are right, I did dat. I can na undo whah I did ta ye, but I learn from me mistakes," he says in a gentle tone. "I jus want ye da way dat ye are…if ye want ta be Gancanagh later, den I will turn ye, but for now, let's jus get ta know each other. Dat's whah I want."

"I don't trust you," I reply, staring into his eyes and seeing them soften in the corners.

"Ye do trust me, jus a wee bit, and dat scares ye," Brennus replies, his green eyes shining with amusement.

"You are insane," I sigh in frustration.

"Na insane. I am right," he says, smiling.

"Loco," I reply, raising my eyebrows and twisting my finger near my ear.

"Do ye want ta learn a spell?" Brennus asks me coaxingly. My heartbeat picks up again.

Do I? I wonder. *Yes. I want to learn it all…everything that will help me to survive.*

"Yes," I reply grudgingly.

"Ye are very powerful, I can see dat in ye, but ye use yer power differently dan us," Brennus explains. His dark hair falls forward a little on his forehead, making him even more attractive.

"What do you mean?" I ask, trying to ignore how sexy he looks.

"Ye give it. We take it," he says with a rueful look. "I can na walk near ye wi'out ye giving me yer energy, 'tis like a drug. I crave it now," he says seriously.

"Really?" I ask, wrinkling my nose.

He smiles at me tenderly. "I crave ye in ways ye can never truly know," he says and I blush. "Come here," he says, crooking his finger at me.

My eyebrows draw together in suspicion. "Why?" I ask.

He sighs, saying, "Jus come here."

When I come nearer to him, he pulls me back gently into his chest, wrapping his arms around my waist. He speaks into my ear, saying, "I'm going ta pull da energy from dis room ta me. I want ye ta try ta feel whah I'm doing as it passes through ye ta me."

Brennus concentrates and the magical scenery in the room begins to swirl and twist out of shape, like a watercolor picture that is saturated with water and bleeds into a mess of colors and distorted shapes. As he pulls energy towards us, I feel it filtering around me, but some of it I am managing to absorb as well, blocking it from going to Brennus.

"Good," Brennus breathes in my ear. "Try ta keep it from me, if ye can. Dat's a good strategy when fighting an enemy. If ye can block him from getting energy, ye can block him from creating a spell ta harm ye. And, if ye can take his energy from him, den ye hold all da power."

I feel electric, like I might burst into flame, for real, at any moment.

"Stings a wee bit at first," Brennus says airily as I begin breathing heavier. "Tink of someting ye want ta create...anyting...like fire." Brennus suggests, holding his hand out in front of me. "Den ye say da words ta make it so," he says as a ball of fire erupts in his hand.

"What words?" I ask.

"Dat's personal ta ye. Sometimes 'tis easier ta rhyme someting, like 'give me fire for whah I desire,'" he says and I wrinkle my nose again.

"That's an awful rhyme," I reply. "Poetry is not your thing."

He chuckles before he says softly, "Jus try it."

I'm no poet either because I can't think of anything that rhymes. Then, a thought enters my mind. Listening to it in my head, I begin to whisper low.

Suddenly, a *whoosh* of fire shoots wildly up from the first floor. It looks like a comet spiraling madly out of control in front of us, as it careens around Brennus and me, circling us with intense heat. Shielding me with his body, Brennus pushes his energy outward, creating a barrier between the fire and us.

It takes a few minutes before Brennus manages to snuff out the roaring inferno that I had created. He straightens up then, pulling me with him and checking me for injury.

He grasps me by the shoulders, asking with eyes wide, "Whah did ye jus say?"

"You said to say anything about fire," I retort defensively, trying to pull away from him.

"I did, but dis is yer first attempt at it so ye should na have been able ta create more dan a little spark—a flickering flame. Whah did ye say?" he asks again in awe.

Just then, Eion, Lachlan, Faolan, and Declan burst onto the landing, "Whah are ye doing up here? Redecorating?" Declan asks when he sees that we are both okay.

"Don't blame me. Brennus told me to say anything,'" I mutter.

"Eh?" Declan asks, sounding just like a Yooper.

"I made up a stupid song and the fire went crazy," I say in all seriousness.

"A song?" Brennus says with a skeptical frown.

"Yeah…like lyrics," I mutter, looking at the smoldering book on the sofa where I'd been sitting with Brennus.

"Sing me dis song," Brennus orders.

"Fine," I exhale deeply, clearing my throat. "Um…Your smile has shades of sweet…It touches me with its heat…" Color floods into my cheeks as my tone becomes pitchy. "The smolder in your eyes…Encircles me with your lies. I am caged by your desire…" I falter for a moment, trying to remember the rest of what I'd sung. "Surrounded by its fire…Love burns as you conspire…it burns like fire."

They all look at each other incredulously. "Ye jus made dat up—are ye a sorceress?" Declan asks with suspicion.

"No…at least, I don't think so," I reply, picking up the book I was reading and seeing that it's completely charred.

"Ye ca na sing well," Declan points out.

"Ye are a horrible singer," Eion agrees with a nod of his head.

I wrinkle my nose at them. "I wasn't aware that this was American Idol—"

"Ye wove love and desire into yer spell of fire," Brennus says in a thoughtful tone. "Dat's yer strength—yer ability ta create love and desire and den ye added fire ta it. Whah was it dat ye said? 'Tempted to die within its seething-hot fire'—ye nearly blanketed us wi' da fire. 'Tis yer ability to pull energy ta ye—ye rivaled whah I can do on yer first attempt."

Raising my hand, I say, "Overachiever," while glancing around at the destruction I caused to my library room. "I think we should go outside when you teach me other spells," I add, seeing that the sofa is still smoldering.

"Ye canna teach her anyting else," Eion says seriously, "she'll kill us all."

"Starting with you, *nevarache* lover," I say, crossing my arms and glaring at him.

"Dat's na funny," Eion replies in a sour tone, putting both his hands up defensively.

"Can ye try another spell? Can ye make it rain?" Brennus asks with excitement in his voice, ignoring Eion's scowl.

"I don't know. Are you sure you want me to try again?" I ask, looking around at the disaster in my room.

Brennus waves his hand negligibly around him, saying, "I'll fix dis."

"You want rain?" I ask, searching my mind for something to rhyme with rain.

Brennus nods.

I start to pull energy in the room to me while I try to think of something that rhymes. "It is love that can sustain the ache of two hearts parted. It is love that will make it rain upon the cheek of the downhearted."

Soft drops of rain begin to fall from the ceiling above us, wetting everything in my tower and causing the smoke in the air to dissipate. As water drips from the fellas' hair and trails down their stunned faces, I say, "I made that up, too. If you like it, wait until you guys hear Ozzie Osbourne."

Before I can evade him, Brennus catches me by the waist and twirls me around and around. When he stops, he hugs me to him. "Ye're so grand, Genevieve! Where did ye come from?"

"Detroit," I reply, feeling strangely happy as they laugh at my comment.

As I look over Brennus' shoulder, I see Finn standing near the staircase. He is getting very wet, just like the rest of us. A soft growl comes from me and Brennus stiffens, pulling me behind him. When he sees that it is Finn I'm growling at, he relaxes and puts his arm casually around my shoulder. I'm not fooled; he is doing that so he can catch me if I decide to attempt to murder Finn again.

Sizing up Finn, I can't miss the battle-axe in his hand. It's like the one that Brennus created, with a long, silver and gold etched shaft, but the head of the axe is different. It's more like a hammer than an axe. As he approaches me slowly with the weapon, his pale-green eyes look haunted.

Finn stops in front of me. Holding his weapon at arm's-length, he says, "Please."

"No," I reply abruptly, knowing that he wants to hear his song from it. He wants to hear his home again. "She will never go home again, either. You stole that from her," I say softly of what he has done to Molly.

"Lads, wait downstairs." Brennus says, sending the fellas away as I glare at Finn.

Brennus says something to Finn in their language that I don't understand. Finn nods, never looking away from me. Brennus turns to me and says, "I will be jus downstairs, *mo chroí.*"

I'm not sure if that is meant to be reassuring or a threat not to attack his brother, but I nod my head to him.

When we are alone, Finn says, "I love her."

"Is it love or did you just want an object to crave, Finn?" I ask.

He scowls at me. "I am capable of love. You are na da only being fortunate enough ta experience it," he utters softly.

"Her family loved her, too," I reply. Finn's scowl fades to be replaced by sadness again. "You are her *máistir* now—her judge, jury, and executioner who condemned her to another life—a life of death."

"What would ye have had me do?" he asks with pain in his eyes. "I watched her for days, wi' Eion and Keefe. We were going ta have her, no matter whah. Nuting would have stopped dat—she is yer friend…she would bind ye ta us." I feel the stab of guilt that I will always have for not protecting her—for making her a target. "Eion and Keefe both asked for her, too."

I pale, thinking of Eion or Keefe as Molly's *máistir* instead of Finn. I sit down numbly, feeling rain soaking through my thin shirt and clinging to me. "I know that this is my fault. It's just easier to blame you for it," I whisper.

"I love her...I really love her," Finn says, sitting down next to me. "She...she fills dat void in me dat has been empty for eternity—since I condemned me brother ta die wi' me."

"That wasn't you. That was Aodh," I say.

"'Twas me. Brennus would na have become Gancanagh if it were na for me. He would na have chosen dis," Finn says, hanging his head and holding his hammer in front of him.

From near the staircase, Molly says, "Enough with the guilt, you two, sheesh." She pushes herself off the wall she has been leaning against listening to us. Striding to the sofa, she squeezes between Finn and me, putting her arms around both of us. "My two favorite people turn out not to be people at all and you both want to whine about it. I don't miss being human," she informs us. "A second of this life is worth an eternity of the other one. You can either live above this mess or you can live under it. Embrace destiny or be buried by it."

"Molly, I always thought you were a vampire," I say with honesty, hearing Finn hiss at me, like I just insulted her.

"Yeah, but now I can kick vampire booty," Molly smiles, letting her fangs engage. She shows me her impressive weaponry.

"Wicked," I remark, like she is showing me new shoes that she bought at the mall.

"So, Eaves, are you going to stop the rain now? Because we get it," Molly says, holding her hands over her head like an umbrella.

"Err...sure..." I stammer, trying to think of a rhyme. "Rain, rain, go away, come again some other day," I sing in a rush as I pull the energy in the room towards me and then release it.

"Kindergarten rears it ugly head again," Molly says, because she knows that rhyme as well as I do.

"Nursery rhymes make great spells apparently," I shrug, while the rain stops pouring down on us.

"Good to know," Molly replies, wringing the water out of her shirt and looking around at the disaster. "So are you going to stop being so lame, or what?"

"I was not being lame," I reply defensively. "I was avenging my friend."

"I can take care of myself and I don't want to be avenged," Molly replies. "I chose this. So, do me a favor. Forgive Finn before the guilt finishes him off. I'm the only person he has ever turned." I watch Molly rub Finn's back as she says that and the look that passes between them is hot.

Sighing, I say, "I will try to forgive you, Finn."

Finn's smile is angelic when he says, "Tanks, Genevieve."

"If you turn anyone else that I love, I will kill you," I add softly.

"Ye would try…" Finn trails off, showing some of the Gancanagh arrogance as he smiles at me teasingly.

Getting up from the couch, I look around. Everything is charred and wet. Sighing again, I wonder how to clean it up. That may take a while to figure out.

Feeling a crackle of energy stirring the room, I turn towards Finn who is drawing energy to him. He is mumbling words that I cannot make out as things in the room are beginning to spin like tops. The couch we had all just vacated is now spinning around like a cyclone. Coming to an abrupt stop, it is completely back to its original form, without any hint that it had been touched by fire. The beautifully woven carpets are all clean and dry now, no longer making squishing noises when I step on them.

"Finn, that's amazing!" I breathe, grateful to have the mess gone. I page through my book that was charred to see that it's as good as new. "Thank you."

"Ye're welcome," he says, before he and Molly head for the stairway together.

"Wait," I say, catching up to Finn.

I reach for the battle hammer in Finn's hand and he slowly relinquishes it to me. As I touch the etched metal, it vibrates with an energy that I can only describe as charismatic. Placing the menacing hammerhead between Finn and me, we both listen to its melody. Finn's weapon is different from the other fellas'. The song is more lively and carefree—more like a rock-star's would be, if I can compare it to any of the music I know.

"Finn, you must have had all the ladies chasing you with mad beats like this," I giggle. "We should put this on 'Guitar Hero.'"

"I had my share," Finn replies, trying to cover his sorrow at hearing the music of his past again.

If I still felt animosity toward him for what he did to Molly, it is gone when he looks into my eyes after having looked towards Molly. He still has regret for what he has done to her and that is its own revenge.

CHAPTER 16

Casimir

I spend my nights in Brennus' room, trying to sleep alone in the huge bed, always pretending that I'm lying next to Reed. Sometimes, the longing that I have for Reed is so intense that it feels like my heart might stop beating. On those nights, I wake up to find Brennus sitting in my room, watching me sleep. He knows that I'm in pain. We don't talk on those occasions. It's like Brennus wants to replace the image of Reed in my mind, so that when I see him instead of Reed as I awaken, I'll forget that Reed is out there somewhere. A part of me thinks he's insane for thinking he can ever replace Reed and another part of me is afraid that I will lose the image of Reed that I am pushing really hard to keep ingrained in my mind.

At least Brennus hasn't tried to kiss me again, not since the day when he kissed me in front of everyone in the hall. He likes to touch me though. I almost feel like a favorite pet at this point. He likes to play with my hair or stroke my wing when we are in my tower reading or when I'm eating breakfast in his office each morning before I get dressed for the day.

Brennus goes out of his way to spend time with me, even when someone is constantly trying to gain his attention for this or that problem. He takes me for walks around his huge estate. He shows me the cliffs where the sea meets the rocks far below. I love to go there now, even though it's getting colder and windier as winter is creeping in. I want to fly around those cliffs, see what is in the caves far below us, but I'm not that good at flying yet, so I stick to practicing away from where the wind can toss me into a wall of stone and then down to the deep, treacherous water below.

Brennus is getting better at knowing me, too. I can tell by the gifts that he gives me. At first, he gave me things like a ridiculously expensive car that is more elegant than any I have ever seen before. It has seats that are more comfortable than a recliner. But, since I can't go anywhere but around the grounds, it's pointless. I can run faster. Then he presented me with more jewelry than I have places to put it. Every shape, facet, color and carat is covered, but when he notices I don't wear any of it, he gets smarter.

Eating my breakfast in Brennus' office, I watch him slide a perfectly wrapped box towards me with an expectant look. I eye it like it's my nemesis. Continuing to spread jelly on my bagel, I ask, "What is it?"

"A gift. Jus open it," he says casually, watching me with a small smile on his face.

Licking the jelly from the tip of my finger, I roll my eyes at him and reach for the box, hoping it's not more jewelry. Unwrapping it quickly, like tearing off a band-aid, I open the lid of the box and a small gasp escapes me when I find a pair of running shoes in it. I've had nothing to wear on my feet lower than a four-inch heel since coming here two months ago.

Has it really only been two months, I ask myself. I feel like it's been an eternity since I have seen Reed—since there has been something to hope for when I get up in the morning.

I gently reach into the box, pulling the shoes out and hugging them to me. I haven't felt like me since I have been here. The strange surroundings, the strange clothes and the even stranger fellas have made living here day to day a constant balancing act. I have been feeling like, at any moment, someone will jump on my tightrope and cause me to plummet from it.

"Ye are da most confusing craitur," Brennus murmurs, shaking his head. "I give ye jewels and ye canna be bothered ta put dem on; but I give ye trainers and ye act like dey are da most precious tings ever created."

"I'm not a toddler, Brennus," I reply, smiling at his comment. "Just because it's shiny, doesn't mean I want it. But these will make me feel more like me."

"Dere are more tings for ye in our bedroom. Denim—" Brennus says, like he has lost some fierce battle and he is surrendering to the enemy.

Not thinking, I rise from my seat, letting the silk robe part and expose the slinky little nightgown underneath. Throwing my arms around his neck, I hug Brennus tight, saying, "You bought me jeans?"

"I did," he replies smugly, hugging me back just as tight.

"Thank you," I say delightedly, kissing him quickly on his cool cheek and pulling away from him.

I bolt from the office, materializing in the bedroom in seconds and see a ton of new clothes hanging in my wardrobes. Some of it is still very edgy, but there is also more practical clothing for training and fighting, which I have been doing more and more of with Finn and Molly and my personal guard.

Pulling a black, designer workout outfit from the closet, I hold it up to my body, trying to see what it will look like on me. I race to the bathroom to change, hearing Brennus chuckling behind me.

"Are ye training wi' Finn again?" he asks through the bathroom door.

"Yes, I'm supposed to meet him near the war room," I call back, pulling on the tight black pants and matching top that hugs every contour of my form. I let my wings shoot out of my back, thinking Molly must have helped pick this stuff out because it fits perfectly and is made to accommodate my wings.

"Da war room?" Brennus calls back, sounding confused.

I open the door and step out, pulling my hair up into a ponytail so it won't hang in my face. "Yeah, that's what I call it. You know the room that no one uses? The one that has the lovely hand-painted maps on the walls? It has a grand piano in it…" I trail off because he is looking at me weird, like I have grown horns or something. "What?" I ask him.

"I was wrong," Brennus says, walking in a circle around me.

"As you often are, but what is it this time?" I ask, smiling at him.

"Dese clothes are really sexy," he says softly, sounding amazed.

"Oh," I say, blushing.

Click.

I step back from him when I hear his fangs engage. It is a knee-jerk reaction because I'm used to trying to avoid being bitten by them. I have been unsuccessful at locating any venison blood I need to sustain a bite. For undead faeries who feed on blood, there is surprisingly no supply of blood around other than the human supply and I can't bring myself to try to get some of it.

I have been storing my own blood in the perfume bottles in my bathroom. I take a little at a time, when I'm alone in the shower. I use my razor to prick my finger. I don't have a lot collected yet, only a little more than two small perfume bottles. I can't afford to get caught, so I only cut myself a little so I can heal fast. It completely grosses me out to think of drinking my own blood, but the alternative is much worse.

Brennus sees my reaction to his fangs and immediately retracts them. "Come, I'll walk wi' ye and ye can show me dis 'war room' dat ye are using," he says, extending his hand to me casually.

We walk out to the hallway where my personal guard waits for me. Two more *clicks* resound in the hall, one from Faolan and one from Eion.

"Banjax," I hear Faolan mutter under his breath as we move down the hall.

Our suite of rooms is located in the North Tower and my archive of rooms is in the West Tower. They have the best views. The East and South Towers I have not had a tour of at all. I think that most of the fellas that live here full time live in these two towers…along with the wans. The war room is located just past my West Tower, on the long corridor that leads to the South Tower.

We are just coming to the doors of the West Tower when Finn and Molly meet us in the corridor. Finn has on his concerned-look as he stops near us.

"I was jus coming ta see ye. We have a guest who has asked ta speak ta ye directly," Finn says to Brennus, looking a little grim.

"Should I see ta dis guest directly or will it wait?" Brennus asks, watching Finn.

"Directly," Finn replies immediately.

"Are ye going ta train dis morning?" Brennus asks Finn.

"I go wi' ye. Da girls will have ta find someting else ta do for now," Finn replies. Turning, Finn says to Molly, "Ye stay wi' Declan. Do na leave his side. I will come find ye later." I see her nod to him before he reaches up to stroke her face, not like a victim, but like a lover.

"Is there a problem?" I ask Finn, my heart kicking up a notch because he is acting strange—threatened.

Brennus smiles, saying, "Dere are always problems, *mo chroí*, but dere are none dat I have na seen before, so do na look so worried."

Brennus speaks quickly to Declan, saying something in Faerie that I don't understand, and red flags start going up in my mind. Declan nods, looking at me, and then at the other fellas in my entourage.

"Lachlan, go get Keefe and Leif. Meet us in da *Aingeal* tower. Make sure ye lock da doors ta da West Tower after ye let yeself in," he instructs and Lachlan shoots away to do as ordered.

"What the—Brennus! What is going on?" I ask, watching the fellas move closer to me.

"Uninvited guest. Just a precaution," he says softly, looking completely calm.

"I should go with you?" I ask, feeling threatened.

What if something happens to him? Then it will happen to me, too. We are linked, Brennus and me. I feel like I need to protect him, if for no other reason than self-preservation.

"Why?" he asks, looking intrigued.

"What if something happens to you?" I ask nervously.

Pushing a strand of my hair behind my ear, he counters, "Whah could happen?"

Narrowing my eyes at him, I say, "You tell me." Crossing my arms in front of me, I wait for him to tell me what's going on.

Laughing softly, he leans nearer and kisses my neck, just below my ear, before whispering to me, "Ye are perfect. I will see ye soon. Try na ta fret." Looking at Finn, Brennus nods his head and they leave together, heading back towards the North Tower.

Declan takes us to my tower and I wait there with two extra guards posted inside with us and several more outside the doors of the tower, patrolling it. Finally, after hours of waiting, Finn comes to tell me that Brennus would like to speak to me in his office. He carries with him a beautiful, red silk dress and heels that are incredibly elegant.

Handing them to me, he says, "Brennus would like ye to wear something more appropriate."

"Why? What's happening, Finn?" I ask, wanting an explanation.

"He will tell ye when ye get there. He wants ye ta meet someone," he says, without elaborating.

"Who?" I ask Finn, holding up the dress to see what it looks like. It's elegant and sophisticated, but it has a neckline that is a little *risqué*.

"Someone ye need ta meet," Finn says cryptically, and I give up because he is not giving anything away.

I change quickly and meet the fellas outside my tower room doors. I walk with my extensive entourage to the North Tower, trying to read their faces.

Approaching Brennus' office, I still before reaching for the handle as my hand reaches up to cover my nose. A rotten, grotesque odor seeps out from under the door ahead of me. If I had hackles on my body, they would be raised, but as it is, I have goose bumps running the length of my body.

Fallen, I think, feeling dread eat at me.

I know their stench. I remember it from the 7-Eleven where Gaspard, the fallen angel, tore apart all the people in the store.

What are the Fallen doing here? I wonder feebly.

I know that Brennus is evil, but he doesn't make a habit of hanging around with the Fallen—at least, I don't think he does. I never really asked him.

"'Tis all right," I hear Finn murmur from behind me. "He would never call for ye if 'twas na safe or at least necessary."

Nodding my head, I make myself reach for the door handle while all of my senses are telling me to flee. As I open the door, I try to inhale in shallow breaths because the stench in the room is enough to make my eyes water. Knowing that I have to hide every weakness and vulnerability that I possess, I stride confidently into the room as if I am the most powerful being ever created.

Seated behind his desk, Brennus rises as I enter. Looking towards the doors across the room by the balcony, it is easy to spot the one who has created the stench. He is standing in a shower of light from the sun, looking out at the view of the sea beyond. He turns when I stop just inside the doorway.

If I had thought that I had seen true physical beauty before, I have to admit that I have been mistaken. The Seraphim angel standing before me now has corrected that notion in an instant.

His skin is perfect, not pale like mine, but a golden, sun-kissed hue that looks supple as it curves over the masculine planes of his face. He is wearing the same kind of black body armor that Reed and Zee had worn when they knew that the Gancanagh were arriving. His armor is more gothic looking than theirs was, with elaborate emblems etched into the chest area and on his broad shoulders. It clings to him, outlining all of the powerful contours of his physique. He is as tall as Russell, but not as thickly muscled.

His tawny, golden-tone hair has honey hues throughout it and his eyes—I know that I have never seen eyes the color of his before. They are golden brown, but with gray and green flecks in them. His eyes stare back at me from beneath eyebrows that incline gracefully on his brow, but they are impossible to read. His eyes register no surprise, no shock at seeing me here. There is no emotion in them whatsoever.

His wings are—extraordinary. They are the same crimson hue as mine, but they are huge, reaching the entire length of his body, and stopping just before the floor.

But, the most beautiful feature that this angel possesses by far is his mouth. It's perfection in its fullness and the sensual way that it turns down in the corners, like he finds displeasure with most things. His disapproving expression creates an intense desire within me to see if I can change it somehow.

That last thought shocks me and I tear my eyes away from his mouth and bring them back to his eyes. His expression hasn't changed at all since I have entered the room. It's like he has been injected with Botox and now his face is relegated to one expression: exquisitely beautiful disdain.

Feeling ugly in the presence of such allure, my wings flutter around me.

A loud *snap* sounds as the beautiful angel's wings unfold in front of me, blotting out the sunlight behind his back. At full extension, his wings are fierce and awe inspiring.

Startled by such a display, my heart accelerates and I take a small step back from him.

Instantly, Brennus' fangs engage with a deadly *click*.

My eyes go to Brennus' to see that his expression is equally disapproving. He extends his hand to me, indicating that I should come to him. Wanting his protection from the lethal predator in our midst, I walk to his desk. Brennus takes my hand in his before he sits down. I allow him to pull me onto his lap, and I am surprised to find that I feel safer near him. Brennus retracts his fangs as he brings his hand up to my cheek to gently stroke it.

As I glance back to the angel across the room, he slowly lowers his wings to a resting position, but his expression remains the same.

"Genevieve, dis is Casimir. He has come ta meet ye," Brennus says, introducing me to the angel.

Casimir steps forward, nearing the broad desk. My mind tumbles over itself as I roll the name 'Casimir' around. I know that name. It's familiar to me for some reason, but I can't place it.

Since I don't know how I should greet my enemy, I say, "Oh?" as I look from Brennus to Casimir. "Well, here I am, Casimir. I would say, 'Nice to meet you,' but..." I trail off, wrinkling my nose at him.

An intense, predatory glint enters Casimir's eyes as his chin drops down slightly. His eyes don't leave me as he speaks to

Brennus in Latin, "You are to be commended, Brennus. You have found her. We are all quite pleased with you. You will be rewarded."

Intense fear overcomes me in that moment, causing heat to flush my face and my hand to squeeze Brennus' tight. Brennus uses his other hand to stroke my hair softly before he, too, replies in Latin, "She is the reward, Casimir."

"She is if you can hold her. You cannot," Casimir replies emphatically. "She is ours. She has always belonged to us."

Brennus laughs softly, smiling at me as I look at him. My heart is beating like a drum. I feel ill, understanding that Casimir is here to bargain for me.

What will happen to me if Brennus hands me over to the Fallen? I wonder.

"Ye lie," Brennus responds in English this time.

"Do I?" Casimir asks, switching to English as well, but his is refined, elegant.

"Ye do," he says, smiling as his hand brushes my cheek lovingly.

His fingers trail down my neck and over my clavicle towards my heart. Casimir watches everything that Brennus does with the same disdainful expression. Brennus' fingers slow, trailing over the plunging neckline of my dress. Pulling the red fabric aside, he exposes the mark branded over my heart. Seeing Reed's wings etched in my skin, an intense yearning claws at my heart, making it difficult to breathe.

A low, deep growl issues from Casimir at the sight of my binding brand. Instinctually, I growl back at him, letting go of Brennus' hand and putting both of mine lightly on the desk in front of me. I lean forward like I could spring over the desk at Casimir at any moment. Then, I drop my chin a notch, staring at Casimir with the same intensity that he is staring at me.

"You have bound yourself to a Power," Casimir says with deadly intensity, like it's a capital offense.

I smile because I have managed to wipe the lofty disdain from his face and swap it for true, raw anger. It is horrifying on the most basic levels, but the angel in me is completely gratified by his response.

"It's the one decision that I have made in my life that I do not question. Ever," I respond truthfully.

"Who is this Power? I shall make him question that decision," Casimir asks.

Brennus' arms wrap around me tight just as I spring towards Casimir, intending to bash his head in with the statue Reed carved of me clenched in my fist. His words are a thinly veiled threat to Reed and I'm not having it.

"I tink we have had dis conversation before, *mo chroí*, but maybe it bears repeating. Ye can na kill me guest," Brennus breathes against my ear. "'Tis bad manners." To Casimir he says, "She bears a mark of Paradise. She is na yers."

Casimir switches back to Latin, "Everything will be ours eventually. You know this. The Reaper contacted you, did he not?"

"You sent Alfred," I state in Latin, letting them know that I can follow them in this language, too.

Casimir replies, "Mr. Martin, your Latin instructor, said that you excelled in his class on all of the progress reports that we had from him."

I clench my teeth at his words so that my jaw won't drop open because he is talking about a teacher I had in high school, *before* I attended Crestwood. They have been watching me for a long time, but Alfred betrayed them and tried to take my soul from me, without their permission. They have plans for me. No one just watches someone else. They want me for something— they have always wanted me.

"Alfred was a poor choice," Casimir says. His calm demeanor is back now.

"Gaspard and Cade were poor choices, too," I reply.

"You didn't enjoy them? I'm surprised, you seem to champion mediocrity," he counters. I bristle because his eyes drift to my binding mark again, and then his eyes move towards Brennus.

"I don't *enjoy* you, and you seem to be a complete failure, so what does that tell you?" I ask him calmly, mirroring his demeanor.

A slow smile begins to pull the corners of his mouth up, making him look achingly beautiful, but there is no magic in his beauty for me. I am repulsed by it, not attracted to it.

"Name your price, Brennus," Casimir says softly. "I wish to take her with me when I go."

"Dere is no price," Brennus replies in an equally gentle tone. "But, if I find another like her, I will be sure ta let ye know."

"There is no one else like her," Casimir replies as his top lip curls in a sexy sneer.

"'Tis true," Brennus agrees with a shrug. I could kiss him for not exposing Russell to Casimir. "Dis has been an interesting and informative meeting, Casimir. However, I am afraid dere are pressing issues dat call for me attention," Brennus says, trailing his finger over the line of my clavicle, making me shiver at his cold touch. "Declan…"

Declan opens the door and steps into the room, followed close behind by Eion, Lachlan, and Faolan. They stand just inside the door with their fangs clearly discernable.

"Brennus, you have done well for yourself. Why would you want that to change? There is always a price. You should name it or you may end up paying it," Casimir says seductively.

"Are ye going ta try ta make me pay dis price, Casimir? Ye must be tired of livin' in yer hole, or are ye jus tired of livin'?" Brennus asks, looking completely calm and amused.

"It could be me who makes you pay, or it could be the little jewel sitting on your lap. I heard you tried to make her grovel at your feet…that didn't work out so well for you, did it? And she is just getting started. You have no idea what you have there, do you?" he asks.

"I'm learning someting new every day, Casimir. Life has suddenly gotten worth living again," Brennus replies.

"It's too bad for you then that you are already dead, is it not?" Casimir replies.

"Da next time ye come here, Casimir, ye best na be alone," Brennus replies coolly. "Do ye need more tellin'?"

Casimir growls in response, which elicits a hissing sound from the fellas who move towards him menacingly. Casimir backs to the balcony doors. He takes one last look at me and then he leaps into the air and is gone.

"ARRGH, someone open da windows, would yous," Eion says, holding his nose like it stings. "And dey say we stink."

"Any of yous see him again, ye have me permission ta kill him," Brennus says to my personal guard. "He wants yer queen. Drain him if ye like."

Brennus touches my chin, turning my face to meet his eyes. "Remember his face. If ye see him again, ye run, ye tell us and we will take care of him. Do na try ta face him yeself. He is dangerous for ye, do ye hear whah I'm saying?" Brennus asks me and I nod, feeling terrified and grateful. "I did na want ye exposed ta him, but I had ta make sure ye saw him and understood whah he is. Seeing is easier dan saying."

"You…you weren't lying to me," I say softly, looking into his eyes. "You plan on protecting me—for real."

Brennus looks at Declan and says, "Take da fellas and tell Finn I want ta see him after I speak ta Genevieve alone." Declan inclines his head and they look grateful to be leaving the office—to be getting away from Casimir's foul odor.

"I will protect ye. Ye are safe here. Do ye know whah da Fallen plan for ye?" he asks me, deadly serious. I shake my head at his question. "'Tis important now dat we find out exactly why dey want ye. If 'tis jus for yer soul, dat could be changed, but I have gotten de impression dat dere is more ta dis dan jus dat."

"Why do you think that they would want more than my soul?" I ask.

"Did ye na see whah ye were doing ta da Seraph? Ye walked into da room and ye owned Casimir. Ye fluttered yer wings and he responded ta ye."

"I'm sorry…I don't know what you're talking about," I say. I watch Brennus smile broadly.

"Ye do na even know ye're doing it, do ye?" he asks.

"Doing what?" I shake my head.

"When ye came in, yer wings asked him a question and his wings answered ye," he says.

"What did my wings ask?" I inquire breathlessly.

"Dey asked, 'Do ye desire me?'" he says, watching me blush.

"I'm going to have to have a little chat with my wings later," I mutter. "What did Casimir's wings say?"

"His wings said, 'I will kill anyting dat keeps me from having ye,'" Brennus replies. "Ye really riled him, too. Seraphim never show emotion, 'tis like 'tis beneath them. Dey usually seem more dead den we do—ye can na read dem."

"They are good at giving nothing away?" I ask, thinking of Reed and how good he is at that when he has to be.

"Ye can say dey wrote da book on it," he replies. "Ye made him growl, twice. I never tought 'twould be possible. I have seen Seraphim kill dere enemies wi' dat same blank expression dat Casimir had in here, but he could na hold it in yer presence. Ye got ta him—he was emotional. Bringing ye in here was da best ting I could have done because it showed me how desperate he is for ye."

"You think he will come back?" I ask, fearing his answer.

"I'm certain dat he will and he will bring his army," he replies casually.

"Why not just give me to him then? You could avoid all of this and they will probably give you whatever you want in return," I say, feeling cold at the very thought of being handed over to Casimir. Declan was right, the devil that you know is far, far better than the devil that you don't. The Ifrit, Valentine, proved that to me.

"He will na have ye. Ye're moin. I am na weak. I do na have ta do whah I'm told," he replies. "Power has its privileges. Ye are me queen. Ye are very powerful, too. Ye do na have ta do as ye're told, except when I'm tellin' ye," he says, smiling at me.

Without thinking, I wrap my arms around his neck and snuggle into his chest, hugging him tight. Resting my head against him, I whisper, "Thank you for protecting me from Casimir. I want to learn everything that you can teach me—magic, fighting, weapons, strategy. I have to become more powerful. If Casimir is responsible for sending Alfred, then he is ultimately responsible for my uncle's death. I want to crush him…slowly, painfully…" I stop speaking when I hear Brennus' fangs *click* in his mouth and his body grow still.

Slowly, I pick my head up off his chest and turn to look in his eyes. Desire and pain war in his eyes, as he says, "I had better go feed now, *mo chroí*. I…I like it when ye speak to me of vengeance and…when ye lay yer head on me chest. I should be able ta control dis, but lust and bloodlust are entwined in whah I am, ye see?" he asks, afraid that he has scared me.

I nod. "You should try venison blood. It tastes a little piney, but it stops the craving," I say seriously. "It's probably healthier too—humans are full of cholesterol."

Brennus laughs. "Would dat please ye—if I stopped feeding on humans?" he asks, squeezing me tighter.

"Yes," I respond immediately. "Can you, I mean, it wouldn't hurt you to eat something else, like cows?"

"Blood is blood. It all nourishes," he says. "Da taste, however, 'tis someting else entirely."

"That's epic, Brennus! You can all start eating beef blood! We can get our own cattle! Get rid of the wans!" I say, grasping him by the shoulders and looking at him happily.

"Whah, no, 'twill never work, Genevieve," he replies. "I might be able to cross over eventually, but the fellas will never be convinced ta do it."

"Why not?" I ask disappointedly.

"I told ye dat lust is entwined wi' bloodlust—we get both from da wans. If I told da fellas dat dey had ta feed on animal blood, dey could probably do it, but ye would be asking dem never ta touch a female again. In order never to harm a human, we could never touch dem. I would be saying ta da fellas dat dey had ta be monks from now on. 'Twould make me more despised den Aodh ever was."

"Oh," I say dejectedly.

"Ye see why ye are so special? Na only are ye na affected by me touch," Brennus says, running his fingers down my cheek and over the curve of my neck. "'Tis like ye were made jus for me. Ye can have a soul, ye can have life and be touched by me and na change—na become a compliant shell dat does anyting I want. Ye have a mind and ye use it and ye sass me and ye rage at me and ye…love…and ye make me want tings I never knew I could ever have again—tings I tought died when I died."

"Brennus, you're asking me to be the queen of the wild things," I murmur sadly. "And you're asking me to give up everything that I already love to do it."

"I'm na asking," he says softly, his lips hovering inches from my neck.

"No, you're not asking," I agree, before feeling his cold lips press softly against my neck.

My heartbeat increases instantly. Brennus pulls back quickly, like I burned him. As he searches my face, his brows draw together with desire. He picks me up in his arms and then seats me on top of his desk. He grasps me firmly by the back of the neck, tipping my face up to meet his, his cheek grazes mine. When Brennus presses his lips roughly to mine, my mind races.

If he bites you, he breaks the contract. Make him bite you—make him lose control, my mind whispers to me.

The blood I have collected will be enough—it will have to be. I wrap my legs around his waist, pulling him to me and kissing him back with unrestrained fire. With one hand on his back, I reach out with my other hand, touching the statue on the desk and feeling its cold stone beneath my fingertips.

Reed, I think, closing my eyes and pretending that it's his lips on mine.

My fingers grasp the base of the statue, ready to hit Brennus with it the moment he sinks his teeth into me. I feel his fangs scrape my bottom lip, but not enough for it to bleed.

What if I do make it back to Reed now and Casimir follows me there? Will he bring his army with him so that Reed will have to fight not only the Gancanagh, but the Fallen, too? Reed will be crushed, I think, feeling my heart twist painfully.

If I stay here, the Gancanagh might wipe out the Fallen for me— both my enemies pitted against each other. But, the longer I stay here, the less the Gancanagh feel like my enemy. Can I live above this mess or will I be buried by it? I wonder as my hand balls into a fist.

"Genevieve," Brennus whispers against my skin, like he would worship me if I would only let him.

Something twists inside of me at the sound of his voice, the passion and the need within him is calling to me. This is love— a version of it and I wonder when that happened.

When did I start loving him? I ask myself. But, it doesn't really matter. It's the bottom of the wave, not the top of it where love crashes over me and washes me way, like it does with Reed. Nothing can compare to that—nothing.

"I can't be what you want me to be," I whisper to Brennus, while trying to pull away from him.

"You already are whah I want ye ta be," he replies softly as he tries to halt my retreat. "Give it more time. Ye will see dat I am right." Shaking my head, I rest it against his chest.

From somewhere outside on the grounds, shouts erupt from the fellas. Brennus tenses as his arms tighten around me. Lifting my forehead off him, my eyes go to his face to see his expression harden.

"What's wrong?" I ask, following his eyes to the open doors where Casimir had left.

In the next instant, Russell enters through the doors and moves rapidly towards me. The shock of seeing him again is overwhelming, bringing tears to my eyes.

I don't have time to even take a breath before Russell's clone enters my body. Then, a comforting sense of being home, a calm and a peace that my soul has been silently begging for, floats through my body.

"We're searchin' for ya, Red," Russell's voice whispers from somewhere deep inside of me. "We need ya. Yer ours. I love ya...and so does Reed."

CHAPTER 17

War Of Hearts

As Russell's voice speaks to me with the resonance of a dream, I feel like, for just one moment, some of the pieces that have gone missing from me are filled. I must have a look of bliss on my face because when I lift my eyes to Brennus', his scowl startles me.

"Da other needs more tellin'," Brennus growls, while stroking my cheek. "I tought da Ifrit would have been enough ta convince him dat he is way out of his element, but he is having a problem dealing wi' reality. Whah did he say ta ye?"

I lower my chin and look away.

"I'm na used ta open defiance," he says sternly, pulling my chin back so he can look in my eyes.

"I'm not used to betraying my friends," I reply coolly.

"Ah, da Seraph has already taught ye something, has he na?" Brennus says wi' equal cool. "Ye're practicing yer poker face?" he asks with a smile that isn't reaching his eyes. "Remember dat dey all have someting ta learn from ye, na ye from dem." Letting go of my chin, he turns towards the door to leave.

"What are you going to do?" I ask worriedly, leaping off the desk and following him.

"I'm going ta speak ta Finn ta make sure dat ye do na spend da rest of yer life in Sheol wi' mentors like Casimir," he says abruptly, turning on me in frustration. "So dat dey do na get dere hands on ye and pluck all da feathers from yer wings one by one, jus for fun—jus because dey can. Ye wonder why I do na want ta turn ye now? 'Tis because I do na want dem ta get dere hands on even a piece of ye. Whah dey would do ta a soul like yers is…unimaginable. I will turn ye, if I have ta—if it saves even a piece of ye. But now I crave all of ye; I want everyting, na jus da *aingeal* part," he says, wiping his mouth like he is trying to wipe away the words he just spoke to me.

"I want to come with you when you talk to Finn. Please?" I ask, putting my hand on his arm to stop him from leaving without me.

"I'm na going after yer soul mate. He probably canna help himself," Brennus says reluctantly. "If he comes here, I will deal wi' him, but truly, he is da last of me problems."

"I believe you, but I still want to come with you. I need to learn everything I can from you. You're an expert on strategy and you know my enemy well. I have no idea what Casimir will do next, but you have some idea, don't you? Teach me. Please," I beg again.

Brennus' face changes when he sees that I'm absolutely sincere. I need someone to teach me how to fight my enemies. I cannot sit back and hope to be protected any longer.

"Whah do yer instincts tell ye about dem?" Brennus asks, linking his arm with mine as we walk from the office. I squeeze his arm gratefully as we enter the sitting room and are met by Finn and my personal guard. "Let's convene in da kirk," Brennus says to them, and when I look at him in confusion, he says, "Da Knight's Bar, as ye so aptly named it."

We walk the corridor together arm-in-arm, while I think about what Brennus had asked me. When Brennus opens the doors next to the medieval suits of armor, I step into the softly lit chapel. Brennus seats me at a table and then goes to the bar. He pours me a glass of a clear liqueur. Sipping it, it tastes a little bit like black licorice.

"I don't know what Casimir will do, but…" I trail off, taking another sip and feeling a little calmer. "He is kind of a snob, isn't he?" I ask as Brennus sits next to me. "He looks down on Powers and Gancanagh, like you're beneath him, which I really can't figure out because he is the one who reeks like rotten garbage."

Brennus smiles. "So, whah does dat tell ye about how he will proceed?" he asks me, lifting his eyebrow in question as he leans back in his chair studying me.

"Well, he doesn't seem the type that enjoys getting his hands dirty. After meeting him, I'm surprised that he even deigned to come here himself. He must really want me…or he really needs me for some reason. He was willing to come here alone and take the risk to bargain for me himself. It makes me wonder if the higher ups are breathing down his neck. He kept saying 'we' and at first I thought that maybe he uses it like the royal 'we' to mean himself, but now I don't think so. I think he is truly reporting to someone else," I pause and take another sip of my drink.

"Good," Brennus says encouragingly.

"So he is a 'snob' and he 'doesn't like to get his hands dirty,'" Finn recaps. "Whah will he do?" he asks me.

"He will look for someone else to do the dirty work for him," I respond. Then I turn to Brennus and say, "Need teaches the plan. He will try to cultivate an ally within."

"She warms da heart, does she na?" Declan says, like a proud papa.

"Whah lengths will he go ta?" Brennus asks me.

"Huh?" I ask.

"How far will he go wi' dis plan?" Brennus restates the question.

"I don't know. Do you?" I counter.

"I do," he says. "Casimir told me dat he sent da Ifrits ta search for ye. He wouldna have done dat unless he plans ta go ta any length ta have ye or ta see ye dead."

"So, if a traitor cannot get me out alive, he will turn assassin?" I ask, feeling ill.

"Casimir wants ye, but he is willing ta see ye dead if he cannot control ye. I have na seen dem so concerned about anyting like dey are wi' ye," Brennus says, and his words chill me. I take another large gulp of my drink, trying to get rid of the goose bumps that are running the length of my body again. "When he fails wi' his plan to kidnap ye, den whah will he do?" Brennus asks me.

I look over at him, feeling surprise that he asked me that question.

Brennus smiles encouragingly. "Ye have ta keep looking ahead—keep anticipating da future moves. Staying ahead of yer enemy is how ye win."

"Uh, okay," I reply, thinking. "Well, if I'm Casimir, I have been sitting in a stinky hole, waiting for someone to deliver that irritating angel to me and when she doesn't show, I come out of my hole…like an angry wasp, looking to bust some heads? Toting my army with me?" I ask them, looking at all of their faces.

The fellas all start laughing again. "Maybe," Brennus says, grinning. "Anyone else have any ideas?"

Finn leans forward in his chair. "He tries again, but dis time, he comes ta Genevieve. He is staying away from Sheol for now—letting da stink wear off and keeping a low profile from the divine Powers who would like ta tear him apart. He wants ta come ta her as a friend, a savior. He will protect her from da bad Gancanagh—da ones dat tried to kill her, hoping she doesn't know he is da one who sent da Ifrit," Finn says, while watching me.

"I've got some candy for you, little girl?" I ask Finn, understanding what he is teaching me.

Finn's eyebrow rises cunningly. "Or, I'm really na a wolf, little girl, jus disregard dese fangs, would yous?" Finn replies wi' a wink.

"Or he starts recruiting again," Declan counters, "but dis time from da outside. He doesn't want ta bring his army—dere's too much risk dat da divine angels will get wind o' it and be dere ta do deir jobs. But if he uses non-angels, dat may buy him some time—where da Divine are concerned. Dey are na so concerned about whah, say, da trolls are doing. It could stir dem up, but na like da Fallen amassing."

"Come on! Trolls!" I exclaim, irritated. "The ones that smell like arse and have really sharp teeth that will tear you apart if you get too close to them?" I ask, looking at Eion.

"Dey do na have purple hair either," Eion says, pointing at me. "Dey are usually bald or dey have jus little tufts of hair comin' out of dere ears."

"Gross," I mutter.

"And troll breath…" Eion goes on before I hold up my hand.

"I get it," I say exasperatedly. "What kills a troll?"

"*Gula*," they all say in unison.

"Gluttony?" I ask, translating the Latin they spoke.

I must look confused because Finn says, "It depends on da troll. Ye have ta find out whah dey canna resist, and den ye give dem more of it den dey can possibly handle."

Still confused, I look at Brennus and his face breaks into a sexy smile. "If a troll canna resist a beer, ye give him a tousand of dem. He will drink himself ta death in a matter of hours," Brennus explains. "If dat does na work, den ye cut his head off. Fire is no good. Dey have skin more resistant den ours ta it."

"Huh," I say, trying to process this new information.

"Steps?" Brennus asks the group.

"Watch for da disgruntled, some of da new fellas—da ones who have da crap jobs," Lachlan chimes in. "Ye smell anyone dat smells foul, like dey have been talkin' ta da Sheol Shiners, ye pound him 'til he squeals."

"The Sheol Shiners?" I ask Lachlan.

"Da pretty boys from Hell," he smiles at me, speaking of the fallen Seraphim.

"What defeats the Sheol Shiners?" I ask him, seeing him tilt his head, considering my question.

"*Superbia*," Lachlan replies, meaning pride.

"*Vanitas*," Faolan adds, meaning vanity.

"*Invidia*," Declan says, meaning envy.

"*Iram*," Eion chimes in, meaning wrath.

"*Avaritiae*," Finn says, meaning avarice.

"*Libidinem*," Brennus says, meaning lust.

"What defeats me?" I whisper to Brennus.

"*Tristitiae*," Brennus softly utters the word that means "sorrow." "Especially when 'tis da sorrow or suffering of someone dat ye love."

My throat tightens because I know that he is right. Gently, he places his hand over mine on the table. A sad smile comes to my lips when I say, "You have a lot to teach me."

"Dat I do," Brennus agrees, lifting my hand to his lips and kissing it. "Ye need me, whether ye tink ye do or na."

"Steps," I say, reminding him that we have issues to discuss.

Brennus' eyes soften in amusement. "Finn, make sure we know who Casimir plans ta cultivate as outside allies. Send da word out dat we are in da business of making dem jus as happy as da Seraphim are ta remain loyal ta us—more willing." Brennus instructs.

To me, he says, "Information is da key. We try ta be respectful ta da other beings out dere, insomuch as we can be respectful, so dey tend ta reciprocate, insomuch as dey can reciprocate. Most demons and lower beings are tired of da Seraphim. It makes it easier."

"I think that is called the 'Golden Rule,' Brennus. 'Do unto others as you would have them do unto you,'" I say with a crooked smile.

Faolan looks at me strangely, asking, "Dat's a rule? Den whah's da 'Silver Rule?'"

Before I can answer, Eion chimes in, "Da 'Silver Rule' must be whah ye do when the 'Golden Rule' does na work. It must be, 'Kill all da others before dey kill all of yous.'"

Lachlan smiles at me and says, "Da 'Golden Rule' should really be, 'Ye will bleed if ye do na do whah I'm telling ye.'"

I roll my eyes at them and Brennus smiles at me possessively. "We need ta tighten da security. We lock da corridors from now on. Only fellas dat have business in da North or West Towers are ta be dere. Post only well-trusted fellas at da doors, but do na trust dem either," Brennus orders Declan.

"Do ye want more personal security for da queen?" Declan asks Brennus.

"NO!" I respond, looking from Declan to Brennus. "Four is enough. I'm used to you guys. I don't want more fellas staring at me. Can't we just get cameras on the door or something?" I ask and they laugh.

"Anyone can get a feed on da cameras. Even closed-circuit can be breeched and den dey know everyting," Brennus says. "We will need ta question everyone dat comes near ye for a while. Do na assume dat dey have business dere. Challenge dem ta prove why dey are dere."

"I think it's time you showed me how to use that axe you gave me, Brennus," I say quietly. "How about joining us in the war room when you're free?" I ask him, looking up from my clenched hands.

"'Tis na a bad idea, *mo chroí*," he says, covering my hands with his large, cool one. "We will begin tomorrow. We will see ta it."

I nod as the meeting adjourns.

Just after nightfall, I crawl into bed, hugging the pillow tight to me. As I lie there, I try to will myself to sleep immediately, so that I won't think about all the scary things I learned today. I don't want to analyze my future because it's grim. The possibilities of winding up steeped in evil are endless. I have to prepare myself for the worst-case scenario. I have to be prepared for Casimir getting me. I need to decide now if I allow that to happen, or if I take option B, like I chose in the caves in Houghton. I can't let Brennus turn me and I can't let Casimir have my soul for eternity.

My life is so out of control now. If I try to leave my new home, I put everyone I love at risk again—Casimir will try to figure out a way to kidnap or kill me. I have managed to remain cool all day, not letting anyone around me see how afraid I am. It's been like trying to tread water while holding a brick in my hands.

My heart is begging me to try to find a way out of this place. I need Reed and I need Russell, probably more than they need me. But, there is something so right about letting the Fallen and the Gancanagh battle each other, while keeping my angels safe. I'm just afraid that I will lose Reed and Russell forever if I get caught in the middle of it.

Maybe that's a good thing, my mind whispers to me. *Maybe they are better off without you.* Tears blind me, so I close my eyes and let them leak from beneath my lashes. *Is there really any question that they would be safer without me?* I think.

Exhaustion finally makes me sleep and I am having the best dream about Reed when I begin to wake up from it. As I try desperately to cling to the dream, I feel fluttering butterflies in my stomach, like he is here with me and it's the sweetest torture. Refusing to open my eyes, fearing that it will be gone the moment I do, I breathe in deeply, smelling his sexy scent that causes a primal ache to spread throughout my body. I become aware of warm arms around my waist, pressing me back into an equally warm chest, my heartbeat races within me.

I open my eyes to the predawn light of the room and I glance behind me, seeing Reed holding me tenderly in his arms. There is a storm of emotion in his dark green eyes, but I immediately have to turn away, not because I want to, but because some force within me is making me. It's the magical contract.

Reed is here!

He is so close to me and all of my senses are screaming out to touch him, to taste him, to tell him that I want him—I need him—I crave him—that I'm sorry for what I have done to him, but I can't move now. I can't turn to him or speak to him. It's like I have no free will. I am a prisoner within my own body. A thousand thoughts pulse in my head, but there is nothing I can do. My jaw is clenched tight, my throat is taut, and I can only breath in shallow breaths now.

"Evie, love, I know that you can't speak to me—it's part of the deal that you made to save Russell," Reed breathes quickly in my ear, while I remain still, an unwilling statue of apparent indifference to the beautiful creature next to me. "That does not mean that *I* cannot speak to *you*," he says in his sexiest voice.

I close my eyes, savoring the feeling of his arms around me, the scent of his skin pressing to mine.

He nuzzles my neck. "I'm sorry that it took me so long to find you," he says, while running his lips softly over my skin.

An ache of longing breaks out inside of me, wanting to kiss him back, but I can't.

"The temptation to pick you up right now and carry you away with me is nearly overwhelming," Reed says with torment in his voice. "If I take you from here, you will be trapped inside yourself…you would remain like this, not eating or sleeping until you were returned to him or we found a way to break the contract…or you died," Reed explains. "It's too great a risk, without a sure means of breaking the contract."

His fingers smooth my hair back from my neck, trailing a line down it and over my shoulder, to pass slowly down my arm, making me shiver.

"I have missed you—every moment that you have been here has been…I need you, Evie," he says in a near whisper, kissing the curve of my shoulder.

A tear escapes my lashes to run down my cheek.

"Don't cry," he breathes, hugging me tight, while wiping the tear gently from my cheek with the back of his hand. "I will find a way to get you out of this. Trust me, I will. You are mine and I will never give up. I promise you."

I want to tell him that I believe him—that I trust him. I want him more than I have ever wanted anything. Just hearing his voice makes me want to fight harder for him.

"I think that I have come up with a way for you to communicate with us. This contract will make it seem as if you are locked inside yourself when I am near, but I think that Russell can speak to you, from within you. I will ask him to try. He has been working with Phaedrus. He can control his clones now. He will send one to you soon. If he can step into you, maybe the two of you can speak from within you, where they cannot stop you. Tell us your plans, what you have seen, so that we can help," he says, holding me close, while stroking his hand down my side hypnotically.

Hope kindles in me at his words. He knows about my contract—how it works. He knows that I'm not being cold to him—that I can't respond no matter how desperate I am to react to his touch.

"Keep playing along, Evie. I know that you have probably figured out that we only have a few months left before Brennus has to find another way to keep you with him," Reed says.

Inside, I rejoice that he understands that, too. He is aware that Brennus has no intention of ever letting me go.

"Make him believe that he is becoming what you want. What you desire. Lull him into complacency. Make him believe that you are outgrowing me. Do whatever you have to do to survive. Anything, so that he doesn't try to turn you," Reed advises me in a whisper.

Holding me in his arms, his exquisite body is spooning mine, as he inhales the scent of my hair. I want to lie here forever with him, just the two of us.

"I'm sorry that I was not there when everything was falling apart," he whispers and I hear pain in his tone as he speaks of Valentine. "I was too late…I won't be too late again," he promises, like he is choking on the words. "Hold on to the string, love, until the current shifts and we can be together again." His words, spoken so urgently, bring tears to my eyes again.

My eyes widen as I hear footsteps coming down the hall. I want to scream to him that he has to go. He has to leave before one of the fellas finds him here and touches him.

REED, RUN! My brain screams in panic, but I can't make a sound, I can't move to even tell him with my eyes.

"This is for you," he says against my ear as he presses a scrap of paper under one of the feathers of my wing, "for when it becomes hard to breathe."

The door of my sitting room opens and someone enters the outer room, turning towards my bedroom door. Reed rises quickly from my bed, uncapping a bottle of perfume; he splashes some on me and on the bed before smashing the bottle on the floor and diving to the open window. Instantly, I turn towards the window, seeing that he is gone as the door of my room opens and Brennus steps in.

"Whah happened?" he asks suspiciously, sniffing the air. Seeing the broken perfume bottle on the floor, he asks, "*Mo chroí?*"

I don't answer him; I just stare at him, hoping that he won't detect Reed's scent. I have to give my angel time to get away. Pulling the blanket up to my chest, I look grimly at Brennus who is frowning at me.

"Are ye crying?" he asks me as his eyes soften with concern. Brennus walks to my side and sits in the exact place where Reed had been just seconds ago. My heart palpitates in my chest as fear for Reed makes me ill.

"Whah's wrong, 'tis jus perfume. Ye can have another one," Brennus says tenderly, reaching over to cup my cheek.

"I..." I say, before breaking into a sob. Brennus pulls me into his cold chest, letting me cry.

"Are ye afraid?" he asks, and I nod because I am.

Seeing Reed again has left me feeling like I can't last one more second without him. The ache inside of me feels like it will soon get so bad that there will be no point in surviving. It's like he just reminded me why I'm alive. It's to be with him and now that I can't do that I feel crushed.

"I will protect ye. Casimir will na have ye. Ye do na have ta be afraid," he says, rubbing my back to comfort me.

I sniff, trying to stop crying. *Brennus doesn't know that Reed was here. He can't smell him.*

That is what the perfume was for, to cover the scent of him. I will have to begin carrying some around. If Reed is planning to have Russell send me a clone, I will have to mask the scent of it. It will smell just like Russell does, lingering in the air for them to detect.

"I'm all right, Brenn," I say, trying to pull myself together. "I'll be fine...I'm going to take a shower now."

"I'll order ye some coffee. Would ye like dat?" he asks.

"Mmmm," I nod with a watery smile.

I walk to the door of the bathroom and I pull it closed behind me. As I lean against it, I listen for sounds in my room, but I hear nothing. After I turn the shower on, I move to the vanity. I pull the scrap of paper from beneath the feather of my wing where Reed had placed it, I unfold it, reading the message written on it in Reed's beautiful script.

It's the quote from Shakespeare: *Doubt thou the stars are fire; Doubt that the sun doth move; Doubt truth to be a liar; But never doubt I love...I love thee best, O most best, believe it.*

Reed loves me...he still loves me, my mind whispers like a prayer. I have tried for the last two months not to let fear and doubt overwhelm me. But, having proof that Reed still loves me, even after I shut him out, is making tears spill from my eyes again. I hide the paper under one of the perfume bottles on the vanity before I enter the shower and let the water wash away my tears.

Reed came here to fight for me. He wants me to continue to fight for us, so that I won't give up and just let them make me an undead creature. He could've just let Russell come here and speak to me, but he didn't. He risked everything to tell me himself. He entered the lair of hundreds of killers to show me what I mean to him. He's...insane. The most perfectly insane creature ever created...and he's still mine.

But for now, I can't have Reed. He wants me to lull Brennus into complacency so that he can find a way to get me out of here. I will have to try to do that. I have to use the weapons I have, thinking about what Buns taught me about feminine mystique. I am going to make it really hard for him to kill me—to let any piece of me get away from him.

At the same time, I have to learn how to run with the darker side of this world. To think like them—to kill like them. If I had remained with Reed, I would have allowed him to take care of me. I would have let him kill for me—protect me. Now, I have to learn how to kill...and mean it. Brennus may be the best one to teach me how to do that, since he seems to be so good at it.

I dry myself off quickly, and then I pull the piece of paper from beneath the perfume bottle. I tuck it back under one of my feathers and make sure that the edges of it don't show, and then I dress in a workout outfit. I head directly to Brennus' office and find him seated behind his desk.

"Planning a hostile takeover, Brenn?" I ask, breezing into the room.

As I walk to Brennus, I force myself to give him a quick kiss on his cold cheek before sitting at the table and pouring myself a cup of coffee. Glancing up at him, he looks a little shocked by my affectionate greeting.

"Every takeover is hostile," Brennus replies, snapping out of the stupor and grinning at me, "or dey would call it surrender."

"Good point," I say, sipping my coffee that has gotten better than when I first got here.

Maybe the staff in the kitchen has turned over, I think grimly.

I smile at Brennus. "You remember that you promised to teach me to fight, starting today," I remind him. "You should change or I'll ruin that beautiful suit," I quirk my eyebrow in challenge, eyeing his exquisite dark suit that fits him like his own skin.

"I'm afraid I will have ta meet ye later. I have a meeting planned for dis morning," he says, coming around his desk and sitting next to me at the small table where my breakfast is spread out.

"Who are you meeting?" I ask, feeling his leg brush mine under the table.

"Da leader of da Werree," Brennus replies, watching me pour a little milk on my oatmeal.

"The Weary?" I ask, wrinkling my nose.

"Na Weeree, Werree," he says, making it sound almost the same.

"The Wary?" I ask, seeing his light green eyes soften as I try to understand him. "Wary? Like 'to be cautious?'"

"'Tis," he replies. "Dat's probably how dey got deir names, because dat's exactly whah ye have ta be around dem."

"What's a Wary?" I ask.

"A Werree is a craitur dat ye do na want ta meet. 'Tis best dat ye eat yer breakfast and go wi' da fellas," he says, looking at his watch.

"Why? Are they mean or something?" I ask, feeling a pang of dread. "Maybe I should stay with you." Thinking I may need to protect him.

"No, dey are envious," he replies.

"Describe one for me," I ask, trying to picture a Werree. "What are they like?"

"Depends on da Werree, but I suppose da best way ta describe dem is dat dey are like scarecrows," Brennus says. Goose bumps rise on my arms instantly. "Dey find a trait dat dey envy, and dey take it from whoever has it. So dey look cobbled together…like a scarecrow who takes da castoffs of someone else."

"WHAT!" I ask him, putting down my spoon before it reaches my mouth, feeling instantly cold inside.

"Some of dem appear grotesque. 'Tis like dey do na know whah looks good together. So, dey may take da arms off of a extremely powerful ogre, but den put it on a smaller body, so dat da proportion does na look right…or a feminine head on a masculine body…ye know whah I am saying?"

"You mean, they steal body parts from other beings and swap them out for their own body parts?" I ask, pushing my bowl of oatmeal from me. Fear at the thought of a creature like that coming here is making my stomach hurt.

"Dat is exactly right. I do na want dem ta see ye. Dere are so many tings about ye dat dey could covet—yer eyes, yer skin, yer hair, yer wings…" he says, reaching out and stroking my wing reverently.

"You are not going to be alone with it, are you?" I ask, fear bleeding into my tone.

"I have nuting dat a Werree would want, *mo chroí*," he says, his beautiful face looking less pale in the soft lighting of the office.

"You have a nice face," I murmur, reaching out and touching his cheek gently.

Studying him, there are no lines of imperfection in his immortal skin. *He has the kind of beauty that draws you in at first glance and keeps you enchanted forever.*

My touch is affecting him, as the darkness in his eyes grows with desire. I whisper, "Do not let the Werree covet your face… I'm growing accustomed to it."

Brennus stills. "He couldna take it. He will be me slave if he tries ta touch me…his flesh canna abide mine. Ye are still da only being I have met dat can withstand whah I am—ye and da other," he says, looking completely happy about what I just said to him.

"I never thought I would say this but, 'good,'" I reply, leaning forward slowly and kissing his lips lightly, feeling the cool texture of them against mine.

Brennus groans then, leaning into me and putting his hand on the back of my neck. His other hand snakes behind my back, scooping me off of my chair and onto his lap. He deepens our kiss, demanding more from me than I am prepared to offer. I am just about to pull away from him, when I hear *click*. It makes Brennus pull back from me.

When I open my eyes, I see heat in his. "Hungry?" I whisper to him, rubbing my nose gently against his.

"Ye offering?" he asks with a sensual smile, cupping my face with his hands and using his thumb to brush over my bottom lip.

My heartbeat increases, feeling a pull towards him. "Sure, there is still plenty of oatmeal left. It's yummy," I tease him, nipping at his thumb. I know I am playing with fire as I use my finger to trace his bottom lip.

"Do na play wi' me, *mo chroí*. Ye will lose," he warns me softly, before nuzzling my neck, making my heartbeat dance wildly in my chest.

"And then you will have just an empty cage, Brennus, if you kill the bird," I whisper as I feel his sharp teeth press against my neck.

The pressure increases for a moment, and I tense, ready to try to fight him off and get to my stash of blood. Brennus rests his lips against my neck, as if deliberating, then he pulls them away from my throat, retracting his fangs and smiling at me, but it looks like more of a grimace than a smile.

"Ye are a dark, wicked little ting, wrapped in a sweet, naïve *aingeal*. It's hard ta say whah I love da most about ye," he says, his eyes softening.

"You love the sweet part the most, or you would have killed me already," I reply, feeling his reluctance to let me go as I rise from his lap, and begin moving towards his office door.

That was just too close, I think, feeling like I just barely escaped a trap. I meant to try to lull him into complacency, but I think I pushed him a little farther than either of us intended to go. He is way too smart to take anything at face value. He will need proof that I love him before he becomes complacent enough to break our contract. I just don't know how I can prove something like that to him.

How do you make a demon believe that you love him? I wonder, listening to the soft chuckle coming from Brennus behind me as he watches me retreat.

Finding the fellas waiting for me in the hallway, I say to Declan, "Brennus has a meeting planned with a Werree this morning."

"I hope dey have orders ta lock up da wans," Eion remarks to Lachlan as we start down the hall towards the West Tower. "I like me wans wi' deir heads still attached."

Stopping in my tracks, I turn to Declan. "Okay, that's just too creepy," I say as a massive shiver runs the length of my body. "Someone has to stay with Brennus. I'm not letting a Werree make a toupee out of Brennus' scalp."

"Whah did she jus say?" Eion asks Lachlan, scratching his head.

"I said, someone protect Brennus' back or I am staying here and meeting the Werree myself," I reply, crossing my arms in front of me.

"Ah no ye're na," Declan says sternly. "Dat's da last ting we need. Dat ting sees ye and 'twill be lucky if he leaves wi' whahever he came in wi'. We will have ta kill him, and since he is likely coming ta give us intel on da Seraphim, dat's na going ta help atall."

"Eion," I say, but looking at Eion's confused face I change my mind. "Faolan, please stay here with Brennus—at least until Finn gets here. I don't want him to be alone. Please?"

"Ye are worried about him," Declan says softly.

"No. Don't be silly—it's self-preservation. Magical Faerie contract, remember?" I ask, feeling myself blush.

"Ye lie," Declan accuses, smiling.

"Fay...just stay with him," I plead, while placing my hand gently on Faolan's arm.

Click. Faolan's fangs shoot forward in his mouth. "Banjax," he says, looking at Declan.

Declan scowls and shakes his head. "Ah, ye might as well stay now. Maybe after, ye can feed before ye come back," he says, before he looks at me and points his finger accusingly. "Oy, no touching da fellas. Ye're too tempting."

"Sorry," I wince, letting go of Faolan's arm contritely. "Thank you, Fay."

As I stride down the hallways with Lachlan, Declan, and Eion, I can't shake the eerie feeling I have been having since leaving Brennus' office. Everything is the same. We pass by several fellas on our way to my tower and they all step aside, allowing us to pass them, but the goose bumps have not receded on my arms. I feel stalked.

I wait beside Declan as he whispers the words to open the doors to the West Tower. A dark shadow catches my eyes and I think for a second that I am watching my own shadow pass me by to enter through the doorway without me. No one else seems to notice it. My eyes grow big and my mouth goes instantly dry. As Declan takes a step forward, my hand grabs his upper arm and stops him from entering the passage ahead of us.

The look of annoyance crosses his face until his eyes meet mine. I stammer, "I...I, shoot, I left my...my iPod back in my room...I can't train without it. We have to go back and get it, Deck." My hand is like a vise on his arm.

I pull him back with me from the threshold of the door. Seeing Eion about to enter, my other hand lurches out to grab him and pull him back into Lachlan. Declan's fangs engage instantly, catching on to what I'm telling him. Eion and Lachlan quickly follow suit as we all back up from the doors in a defensive posture.

A signal sounds, like a distant scream, causing the darkness that had appeared to be shadows shrouding the interior to my tower to move forward *en masse*. I can now discern a score or more distinct shadows separating from their hiding places on the ground and walls.

"Werree," Declan mutters and a chill runs over my skin as we continue to back away from them.

"What kills them, Deck?" I whisper urgently to him.

"Disembodied like dis, ye need magic ta hurt dem," he says, before getting in front of me to block them from lunging at me as we move back.

Dark, twisting shapes scurry over the deep-red tapestries lining the walls on either side of us. Following the progression of the inky bodies to the ceiling, three of them attempt to get over us, either to get behind us, or to drop on us from above.

Two of the shadows make a lunge for Lachlan, but they fall back as flaming light bursts forth from Lachlan's hands, setting them on fire. But, it's not like real flames; it's more like magical light with no physical heat. The effect of it, however, seems to be more than sufficient to stop them as they drop to the ground, writhing.

Several of the awful, faceless Werree stop just inside the doorway ahead of us. Planting their feet like archers, they poise before us, aiming shadowy bows with black, wicked arrows. The weapons look like extensions of them, since it's all comprised of their "essence."

Declan immediately whispers magical words, erecting a barrier between the Werree and the two of us, but Lachlan and Eion are using their own magic to battle the ones ahead of them, so Declan can't cover them, too. Declan tries to warn them at the last moment.

"Arrows," he cries.

The dark, shadowy, shafts make no noise as they spiral through the air, striking Lachlan in the chest and making him stagger backward. Eion goes immediately to Lachlan as he falls to the floor. Grasping Lachlan by his shoulders, Eion pulls him backward, continuing our retreat. Lachlan's jaw clenches in agony while he attempts to grasp an arrow shaft adorning him, but it slips through his fingers like the night sky.

My feet freeze beneath me and I stop retreating. Lachlan's back arches in pain, as his arm stretches out to Eion for help to remove the arrows. Eion continues to shield him, trying to protect him from the freaky archers who are drawing back and aiming to shoot at us again.

As I pull energy in the room to me, I feel the Werree fighting me for it. They are trying to block me from creating a spell, but the more I concentrate, the more the energy is flowing to me, like it wants to come to me instead of to them.

"Get behind me, Deck," I pant. The intensity of the energy I have pulled into myself burns me.

"Whah?" Declan scowls. But then he feel the energy I'm pulling towards me beginning to shift, because he retreats to a position behind me.

Without any time to create a spell, a thought occurs to me and I latch on to it. Softly, I sing, "Ring around the rosy A pocket full of posies, Ashes, ashes, They all fall down."

When I finish the singsong nursery rhyme, I flip the switch on the energy, just as Brennus taught me, expelling it from my body. A rippling current explodes out of me, striking the Werree ahead of me. Their murky figures darken to a pitch-black hue. Slowly, their bodies begin crumbling to ash while a desolate wind blows through the corridor, sending the scattered remains of several of my victims to cover everything with a coating of grit.

The Werree that I have missed with my spell, stop dead in their tracks. The same kind of scream issues from one of them. It is a signaled retreat. The shadows creeping on the ceiling continue their movements over our heads, beetling above us towards the North Tower.

As I close my eyes to attempt another spell, a sharp, piercing pain stops me as it twists in my side. When I glance down, there is nothing there to indicate that I have been hit, except for the blood that begins to seep out of my abdomen.

"Deck?" I say in confusion, placing my hand on my hip and trying to stop the blood.

He hisses near me, smelling my blood while a look of longing crosses his face. Eion, on the other side of me still holds Lachlan, but he freezes, seeing the blood on my hands as it flows from between my clenched fingers.

"It's Brennus—he's been hurt," I whisper.

Another stab of pain spreads through my shoulder, causing a circle of red to appear on my shirt as I double over in agony.

"Banjax!" Declan mutters, before covering his mouth and nose with his hand. Speaking through his hand, he orders, "Get ta yer tower. When ye are in, seal da door shut and find a place ta hide until ye heal. Eion and me will take care of da few Werree dat are left, and den we will see ta Brennus. Can ye make it dere on yer own?" he asks, still trying to block the aroma of my open wounds.

I nod before I pivot and stumble back towards the West Tower, away from Eion who is watching me like a cat watches a mouse. Moving toward the door where my enemies, the Werree, just formulated their attack on us, I assess the area behind me in short bursts to make sure that no Werree are there to jump on me. I also have to keep Eion in my sights because he is having trouble letting me retreat.

Eion's hands are balled into fists as he hangs on to Lachlan's shirt now like an anchor. He's panting with the exertion it's taking him to remain crouched near his fallen friend and not pursue the meal that is backing away from him on trembling legs.

Losing the battle to remain where he is, Eion shoots up out of his crouch, and begins to move with stealthy grace towards me. Fear makes the blood drain away from my face as I bump into the wall at my back, near the doorway to my tower. I feel frozen, not knowing if I should try to fight him off, run, or try a spell.

He's my friend, I don't want to hurt him, I think feebly.

I flinch when a warm hand reaches around the doorway that leads to my tower. It pulls me through the archway effortlessly and into a tight embrace before the door slams shut between Eion and me.

Whispering softly in my ear, I hear Reed say against my hair, "I have you, love. I'm here."

CHAPTER 18

My Angel

"Zee, block the door. Russell, help Zee, and then meet me upstairs in Evie's tower," Reed barks out orders. He reaches his arm down and lifts me off my feet to hold me close to his chest. I can't move now, since Reed is here I have to retreat inside myself due to the contract. "We took care of the rest of the Werree in here, love." Reed says, kissing my cheek as his incredible scent settles around me.

I wonder how he did that without magic, but I can't ask him. I'm a prisoner inside myself, as I lay listless in Reed's arms.

Reed's strong wings elevate us from the floor as he flies us to the doors with the angel wings carved into them: my tower rooms. He pushes the doors open and leaves them wide for Zee and Russell to follow us in. Reed seems to know where to go as he lifts us into the air again, flying to the highest level of my archive: my bedroom. We land easily on the platform and he strides to the bed, easing me onto it.

He tears my shirt from me, exposing the bleeding cuts that feel like someone stabbed me with a bayonet. Pulling the sheet from beneath me, Reed shreds it in strips, wrapping one tightly around my waist. He then binds my shoulder, pulling it tighter than I think is absolutely necessary. I scream out in my mind, but otherwise I make no sound.

"That will stop the bleeding. You should heal now," Reed murmurs to me, placing a blanket over me.

I'm fighting for air now. The pain from being magically stabbed is nothing compared with the fear I have for Reed,

Russell, and Zee. *What are they doing here? They have to get out of here before the Werree or the Gancanagh converge on us.*

"RED!" Russell yells, panting a little as he bursts from the stairwell to my room.

I can't see him, my head is turned away from the stairs, but just hearing his voice is taking some of the pain that I feel away, replacing it with worry.

"How is she?" Russell asks Reed as he kneels down in front of my eyes so that I can see him.

His beautiful, brown eyes are concerned, well, what I can see of them because his hair is long and getting in his eyes. I want to brush it back for him and tell him that he should get a haircut.

Reed comes to kneel next to Russell, so that I can see both of them. Staring into their lovely faces, I want so much to throw my arms around them and tell them both how much I miss them…that I love them, but I can't.

"We should've let that creepy Gancanagh bite her. Then we could've killed him and taken her outta here," Russell says to Reed.

Reed speaks rapidly to Russell, saying, "I thought about that, but she's wounded. I didn't want to take the chance that he'd drain her quickly because she already lost a lot of blood. He is one of her personal guard. That means he's elite, an excellent fighter. We need to get a lesser Gancanagh: one that has recently been turned. If we take him and then starve him for a few days, he'll bite anything we tell him to, even his forbidden queen. Then, it will be easy to pull him off of her and destroy him before he can really hurt her, but we need to do it with assurances that we'll be able to get her blood to drink and then protect her as we escape."

"I get it, ya can't touch them and ya think I couldn't take that stinky bastard myself," Russell says with a grim look, translating.

Neither Russell nor Reed is wearing any protective armor against the touch of the Gancanagh. It's like they were caught off guard and not able to put it on.

"Zee, are they coming?" Reed asks Zephyr who is somewhere below us.

"Not yet," Zephyr replies, sounding calm. "I'll let you know when they get in the West Tower corridor."

"Do you think you can do it now, Russell?" Reed asks. "You have to be fast. I doubt we have much time. Brennus knows she's bleeding and he knows he has to get to her before one of his men does."

"Yeah, I'm ready," Russell says, sitting down in front of me and closing his eyes.

I watch in silence as Russell's face loses some of the concern and begins to look calm. All at once, a golden, glowing image of Russell steps out of his body, turning towards me. As Russell's image enters my body, I hear his voice say aloud and in my head, "Ah Red, shoot…Reed, she needs some pain killers and can ya please loosen the bandage on her shoulder, yer cuttin' off her circulation." It is like he is speaking in stereo.

Reed immediately loosens the binding on my shoulder, saying, "I'm sorry, love. Is this better?"

I think, *Yes, thank you.*

"She said, 'Yes, thank you,'" Russell says to Reed.

You can hear me, Russell! I shout in my head, elation hitting me in waves.

"Yeah, I can hear ya," Russell says aloud, grimacing. "I can feel what yer feelin', too."

Okay, I think as my brain begins to tumble over itself, trying to figure out where to begin to explain to him all that has been happening. Images of things that have happened flash rapidly in my mind…Molly and Finn, Brennus and the gathering of fellas in the hall, the Gancanagh archive room with the singing weapons, my meeting with Casimir and his attempt to bargain for me, receiving Russell's clone while wrapped in Brennus' arms, the strategy meeting with Brennus and the fellas, lying with Reed in my bed this morning, Brennus at breakfast, and then the Werree attack. Image after image pulses in my mind and it's taking a toll on Russell. His face looks pale and shocked.

"Yer killin' me, Red, slow down…" Russell mutters in pain.

"What is it?" Reed asks Russell urgently.

Russell shakes his heads. "Ya don't want to know half of it, Reed," Russell says with a frown. "Do ya know Casimir?" Russell asks him.

A growl escapes Reed. "Did he come here? Does he know you're here?" Reed asks me, putting his hand on my brow and sweeping my hair away. His green eyes look haunted and I know I have to explain what has been going on.

I tell Russell: *He came here to bargain for me, but Brennus told him I'm not for sale, at any price. Casimir warned Brennus that he should turn me over to him. I think he probably sent the Werree. They were coming here to give Brennus intel, but they attacked us instead. Brennus thinks that Casimir will go to any length to either get control of me or kill me so that I'm no longer a threat to the Fallen. But, we haven't figured out why they are so threatened by me,* I think and then listen as Russell translates what I'm thinking word-for-word to Reed.

Reed's eyebrows draw together in thought. "We saw the Werree arrive this morning while we were preparing to have Russell send you his clone. Zee, Russell, and I watched them shed their flesh suits outside. They only do that when they're planning to attack. They cannot remain outside of their suits for long, they need them to survive, but they're more agile outside of them," Reed explains.

How did you kill them without magic? I wonder.

"She wants to know how we killed the ones in her tower," Russell says.

"Sunlight kills them. That's why they came before the sun came up, they cannot be without their flesh suits in the sun," Reed explains. He pulls a mirror from the pocket of his jeans and angles it towards my face, flashing light on it. "We didn't have time to put our armor on after we saw them. We just had to take our chances."

That was stupid. Don't ever take your chances again, I think.

"She just called ya stupid," Russell says, grinning.

"Company's coming," Zee utters from below. "They just entered the West Tower."

"Okay, Zee," Reed says over his shoulder. "You have to take Russell and leave now. I'll follow you in a minute."

"I love you, Red," Russell says out loud and it echoes in my head.

I love you, too, Russell, I reply desperately in my mind. *Please tell Reed that I love him, too...and Zee and Buns and Brownie.* And then, my mind says things to Russell that I would never say out loud because I know that it's not right to say them...desperate, pleading things. I beg him to stay with me, to make Reed stay with me, not to go and leave me here alone with them again. I tell him how afraid I am of Brennus winning and Casimir coming for me. And then, the worst thing happens: my soul speaks to him, pleading with him to stay with me—to love me—to never let go of me.

In an instant, the connection to Russell ends as he opens his eyes. The pain that I see in them is brutal. It is beyond anything I have ever seen in them as we stare at each other across the small space.

Zephyr lands on the platform and comes to kneel by my side. After kissing my cheek tenderly, he pulls back to look in my eyes, saying, "I have missed you, Evie. I will be back for you–I swear it to you. Just a little longer. Be brave. Buns said to tell you that she loves you and that she will see you soon. Brownie, too."

Straightening up, Zephyr turns to get Russell so that he can fly him out of here. Russell steps back from Zee, pulling his arm back forcefully from him when Zee tries to pick him up.

"Naw, I'm stayin' here," Russell says with his brows drawing together, pushing against Zephyr when he reaches out for him again. Russell's wings arch out as he scowls at Zephyr.

"Do not be stupid, Russell, you cannot stay here," Zephyr replies in a calm manner, like he is talking to a child.

"She needs me! I can't just leave her here alone! I'm stayin'," he says in desperation. He wrenches his arm back again from Zephyr and scowls at him. "Y'all don't understand! She's scared. They're gonna hurt her, break her!" he argues, backing up so that Zee won't be able to just grab him and go.

Zephyr frowns. "We have no choice, Russell," he says. "They will kill us if we stay. I cannot allow myself to be taken by the Gancanagh. If they could turn me, I would be a lethal monster. I have a duty to make sure that does not happen and I have a duty to see that they do not make you a monster as well. So, we must go. I do not want to have to make you leave," he says in a low tone.

"I'M NOT LEAVIN' HER HERE ALONE," Russell shouts, stabbing his finger towards me in agitation.

Tears escape my lashes to drip down my cheeks. I didn't mean to do that to Russell. I don't know how to sensor what I'm thinking so that he can't hear it. Begging him to stay like that is nothing short of torture to him. He has to leave here, before Brennus arrives. If he stays, there is no question that Brennus will kill him this time and maybe Zephyr and Reed, too, if he can get to them.

A loud bang startles me as something pushes against the doors downstairs. Time is up for them. They have to leave now.

"Sorry, Russell," Zephyr mutters, right before he punches him hard in the face. He catches Russell in his arms as Russell falls forward, unconscious. Zee turns to Reed and says in a menacing tone, "Be right behind me. Do not make me come back here for you."

Reed nods to Zee. Zephyr launches into the air, cradling Russell in his arms and flying towards the skylights in the rooftop ceiling. Glass smashes and falls as Zephyr and Russell break through the roof and make it outside.

Kneeling down, Reed looks into my eyes again as he whispers to me, "I will be watching you. We have a plan to break the contract," he says as another loud *crash* sounds from the doors downstairs. "I will smuggle some animal blood in for you. You have to locate places to put it that you can get to quickly, in case you are bitten before we can execute our plan. I will not let him have you. You are mine. We are one. I love you, Evie," he breathes against my lips, and then he brushes his mouth tenderly over mine.

As he pulls back from me he gazes into my eyes. I try hard to scan every detail of his face, so that I can remember it later when he is gone. "I miss the outline of your body pressed to mine and the feel of your breath on my neck when you sleep. I miss the sound of your voice. I need you. I have to go soon, but I will be back for you. I promise you. Then, I will show you that

there is still beauty in the world—not a future full of despair…
I promise you, I will," he says, cupping my cheek as my heart
contracts in my chest.

"Before I go, I'm going to have a conversation with your
warden. Do not worry about me. I will never allow him to touch
me," he says, trying to reassure me.

NO! I scream at him in my mind. *That's completely insane!*
I think, but I'm powerless to do anything but lie here like a
paperweight.

BOOM! The doors to my tower explode open, stealing my
breath from me.

"GENEVIEVE!" Brennus calls from the entrance to my
archive, sounding panicked.

"She is still healing. It's better if you and your brother
remain down there," Reed replies calmly, standing at the balcony railing of my room.

Brennus' tone is unshaken, the gracious host, as he says,
"Look, Finn, 'tis da *aingeal.* I do na remember inviting ye here,
but now dat ye are, why don't ye come down here so dat we can
be properly introduced."

"As much as I would love to, Brennus, I will have to decline
for now. When Evie's contract is not in play, I am hoping that
we can get better acquainted. I will crash your party then."

"No need to crash, I will send ye an invitation," Brennus
replies. He sounds closer, like he has moved forward into the
room and is standing below the balcony on the first floor.

"I have already received a few of your invitations. They are
not very exciting," Reed replies.

"I noticed ye killed da messengers," Brennus replies and I
begin to understand that Brennus has been sending fellas to
kill Reed. "I was hoping ye would want ta come ta more of me
parties. I was afraid ye would refuse ta after da one I hosted for
ye in China," Brennus says with a smile in his tone.

"I had to come to the surprise party that the Werree just
threw for you. Was it funded by Casimir?" Reed asks without
emotion.

"We are working on dat question right now," Brennus
replies, and he sounds closer. "Da Werree dat stabbed me wants

ta tell me everyting, he jus doesna know it yet. Da fellas are working ta remind him right now. I instructed dem na ta touch him wi' dere skin, so dat he can enjoy da pain a little before I find out all I want ta know from him."

"It would seem that we have a common enemy, Brennus," Reed murmurs.

"'Tis true," Brennus agrees. He sounds really close now.

My heart is pounding against the walls of my chest. *What is Reed thinking, letting Brennus get this close to him!*

"If it's Casimir, then you need us. You just tell us where and when," Reed says.

Brennus rises up by the railing in front of Reed, levitating in the air. He is still attired in his dark suit without a hair out of place. Brennus ignores Reed while he floats casually before us. Then, his eyes meet mine. Unable to even sit up on the bed, I am helpless to protect Reed from Brennus' magic or the malevolence in his eyes.

"Whah makes ye tink I need yer help, *aingeal?*" Brennus asks. The energy in the room is shifting, being drawn towards Brennus in crackling waves.

"The stab wounds in *my* angel," Reed replies with his back to me now, standing between Brennus and me.

I can't gauge what Reed's planning to do next. He appears relaxed and focused as he watches Brennus drifting idly in front of us. I, on the other hand, can feel my lungs constricting in panic.

"She is na yers. Ye were na strong enough ta hold on ta her," Brennus replies with friendly malice.

"Free her from the contract and let's see who she comes to," Reed replies. "The queen you think you own is mine—will always be mine."

Brennus smiles. "If she is yers, den ye should take her wi' ye," he says in a soft tone. "Oh…dat's right—ye canna because she gave herself to me. Give me a few more months wi' her and I may free her. Den we will see if ye are correct," Brennus says, not looking upset in the least.

"In a few months, all of your faeries will be turned to dust," Reed says calmly. "You need our help with Casimir. Evie knows how to contact us. Take the offer, it expires with her contract."

Brennus smiles again, right before he begins whispering something. Then, he winds his arm back quickly, like a pitcher on a mound before throwing something forward as fast as a bullet at Reed. My heart refuses to beat for a moment, but Reed hardly reacts at all as an enormous, slate-gray gargoyle unfolds in midair between Brennus and Reed. Its sharp, white fangs drip saliva as it lets out a horrifying screech that makes me quiver on the inside.

Wind gusts from its bat-like wings blow my hair back from my face in short bursts as the talons of its feet reach out to grasp Reed's body. The gargoyle's wings simultaneously wrap around Reed, shrouding him from my sight.

A soft, amused chuckle comes from underneath the gargoyle as its scale-ridden flesh melts from Reed like a wax candle, dripping harmlessly away from the flaming wick. As I realize that Reed isn't hurt by Brennus' spell, I'm able to breathe again shallowly, but I feel really sick now, worse than when I was first stabbed.

"Brennus, you know your Faerie magic doesn't work on Angels. Why bother?" Reed asks, perplexed. "It's why you had to have Safira freeze us, because you couldn't do it yourself. I enjoy your enchantments, however, like the one you used at the chateau when you sent your men to get Evie. It was nice not to have to smell you coming."

"I jus had ta see if anyting has changed. Tings do na seem ta be working out so well for *Aingeals* lately. I was wondering if ye have all lost favor…or if dere is a new species dat is meant ta replace all of ye." Brennus says, looking past Reed to me. "But, we do na need magic ta kill ye now wi' all da human technology out dere. Rocket launchers seem to work well on *aingeal* hives. And den, dere is still me skin dat ye canna handle," Brennus replies.

Brennus' magic doesn't work on Angels! He never told me that! It works great on other beings though…like the Werree and Ifrits. But if his magic doesn't work on Reed, then it may not work on Casimir either, I think, feeling more vulnerable than ever, not less.

That means the fallen Seraphim don't have a lot to fear from the Gancanagh except being touched by them, which is a detriment, but they have ways to combat that. Remembering how much faster Reed was when he was fighting the Gancanagh in China, I have no doubt that the Fallen are nearly as good.

"Me magic works on me half *aingeal* well," Brennus says, nodding towards me. "The contract will na allow her ta even speak ta ye. I wonder if da magic she is learning will work on all ye *aingeals*. She controls na only da lower energy, but da pure energy, too. 'Twill be interesting ta see jus whah she can do ta yer kind when I'm done teaching her whah I know," he says, looking like he is anticipating that day.

"Is your plan to unleash her on your enemies?" Reed asks him coldly.

"I plan ta unleash her on *her* enemies," Brennus replies, coming closer to Reed as he nears the platform. "She will be very powerful. The world could be hers ta command."

"You think that's what she wants?" Reed asks.

"She wants ta be safe. Dat will make her safe," Brennus replies.

"No, that will make her the only target worth going after," Reed replies.

"She is dat already…or ye wouldna be here," Brennus counters, stepping onto the platform of my room, forcing Reed to shift away from him.

"I would be here without any of that. I'm here because every time she smiles, it's like Paradise opening up to shine upon me. I'm here because of the way she loves me with no reservations. She doesn't hold anything back, but gives it all to me as if there was no one else like me in the universe. She has no idea that she alone is the unique being," Reed explains while defensively moving to the side as Brennus walks forward towards the foot of my bed.

Brennus effectively comes between Reed and me, making my heart twist as Reed is forced to back away from me.

Yawning like Reed is boring him, Brennus tucks the blanket snugly around me. "First love is like dat," Brennus says tiredly. "But, den ye mature and find a deeper love, one dat was created jus for ye. She will never forget ye—her first love, so ye can take some comfort in dat, *aingeal.* Ye should be going now. I would like ta speak ta her and I canna do dat wi' ye here."

"She's in my blood. I will never stop fighting for her," Reed promises, but he sounds like he's in pain now, tortured by his inability to stop Brennus from touching me.

"Den we will see each other again," Brennus says, sounding a little weaker.

Brennus sits down on the bed next to me, pulling me into his arms tenderly. Reed growls, but he doesn't move towards Brennus and me. He is fighting with the knowledge that if he harms Brennus, he harms me, too.

"Reed," Zephyr says from behind him. He must have come back in through the skylight in the ceiling. "Time to go," he orders with authority, while his light brown wings beat steadily just beyond the railing of my balcony room.

Reed growls again. *Click,* Brennus' fangs engage as he waits to see what Reed and Zephyr will do next.

"REED!" Zephyr barks. I flinch inside at the sound, because Zee is scary when he wants to be.

Reed pulls himself together then, enough to whisper to me, "I will be back. I promise, Evie." He launches into the air and Zephyr follows directly behind him, making sure that Reed doesn't change his mind and turn back to us again.

The moment Reed is gone, I inhale a deep breath, and then instantly pay for it as shooting pain in my abdomen and shoulder remind me that my heart is not the only thing bleeding.

"Ah, Genevieve, I'm sorry, lass, truly," Brennus whispers against my hair, pulling me to him tighter. "Dis should never have happened. I missed all da signs. I was arrogant and toughtless. Nuting has attacked me in ages. I didna take da proper precautions against da Werree," he admits, stroking my hair. He settles me against his cool chest, lying back on the pillows of my bed. "If it were na for ye sending Faolan ta me…" he starts to say, but stops.

His cool chest feels good against my throbbing shoulder, so I press closer to him. "I think you need some personal guards from now on, Brenn. You can definitely have Eion, but I want

Faolan back," I whisper. "How's Lachlan?" I ask softly, remembering Lachlan's chest filled with inky, black arrows.

"Lachlan is gone…we couldna save him," Brennus replies, squeezing me tighter.

"What!" I whisper, feeling my throat grow so tight that I am fighting for air again.

My reaction is shocking me. Somehow, Lachlan had managed to become like a friend to me, even as he was there to make sure that I behaved myself. Feelings that I have been denying that I have for them rise up in me. Rage and pain overwhelm me at once, as I murmur, "I will kill Casimir, I promise you. We'll have revenge for Lachlan." Tears stain my cheeks again, wetting Brennus' jacket.

"*Mo chroí*, ye are like a dream. I canna believe ye exist," he breathes against my hair, petting my back soothingly as he tries to calm me.

"Brenn," Finn says in a gentle tone, poised on the platform ahead of us. "Ye need ta feed so dat ye can heal. I will stay wi' Genevieve while ye see to it. None of da other fellas will come in here. Declan and Molly are guarding da door. 'Tis okay now."

"I'm na leaving her 'til she heals," Brennus replies and I still, realizing for the first time that he is just as broken as I am. I reach up under his suit coat, feeling the cold stickiness of his blood seeping through his shirt.

"Brenn, she just blew away a dozen or more Werree, like dey were paper dolls. Da last ting we should be worried about is protecting Genevieve. Anyway, she canna heal until ye do, remember?" Finn asks him, with a concerned expression in his pale green eyes. "She is starting ta look as pale as ye. Ye have ta do someting before she gets worse."

"Den bring a wan here. I'm na leaving her alone," Brennus says, assessing my face. "Hurry."

"I will," Finn agrees, watching me rest my cheek against Brennus as I cry. He signals to Declan at the door before turning back to me, saying, "'Twill be better soon, Genevieve. Da pain will be less once Brennus feeds."

"No, it won't. They killed Lachlan," I reply in a whisper, seeing the surprise in Finn's eyes that my tears are for my friend.

Turning my head into Brennus' chest, I try to choke back a sob. I rub my face against Brennus' jacket, wiping my tears and then I whisper, "From now on, we invoke the 'Silver Rule:' Kill all of them before they kill all of you."

"Nuting would please me better, *mo chroí*," Brennus breathes against my hair.

"We have to find Casimir's hole," I say, feeling tired because I keep losing blood.

"He will seek ye out soon," Finn informs me, "he did na succeed, so he will have ta try again."

I close my eyes, seeing Casimir's face in my mind and feeling lethargic and muddled. I feel set adrift, floating away from the safety of my home and there is nothing to hold on to anymore.

Like an answer to a prayer, Brennus whispers, "Hold on to me. I'm here." He traces his finger over my cheek and then he holds me as the pain in my shoulder and abdomen oscillate between severe and dull.

"Who is this, lover?" A feminine voice cuts the air in accusation from the stairway of my bedroom.

Opening my eyes a little, I try to raise my head, but my vision swims, so I put it back down limply.

"Why does *she* have her hands on you? Doesn't *she* know that you're mine?" The scantily clad, lithe woman asks as she walks to the bed.

His hand reaches up to touch her cheek and she loses her snarling demeanor. It is replaced by a dopey, little smirk.

"Missed you...lover," she breathes. As she leans forward to kiss his mouth, her dark hair falls on me as I rest against his chest. "You haven't made love to me since this morning. Where have you been hiding?"

This must be hell, I think dizzily as Brennus sinks his fangs into the girl at his side.

She exhales in ecstasy and it only takes a matter of minutes before she slips from his arms to the floor, unmoving.

Brennus snuggles me closer, saying, "'Twill be all right now, Genevieve. Rest, *mo shíorghrá*." My fuzzy brain holds on to his last words because I know what they mean now. He just said, "Rest, my eternal love" and I can do nothing but obey.

Nineteen

I awake in Brennus' room, but it's impossible to tell by the light from the window what time it is, since it's mostly gray here. My fingers skim over a blanket, while I feel a cold body radiating icy air next to me. Vague memories of what had happened come to me. I give a small gasp, starting to sit up, when Molly crosses her feet in front of her on top of the blankets.

Smiling into my eyes, Molly puts down her fashion magazine. "How do you feel? Better or worse than the time we got the peach schnapps?" she asks me, studying my face and looking concerned.

"Umm…not sure. Give me a second," I say, trying to move again and feeling stiff. My shoulder definitely still hurts, but not nearly as bad as before. My stomach is better, too, but it still feels tight and sore. "Better," I reply, pushing myself up to a sitting position.

"Better or worse than sledding with cafeteria trays?" she asks.

"Worse," I decide, grimacing a little and remembering our escapades in high school.

"Worse than the trays?" she asks. "That blows, 'cuz those trays super sucked. Remember how mine broke in half? I think I still have a piece of one in my shin," she says, pulling her leg up and yanking down her kneesock so I can check it out. She is dressed in a sexy, punk outfit consisting of a short, pleated skirt and tight-fitting top with kneesocks and Doc Martins.

Her skin looks flawless now, like she never skinned her knees in her life. "That's all in your head, Molls," I reply, not seeing anything remotely wrong with her pale skin. "So, where is everyone?" I ask, because it sounds really quiet, like a morgue.

"Eaves, the whole place is on total lock-down now. It's worse than airport security around here. I swear, I feel like a terrorist every time I try to get near you. Finn has gone totally parental on me. I can't leave without his permission, and then I have to have five or six fellas go with me everywhere I go. It's so lame," she complains, crossing her arms with a pouty face.

"Welcome to my world," I mutter.

"I know, right?" she says, giving me the there-you-go gesture. "It's like we're grounded or something. I can *so* have more fun being *alive*," she whines and I try not to smile. "Oh! You totally missed *it*! I had to save *it* for you because *it's* just too funny! Brennus nearly went postal when he saw it. I think I like your new friends, Eaves! Check this out!"

Molly bounces off my bed and goes to the bedroom door. She cracks it to see if anyone is coming. She closes the door quietly again and turns to my closet door where she pulls out a gilded frame from it. When she turns the frame around, I recognize it as the one that held my 'goddess portrait.'

Someone had cut the portrait out of it and replaced it with the same smiley face poster that we left in the Delt composite. The smiley face is flipping us off, while the caption reads: 'HAVE A NICE DAY.' Below the caption, I recognize Buns's handwriting that reads in bold, red lipstick: *We Love You, Sweetie. See You Soon.*

Tears brighten my eyes as a laugh escapes me. "It's perfect," I murmur. "That's Buns and Brownie. They have the best sense of humor."

"Well, they're certainly little kleptomaniacs because they stole all of your pictures in your archive. It was sabotage," she smirks, enjoying the chaos.

"Yeah, that sounds just like them," I say, not able to hide the smile on my face. "How long have I been sleeping?" I comb my fingers through my hair to get the tangles out. I glance again at the window; it's gray and raining.

"I'm not sure—awhile—nearly a day. You just missed Brennus. He was here for most of the time with you, but he had to deal with all the issues," she says. "You know, I think it's kind of hard to be an evil emperor. Everyone wants his attention. He had to change all the plans now. We were all set to have this huge surprise birthday party for you, and now everyone is packing up their gear for the move instead. So, I might as well give you your present now." Molly says, tossing a small, wrapped gift onto my lap. I let it sit there as I gaze at it dumbly.

"What?" I ask.

"Happy Birthday, Eaves," Molly grins, watching me as she hugs one of the tall posts at the foot of my bed.

"We're leaving?" I ask, latching onto the most important information she imparted.

Molly nods, "Yeah, soon. I think we're going to do the tribute thing for Lachlan, and then we're gone," she says casually, watching me to see if I'll open her gift.

"Lachlan," I breathe, remembering him hitting the ground with shafts of arrows peppering him. Tears immediately spring to my eyes.

Molly shrugs, "They're having some kind of funeral thing for him. The way Finn described it to me, it sounds kind of Arthurian–or Viking. They're having a funeral pyre–it's a Faerie rite," she explains.

"When?" I ask.

"Today, before we go," she says. "Are you okay? You look pale again. Do you need something to eat?" she asks, looking concerned.

"No, I'm fine," I lie, giving a ghost of a smile.

"Aren't you going to open it?" Molly prompts me, seeing me frozen on the bed. "Nineteen. I bet you never pictured yourself here a year ago," she says, holding her arms out palms up. "Nineteen–medieval castle–undead friends…"

"Uh, yeah. Surprise, right?" I agree feebly, while numbly opening the silver paper.

I unwrap the package and lift the lid of the small box. I push the tissue aside and blink back tears again. My fingertips glide tentatively over the blood-red jewel, shaped like a shield in a platinum setting. Next to the red diamond, strung on the same necklace, is my Uncle Jim's class ring that I had given to Reed last Christmas. "How?" I ask breathlessly.

"They came with all of your stuff. I found them when I was going through the items for your room. I was afraid that Brennus wouldn't let you have them, because it's obvious that Reed gave you that necklace. It's worth a large fortune—not something you would buy for yourself. And then, I had sent you your uncle's class ring for Christmas last year, remember? You said you had someone you wanted to give it to. Two and two equals four," she smiles.

"I don't understand. I thought…" I trail off.

One of Molly's eyebrows quirks. "Ohhh, you thought I'm one of 'them,'" she says. "Well, I am and I'm not. I'm not a Faerie, so that makes me…more the calibre of a vampire because I was human once, not Faerie. You've seen what they think of vampires," she says, rolling her eyes. "But, since I'm Finn's vampire, they treat me like a pet…but not really an equal."

"So you're saying that if you're not 'one of them,' then you're free to do whatever you want?" I ask, seeing the gleam in her eyes.

"Dat's right," she agrees, sounding just like a fella. "I'm me own island—human-Gancanagh. Ye jus say da word and I'll give ye a get-outta-jail-free card."

"What?" I ask, exhaling my breath in a rush.

"Ye heard me. Do ye need more tellin'?" she asks with *faux* menace, as she lets her fangs shoot forward with a *click*. "Ye look like a tasty morsel and I promise na ta have more den a wee nip of ye."

"They will kill you, Molly, if you break the contract," I whisper, afraid for her. I look towards the door, just to make sure that no one is listening to us.

"They would try," she responds honestly, giving me the cheeky smile that always accompanies the arrogance of the Gancanagh, while retracting her fangs.

"No way," I reply, shaking my head. "Why would you even consider that?" I ask and I feel scared even talking about it out loud. If someone hears her, she is done.

"You almost died—for real. Not undead and happy, but dead and buried," she whispers. "You weren't even the one hit. It was Brennus. How are you supposed to defend yourself against that? Finn said the Fallen will be back for you *or* Brennus because it doesn't matter. Hit one and you both fall. I just want to give you some better odds. Finn seems to think they can handle it, but I saw those Werree," Molly shudders, looking a little haunted.

"You can't help me," I say, clutching her gift in my fist. "But, I will never forget that you offered." I crawl from beneath the blanket to the other end of the bed, hugging Molly where she stands by the post. "And I will never forget your gift to me either."

"You're my family," Molly whispers, and I nod my head, unable to respond at all because my throat is too tight. "You and Finn."

"I love you—even if you're a vampire," I whisper.

Molly laughs softly at my joke. "And I love you—even if you're a half-breed," she whispers back.

"When is the funeral for Lachlan?" I ask, pulling back, but having a hard time seeing through my tears.

"Soon. Do you plan on going?" she asks. "Everyone is expecting that you will miss it because of your injuries. It takes you forever to heal," she teases me.

"Yeah, well, I had to wait for Brennus to get better before I could, so I can only move as fast as what's in front of me," I reply with *faux* defensiveness. "I need to go to the funeral–tribute thing. He was my…personal guard—my friend," I say, swallowing past the aching lump in my throat.

"Okay. I'll go with you. Get ready and I'll meet you back here. Wear a coat. I had them modified to fit your wings. It's going to be out by the cliffs," she says. "You still get cold, don't you?"

I nod, "You?" I ask.

"Not so much," she says, shaking her head. "Formal attire?" she asks.

"I'm betting they won't be in jeans and trainers," I reply. I only ever see the Gancanagh in tailored suits or elegant attire since coming to the castle. They dressed down when they were in the Upper Peninsula of Michigan, but I think that was so they would blend in there.

"I wouldn't wear the present I gave you, Eaves," she warns as she walks to the door. "He might freak."

"You think?" I ask her sarcastically, hearing her giggle as she leaves Brennus' room.

Going to my closet, I pull out a silk robe and wrap myself in it. I stash my necklace and ring that Molly gave me into one of my shoes. I walk to the outer door that leads to the hallway and find Declan and a score of Gancanagh that I vaguely know waiting for me outside.

Surprised to find so many of them, I try to recover as I turn to Declan and say, "I need your help, Deck."

Surprise flickers in his eyes as he glances at Faolan, and then he pushes himself off the wall he had been leaning against. I hold the door wide for him, allowing him to enter my sitting room. Leaving the door open, we sit down in the chairs that face each other.

"I need to go to Lachlan's tribute, but I don't know what I should wear or what I should do to honor him," I explain. "Can you help me?" I ask.

"Why?" he asks, looking puzzled.

"Because he was my friend—because it's my fault that the Werree murdered him," I reply, looking away as a tear escapes my eyes. I clench my teeth, trying really hard not to cry again.

"'Tis na yer fault, lass. Ye pulled us all back. We would've all walked through dat door wi'out ye figuring it out," Declan says in a gentle tone.

"They were there for me," I reply, gazing in his eyes.

"And ye took care of dem, did ye na?" he says with a look of admiration and respect.

"I did," I reply, and he smiles. "So, will you help me?" I ask again.

"I will," he replies. "Ye go take yer shower and put on a nice dress. Den, meet me in here and I will get ye ready for it. I'll order ye some food, too. Ye still look pale."

"Look who's talking," I tease him tiredly, before getting up from the chair to do as he instructed.

I shower and then put on a sleek, black dress that allows my wings to be out. I select the matching coat from the closet and impulsively retrieve the necklace and ring Molly had given me, shoving them in the pocket of my coat.

I lay my coat over the back of the chair in the sitting room before I sink into the chair facing Declan again. He has a pot of an inky, dark liquid that looks a lot like henna waiting on a small table near us. A wooden, pen-like implement rests inside the pot.

Picking up the pen, Declan says, "Dis is da story of Lachlan's life, his death, his rebirth as a Gancanagh and his final battle." Using the pen, Declan begins drawing lines upon my face, stopping occasionally to dip it in the pot. "We would do dis ta da wife, mother, and sisters of da warrior dat died, so dat dere tears would wash away da pain of dis life, making him clean ta face his next life."

"This is a Faerie ritual, not a Gancanagh rite?" I ask.

"'Tis Faerie," he replies, continuing to work as I try not to cry and ruin what he has already done.

It takes a long time to apply all of the symbols. When Declan is finished, he holds up a mirror for me to see what he has done. My face resembles an intricate labyrinth of interconnected lines and rune-like symbols. I look textured, in a way: pagan and otherworldly. The lines trace down my neck and on my hands and arms.

"Are ye ready?" Declan asks me, and I nod, swallowing the last bit of food he had ordered for me. "Den, we should go downstairs. Dere will be a processional out ta da cliffs."

"I said I'd wait for Molly," I reply.

"I'll send someone ta fetch her," he says.

We step out in the hallway and Declan quietly speaks to one of the fellas. The rest of the fellas stare at me like I'm an alien. Fidgeting a little, I begin counting them. There are fifteen that I can see. I recognize some of them: Torin, Goban, Ninian, Faolan, Lonan, Alastar, and Cavan.

"Faolan," I say, making eye contact with him and trying not to tear up. "Thank you," I murmur in a half-whisper. Brennus said he helped him against the Werree, saving our lives.

Faolan nods, looking pleased.

"Where is Eion?" I ask Declan, not seeing him.

"He will guard Brennus from now on," Declan replies gruffly, like he approves of the change. "We should go."

I walk in the center of a swarm of fellas, following Declan to the front doors. As I step outside, the air blows crisp and damp against my cheeks. I put my coat on, tying the belt tight. Molly sidles up to me, whispering in my ear, "Nice tattoos, half-breed."

"Jealous, vampire?" I ask with a ghost of a smile, hearing her smother a giggle.

"Hey, I picked this up for you on the way through the hall. It was delivered this morning," she says, handing me another wrapped box.

"What is it?" I inquire, looking at the small, blood red box with a bow that resembles my angel wings.

She shrugs. "Another birthday present. They checked it. It's not ticking," she says, grinning.

"Who is it from?" I murmur.

Molly frowns, "I don't know. Maybe there's a card inside, but I'm sure it's for you. Look at the wings," she replies. "Open it."

I unwrap the bow from the box and lift the lid. Reaching in it, I pull out a large, golden compact. My heart begins to pound in my chest as I feel the cold metal in my hand. On the lid of the compact, there is a set of ruby encrusted angel's wings. It is exquisite...exquisitely evil...a Trojan horse.

"Oh, it's make-up. That's kind of fierce," Molly says, seeing the gift. She takes the box from me as I hold the compact in my hand, studying it numbly. "I don't see a card. It's probably from Brennus. Maybe we should put it back in the box, so he can give it to you."

"It's not from Brennus," I reply, putting the compact into the pocket of my coat and feeling myself growing pale. "It's not make-up. It's a mirror."

"Oh, very swank," she smiles absently, looking around for a place to set down the box. She stashes it behind a towering gargoyle.

Shoving my hands in my pockets, I can feel my gifts from the angels. In my right hand, I hold my necklace from Reed. In my left hand, I can feel the smooth, gold metal of the compact from Casimir—the portal that will link me to him when I open the lid and allow him to pass through it to me.

"*Mo chroí*," Brennus breathes near my ear and I jump.

As I turn to look at him, my heartbeat picks up for a different reason than being scared. Brennus looks like a pale, Greek god who has come down from Mt. Olympus to grace us with his presence. On his head is a golden crown that resembles a laurel wreath. The gold against his black hair is striking, making me want to reach out and touch it.

"Whah are ye doing here?" he asks with concern in his tone. "Ye should be resting. I'll see ye back upstairs."

"No," I say, stepping back as he tries to guide me back inside. "I need to go—to say goodbye to Lachlan. Please?" I ask, feeling almost desperate. I can't even tell him why it's important to me. My emotions are so chaotic and taut. I feel frayed. I think he realizes this because he pulls me into his arms, hugging me tight.

"Ye do Lachlan a great honor by mapping his story. Ye are his queen and 'tis a sign of great respect dat ye mourn his loss," Brennus says, rubbing my back under my wings. I have to choke back the tears again, so I just nod to what he is telling me.

"Will ye walk with me out ta da cliffs?" Brennus asks and I nod again. I look up at his face and I'm shocked to see his radiant smile. He looks completely happy and I feel confused because we are walking to a funeral.

Brennus' arm wraps more firmly around my back as we walk together towards the cliff and the sea. Fellas surround us, strolling at a respectful distance, but forming a barrier so that we're well protected. Machine-gun and rocket-launcher toting Gancanagh are posted at different intervals along the way to the cliffs, bringing awareness to the fact that there are lethal threats to me and anyone who shelters me.

Nearing the cliffs, I catch my first glimpse of Lachlan. He is lying on an altar of fallen stone. They dressed him in a suit of ancient, silver armor and in his hands he holds the diamond-headed spear that I had held with him in the archive room. My throat immediately closes as tears fall from my eyes.

Brennus' arm around me tightens. "He died a good death, *mo chroí.* He was a warrior and he died fighting. 'Tis all any of us ask," Brennus says, pulling me closer to his side.

I know that it's Lachlan laying there, not my Uncle Jim, but images of my uncle enter my mind at that moment, along with flashes of his pain. *How did Alfred kill him? Was it slow? Did he try to fight back with his inadequate human body?* my mind asks me, seeing many of the torturous things that could've happened.

We stop near the fallen stone. Brennus squeezes me before letting go of me to move to the head of the stone. He begins speaking in another language; a language that sounds different than anything I've heard them speak before now. It must be Faerie. It sounds soft and mellow, like the gentle flow of water over stone. But I can barely listen to the sound of his voice. My thoughts are far way: in my Uncle Jim's house the night he died.

Did Alfred go to him alone, or did he bring others to help him torture Uncle Jim? Did Alfred tell him why he was killing him—that it was because of me? Did he know that he was dying for me—in my place? Did he scream out for help—for someone to save him? I wonder, vaguely feeling tears dipping from the curve of my jaw.

Gruesome images of how Uncle Jim could've died continue to float in my mind, making my head pound and my stomach feel nauseous. The grief from his loss is more painful than the stabbing I recently endured. I raise a shaky hand to my face to dash away some of my tears.

Looking again at Lachlan, I know that his blood is on my hands as well. Casimir sent the Werree for me and he sent Alfred, too. Something inside of me feels broken, like there is a shadow between my heart and my soul now. It's a dark place: a place filled with yearning and need—a place that craves revenge. I want to see Casimir suffer brutally and painfully without any mercy. None.

When Brennus finishes speaking, Finn addresses the gathering. He is brief and then he looks past Molly at his side to Faolan next to her. Faolan speaks then, and the procession continues around the rock, each Gancanagh speaking in turn. I feel disconnected from the rest of the gathering as I stand next to Brennus, not knowing what the fellas are saying, because they are still speaking in a language I don't understand.

Soon, Declan, standing next to me, finishes speaking and everyone shifts their eyes to me. Brennus leans near my ear and asks, "Would ye like to say anyting to the gathering before we move on?"

I am quiet for a moment, looking at Lachlan's face, remembering him as he was with us in my archive, playing cards and teaching me to cheat with no expression on my face. Or, when he was telling us about the first time he tried a wind-charming spell and just about blew the doors off his parent's dwelling. Or, at the strategy meetings, where he taught me alternate ways of looking at a problem. Or, when he stood by my side and tried to protect me from the vicious, shadowy creatures that covet the body parts of others. He is gone now…and he won't be coming back.

Wiping the tears that are still coming from my eyes, I say softly, "I don't know which is more difficult: going on alone to an unknown destination, or having to remain behind to watch the one you love leave. Those of us who have had to remain behind, we know that it's a cut that never heals…it just continues to bleed—to burn inside of you." A twist of pain cuts through me, thinking of my uncle.

"We have lost someone that we cannot replace. There is no one like Lachlan. He was unique…an original. I hope that wherever he travels next there will be someone there for him, to guide him home," I whisper, feeling my throat getting really tight again.

Breathing in deep, I continue, "Since we are forced to let him go, to bleed inside for him…I want payment. I want retribution in the form of pain…I want revenge and I will have it. I promise you, Lachlan," I end.

Click, click, click, click, click, click—my call for vengeance has elicited a visceral response from the fellas. I ignore them, lost to my own raging desire for revenge. I move towards Lachlan's side and reach my hand out to touch the spear in his grasp. The weapon begins to sing its gentle lullaby. It is barely discernable over the rhythmic swaying of the sea below the cliffs, but I can hear it and those closest to Lachlan can hear it, too. After a few moments, I pull my hand back, letting go. I turn away from Lachlan and walk to Brennus' side. His eyes are soft, like he has been given the greatest gift imaginable.

Brennus embraces me, leaning down, he whispers in my ear, "Ye really are da queen of hearts."

I place my hand on his chest and shift to look at him, whispering, "Bring me Casimir and I will be anything you want me to be."

Flames of desire ignite in his eyes as he replies, "Now dat is an interesting proposition."

Finn clears his throat then, causing Brennus to straighten up slowly. With reluctance, Brennus lets go of me before going to the stone and laying his hand upon Lachlan's head. He closes his eyes as energy in the air shifts towards him. Whispering words I don't understand, Brennus steps back a few paces from Lachlan. A green flame ignites around Lachlan, licking at the sides of his armor and causing plumes of smoke to curl up in the air. Inhaling it, it smells like burning candy.

I turn away from the sight of Lachlan's burning corpse and walk alone towards the edge of the cliffs and the sea far below them. The terrain is rocky and covered in a moss. When I almost reach the edge of the cliff, I feel fluttering butterflies taking flight inside of me. Pausing in my tracks, I take a deep breath, clearing the burning scent from my nose. I take another step forward, the fluttering increases. My legs grow heavy, making it difficult to take the next step towards the sea.

Reed is here somewhere, I surmise as my heart races in my chest.

The next step is nearly impossible. It feel like I am trying to trudge through quicksand. Reaching out, I use the jagged edges of the rocks to pull myself forward. Reed must be hiding beneath the cliff's edge on one of the shelf ledges. I want to call out to him and tell him that I know he's there, but I can't. I can barely move now as I pull myself the last few feet to the edge of the cliff.

The butterflies inside of me are beating wildly now, comforting me with the assurance that he's here—that he still exists. Things are blurring for me now. I can't see the lines that were drawn so clearly before. Right and wrong aren't making sense to me. I don't think that I know exactly what evil is anymore. It used to be so black and white, but now it is just shades of gray. I'm so far from where I intended to be. I need Reed. I need him to pull me back from this edge of evil because I think that once I fall, there will be no going back.

I exhale, trying to say his name, hearing him whisper in return, "I'm here." Closing my eyes, I savor the sound of his voice that reaches the raw, dark place inside of me between my heart and my soul.

Icy air radiates from behind me as Brennus says, "'Tis time we went back ta da house. Ye look so tired; ye need ta rest."

I shove both my hands in my pockets and I clutch a gift in each of them. "If I jump, will you catch me?" I ask, looking out at the sea ahead of me

I hear both Reed and Brennus answer me in my next breath, "I will."

Reed's answer is so low, that I don't think that Brennus can hear him. It pulls at my heart. I want to be with Reed so much, but I'm beginning to believe that it will never happen. *I have to leave now, or all I will have is the burning desire for revenge inside of me*, I think.

I move forward towards the sea—towards Reed. Brennus catches me from behind before I can jump.

Shifting in his arms, I hold out the gift from Casimir for Brennus to take, saying, "Then this is for us."

"Whah is dis?" Brennus asks, taking the compact from my left hand and running his fingers over the blood red jewels encrusted on the cold, metal lid.

"Revenge," I breathe, looking into Brennus' green eyes and seeing his desire for me. I allow the necklace in my other hand to slip from my grasp, hoping that Reed will catch it before it falls into the sea below.

CHAPTER 20

The Gifts

Curiosity registers on Brennus' face as he holds the shiny, metal compact I have given him. He turns it over, studying it. I don't need to hold it to know that it's from Casimir. The jeweled red wings encrusted on the lid have a way of making my extremities go numb, just like Casimir had when I met him.

"Where did ye get dis?" Brennus asks.

"I think that Casimir sent it to me," I reply, surprised that I sound so calm. "Don't open it. It's a very clever little trap," I warn him.

Butterflies are still fluttering around in my stomach, denoting Reed's presence, but I can't be positive that he is there, so my reasoning must be enough to allow me to still operate within the realm of the magical contract. I pray that he is there and was able to catch the necklace that I just dropped down to him. I hope, too, that he is still listening to what I'm telling Brennus.

"How does dis trap work?" Brennus asks as his arm tightens around me protectively.

"It's a portal—a link between two places. This mirror has a mate. When they are both opened, they connect like a hallway to one another, allowing an angel or other being to shapeshift and pass through the hallway to the other side," I explain.

"You tink dis is from Casimir?" he asks for clarification.

"I'd say that it's a good thing that it's metal, otherwise it would smell like rotten garbage," I reply. I quickly tell Brennus about the portal I unexpectedly opened, given to me on my last birthday by Alfred. I explain the shadow man who had popped out of it and tried to strangle me. "Casimir must not know that Alfred already tried this. Old boy needs a new bag of tricks."

"'Tis a perfect trap because I've never heard of it," he says. His eyes rove over my face lovingly and I just realize I must look like a frightening mess. I'm covered in inky tattoos that have probably smeared and run because I have been crying over the loss of Lachlan…and my uncle. I self-consciously touch my cheek, seeing the inky lines on my fingers when I draw them away.

"I think it's an angel thing. They don't broadcast their escape routes. I had to open one to find out about it," I reply, looking away because Brennus is so handsome with the crown of laurel in his thick, black hair. My wings flutter a little and a rumbling laugh comes from Brennus.

"I *do* desire ye, *mo chroí*," he says thickly with a possessive smile. "Ye have no idea how much, do ye? Ye have never looked more beautiful ta me dan ye do right at dis moment. Ye look Fay—like a Faerie wi' da ritual mapping on yer body. Ye look like ye belong in dat time, long ago, when I was a lad. I would've fought for ye den, too. In dis world or dat one. Heaven could be here. We could make it here, together."

"Casimir is standing in the way of that," I point out, feeling an intense pull towards Brennus. My desire for him is growing every day. "He will be back for me."

Brennus holds up the compact for me to see. "I see so many ways ta send him a message wi' dis. Let us go back ta da house and we will explore dem," he says, guiding me away from the edge of the cliff and away from my angel.

I lean against Brennus on the way back to the house. We don't discuss the compact. I still feel as if I've just been in some sort of horrible accident. I'm sore and shaken and the dreadful consequences of the attack have left me filled with sorrow and grief.

Brennus holds me close to him, trying to comfort me, and he does, much to my surprise. When we enter the house, Brennus pauses near Finn, saying, "Genevieve has received someting very intriguing. Can ye meet me in me office in a few minutes, I would like ta discuss it wi' ye."

Finn nods, looking past Brennus to me. His eyes soften as he says, "Ye look grand, Genevieve. Jus like a Faerie."

"Tanks, Finn," I smile, using his accent. "Take a good look, because I'm going upstairs to wash it off now."

"Ye did us proud today." Finn replies, smiling as I blush at his compliment, ducking my head.

"Don't get used to it," I advise, seeing him smile and shake his head.

"I'll walk ye upstairs, *mo chroí*," Brennus says, guiding me to the stairs. My entourage follows us up. Declan checks my rooms before winking at me and leaving to wait in the hall.

When we are alone, Brennus says, "Ye go and take yer shower now. I have someting I want to discuss wi' ye when ye're finished."

Thinking he might be about to tell me where we will be moving next, I try to hurry through my shower. It takes me longer than I thought to get the henna off my skin. Faint lines of it remain, but I give up, putting on a silk robe before drying my hair. Feeling tired, I pull on a pair of yoga pants and a tank top I modified to fit my wings.

Going back to the sitting room, I sit on the settee that faces the chair Brennus is in. "You wanted to talk to me?" I ask when he doesn't say anything right away.

"I do," Brennus says, searching my face. "I jus do na know if I should tell ye dis now."

"What is it?" I ask, my heartbeat kicking up in reaction to his serious expression.

"Do ye remember da note I wrote ta ye? Da one when ye were in China?" he asks.

"Yes." I reply.

"In dat letter, I promised ye someting. I want ta give it ta ye now, but I do na know if 'tis a good ting or a bad ting," he explains. "I planned for it ta be part of yer birthday present."

I search my mind, trying to remember what he promised me. I go over the letter, like a faint echo in my mind: *The needs that you hide deep inside of you, I know them all. You want a family above all else. I will provide that family for you. You want other things as well, things you don't speak of to anyone. Ever. I will find your sire for you, I promise…*

"You found my father," I state, feeling scared, excited, and ill all at the same time.

"I did and I did na," Brennus says. "I believe I know who he is, but I have no idea where he is now."

"Who is he?" I ask in a small voice, not able to make eye contact with Brennus.

"His name is Tau," Brennus says and my head snaps up.

"You're kidding me?" I ask, thinking of my birth certificate. There was only a letter 'T' in the spot where the father should be indicated. I always thought that it was a way of not leaving the document blank. It was a name all along. "I have a father," I breathe. Brennus smiles at me when I look at his face again. "Do you know anything about him?" I ask, leaning towards him and searching his face.

"I do. He is well-known," he says.

Hundreds of questions bounce around in my head, until one hits me like a punch in the stomach. "Is he evil?" I ask before I can stop myself.

"Depends on who ye talk ta, but, no. He is Divine. Dat is what ye meant, was it na?" Brennus asks. I nod numbly, feeling the kind of relief that only comes when the worst-case scenario that you've held in the back of your mind for a long time turns out to be just a scenario.

"He is Divine," I whisper. "Do you know what he is like?" I ask, hoping for a glimpse of his character—some small piece of information that I can hold close to me, like a secret treasure.

Brennus smiles, saying, "He is a Seraph, of course. Some of his exploits are well known. He is elite. Tau is a commander."

"Is he brave?" I ask.

"Let me put it ta ye dis way. When dere is a parley between da Seraphim in Sheol and Paradise, 'tis Tau who goes ta Sheol ta speak with dem. Alone," Brennus says. Every hair on my body stands up in that instant, imagining the type of courage it would take to walk into Hell alone to speak to the enemy. "Now we know where ye get all of yer courage," Brennus says.

I bristle. "Yeah, my mother and my Uncle Jim," I retort, not knowing where the anger in me is coming from, but feeling it intensely.

"I know dat dis does na seem like much of a gift ta ye right now, but 'tis someting dat ye crave. 'Twas such a strong need dat 'twas in yer blood," Brennus says softly. "Ye could na hide it."

I pepper Brennus with questions, finding out what he has learned about Tau. All that he can tell me are stories of some of the battles against the Fallen that Tau had led. He can't tell me anything about why he chose to have a baby with my mother or why he hadn't stayed to help raise me. He can't tell me why I was left in the dark about being part angel either.

"What am I supposed to do now, Brennus?" I ask, feeling lost and desperate. "I don't know what they want from me. Do you know what they want from me?"

"It does na matter whah dey want from ye," he replies, coming to sit next to me. He pulls me to him, letting me rest my head on his chest as he gently strokes my back. "'Tis whah ye are willing ta let dem have dat matters. Ye have our protection. Ye are da queen." Something in what he just said touches that dark place in me again, making it feel less raw, less sore—less alone.

"There are times, Brennus, when you seem to say exactly what I need to hear," I whisper against the skin of his neck.

His arms tighten around me, and in this moment, I feel safe. "I do na know how I lived wi'out ye for so long, *mo chroí*," Brennus replies.

"Thank you for my gift, Brennus," I murmur, feeling small because I have never given him anything. I know that I have been a hostage here, his prisoner, but I'm so confused now about everything. He is seduction in the flesh. He keeps finding all of the things that I crave and giving them to me. That is a powerful drug. It was easy to resist him when he didn't know me, but now that he does, it's making things much, much harder. I have to do something to shift that power back to me, because he is taking it away from me.

"I have a gift for you too, Brennus," I say, pulling away from him.

Looking surprised, he asks, "Ye do?"

"I do. Wait here and I'll get it," I say, getting up from the settee. I go to the bathroom in our room. Selecting the larger of the perfume bottles that contain my blood, I walk back out to the sitting room with it in my hand.

"Whah is dat?" Brennus asks as I extend it to him, waiting for him to take it from me.

"My insurance policy," I reply as his cool hand brushes mine, taking the ornate bottle from me. Unstopping it, he brings it to his nose, passing it under slowly. Immediately, his fangs engage with a forceful *click*.

"Dis is…ye are giving me yer blood?" he asks with a sultry look I can feel.

"I'm giving you my trust. That is the blood I planned on drinking in order to stop the craving of being bitten. You can do whatever you want with it—my blood. I just ask that you protect the trust I have given you," I say, watching his eyes grow dark as he puts the stopper back on the bottle.

"Do ye know dat no one has given me anyting since I died?" he asks, extending his hand for me to take. I sit next to him again. "Everyting dat I have I have had ta fight for or earn."

"You've had to earn my trust," I point out, hearing him laugh.

"I did and 'twas da hardest ting I've ever had ta do, too," he agrees, smiling. His fangs don't seem as scary when he's amused—but they are still scary, just not freakishly so.

"Now that you have it, what will you do with it?" I ask him tiredly, resting my head against his shoulder.

"Try na ta lose it," he murmurs before kissing the top of my head.

I yawn in exhaustion before saying, "Good." In my next breath, Brennus picks me up in his arms, walking slowly towards the bedroom with me.

"What are you doing?" I ask, panicking a little.

"Putting ye ta bed. Ye look as if ye will fall asleep sitting up in a minute. I had planned on us leaving here tonight, but I will have ta put it off for a few days until ye are better. I forget dat da living are so frail," he says, teasing me.

"Are you attempting to make being undead sound appealing?" I tease him back.

"I am na. I have a new plan now," he says, brushing his lips against my neck.

"Oh? And what's your new plan?" I ask, feeling my heartbeat pick up from his kiss.

"Da old plan was centered around da time 'twould take before I could make ye undead…one of us," he admits, lying me down on the huge bed. He pulls the blanket over me, sitting next to me and gazing into my eyes that probably show my fear. "Da new plan is centered around keeping ye from ever having ta become undead."

"I like your new plan," I whisper. Even when I already knew the old plan, hearing him say it aloud scares me. He brushes his fingers over my cheek.

"I tought ye might," he replies ruefully, brushing his lips to mine. He pulls back, getting up from the bed and walking towards the door. "Finn and I will discuss the compact. We'll brief ye later, after ye rest. Happy Birthday, me sweet *aingeal*."

"Thanks," I say, feeling sleepy. Hearing the door shut, I snuggle down in the bed.

In the twilight between sleep and wakefulness, I hear someone whisper to me, "Red."

As I open my eyes, I realize right away that I'm looking into Russell's chocolate brown eyes. "Russell," I mumble. My eyes bolt to the door to see if anyone is coming. "What are you doing here?" I ask when I am sure no one has been alerted to his presence yet.

"What are ya doing, Red?" Russell asks, not answering my question. "Ya got another one of those doors from Casimir and ya turn 'round and give it to the vampires?" he asks, sitting next to me in my bed with a disapproving look as he shakes his head at me.

"You can't be here, Russell," I say, pushing myself up against the pillows.

Russell gives me a worried frown. "I'm not here, technically. This is just a clone," he explains. "What's yer plan? Are ya fixin' to open that portal thing and let Casimir come to ya?"

"Probably something like that—I don't know. We haven't talked about it yet," I reply, scrubbing my face, trying to wake up a little.

"They're lettin' ya make decisions now?" he asks me with a skeptical frown.

"We discuss strategy," I say vaguely, because for some reason, I feel like I shouldn't tell him how we operate.

"You know I used to think you were smart, but yer fixin' to change my mind, aren't ya? These things aren't yer friends, they're monsters. *We* are yer family, not *them*," he whispers adamantly, pointing at my bedroom door. "Without tall, dark and stinky 'round, you would be their dinner—or maybe just a snack."

My eyebrows draw together at his insult. "I think I'm a better gauge of what I am to them then you are," I say sullenly, not liking what Russell is saying to me.

"Maybe yer perception is a little off, 'cuz it looks like yer becomin' quite the little queen to me," he says, watching me. "Do you remember Houghton at all, Red?" he asks me. "He tortured you nearly to death. When I found ya, you could hardly talk. Do ya remember runnin' for our lives from him?"

"Do you remember him saving our lives, Russell?" I retort in a harsh whisper, feeling myself flush with anger. "He didn't let Valentine tear us apart."

"I'm not gonna argue with ya 'bout him. We're gonna come and get ya outta here. We have one of yer new buddies. Zephyr and Reed caught him and he's startin' to look pretty hungry to me. Zee just wants to make sure he'll bite ya so that ya don't have to be 'coma girl' for very long," Russell says, watching my reaction.

"When do you plan on coming to get me?" I ask.

"Why?" he asks. "Ya fixin' to tell yer new pals?"

"No!" I whisper back defensively. "I just…I just don't know if I can leave yet," I reply, looking away from his face.

"Yer completely kiddin', right?" he asks, running his hand through his hair like he does when he is really upset. "Yer not stayin' here! We're comin' to get ya. We didn't have to tell ya. This was supposed to be to reassure ya, not to convince ya."

"You don't understand, Russell. If you let me stay, then I can see if I can kill Casimir. He doesn't know that I know about the portal. He will expect me to be as lame and unsuspecting as I was the last time I opened one," I explain, trying to make him see reason. "I would rather do this here. The Gancanagh are wicked at strategy. We might be able to take Casimir out."

"You know, I'm almost tempted to tell Zee what ya just said 'bout their strategy, but I enjoy *livin'*," Russell retorts, looking stunned. "Red, listen to me carefully. *We* have been infiltratin' their security for days. They have huge holes everywhere. They aren't as fast as us and their magic doesn't work on the angels. The only thing they have going on is their skin and the fact that we're watchin' their backs. Reed and Zee have been takin' out all of the Fallen who have been sent to watch this nest. They also took out the Fallen who were amassin' near here, waitin' for all y'all to move. Reed hardly sleeps. He just works," Russell says, and my heart drops.

What is this doing to him? I wonder numbly.

"If I come back now, Casimir will follow me to you," I whisper, feeling guilty for wanting to stay and guilty for wanting to go.

"Good. We'll be ready for him," Russell replies without missing a beat.

"No, Russell, you don't understand. If you take me back, then we lose this chance to get Casimir. If I'm with the angels, Casimir will assume I know that the compact is a portal because the Powers would warn me. Since I'm with the Gancanagh, he thinks I don't know and will proceed with his plans. If you take me now, we lose our edge." I see Russell waver, so I press my advantage. "It's personal for Casimir. I don't know why, but I think he will come for me himself. Maybe he knows my father, Tau," I say, thinking that maybe Casimir knows who he is and has a history with him.

"That stinky devil found yer dad for ya?" Russell asks for clarification.

"His name is Tau," I whisper.

"Hang on…I'm gonna tell the angels all of this. Wait a sec," Russell says with a pained expression.

"They are with you?" I ask, feeling myself blush, because for some reason, I thought this was a conversation between Russell and me. Knowing that Reed is with him makes me curl up and have to retreat inside myself again, like "coma girl."

"Ah shoot, Red," Russell says next to me, seeing that I'm inert again. His clone moves to me, entering my body so we can communicate again.

I hate that contract, Red, Russell's voice sounds inside my head.

You're preaching to the choir, Russell. Try being subject to it, I reply.

Red, don't they let ya sleep 'round here? Russell asks. *Yer exhausted and hungry. Ya should eat. How do ya live like this? Order a cheeseburger or somethin', please!*

I relax immediately, wanting to laugh. *I was trying to go to sleep when you came in.*

Yeah, well, order an aspirin while yer at it 'cuz yer still sore, too, he says with a concerned tone. *Hang on—Buns is tellin' me somethin'.* I wait, trying to still the rush of questions that are pulsing in my head so that it doesn't interfere with him hearing Buns, but it's hard not to think. *All right, Buns said that yer dad is as popular as a rockstar in Paradise—very stellar pedigree ya got there, Red,* Russell says.

Somehow, I'm having a hard time picturing him as a hero, Russell, I reply, feeling anger and pain. *He made me ashamed of who I am for so long. He left me to face all of this alone.*

Ah, Red, yer pissed! I thought you'd be happy that he's not like Alfred, a fallen freak, Russell says.

I don't want to talk about him anymore. He's not here, is he? I ask rhetorically.

Okay, hang on again. I'm tellin' Zee and Reed all 'bout what ya said, 'bout wantin' to stay so ya can trap Casimir with the vampires, Russell says absently. *Reed just crushed his glass…he's freakin' a little…a lot…take it easy, killa, I'm on yer side, Reed…okay, okay! Uhh…Red, Reed said, "no."*

I can feel the anxiety building in me. *This is my mission, Russell,* I reply. *Talk to Zee. He'll see my point. I can do this. Stop getting in my way.*

Gettin' in yer way! Ya did NOT just say that to me! Russell says with disbelief in his tone. *The last time I was here, you were beggin' me to stay—not to leave ya here alone. Reed's right. He just said, "Ya don't kick a wasp's nest and then stand 'round waitin' to see what's gonna happen."*

I'm getting Casimir, I say angrily in my head as that dark place between my heart and my soul flares up, overwhelming me with rage. *He killed Uncle Jim, who was my REAL father, when he sent Alfred to me. He's mine and the GANCANAGH are going to help me. Do you understand? I'm tired of these evil, fallen a-holes. They get to walk around and threaten me and kill my family. Am I supposed to hide behind Reed and Zee and take it? What will Casimir send for me next? An army of Ifrits? Don't even think about coming to get me, Russell, until I do this. Now, get out of my head,* I say, before booting Russell's clone out of me, feeling pissed off and completely exhausted.

The connection to Russell is broken as his clone disappears from my room. It only takes about a minute for me to feel the massive tidal wave of guilt that hits me. I pull the pillow to me, hugging it tight and trying not to cry again. I'm sick of crying.

Slowly, I relax and I must have fallen asleep, because the next thing I know, there are warm arms around me, spooning me as I lie in my bed. Not thinking, I turn over, finding the warm, perfect lips of my angel, and kissing him deeply with all the longing I have had bottled up inside of me. Unfortunately, it isn't long before I become fully awake and I have to retreat inside myself again as whatever magical power the contract has over me kicks in.

Reed groans softly, expressing the ecstasy of our shared kiss and the frustration of having it end. He leans his forehead against mine and tightens his grip on me.

I must be insane, I speculate, thinking about how impossible it seems now to stay away from him even one second longer.

"I miss that, Evie…you have no idea how much I crave a response from you—any type of response," he murmurs, trying to hide the pain in his voice. "Don't worry, I'm not here to make you come with me now. I had to come here and tell you that I need you to come back to me," he breathes against my cheek, and the scent of him is doing lovely things to my insides.

"I'm just getting by without you. I ache from not being able to hear your voice, to see your smile, to feel your caress."

"I understand duty—it is the one thing that makes sense to me. You feel you have to try to kill Casimir for what he did to you. You have forty-eight hours," Reed whispers, looking into my eyes. "Whatever you plan to do has to be done in that time because that is all I am willing to give up. That is it. *I* can't be without *you* any longer than that. Buns and Zee think that I need to give in a little on this and trust your instincts. That is the only reason I am not taking you out of here now. It was suggested to me that if I hadn't been overbearing with you, then you would have come back to us instead of going into the church alone," Reed says with a grim expression on his face, making me swim in guilt for doing this to him.

"I'm trying to change, but you have to understand that I'm used to being in control of every situation. It is difficult for me not to protect you from every threat I see coming at you—nearly impossible," he says with a humorless laugh. "Everything seems like too great a risk when it comes to you. The thought of you here with him for even one more minute is…excruciating to me. If something happens to you before this is over…" he trails off as his jaw clenches and his wing covers my body protectively.

"I know you have a job to do—a mission, but you are still so new at this and still so breakable," Reed says, kissing my neck as he snuggles me to him, causing my heartbeat to accelerate and my cheeks to flush. "Really think about what you are doing when it comes to Casimir. He is older than me. He did not get to be that old by taking chances. He is arrogant, though, and you said you believe this is personal for him. Russell explained the meeting that you had with Casimir. He saw it all in your head and I think you are right—you rattled Casimir."

"I will be nearby from now on. You may feel me here at times. Zee is here too and some of Dominion—Preben, Sorin, and Elan among others. We are taking out the Fallen as they come, but once you spring your trap on Casimir, you should expect retaliation. Do not wait for it. Once your plan is completed, I will come for you and take you from here. The Fallen have many allies that have no loyalties to the Gancanagh, as you have seen," he says, leaning in and kissing my shoulder where I was magically stabbed. "Brennus has been too focused on you. It has blinded him to what is coming," Reed says as he strokes my wing hypnotically, making me feel weak for him.

"We have been protecting the Gancanagh. When the magical contract between you and Brennus is severed, that will end. Then, I will bury him so deep, the cries of Sheol will reign above him," Reed whispers to me.

A chill passes through me like a knife. I should want that—I should want Brennus to suffer, but I don't. He is in my blood, too, whether I want him there or not and now—now the thought of his suffering makes me suffer, too. There is no choice; I have to be with Reed. He is what I want—what I need, but Brennus is...

"I brought venison blood. It's under your bed. If you are bitten...if they turn you..." he whispers through clenched teeth, squeezing me almost painfully tight. "Then find me—I will make a good first kill. Dying in your arms sounds like bliss to me," he says, and my throat tightens painfully, hearing what this is doing to him. He brushes his lips to mine tenderly, before letting me go.

Reed gets up from the bed and gestures towards the small table in my room, saying, "Russell told me you were hungry, so I brought you something to eat." He seems to waver, looking at me in the bed, his hands ball into fists. I notice for the first time that he has the ring that I gave to him on his finger. He had caught it when I dropped it to him today. "Forty-eight hours, Evie...I love you," he whispers, and then he is gone in a fraction of a second.

As I sit up in the bed, I want to scream his name so that he will come back and take me with him. This is insane. I'm insane. *Revenge is not as important as Reed,* I think, resting my forehead on my drawn up knees. But this is more than just revenge. This is destroying Casimir before he destroys anyone else that I love.

I rise from the bed and walk to the table. As I open the carton on it, the aroma of gourmet mac and cheese assails me. A box of Twinkies is lying on the table, too. I set down the mac and cheese and pick up a Twinkie. Unwrapping it, I try not to let tears fall from my eyes as I bite into it.

CHAPTER 21

Plans Within Plans

"I still say me plan has merit—it lulls dem into a sense of complete control, and who could resist her naked body?" Eion asks from across the table, while gesturing towards me with a flick of his hand. "Dey would be fighting each other ta get inta da mirror and through da portal ta her."

"I'm not opening the compact completely naked, Eion," I say, rolling my eyes at him. "How am I supposed to fight back naked?"

"I do na know, but 'twould be interesting ta watch," Eion replies, grinning wolfishly.

"Maybe ye do na have ta be naked…jus da illusion of being naked would do," Brennus says in a thoughtful tone.

"You guys just want to see me nekkid," I say suspiciously, watching their faces grin nefariously.

It's a larger group than I'm used to seeing for a meeting in the Knights Bar. In addition to Brennus, Finn, Declan, Eion, and Faolan, we now have Goban, Lonan, Ninian, Alastar, and Torin sitting with us at the tables we pushed together in the kirk. But, even with the new faces, I'm exceedingly aware that one face is missing among us: Lachlan.

"I still say we should use a clone instead of Genevieve," Declan says.

"A naked clone?" Eion asks, seeing Declan scowl at him.

"Na a naked clone, jus one of her clones. Dat way, she can be safe somewhere else while we sort out da Sheol Shiners for her," Declan says, looking from Eion to me and seeing my scowl.

"I'm not useless, Deck. I can do this," I say angrily. "I want to be there if Casimir comes through." *I want him to know why he's dying—that it's personal for me, too.*

Declan gives me a wary smile. "Dere is no question dat ye are useful. Ask da Werree and dey will tell ye dat, but I still do na like it. Dese are *aingeals* we're talking about, na Werree—auld and ancient *aingeals*. I'd still be nervous if yer body was made from iron and yer heart of steel," Declan replies, looking me over as if I am made out of paper. "Dis is na a game, lass. Dese tings are da very embodiment of evil," he says, shaking his head.

"Thanks, Deck, but I just put on my boots, so I'm not very concerned where I put my foot," I reply, hearing the fellas try to suppress their laughter. Declan glances upward, like he is looking for guidance from above.

"Ye're starting ta sound like one of us," Finn says, shaking his head at me with a wink.

"Da more I tink about Eion's plan, da more I like it, *mo chroí*," Brennus says, bringing us back to the discussion of how to use the compact that Casimir sent to me. "It makes ye appear naïve and vulnerable, two tings dat are almost irresistible ta dem. 'Tis my favorite kind of trap—lust, being caught in a web of desire," he says in a seductive tone. "Da place is small and intimate, too. 'Twould appeal ta Casimir's nature…'tis sensual and erotic…" Brennus says, watching my cheeks flush wi' color as I squirm a little.

I rub my forehead in frustration. "Can't we just open it in the war room and when they come out, we throw the kitchen sink at them?" I mutter, seeing them all look confused by my comment, because sometimes they are all so literal.

"Whah…Why would we trow a sink at dem when we have charmed automatics and missile launchers?" Ninian asks in confusion. "Faolan, I tought ye said ye showed her da weapons room. Ye said ye taught her how ta break down da armor piercing fifty calibers and rebuild dem. Why is she talking about sinks?" he asks, stabbing his finger at Faolan accusingly.

"FINE!" I say, holding up both my hands so they won't begin to argue. "We will do it Eion's way, but it will have to be the 'illusion of naked' and we have to do it soon—tonight. I don't want Casimir to get suspicious as to why I haven't opened his gift. The sooner the better." I'm running out of time. Reed said forty-eight hours and several of those hours are already gone.

"'Tis da plan den?" Brennus asks me for verification. I nod, feeling fear beginning to set in now that I have a course of action. I don't know what makes me more terrified, failing or succeeding. Failing means Casimir survives to hunt my friends and me. Succeeding makes me a true killer. Once I cross the line into the realm of stalking my prey, I can't go back. I will no longer be hiding. I will be hunting.

"Dere are a few hours of light left. We execute when darkness falls," Brennus says, scanning our faces. His eyes remain on my face as the others get up from their seats. "Go and feed. We meet in da North Tower when ye are finished," he says, watching me as I remain where I'm seated.

"Aren't you going with them?" I ask, feeling edgy. I rise from my seat and push it back in before heading for the door.

"Na now," he says, smiling slowly and following me to the door. "Ye need a distraction. Ye are too tense. Ye will have ta relax or Casimir will sense dat dere is someting wrong. Yer body language will tell him all he wants ta know. Ye have ta make him trust dat ye do na know dat he is watching ye when ye open da portal."

"How am I supposed to do that?" I ask as I turn to look at his face. Grinning at me, Brennus takes my hand in his, bringing it to his lips. I lean against the door to the Knight's Bar biting my lip. I want to pull my hand back, but it will make him angry.

"I know several ways ta make ye feel very…" he kisses the palm of my hand, "very…" he kisses my wrist, "relaxed." He says, kissing the sensitive skin at the crook of my elbow.

"Oh," I breathe, feeling my body reacting to Brennus' touch. "I had a soccer coach, growing up, who always said it was better to play with an edge," I whisper. Brennus ignores my comment, pulling me into his arms and kissing me with just a whisper of a touch to my lips.

"Wait," I murmur breathlessly against his mouth, trying to find a way to stop him from kissing me. "There is one thing that you promised me that you haven't given me yet…" I pull back from his mouth and see his sexy smile, his eyebrow goes up like he is intrigued.

"Whah have I promised ye dat I have na given ta ye?" he asks, toying with a piece of my hair. I can feel the cool air between his body and mine, touching me like a caress.

"You haven't shown me how to use the weapon you gave me," I reply, referring to the axe he gave me in the archive.

He shakes his head and closes his eyes. His smile turns into a small grimace. "Ye want ta fight wi' me now?" he asks, seeing me nodding my head with a devious smile.

"Yes, I need to break something and you look like a fragile, little flower—you smell like one, too" I add, sniffing the air around him teasingly, trying to find a way to redirect him. "Maybe I should get Finn to show me instead," I say, raising my eyebrow to mirror his.

I feel energy in the room shift. It should have prepared me for the ring of thorny rose bushes that are magically growing out of the floor, encircling us. Startled, I move nearer to Brennus, hearing him chuckle as his arms go around my waist. "Even flowers can be deadly, *mo chroi*," Brennus says, reaching over and plucking a deep red bloom from the foliage. Holding the flower to my cheek, he strokes the pedals over it sensually. "Tell me dat ye love me," he says, allowing a thorn from the stem to trail threateningly, but not painfully, over my neck as he brings it lower.

"Why?" I ask, feeling restless and cornered, but underneath that, a thrill of danger courses through me like a drug.

"Because I want ta hear ye say it," he replies, allowing the petals to trail a path over my clavicle. "I need it."

"You don't need anything, Brennus. You have proven that to everyone for centuries," I reply, resisting his will, but there is something inside of me that wants to give in—to give him anything he wants. Everything he wants.

"Say it…" he whispers, leaning near my ear and causing my heart to contract.

"Brennus," I sigh, trying to sound aloof, but feeling my heartbeat pounding in my chest.

"Why will ye na tell me?" he asks, his mouth inches from mine. "I know dat ye love me. I can feel it when ye look at me now. I can see how yer eyes follow me."

"Maybe I'm making sure that the scary monster in the room isn't in a bad mood," I reply, taking the flower from his hand and touching the petals lightly with my fingertips.

"Ye lie. Why?" he asks, lifting my chin to look in my eyes.

"Go to the South Tower. The wans will line up to tell you how much they love you," I say, surprised and disconcerted to hear jealousy in my tone.

"'Tis meaningless, Genevieve. Dat is intoxication and lust," he explains with a darkness growing in his eyes. His thumb traces my jaw, but my jealousy has softened his eyes, making him look satisfied.

"I don't want to love you," I whisper honestly, pulling my chin back and looking down, seeing that I have crushed the silky petals in my hand.

"Dat does na change da fact dat ye do," he replies with a sultry smile.

"How can I possibly describe what I feel for you, Brennus?" I ask, shaking my head and feeling the painful ache inside of me. "This isn't like the love I have felt before. Whatever it is, it's painful. If this is love, then I love you the way creatures like us ought to be loved—secretly and unwillingly, within the dark shadow between my heart and my soul."

"'Tis how it starts, *mo chroí*. 'Twas like dat for me, in da caves," Brennus replies, his arms encircling me again. "'Tis da kind of love ye want ta destroy, but it grows inta something much, much more powerful den ye can imagine, if ye let it."

"I don't want it to grow," I reply, looking away from him again. "It will only bring me pain."

"'Twill only if ye resist it," he breathes against my cheek. "Let me teach ye about da pleasure within dat pain," he says, stroking my arms. "Let me hear ye cry out jus for me."

"Brennus," I say exasperatedly, "I don't want pleasure. I want to smash something," I say, frustrated by the tumult of emotions within me. A shiver passes through me, fearing that

I won't be able to stop him if he wants to follow through with that thought.

"Ye have so much ta learn, ye have no idea," Brennus groans. "Soon, I will show ye whah I'm saying."

"Seeing is easier than saying?" I ask ruefully, looking up at him and trying to make light of it all.

"'Tis," Brennus agrees with a reluctant smile. "I jus have ta keep in mind dat ye are an eternal being, so dere is time for all da tings I want ta teach ye." I lower my eyes from his, trying not to let him see that he may not be right about that.

"There are some things that she doesn't need to learn from ya," Russell says, while strolling right through the rose bushes like a ghost. "Roses?" Russell scoffs. "Don't ya think that's a little cliché? She's more of a Bird of Paradise—somethin' exotic and unexpected."

"Russell!" I gasp, feeling my face flush, while wondering how much of our conversation he overheard. I know I'm seeing his clone, but I can smell his clean scent and see his smart-ass smirk that I know is his "game face." I want to run to him, but I know I can't do that.

"If you want to teach her somethin', you should take her to the South Tower. But, I can see why ya wouldn't want her to learn 'bout what goes on there, right?" Russell asks Brennus, but his eyes are on me. He is making sure that I'm okay and his concern for me is enough to shake me up a little. "You should see it, Red, it's like a strip club without the money…oh, and of course, all the women are strung out and bleedin'."

I feel myself go pale. *Why do I keep forgetting that they kill people?* I wonder to myself, feeling the line between right and wrong move again and distort.

"Da other. I knew dat I should have killed ye, but I tought maybe ye had more sense dan ye do," Brennus says, rubbing the back of his neck with his hand, then he shrugs, like it's of little consequence. "'Tis time I made ye a priority again. I should know better dan ta na follow tru wi' da killing."

"And I should've known better than to come here without an air freshener, but here we all are, together again," Russell agrees, looking around at the interior of the Knight's Bar and the beautiful rosette windows.

Brennus' arms encircle me again, pulling me into his embrace. Nuzzling my neck, Brennus says to Russell, "Ye are na really here, are ye? If ye were, I doubt ye would be saying much right now and we both know dat. So, ye should tell her wha-hever 'tis ye came here ta say. We have plans dat do na include ye."

"I'm here to see you, vampire," Russell sneers, watching Brennus' fingers trace a line up my arm, caressing me and caus-ing a shiver to pass through me at his cool touch. "Yer place in India has been infiltrated by the Fallen. That is where all y'all were headed next, right?" Russell asks rhetorically.

Brennus pauses, his eyebrows drawing together. "Why are ye telling me dis?" he asks, not letting me go, but no longer kissing my neck either.

"'Cuz ya have my girl," Russell replies with his hands balled in fists while he watches Brennus touch me.

"She's na yer girl," Brennus says.

"Naw, she's not yer girl, stalker," Russell counters. "Yer a pretender. Ya pretend to be good—to be her family, but yer nothin' more than a vampire and she needs to wake up and see that." Turning to me, Russell barks, "Wake up, Red," making me jump a little at the anger in his tone.

"She is awake. Whah do ye want from her? Ye want her ta kill herself for ye, is dat it?" Brennus counters, his fangs engaging as he lets go of me and walks with stealthy grace around Russell's clone, looking for a way to hurt him. "She already tried dat, remember? Ye want ta see her die for ye? She can na stay wi' ye. Ye will get her killed—or worse."

"Naw, that's what yer gonna do," Russell replies. "The Fallen have been all 'round this place, watchin' all y'all."

"Dat is na surprising. So, ye have been killing dem off for us?" Brennus stops circling Russell, coming to stand in front of him. "We're able ta protect her from dem. We do na need ye ta do it for us."

"Now it's yer turn to wake up, Dracula," Russell says between his teeth. "They want her."

"Den let dem come and try ta take her. Dere is no reason ye should have all da fun," Brennus replies, sniffing the air around Russell. He is processing all of the attributes of Russell's clone, trying to find a weakness.

"She's not a pawn," Russell says with menace, leaning towards Brennus.

"Tell dat ta da *aingeals* wi' ye. Dey would like nuting better dan ta use her ta bring da Fallen ta dem ta heat up deir war," he says with an ironic twist of his lips, smiling at Russell and showing him his wicked fangs.

"Yer wrong. We're gonna protect her when we get her back," Russell argues sharply.

"Ye try ta take her and dere will be no place for ye ta hide from me," Brennus says with deathly calm.

"Who's hidin'? We don't have to hide anymore. She fixed that when she went to Dominion. Y'all actually helped, too." Russell replies with a smug smile, crossing his arms in front of his chest with a look of pure satisfaction. "When ya blew the crap out of Dominion, they got on board with whatever Reed wants—an army of angels. They think she's a gift from God now…so, thanks."

"So ye're here ta convince me ta let her come back ta ye," Brennus asks incredulously.

"Naw, I'm not stupid. I know ya will never willingly let her go," Russell says sullenly. "I'm here to ask ya not to be a complete idiot with the Fallen. Don't take chances with her life. Casimir is too powerful to take on alone—we'll help you, if it comes down to her life."

"So, ye're da olive branch?" Brennus asks with a skeptical look.

"Naw, I'm the guy that's gonna whoop yer ass if you let anythin' happen to her," Russell replies, pointing his finger in Brennus' face.

"Ye sound like someone wi' a plan," Brennus remarks, not flinching at all at having Russell's clone so near to him. "Are ye really so confident dat da soldier ye captured from here can be persuaded inta biting her?" he asks with a speculative look. "Ye should really reconsider dat move. Leif knows dat da moment he does so is one of his last moments. Either ye will kill him or we will. He may well refuse ta do it. Den, whah will ye do? Will ye bring her back ta me?" he asks, raising his eyebrow.

Russell's eyes widen minutely, enough to let me know that he's surprised that Brennus knows what they have planned. He glances at me, maybe wondering if I told Brennus the plan. A stab of pain hits me at Russell's distrust of me. "He'll bite her, 'cuz he knows that we will kill him quickly after he does. And anyway, all he needs to do is see her and he will be beggin' us to taste her. You know I'm right," he says, looking back to Brennus. "You can imagine the torment it would be for him not to, 'cuz he has the same look on his face when I talk 'bout her that ya did in the caves when I took her from ya last time—pure agony."

"I still owe ye for dat," Brennus says, his jaw clenching.

"C'mon and find me then, what're ya waitin' for? All y'all keep countin' me out and I can't understand why that is. You see how powerful she is becomin'. I'm just like her and soon I'm gonna be yer worst nightmare," Russell says, grinning as he watches Brennus' brows pull together in a scowl.

Brennus loses his scowl after a few moments, while retracting his fangs. His face changes to mirror Russell's grin. "I tink dat I can see why she likes ye. Ye really are amusing, but 'tis easy ta be tough when ye're na really here. Da next time ye want ta parley wi' me, come in person, like ye did da last time. Ye will get more respect dat way," Brennus says patiently. "Goodbye, da other."

Lifting his finger, Brennus touches it to Russell's clone, making him disappear instantly. Brennus stares at his finger for a moment, and then he smiles before he turns back to me. It's taking everything in me not to show any emotion over Russell leaving. I know I chose to stay, but that decision is haunting me now.

"Ach, I give him points for style. I really like dose clones. I wonder if I could replicate someting like dat wi' a spell?" he says, looking amused by what just happened with Russell.

"You're not mad that they are here?" I ask in shock, seeing the amusement on Brennus' face, while trying to figure out Reed's strategy for sending Russell now.

"'Tis na unexpected. I know dat dey are here from time ta time, checking on ye." Brennus replies.

"Will you let them help us, if we need it?" I ask, allowing him to take my arm as he uses his magic to shrink the rose bushes into nothingness.

"I will do anyting dat keeps ye from being harmed," Brennus replies, leading me out of the Knight's Bar. "But, one day, ye will na need a security blanket because ye will be very powerful. Whah will ye do den?" he asks as we stroll together down the corridor towards the North Tower.

I exhale a breath slowly, not really believing that a day like that will ever come. "I don't know. I'm so used to being afraid all the time, I have no idea what I'll do if that all goes away."

"Ye hide yer fear well," Brennus replies, frowning and squeezing my arm.

"Do I?" I ask with a grimace.

"Ye do. 'Tis one of da tings I admire da most about ye. 'Tis dat, and da fact dat ye are able ta act even when ye're filled wi' fear," he smiles. "Ye faced down an Ifrit wi' little more den yer bare hands. Ye canna teach dat kind of courage. Ye either have it or ye do na."

"You know what I like about you?" I ask, seeing the light enter his eyes as he shakes his head.

"I like the way that you tell me things, like we're equals— partners. I like that you include me in the strategy meetings and don't try to shut me out, like I'm not strong enough to handle what's happening," I reply.

"We are partners. Ye're me queen," Brennus replies. A flush stains my cheeks partly from the embarrassment of the title, but the other part of me is flattered by the way he sees me as someone able to make decisions and contribute to the mission.

As we near the North Tower, a couple of fellas approach Brennus. I recognize one as being Cavan. Cavan gives me a tentative look, and then he leans to Brennus, whispering something in his ear. I hear the word "wans." Brennus scowls at him, and then he casts a glance at me and says, "*Mo chroí,* dere is someting I have ta take care of before we go ta da North Tower.

I want ye ta stay here wi' Cavan while I attend ta it. Ye can wait in da alcove over dere. I'll be right back for ye."

Brennus escorts me to the alcove where there is a small settee beneath the windows. I ask, "What is it?"

"Nuting but a headache, me sweet. 'Twill only take me a moment," he replies, before kissing me on the cheek. To Cavan, he says, "She stays here and no one nears her until I come back." Cavan nods and Brennus is gone in a fraction of a second.

I step back out into the hallway and pace in front of the alcove, wondering what is going on. Cavan walks down the long corridor and guards one end, while a fella that I don't know is guarding the other end. I hear voices coming towards Cavan's end, so I turn to see him intercept three young women from wandering towards me.

Reaching Cavan, the women ask him with sultry voices, "Where is my king? Where is Brennus? I want him—he's been away too long." They are dopey, walking around with little more on than silk robes.

"Ye know ye are na ta be out here. Go back ta da South Tower. 'Tis where ye will find him," Cavan says in a chiding tone, touching each of their cheeks and trying to direct them back towards the South Tower. A chill runs through me watching Cavan herd the young ladies away from me.

I glance in the other direction; the other fella is having a similar problem. A flock of females is attempting to come down the hall in search of Brennus. Goose bumps rise on my arms seeing them all. *Am I becoming one of them?* I wonder. *Am I blind to what he is?* Just as that thought hits me, fluttering in my abdomen rapidly overtakes any other thought.

Black, armor-clad arms encircle me, instantly lifting me off the floor and pulling me back into the alcove that shrouds us from being seen by the fellas at either end of the hall. A soft gasp escapes me as I turn to face Reed. I manage to put my arms weakly around Reed's neck and press my lips to his before I go completely limp. His charcoal-gray wings frame him, making him look like the most powerful being in existence.

My arms slide from his neck, but Reed holds me tight against his body as he breathes in my ear, "I used my persuasion to get the humans to leave their tower. I needed a diversion so that I could see you. We don't have much time because my thrall doesn't hold up for very long to their addiction to the Gancanagh. The women will end up trying to be touched again and once they are, they will obey every command," he says, stroking my wing.

"I need to tell you something very important. The Fallen are near and we are seeing unprecedented numbers of them. They are mostly fallen Archangels and Powers, but a few are Seraphim. They are organized and we believe they are preparing to attack within the next few days. I need to get you out of here before that occurs. We know your plan is going to be executed at nightfall," he says rapidly, briefing me. "Be prepared to leave shortly afterward."

"I need to make sure you know that the portal works both ways. Do not, for any reason, enter the portal Casimir gave you. If Casimir gets back in it somehow, you cannot follow him. I mean it, Evie. Let him go because if he can pull you into Sheol..." Reed's tone is stern, but he trails off and squeezes me to him ferociously, before brushing his lips over mine.

"I know that you are capable of doing this," he breathes against my mouth, closing his eyes tight as if in pain. "You were created to protect and destroy. I want to help you do it," he adds, before opening his eyes so I can see the perfection of them. "Just be cautious. Please remember that you are the only thing that matters. I will be here for you, should you need me, my love. I will not fail you again."

My heart twists in pain because he has never failed me. Never. I just don't want to risk losing him. *I want the Gancanagh to destroy Casimir with me, so Reed will be safe, so that there will be no risk to him,* I think. That is my plan. If he intends to help then he is in danger from the Gancanagh *and* the Fallen.

Reed leans his forehead to mine, whispering, "The next time you see me, we are going home, even if your mission is incomplete. Then, you can tell me everything that is in your heart and I will show you all the love in mine for you. Until then, Godspeed, Evie."

Brennus' voice barks out orders to Cavan at the end of the hall. At the sound, Reed stiffens before placing me tenderly on the settee. Reed's fingers trail over my fingers until just the tips of them are touching, and then in the next instant, he is gone.

"Genevieve?" Brennus says from the archway of the alcove. "Are ye well?" he asks, seeing me rise shakily to my feet. He comes to stand next to me, taking my elbow and leading me back towards the North Tower.

"Of course," I reply, trying hard to hold a smile for his benefit. "Did you take care of the problem?" I ask, trying to distract him.

"I did," he says, his mouth pulling down in the corners. "We will be leaving here as soon as we sort out da Fallen. Our position has flaws. We still retain a superior edge, but 'tis because our enemies are reluctant to attack us. Dat will change soon." Brennus says, guiding me up the winding staircase. "I spoke ta Finn; he is making all da necessary arrangements. Ye fancy a warmer climate?" he asks and I nod my head, trying not to let him see the worry I feel.

What if something goes wrong and the angels lose me again?

"Won't that make it harder for you to blend in with the locals?" I ask with a teasing smile, running my finger over the pale skin of his forearm. "We might have to get you some spray tan."

Grinning at me, Brennus says, "Dere is a solution for everyting. Ye are waking me up ta all the possibilities." He reaches over to tuck my hair behind my ear so that he can see my profile better as we stroll down the hallway together. "Ye take away all of da emptiness of death, *mo chroí.* Ye make da possibility of a true death seem less important den losing ye. Ye have become da only ting dat matters ta me and I know ye are na aloof ta me."

His words make the air feel thin, like it's getting harder to breathe. I want to deny what he is saying and run away from the truth in his words. As we reach our room, he holds the door open for me and closes it securely behind us. He pulls me into his arms, kissing me with a passion that I am wholly unprepared for, while picking me up in his arms and carrying me towards the bedroom.

Laying me on the bed, he follows me down. "Wait," I say, turning my face away from his, trying to slow him down as I feel him begin to pull my shirt up. His cool hand skims over my ribcage sensually, making me shiver.

"No," he replies, ignoring my attempts to get him to stop kissing me when I turn my face away from him. He just moves lower, continuing to kiss my neck, while holding me in his arms.

"I'm not ready to…" I say, but I stop and gasp as he tears the shirt from my body, exposing the sexy little undergarments I have on beneath it.

"Ye're ready," he replies smoothly. "Ye should smell da pheromones ye are emitting. 'Tis like a drug. I feel intoxicated by it. Ye have no idea how ye affect me—'tis almost like tasting ye," he breathes against my skin. He doesn't know that Reed caused those pheromones to leap out of me.

"But, I can't—" I say with a groan, putting my hands on his chest to gain some space between us.

"Ye have no choice," he replies with a sultry smile, kissing me as his hands roam over my body. "Ye are me prisoner."

"I thought I was your partner," I breathe, like it's a soft, little secret between us.

"Dat, too," he whispers against my lips. "Ye are me prisoner as I am yers."

"Oh," I breathe back, believing what he is telling me—he is my prisoner and somehow, I always knew that. "But you're no good for me."

"Come now, I am a guilty pleasure at da very least," he replies seductively. His hands trace my silhouette as if memorizing the shape of me. "Ye are na alone anymore, ye are part of dis family. Together ye and I will be more powerful den anyting ye can imagine." He brushes the hair back from my face with a growing darkness in his eyes. "Can ye na feel me in yer blood?" he whispers against my neck, his cool lips toying with me, causing my pulse to beat harder against those lips. "I can feel ye in me bones. I crave the innocence in ye; even as I want ta take it from ye, so dat I can teach ye whah lies beyond dat innocence. I love ye, *mo chroí*," he whispers. "I will love ye forever."

My heart pounds in my chest, like it will tear at any second. I don't want to love him and I don't want him to love me either. Tears creep into my eyes because I have confusing feelings for him, too, but they are a burden to me. Bonds formed between us when he killed Alfred for me, when he saved my friends and me from the Ifrit, when he protected me from Casimir, and when he told me of my father. But, what I feel for Reed makes all of that pale in comparison.

"Eternity is a long time, me *aingeal*," Brennus responds, undeterred by what he sees in my eyes. "So many tings can happen in da space of infinite time. Ye will forget everyting in time. Ye jus need ta let go."

"I will never forget him," I whisper, feeling Brennus' pain as I push him away from me. "I belong with him." I watch anger and frustration grow in Brennus' eyes as his fangs engaged with a *click*.

My hands tremble, not knowing what he intends to do as he leans nearer to me, holding my arm almost painfully.

"Ye're moin. Ye'll always be moin and soon, ye'll know it. I should break all of yer illusions now and show ye whah I mean, but I want ye ta come ta me—ta ask me ta love ye. I will wait for dat. Do na make me wait much longer," he breathes before placing a gentle kiss on my lips and letting me go. I rise up on my elbows, feeling my blood draining from my face even as relief is swamping me.

As I watch Brennus walk to the door, I ask, "What if I never ask you to love me?" I think he isn't going to answer my question, but then he pauses at the door.

Without looking at me, Brennus says in a low tone, "Den, I'll make ye beg me."

CHAPTER 22

The Compact

The compact gives a soft gasp of stale air as I lift the lid, opening it. I carry it with me across the bathroom and let it reflect the contours of my face before angling it lower to reveal the deep red silk of my robe. I place the compact on the edge of the enormous, sunken spa tub, and then I untie the belt of my robe, peeling it off slowly. The fabric falls in front of the mirror like the silken ripple of sand dunes. My fingers skim the hot water as it flows from the ornate, gold faucet into the tub. I gently ease into the water.

Heat from the water causes my face to flush while the white, frothy bubbles tickle my skin, eliciting a sensual smile from me. I ease back against the edge of the bath. Picking up the mirror, I check the pins in my hair, making sure that they are all secure. I don't want the tendrils to slip down and fall in the water as it laps against my bare shoulders.

I lean to the edge of the enormous bathtub and prop the compact on the marble-tiled shelf by the stone stairs. Closing my eyes, I hum a tune to myself. I try to control the pounding of my heart as I hear soft, fluttering sounds like moths make while flying around a porch light.

As I open my eyes slowly, I try really hard to keep my features blank. I gaze around the room, seeing that all the walls and floors are covered in a variety of different insects. Crickets, locusts, grasshoppers, and beetles are crawling with scuttling movements and extended feelers near my arm where it rests on the edge of the tile. Exhaling softly, like I have been punched in the stomach, my wings shoot from of my back. A cascade of water splashes from the spa, causing some of the insects to wash onto the floor. Immediately, the insects erupt into the air, blotting out the light like shifting, hazy black clouds.

Whirling like water through a funnel, the insects all sort themselves, connecting together to form angelic silhouettes. The dark form of black crickets bursts forth into a leering Power with the dove gray wings of a bird of prey.

Similar things are happening with the beetles and grasshoppers. They both implode into frighteningly strong beings with the white wings of Archangels. The wings of one Archangel fans out, blotting out most of the light behind it when his eyes come to rest on me in the tranquil water. His slow, flawless smile has my heartbeat racing while I struggle to keep fear from showing in my eyes.

The reek that I am expecting isn't as bad as I thought it would be. They still smell rotten, but it's not making me want to hurl.

They must be staying away from Sheol, I think, surprised because that means that this portal doesn't lead directly to Hell. Maybe they are afraid that this is a trap and they don't want to give us an avenue to enter their domain uninvited.

When the locusts pour onto the floor, crawling over each other and twisting into distorted shapes, I can think of nothing but killing scenarios. Then, Casimir's disdainful expression emerges from the swirling chaos, his perfect features giving little away as to what he is thinking.

When his eyes make contact with me, like the Archangel before him, his crimson wings push out to full extension showing me his fierce power. A deeper flush stains my cheeks, because even though I don't know what he is saying to me with his wings, I know it's not good. Fear makes me want to leap up out of the water and scramble for the door. It's really kind of good that my legs are numb with fear, so I don't follow that impulse that would probably get me killed.

"Locusts…that suits you, Casimir," I murmur in a low tone, leaning back against the wall of the spa nonchalantly. "You do sort of remind me of a plague. You guys should try something less disgusting…like fireflies. The crickets are okay. Some people consider them lucky," I add, looking at the terrifying Power angel who hasn't taken his eyes off of me. "I have got to say that in your case, Power, it's a little ominous. I *would* like to know how you can keep your body armor on when you shapeshift. I always wind up completely nekkid. It's inconvenient."

"Is this your way of stalling us so you can figure out which way to run?" Casimir asks in a gentle voice, looking a little more satisfied than he did the last time I saw him.

"I know which way to run, Casimir," I reply, leaning to my side and crossing my arms on the edge of the spa. "Do you?" I ask, quirking my eyebrow while trying to control my breathing because my heart keeps insisting on increasing it's pace.

"Find him and bring him here," Casimir says, barely moving at all from where he is standing in the middle of the bathroom. In an instant, the Archangels are gone, exiting through the bathroom door that connects to my bedroom.

Approaching the spa slowly, Casimir crouches down so that he is nearly eye level with me. He touches one of the drops of water on my arm, following the wet path downward. Then, he shifts his jewel-like brown eyes and gazes into mine, studying me.

"Who are you looking for?" I ask, not moving at all as I watch Casimir's eyes shift again, touching every inch of my exposed skin with his gaze.

"You should ask, 'For whom are you looking?'" Casimir replies, correcting me while he reaches out idly to touch my hair. His pupils dilate a little as he pulls the pins from it, letting it fall through his fingers.

I feel my face flush again at being corrected by this monster, but I play along, asking him, "For whom are you looking?"

"Your master," Casimir replies.

"I have no master," I counter.

"You have too many masters. I am here to begin to correct that for you," he says, his eyes shifting to my wings that I'm trying really hard to keep still so I won't give away any of what I'm thinking.

"So, you are here to help me?" I ask in a cool manner, seeing how my question has brought the corners of his mouth upward just a little more. I knew this would be hard, confronting a compassionless angel, but feeling his breath on my cheek is making me want to cower in fear.

"I'm here to see if you are worth saving…or if you have been tainted beyond redemption," he responds easily, like it's of no consequence to him either way. But, his golden-tanned, flawless skin is growing a little flushed as his eyes continue to assess me.

I let a smile form on my mouth. "Your choice of words is… interesting," I murmur, resting my chin on my crossed arms. "So, what's the verdict, Chief? Am I worth it?" I ask, trying not to hold my breath as I wait for his answer.

"It is not that simple," he replies, studying me. "You have earned some respect for not cowering when we arrived, but that is a minor victory."

"I don't mind tests," I say as casually as possible, knowing that these angels do not respect anything but strength. Showing fear is like begging them to kill me. "My life seems to possess an endless array of them."

"Yes, you do seem to excel when presented with a challenge," Casimir agrees. "You are a lovely, little coquette, with impressive adaptability—something new. You lack the callousness of most angels of our ilk. I doubt that when you kill you feel nothing," he says, like he knows me well.

"I doubt that when I kill you, it will trouble me much," I reply with a smile, trying to exhibit the brashness that seems to attract these monsters.

Casimir looks genuinely amused by my comment; a smile is inching up on his face. "That sounds too innocent coming from you. It is quite difficult to appear dignified, however, when you are crawling on the ground. You have fallen prey to an inferior race. I am here to show you the error of your ways. We do not grovel. We do not allow others to make us their lap dogs."

"There is no 'we,' Casimir. There is you and there is I," I reply. "Why would you ever imply that I am one of you?" I ask, and then I hear the Power who has been observing our conversation begin to chuckle, like my comment amuses him. My eyes shift to his face, his lips form a kiss as he winks at me leeringly. Panic fills me at the thought of him touching me. I take a small breath, trying to calm down as I wrinkle my nose at him before looking back to Casimir.

"If we allow you to become one of us, then you will be most fortunate. I simply meant that Seraphim do not allow others to control us," he explains patiently.

"So, what is it that you want from me, Casimir? Apart from letting me know that you're offended by the company I keep," I ask with no emotion, trying to hide the fact that this is the most important question I have ever asked anyone.

"There is a lesson here, Genevieve. Information is costly. The one with the answers is always valuable. I do not trade what is valuable for anything other than everything I want," Casimir replies.

"And what's that?" I ask with a quirk of my eyebrow.

"You," he replies, causing the hair on my arms to rise up.

"What? Don't tell me you want my soul, like Alfred did. Do you really think they are going to allow you back into Paradise with a stolen soul?" I ask, glancing up at the ceiling and then back down to his beautiful face, like he's crazy.

"Why would you think that I would ever want to go back there, where I am a second class citizen? A servant to lesser beings?" Casimir inquires, tilting his head to the side as if evaluating my logic.

"So, if Paradise is not the goal, then what?" I ask, playing with the bubbles in the tub, picking them up in my hand. I'm trying to hide the fact that his words are disturbing me, but they probably already know that because the blood is draining from my face.

"Why do you think the Divine want you?" he counters.

"They like me," I say, shrugging my shoulders and playing dumb. The true answer is that they see me as a weapon—a powerful weapon that attracts their Fallen prey to me.

"Of course they do," Casimir replies, keeping his face blank. "Why do they like you?"

"Oh…well, I'm funny," I say, hearing the Power behind Casimir burst out laughing, so I give him the there-you-go gesture.

"No, you are evading. If you do not want to know, then do not ask," he says in a casual mien.

"I'm their new, favorite weapon," I answer him, looking at his face and seeing his eyes soften at the edges a fraction.

"Precisely," he breathes. "But, have you noticed that you do the same thing to them as you do to us? We are the same, Divine and Fallen. Our physiology does not differ. We are all Angels."

"So that makes me a gun in anyone's hand," I reason. "If you can pull the trigger, then I'm your weapon."

He shrugs. "There is so much more to it than that, but if you want to speak in layman's terms, I will concede your point. Explore the possibilities where you are concerned. They are endless. If we can lure the Divine to us, then we have the advantage. If we can show you our side in this, because there is always the flip side of the coin, perhaps you will see our point of view. If not, maybe the Divine will. You see? You are a new race. What is your purpose? Is it to replace all of us? How do you think the Divine will feel about being replaced? Do you think they will appreciate it?" he asks me and I can't stop the shiver that courses through me.

If the Fallen can make me look like an enemy to the Divine, they can perhaps persuade them to align with them…the enemy of my enemy is my friend. It sounds absurd, but it's already happened with the Ifrits changing loyalties. It happens all the time in their world, I think, feeling cold.

"What will humans do when they are no longer favored? If they are to be replaced by you?" he continues, enjoying what his suppositions are doing to me. "No matter what you believe, you are truly alone in the universe. You are the only one of your species that exists."

But I'm not…I have Russell, I think, trying to hide my thoughts from Casimir. *What will he do if he learns of Russell?* I feel numb and lower my eyes to hide Russell from him.

"You think I'm a warning from God? A threat?" I whisper in a secretive tone, like the kind I use when I think no one is listening. I glance up grimly from the water around me to Casimir's face. His perfect aching brow softens.

"You are alluring," he says with admiration in his tone. "A very destructive being. It was absolute genius to make you female. If you had been male, you would not have survived this long," he says with absolute certainty.

"Lucky me," I utter numbly.

"Threats work both ways, Genevieve. You will be extremely lethal soon. You could rival anything in Paradise—anything," he says in a low tone, watching my reaction.

I still. "Now you're talking stupid," I reply, feeling my throat tighten in fear.

"Am I?" he asks, his eyes widening in surprise. "You have been given weapons that none of us possess. We suspected that you would be powerful, but to see you begin to realize that potential is…tempting."

I yawn like I have seen Brennus do when someone says something to upset him. "Power is overrated. Have you ever heard the saying, 'Heavy is the head that wears the crown?'" I ask him. "I don't crave that kind of power. It's exhausting."

"And trying to survive the whims of others is not?" he asks me probingly.

"It is preferable to trying to rule them," I reply honestly.

"Dangerous," he whispers, showing me his first, true smile.

He is exquisitely beautiful with his golden hair and his handsome façade, but it's just that, a façade. He speaks in Angel to the Power in the room who then glances to the bathroom door. The Power shrugs, and then steps towards me with a wolfish grin on his face.

"What are you doing," I ask them calmly, but I feel my stomach lurch.

"We are ready to depart," Casimir says, straightening up and towering over me in the tub. "Altair will assist you through the portal."

"I thought you sent the Archangels to find Brennus," I say, watching his eyes darken.

"They will bring him to us. We will make him see that it is in his best interest to break his contract with you. If he cannot see it, then he will feel it. It will be uncomfortable for you, if we have to do it that way, but you seem to adapt well to adversity," he replies easily, like my pain is irrelevant.

"So, you've decided I'm worth saving?" I ask, submerging my hands in the water, so he doesn't just reach in and pull me out. "You change your mind like a I change my clothes."

"How so?" he asks and Altair pauses by the tub to hear my answer.

"The Werree that you sent already tried to kill me," I reply.

"Yes, and you killed nearly all of them for it," he states with a gleam in his eyes. "If I had but one wish, it would have been to find someone like you."

"And if you were a coin, I'd throw you down a well without making a wish," I reply.

"I stand corrected. It is you," he says without his usual disdainful expression.

"What is it about what I just said that is appealing?" I ask with exasperation, shaking my head in confusion. "I *so* don't get any of you."

"No one speaks to them like you do, "Altair replies, grinning.

"Like what? With my mouth?" I ask him sarcastically.

"Boldly—without fear. If they do, they rarely retain the ability to speak again," Altair replies, extending his hand for me to take so that he can assist me from the spa. His eyes are darkening, maybe in anticipation of seeing me rise naked from the water.

"Why should I fear him, Altair, when I intend to kill him?" I ask, ignoring his hand.

"Why would you want to do that when I am going to rescue you from the Gancanagh? I will be your master—" Casimir begins.

I interrupt him. "What makes you think I will allow you to enslave me?" I ask, annoyed by his sheer arrogance.

"How will you stop me?" he counters.

"Painfully," I reply, seeing how my words are affecting him. He has lost the bored look he had before.

"Why would you find my guidance more repulsive than your present predicament?" he asks.

"You stole something from me," I reply.

"I have nothing that belongs to you," he replies, puzzled, his perfect brow showing a beautiful frown.

"You stole a piece of my heart," I say, feeling my throat get tight. "You sent Alfred and he killed my uncle."

"You are referring to the human who raised you?" Casimir asks, his color heightening. He is enjoying my need for vengeance.

"I am," I nod, losing the battle to keep the hatred from my expression.

"But he was merely a human. They all die eventually. Some more gruesomely than others, I will admit. 'Every man wants to go to Heaven, but no one wants to die.' You can think of what we did as sending him to Paradise for you. Now you will always know where he is."

"Joe Louis said that about Heaven," I say, recognizing the quote as coming from the iconic boxer from Detroit.

"Yes, I know. I read it in one of your school papers," he says, causing goose bumps to rise on my arms.

Evil Freak, I think, chilled.

"Joe said something else as well," I reply, feeling something brush up against my foot within the water. "He said, 'Everyone's got to figure to get beat sometime.' Maybe your time is coming, Casimir. Maybe it'll be soon."

"Ah, Genevieve, I will enjoy showing you your place. It is truly something I am anticipating with emotions that I had thought I would never feel again," he says with an angelic smile that is in direct contrast to his ominous tone.

"And where is my place?" I ask, feeling disgust.

"Beneath me," he smiles and I know that he means directly beneath him. His words make fear run through my veins like icy water, but I can't let them know that his words scare me.

"Altair, do you plan on helping him?" I ask, turning to the Power who cannot hide the yearning on his face. "He's going to need it."

Both Altair and I freeze when we hear Casimir laugh softly in amusement. It's a compelling laugh, deep and…honest. The shock on Altair's face lets me know that this might well be the first time he has ever heard Casimir laugh.

Casimir grins. "You have me spinning. I cannot decide what I shall do with you. Shall I show you the savage side of your nature…take you down to the primal level of what you are?" he asks with a delicate lifting of his eyebrow. "You could be the platform on which I rise. But, I will have to tame you first, because right now you are a beautiful disgrace. I will have to make you respond only to me," he says, his eyes tightening cunningly in the corners.

"Altair, does he always speak like that?" I ask, wrinkling my nose again. "I love his choice of words—beautiful disgrace, like he is unaware that he is the embodiment of that."

Altair smiles at me. "He will never be able to hold on to you, Seraph," Altair replies almost reverently, extending his hand to me again. "The other Seraphim will fight for you when they see you—you may well be the one—" Altair is interrupted when Casimir emits a low, terrifying growl.

Just when he does so, Brennus' hand reaches up out of the bath water and grasps Altair's hand firmly, before he rises slowly to bring his dripping-wet face within mere inches of Altair's waning expression.

As water runs off his chin onto his pale, bare chest, he says to me, "'Tis a good ting I'm already dead and do na really need ta breathe, *mo chroí*. Did ye plan ta talk ta dem all evening?" he asks, not looking at Altair who has a dopey expression on his face now, but directly at Casimir. Brennus' face darkens with anger, "Kill him," he orders Athair. I watch Altair straighten up instantly, turning on Casimir and pulling wicked daggers from the holsters strapped to his hips, like a gun slinger pulls out sidearms.

As Altair lunges at Casimir, I hardly see Casimir move but he easily grasps Altair's wrists, halting the attack. Casimir twists Altair's wrist until it breaks, effectively turning the weapon in Altair's hand. He uses the redirected momentum to plunge the long dagger into Altair through the layers of Altair's body armor. Then, Casimir pulls the dagger upward, gutting the Power angel as pieces that belong inside of Altair spill out onto the tiled floor. Casimir does not pause but clutches the knife and cuts the head from the Power as he holds him up.

Shock creeps over me as the scent of blood fills the air and Altair crumbles headless to his knees. It is then that I discover that knowing the plan and executing it are two very, very different things. Seeing the brutality of Altair's death makes me hesitate for a fraction of a second. When I recover, I pull my hands up out of the water and lift the wet, combat-ready, fully automatic machine gun complete with kick ass, banjax charms from the depths of the spa.

Positioning the gun against my shoulder, I point it at Casimir and squeeze the trigger. A spray of bullets bursts forth, honing in on him. When the first bullet penetrates his thigh, spraying his blood on the wall of the bathroom, a small smile forms on my lips.

In the next moment, my smile slips as Casimir literally shatters into a swarm of locusts again.

"No," I breathe, seeing my bullets gliding between the pieces of him.

I drop my gun into the water and scramble out of the tub. My skin-tight body suit drips water onto the floor as I run towards the swarm of flying insects. Batting at the bugs with my hands, I am hurled backward off my feet by Casimir's angelic silhouette of locusts. I crash into the vanity, toppling the perfume bottles and smashing the mirror into large shards of glass.

Stunned for a moment, the flittering of hundreds of small, paper-like wings beating the air is all I can hear. Then, the locusts emit a piercing, insect-like noise. Covering my ears in agony, the noise reminds me of the orchestra of sound that bugs create on a summer night, but LOUD.

I pull one hand from my ear and grasp one of the long, jagged shards of mirror, while getting to my feet. As I glance to the tub, Brennus is hunched over too, trying to cover his ears to blot out the intense noise. Next to him, the portal is still propped open on the edge of the tub.

"BANJAX!" I shout, watching the swarm of locusts moving into the portal I have stupidly left open.

The noise ends immediately as the last locust makes it into the portal. Standing up straighter, I want to scream in frustration. I let the fragment of glass slip from my fingers. It falls to the floor and shatters with a loud twinkling of sound.

Brennus steps out of the spa, watching my face pale as I bend over and put my hands on my knees, trying to calm my frantic breathing.

I failed, I think in anguish.

"'Tis na da only opportunity dat we will have ta kill him, *mo chroí*," Brennus says, trying to console me. "He is na going ta go away anytime soon."

"I know," I pant. "But it was maybe the best shot we can expect."

"Did ye get da answers ye wanted?" Brennus asks, seeing the pain on my face.

I shrug, "Maybe…I don't know. He's a liar and a really good spin doctor, so…I don't know."

The door of the bathroom opens and Declan strolls in with the two Archangels following him docilely. "He escaped," Declan states, looking around and seeing Altair on the floor. He nudges Altair's dismembered body lightly, like he is making sure the angel is dead. "He'll be back," Declan says soothingly to me, like I have just lost my favorite pet. "Maybe I can help." Turning to the Archangels, Declan orders, "Destroy Casimir and bring his body ta me."

Instantly, the Archangels spin into beetles and grasshoppers. They pour into the compact in the space of time that it takes me to exhale.

"Do you think it will work?" I ask Declan with little hope in my tone.

He shrugs, "I do na, but 'tis worth a try."

Straightening, I am about to tell Declan that he should sugarcoat his answers in situations like this, when something in the air begins to shift. It is subtle at first, just a stirring of the air around me. A second later, the pieces of glass on the floor dance and move while the remaining pins in my hair loosen as my hair lifts towards the compact. A moment after that, I lunge for the handle of the faucet near the sink as my legs lift right out from under me.

Everything in the bathroom spins and flings off of the shelves towards the open compact. It's as if a black hole had opened and is now sucking the entire contents of the room into it. All of the perfume bottles rocket towards it, distorting and twisting like food coloring dropped in water, just before they enter the portal.

My fingers slide over the smooth surface of the faucet as I desperately turn my head to see if there is something else I can cling to. Declan is in a similar situation. The door handle bends in his hands as the force of the vortex sucks him towards it.

"OY!" Eion says from the doorway, pulling Declan to him as he grasps his forearm.

I feel one of my hands slip and it whips me around so that I'm facing the portal. Brennus is holding on to the edge of the spa. If he lets go I'm as good as dead, along with him. They will kill him if they get him and I will die, too. Casimir may have changed his mind about keeping me alive now that I have put a bullet in him.

Knowing that fire doesn't hurt Brennus like it hurts angels, I try to pull some of the energy in the room to me. My fingers are beginning to bleed as the metal of the faucet cuts into them in my struggle to hang on. In desperation, I whisper words that can't possibly be heard above the tremendous rush of wind swirling in the room. "Love burns as you conspire, It burns like fire…"

Fire ignites, swirling and spiraling while rushing towards the portal like the tail of a comet. Seconds after the inferno enters the portal, the rush of wind stops dead. I crash to the floor and just lie there limply, panting.

Brennus picks up the open compact, snapping it closed with a grim expression. Tossing it to Declan, he doesn't pause, but scoops me up off the floor, holding me close to his cool chest. "Ye failed ta mention dat dey could try ta pull us ta dem," Brennus says, while tightening his grip on me.

"Sorry. I'm new at this. The learning curve is pretty brutal," I mutter, beginning to shake in his arms.

"'Tis," Brennus agrees with a sympathetic expression. "Declan, I want a set of dose portals. See what we can come up with." Brennus orders. He carries me to the bedroom and wraps me in a towel before he sets me on one of the plush chairs. "Ye need ta change quickly. We are leaving now."

As I look up at Brennus, Finn materializes at the door of the bedroom. "The Fallen are near. Dey have the Kevev with dem," Finn says in a clipped tone.

"Any other allies?" Brennus asks quickly, not taking his eyes off me but rubbing his hands briskly over the towel, trying to warm me up because I'm still trembling. It's not helping because his coldness is seeping through the towel to me. Brennus realizes this and gives up. He walks to my wardrobe, pulling out practical clothing—designer jeans, designer shirt, and leather boots that stop before my knees. He walks to me and places them on my lap. I rise from the chair and change quickly with my back to them because it's apparent that they aren't going to leave me alone now.

Finn continues briefing Brennus. "The Fallen may have also recruited Inikwi—ye know how slippery dey can be."

I feel a shiver run down my spine. After I finish dressing, my hand clamps tight on Brennus' arm. With a nervous quiver in my voice, I ask, "Inikwi? What are Inikwi? What do they do? How do you kill them? What are Kevev? Are they fierce?"

Brennus' eyes scan mine. "Shh, *mo chroí*, 'tis all right," he says in a soothing tone.

"Brennus, when someone tells me it's 'all right,' it usually means we are totally dead," I reply, searching his face for answers.

"We're na totally dead—we are jus na totally safe," he replies easily.

My eyes narrow, "What is a Kevev?" I ask with menace. I hate having this stuff sprung on me.

"'Tis like…" his eyes look upward, searching his mind for a suitable description. "Finn, would ye say dey are like ogres, but dey are na as big or smelly…" he trails off, gazing at Finn.

"I would," Finn agrees with a brisk nod. "Dey have da same grey skin and dey have roughly da same build. Ye know whah dey remind me of when dey have deir latex, human-looking skin suits on?" Finn asks Brennus conversationally.

"Whah?" Brennus asks.

Finn shakes his finger at Brennus, "Dose human blighters dat jump around on da mats in da rings—da ones we saw at da fight night ting dey had," Finn replies sourly.

Brennus appears aghast. "Och, dey weren't really fighting!" Brennus says in disgust. "'Twas a waste of time. Dere was no dismemberment—no real blood ta speak of—" he stops talking when he hears me clear my throat. "Dey wore wan's clothes…" he adds as if disturbed by the memory.

"They look like…um…professional wrestlers?" I ask them and they both point their fingers at me, nodding. "Any other special abilities?" I ask them quickly.

"Brute strength is whah dey are known for, no magic, jus stay away from deir breath," Brennus advises.

"Why, does it enthrall their victim?" I ask, thinking of all the possibilities of his statement.

"No, 'tis jus foul," he replies with a casual shrug.

"What are Inikwi?" I ask rapidly, moving on to the next unknown entity.

Finn frowns. "Dey used ta be human, but deir souls were weak so dey could be taken over by a demon," Finn explains.

"You mean 'shadow men?'" I ask, and see Finn raise his eyebrow in question. "You know—like when a demonic soul from Sheol invades a human host—I call them shadow men," I explain.

"We call dose humans 'possessed,' Genevieve," Finn shakes his head. "Dis is different. Whah is in da human host was never human to begin with—'tis na a soul. 'Tis a true demon and da human does na necessarily have ta be alive ta be inhabited— some of dem are corpses when it happens," he replies, watching my eyes grow wide. "Dey are whah ye might term 'utterly wrong.'"

My mouth has suddenly gone dry so my voice sounds a little high when I ask, "Are they strong?"

"Dey are," Finn says without hesitating. "Dey are unbelievably strong and they act like a unit, hunting in packs for deir prey. If you see one, den dat means dere are several dat ye do na see."

"What kills them?" I ask breathlessly.

"Rip out da heart and dey will die, but it has to be da heart of da demon, na da human heart. Anyting short of dat and dey will be back ta kill ye. Dat is why dey are slippery. Dey look dead because da human host can die wi'out it affecting dem atall. Ye have ta make sure dey are dead," he replies. "Magic will work. Ye jus have ta have a very powerful spell dat will somehow stop da heart from beating. It has ta be very powerful ta penetrate deir armor."

"Is that it?" I ask, looking for anything else they can tell me to fight this new threat.

"Dey taste terrible," Brennus adds helpfully, and I pale.

"Too much information, Brenn," I reply, slipping on my boots and zipping them up.

"Dis is actually good news," Brennus says when I stand up. "Should Casimir attack us wi' da Kevev and da Inikwi, dat will mean he needs dem. It means dere are na enough Fallen for a decisive battle. Yer friends, it would seem, have been making sure dat dere are na enough Fallen getting ta Casimir. He is cut off from his reinforcements. If Casimir reacts ta whah jus happened—emotionally and na wi' da cool precision of a Seraph, den he leaves himself open ta error. But, I do na want ta remain here now. We need ta get ye somewhere safe so dat we maintain our advantage."

Brennus puts his hand on my back, gently leading me to the door. Finn falls in on my other side as an escort. When we enter the hall, there are a score of fellas there waiting for us. "Where are we going?" I ask, seeing that we are, indeed, set to leave.

Brennus is about to answer me when shouts erupt from outside. Battle cries and screams of agony mingle with the rapid report of machine gun fire. The clanging of metal and chaos punctures the tranquility of the grounds. My entourage becomes still, listening to the sounds that eerily remind me of China on the last night I was there with Reed.

Brennus returns to the window in the sitting room and I follow closely behind him. A shiver runs down my spine as I stare outside. Angels covered like Ninja assassins in black, body armor are flying in legions around the grounds outside. Diving at random at fellas on the ground, the angels pluck their victims from their feet, tearing them apart and raining pieces of Gancanagh down on their comrades below. But, that is not all they are doing—they're also killing what must be Kevev, judging by the shredded, latex flesh being peeled from the gray, hulking bodies.

As I watch them with horrified fascination, I flinch when an angel pounces on another angel in midair, hurtling them both into the side of the building with a loud crash. Powerful wings beat near the panes of glass where I stand while one angel uses the other's head as a battering ram, pounding it repeatedly into the wall. As dust falls from the ceiling, Brennus' arm reaches out protectively to block me.

"They are Fallen and Divine," I breathe with fear knocking the breath from me because Reed and Zephyr are undoubtedly out there somewhere. They brought their army to make sure Casimir doesn't succeed in getting me.

As I glance around numbly, I don't even realize Brennus has taken my hand and is tugging on it gently to get me to follow him away from the window and back out into the hallway.

"Dey have changed deir rules for ye, *mo chroí.* Da Divine have never gotten involved when dey consider da war ta be a battle between 'evil craiturs,'" Brennus says, sounding a little thrown by the information.

We head for the stairs at a clipped pace and manage to get down them. As we pass through the main hall, the glass ceiling above us shatters, raining jagged shards and angels down upon us in equal measure.

"Hold dem off," Brennus orders his men. Half my entourage breaks off from us while we continue to move through the castle towards the West Tower.

"Dere are tunnels beneath dis home, *mo chroí.* We will exit trough one of dem and be away from here before dey know we are gone," Brennus assures me, like this happens every day.

"I could use a weapon, Brenn," I say, seeing arms being distributed to the fellas as we pass a checkpoint in the North Corridor.

"Whah sounds good ta ye?" he asks, searching my face.

"A gun," I reply.

Brennus nods to me, before taking a sidearm and holster from one of the fellas. Then, he helps me put it on so that the gun rests near my ribcage.

"Anyting else?" he asks, looking like he is trying not to smile.

"A dagger," I reply.

Instantly, every one of the fellas holds the handle of their knives out for me to take. I choose Brennus' knife because it worked for me before. I killed Keegan with it. As I grasp the handle of the weapon, I feel the eerie power within the blade. I push it securely into the top of my boot.

"Shall we?" Brennus asks me as the chaos of the fight pushes closer to us.

Adrenaline is coursing through me now because I don't know which way I should be going, toward the fight or away from it. *Does Reed want me to leave here and get away from the fray or move towards it where he can get to me?* I wonder in confusion.

"Where are the tunnels?" I ask, taking Brennus' hand and following him down the corridor.

"Dere is one in da kirk—da Knight's Bar," he says, smiling at me.

We enter the chapel and walk to the suit of armor located directly beneath one of the rosette, stained glass windows. When the armor is pushed aside, a spiraling staircase appears, leading below. Brennus gives me the after-you gesture. I step into the stairwell as flashes of memory hit me that this is like being in the caves in Houghton with all of its stairways to torture.

Damp, salty air coming from below causes me to pause on the first step to ask, "Does this lead to the sea?"

I don't hear Brennus' answer because the roar of a gun's report along with searing pain blots out his response. A single bullet rips through my thigh, forcing my leg to fold beneath me. Casimir catches me in his open arms before I fall more than a few steps down the dark stairway. I cry out in agony while Casimir whispers in my ear, "It hurts, doesn't it?"

CHAPTER 23

The Ocean

I brace myself against Casimir's chest so that I don't go crashing down the steep, endless staircase that leads to the sea. I have to close my eyes against the bitter pain throbbing in my thigh. The bullet has gone right through it, but it burns like it's lodged in the muscle. As I breathe shallowly, tears cloud my eyes and I grit my teeth, trying not to faint.

Casimir's voice is cold as he says, "That was a warning, half-breed. What you do unto me, I will do unto you—twofold." Casimir fires his gun again and shoots my other thigh at point blank range.

I almost lose the ability to breathe as he clutches me to him. I can no longer stand on my own and the pain is unreal. Turning me around, so that I'm shielding him, he pulls me the few steps to the top of the stairwell, entering the Knight's Bar.

Casimir drags me just beyond the stairwell. His entourage files in behind us, taking up positions within the room. At least fifteen angels are with him; they are all covered from head to foot in body armor to protect them from the touch of the Gancanagh. They, too, must've been away from Sheol for a while because their odor is not very pungent; otherwise, I would have smelled them before I saw them. Training their weapons on the Gancanagh, the angels outnumber them in the room.

Brennus, who is also bleeding from both of his thighs as I am, is still standing on his own. Fierce pain enters Brennus' eyes when he sees me, pale and broken, in Casimir's arms. I gaze back at Brennus, knowing that there is nothing that he can do now to stop what is about to happen.

Casimir directs his comment to Brennus, saying, "I admire your lair. It is just like a labyrinth down there with tunnels and caves that lead from the sea. You should know, just for future reference, that it is not very difficult to get in here when one has the ability to fly."

"I will remember dat for next time, Casimir," Brennus says slowly.

Casimir, sounding bored, states, "You know what I want. Release her from the contract or you both die."

The fellas in the room begin hissing menacingly at Casimir, but he ignores them. Brennus holds up his hand, indicating that he doesn't want them to try to attack.

"Dere are worse tings den a true death, Casimir," Brennus replies, hiding the pain in his eyes.

"Yes, there are and I know them all," Casimir agrees, before kissing the top of my head gently and smoothing my hair. "Give her to me and I will not have to show any of them to you."

"'Tis really na me decision ta make," Brennus replies, watching my face.

"Excuse me?" Casimir asks, sounding surprised instead of bored.

"'Tis her decision," Brennus replies, staring into my eyes and seeing my confusion.

"You will let her decide your fate?" he asks Brennus, like he doesn't completely understand what is being said. "You are willing to die for her?"

"I am, but I am already dead…'twill jus be da end of me," Brennus replies, never taking his eyes off of me. "If she decides she is na going wi' ye, den she is na going wi' ye, no matter whah ye do."

My lower lip trembles as tears escape my eyes. I begin to understand what Brennus is saying to Casimir. If I decide that dying here is the better option to being Casimir's slave, then Brennus won't break the contract, forcing Casimir to kill us both. He will effectively be dying with me—for me, so I won't have to be a slave.

"You *are* powerful," Casimir breathes in my ear, before he speaks louder. "You do realize, Brennus, that whereas she will undoubtedly be back in one form or another, you will not."

"I know dat better dan ye do," he replies, unaffected by the information. "'Twill na matter. I know ye intend ta end me before ye leave. Ye canna leave me here since ye know dat I will never stop hunting ye. I'll use all of me influence ta find ye and break ye ta pieces. Ye canna have dat, can ye?" he asks rhetorically.

"You paint me in such a sinister form," Casimir replies, sounding bored again. "All I want is the half-breed. You do not have to make this an epic battle. She was never yours. She has always been ours."

"She's moin," Brennus retorts angrily.

"I could just take her…torture her and subsequently you at my leisure anyway…" Casimir says. He produces a knife and holds it to my throat, pulling it down slowly so that it cuts a thin, shallow line in my skin. I clamp my lips together, trying not to make a sound. "But, then I won't be able to hear her cry and that will take all of the fun out of it. With the contract still in play, she won't respond at all."

When his hand passes in front of my face, I notice burn marks on them that are healing. He must not have enjoyed the fire I threw at him earlier through the portal. My body stills as I realize what that means.

My magic works on him, I surmise, feeling my pulse kick up.

"Declan, if he tries ta leave wi' yer queen before we resolve dis issue, ye make sure I'm ended. We canna have him torturing her," he says, looking at me.

Declan, looking grim, chokes, "I will," knowing he will be killing both of us if that happens. Gazing at me, Declan says, "Lass, I figured it out. 'Tis both, lass…'tis both."

It takes me a second to realize what he's saying to me. He once said he didn't know if it was courage or naiveté that made me do all the brave and foolish things that I do. I guess he decided that it's both.

Casimir hands me over to the angel next to him and puts his knife back in its sheath. "So, I will need to convince Genevieve that it is in everyone's best interest that she leaves with me quietly?" Casimir asks, looking up at the ceiling calmly, like he is contemplating nothing more than the architecture of the room. "That shouldn't prove to be too difficult a task, knowing her soft heart."

In a heartbeat, Casimir draws out his gun and points it at Finn. Pulling the trigger several times, he sends bullets into Finn's chest. Finn steps back, grimacing, but he doesn't fall down, which attests to the fact that he is really freaking strong and already mostly dead. Brennus manages to remain standing, too, looking even whiter than he did before.

"The next round goes in his head, half-breed," Casimir says to me insultingly, while sliding another magazine into his gun. I close my eyes against the sight of Finn's blood trickling from him.

"I want you to break the contract, Brennus," I whisper.

When I open my eyes, I see pain contort Brennus' face as his eyes shift from his brother to me. Brennus knows what I'm doing. I'm agreeing to be Casimir's slave so he will spare Finn.

"Your feelings for these creatures is appalling, Genevieve," Casimir says with a grim look, like he finds me unsavory. "I should kill them all to teach you another lesson about being loyal to the wrong ascendency, but the stench in here just makes me want to leave as soon as possible. Brennus, she has made her decision, now unshackle her."

"Is dat yer decision?" Brennus asks me for clarification.

My eyes cloud with tears of fear, knowing what this will mean for me. It will be brutal. Casimir wants revenge and he has eternity to see that it's done to his satisfaction. I swallow hard, nodding my head to Brennus.

"Den I will release ye. I love ye, *mo chroí*, forever," Brennus says, like I'm the only one in the room as his hands form fists.

With tears on my cheeks, I whisper back, "Goodbye, Brennus."

Casimir growls. "From now on, you will speak only to me," he says, pulling me back into his grasp and shaking me roughly.

Brennus and all of the other fellas in the room begin hissing menacingly. I think Brennus would attack Casimir if Finn had not grasped his arm to hold him back. Finn scowls at Brennus, "She has a chance ta survive dis, Brenn. Give her dat chance."

Pain, like I've never seen from him before, crosses Brennus' face as he stills. He wipes his hand over his mouth and settles down a little. Then, staring into my eyes again, he begins pulling the energy in the room to him and whispering words I don't understand. I am not really listening to what he's saying, because I'm concentrating on stealing the energy from Brennus as he gathers it to him. My hope is that Casimir won't know what I'm doing—that if he can feel the energy in the room, he attributes it to Brennus.

Brennus shoots me a funny look as he feels me taking his energy. With the air crackling around us, something within me shifts and eases, like a heavy weight is leaving my body and I know that I'm no longer bound to Brennus or the Gancanagh.

I continue to take the energy, feeling it burning me inside. "Do you like poetry, Casimir?" I ask in a panting breath, holding as much energy as I can.

"Excuse me?" Casimir asks in elegant disdain.

"I'm creating something just for you…here, it goes like this: 'I wish I were like the sea To pull you down, Drown you within me. Breathe wet fire, Feel your fear, Kill you slowly, Shed no tear. I'll call the ocean from its path, To sweep you wildly within its wrath." My voice strains before I release all the energy I have collected at once. I feel it ripple in a tremoring shock through the castle.

"What did you just do?" Casimir growls, holding on to my arm with brutal force.

A rumble beneath the floor saves me from having to answer him, while salt water roars up the stairs behind us, spewing like a water cannon. It knocks me away from Casimir as the room floods with a tidal wave of white water from the sea. In the next moment, I slip beneath the eddy. As I hold my breath, I tumble in the wildly, churning current. I bump into chairs and tables as they spin beneath the water in a chaotic mess of medieval armor, fellas, angels, and other debris.

When I brush up against the rosette, stained glass window, I press flat against it. Pounding my fist on its colorful glass, my lungs burn from lack of oxygen as I feel the panes shatter beneath my hands. I spill out the window of the Knight's Bar, like a tealeaf being poured from a teapot, and I land hard on the ground below me. Water continues to stream from the window while I struggle to crawl away from it.

All around me, another battle is taking place. Angels, fellas, and creatures I have never seen before, are hacking at each other, locked in combat. It's total chaos as mortar shells shake the ground, spewing dirt and body parts into the air. A pair of dress shoes stop in front of me. Glancing upward, I lose my breath, seeing a human-like figure dressed in the suit he was probably buried in standing over me. Milky-white eyes, formed by a film of cataracts, stare down at me. "Inikwi," I shiver, gazing around to see that several of them are surrounding me.

The Inikwi speak to each other in deep, gargled voices, like their throats are filled with water.

A groan is wrenched from me and I shudder as a creepy, half-dead thing reaches down and pulls me up off the ground by the front of my shirt.

Creases form in the black mold on the corners of its mouth as its gray tongue snakes out of it to lick my cheek. My stomach clenches along with my jaw as I cringe away from it, trying to turn my face. As I dangle in his grasp, I hear Casimir's distinct voice behind me speaking the gargling language of the Inikwi.

"I should let them play with you, half-breed. Maybe I will later," Casimir says, watching me squirm to get away from the utterly wrong thing that is holding me.

"You didn't enjoy the swim?" I ask Casimir. He looks a little more disdainful than normal. But, wet and dripping, he still manages to appear even more beautiful than usual—like a young surfer coming out of the water in his wetsuit.

Before I see Casimir's fist move, he punches me in the stomach, causing most of the air to expel from my body. Gasping for breath, I feel myself being handed to Casimir's waiting arms. "What? Nothing more to say?" Casimir asks, snuggling me close to his body. A handful of angels from Casimir's entourage fall from the rosette window, looking equally as annoyed as he does. Casimir barks orders to them, "Find the leader of the

Gancanagh. I want him. Exterminate the rest, except for maybe the brother—I will torture him in front of Brennus…that could be interesting."

I shiver, hearing his plans for Brennus and Finn. The angels nod to Casimir before nervously gazing up at the rosette window of the kirk, probably wondering how they are going to accomplish that task with so few of them remaining.

Casimir doesn't wait to see if they will comply, but turns with me in his arms and moves supernaturally fast towards the building that houses all of the vehicles. I rest my head on his shoulder, feeling painfully intimidated. When we enter the garage, Casimir chooses the car that looks the most like a race-car with doors that open up instead of out. The keys are in it. I guess the Gancanagh never really believe anyone will be dumb enough to try to steal from them. Opening the driver side door, Casimir reaches in and places me in the passenger seat. Then he gets into the car and starts the engine. He turns to me and takes the gun out of the holster on my side, tossing it out his window. Reaching over, he buckles my seatbelt for me.

With strong, manicured fingers, Casimir grasps my chin and turns my face to his. "If you try anything, I will take my knife and impale you to the seat. Do you understand?" he asks me. I nod my head, feeling my blood draining from my face.

He eases the car out of the garage before he presses the accelerator to the floor, rocketing along the winding drive that leads away from the house. "Where are we going?" I ask in a weak voice, hoping to come up with an exit strategy if I know the plan.

"Just to the end of the drive. I have soldiers in position waiting for us. We have a portal to Sheol," he says. Bile rises in my throat while he rubs his thigh where I had shot him earlier, scowling like it hurts him.

I have to fight now, or I'm worse than dead, I think as my hand inches downward to my boot where Brennus' knife is hidden.

As I watch Casimir's profile, a movement catches my eye beyond the driver's side window. It looks like a charcoal-gray missile is coming towards the car and my hand moves to the handle of the door to brace myself just before it flies straight into us.

On impact, the vehicle begins flipping over and over on its side as the momentum of being broadsided propels us in a different direction. As the car comes to rest on its side, I lie against my door that is on the ground. Feeling dizzy and sick, I groan in pain, gazing at the grass covering my window.

The car moves then as something leaps up onto its quarter panel. A sharp groan of metal sounds as Casimir's door is torn off of its hinges and thrown away in a blink of an eye. The car crashes downward as it is righted and comes to rest on all four tires. The car is still rocking as a hand reaches in and pulls Casimir by the throat from the driver's seat.

Charcoal-gray wings unfold by the side of the car to the raspy sound of my shallowly taken breath. There are other, more-distant noises, but they don't make much sense to me—like screaming—the screams of someone in agony.

I look dazedly out the shattered front windshield and blink when an arm falls with a *thump* on the hood of the car. It's bloody and gory, with sinew and cartilage hanging from it. Something else falls then—an ear?

My vision swims, making me see double. Running my hand over the frame of the door, the smooth handle brushes against my fingertips and I pull on it weakly. It won't open. Blood from my head drips onto my arm; I reach up to touch it, but I am distracted by a cracking sound. Outside the car, one of Casimir's wings is being brutally shredded from his body.

I pale even more and I feel like I'm going to be violently ill soon. As my hand goes to my mouth, I see a hulking ogre-like creature ambling towards the car on my side. Just behind the Kevev are three Inikwi, moving fast and overtaking it to get to me first.

They run like animals...dogs, I think as I see them use all four limbs while their strides stretch out the length of their bodies, but they look human. A whimper of fear escapes me while my trembling hands go to my seatbelt to undo it. A warm, blood-spattered hand covers mine, stopping me from freeing myself.

"It's okay, love. We're leaving now," Reed says in a gentle tone, staring into my eyes with his perfect green ones.

He sits in the driver's seat and starts the mangled vehicle. The car purrs like it had in the garage. Reed leans forward and pushes the shattered windshield out of the way. He then uses his hands to push the drooping roof of the car back up. Wheeling the car around, the arm and ear slide off the hood to the ground as we head back in the direction of the estate. In confusion, I rest my head limply against the seat. My brain cannot make sense of what is happening.

How is he here? Why is he taking me back to Brennus' house? I wonder as the scenery whips past the car at an insane speed.

"Hold on, love," Reed says to reassure me as something *thumps* on the roof of the car.

Reed pulls out an automatic weapon, aiming it one-handed above our heads. He sprays bullets and punctures the roof while he maneuvers right past the circular drive in front of the estate and onto the manicured grass. Another *thump* comes from the trunk. An angel is holding on to our car, trying to stop us Fred Flintstone-style—with his feet dragging on the ground.

In the next second, light brown wings shroud the angel holding our car as Zephyr dives at him, impaling the Fallen angel on his broadsword. The back of the car bounces back onto the ground, causing us to fishtail before Reed gets the car back under control.

"Thanks, Zee," Reed says under his breath, looking in the rearview mirror.

Salty wind courses through the open windshield while the performance tires chew up the lawn. My vision doubles again as the rapidly approaching edge of the cliff sends red flags to my brain.

Moving my head to look at Reed again, I say just above a whisper, "Cliff, Reed."

Reed's eyes widen and he looks stunned as he says, "Evie?"

I raise my hand and point at the cliff that we are hurtling towards as I croak, "Stop, Reed!" My brain is swirling. *Why doesn't he see the sea ahead?* I wonder dizzily, as reality is distorting. *Maybe this isn't real…*

Reed places his hand on my cheek. "He broke the contract?" Reed asks, not caring about driving us to what seems like the edge of the world. "You are free?"

I nod slowly, not taking my eyes from the brilliant stars in the big sky ahead of us. "He let me go, so Casimir wouldn't kill me," I say shakily as my hand reaches out to take his.

Reed watches me entwine my fingers in his. His eyes soften as he speaks to me in Angel with a euphoric expression on his lips. It makes me forget what was making me panic as I give all control of my destiny over to him in an instant.

The rotten flesh of an Inikwi leaves a smear on my window when he lands on the car and clings to the roof. Several more *thumps* hit the car as more of his pack joins him. "Don't worry, Evie, I have a plan," Reed says, while reaching into his body armor and pulling out something shiny from it.

"I trust you," I whisper.

Reed opens the compact in his hand the moment the car begins its decent towards the sea below. The interior of the vehicle becomes a swirling, chaotic mess, as everything distorts and twists as if being stretched and pulled in a taffy machine. With no air to breathe, the feeling of being pulled like metal to a powerful magnet consumes me.

I land on the ground on my hands and knees. The moment I am able to take a breath, I can't because I am vomiting everything I have ever eaten onto the ground in front of me. A growl sounds from Reed as he stands with his back to me, facing the four Inikwi that came through the portal with us. They speak to each other with garbled voices.

"Love, can you move?" Reed asks, not looking at me. I push myself up to my feet, but I have to lean against a wall so I won't crash back down. My bullet wounds are healing, allowing me to stand, but my legs still ache.

"Yes," I respond, looking around in a daze and realizing that we are in some kind of underground tunnel. The metal scraping sound of a train pulling into a station registers in my mind as subway cars pulse by me, blowing my hair back from my face with stale air.

"Board the train, Evie," Reed instructs me gently, pulling knives from the notches designed into the thigh area of his body armor.

"Umm…Okay," I mutter, pushing myself off the white-tiled wall and moving in a crooked line across the platform to the entrance of an open subway car. The car is nearly empty, except for a handful of rowdy twenty-somethings that look like they are on their way home from the pub. I can hardly understand what they are saying because of their heavy, British accents.

I hold on to the metal handrail near the open door as I turn to look at Reed. One Inikwi is already dead, lying in a pool of silver liquid that has the consistency of maple syrup. Laughter and jeering comments drift to me from the other end of the car. The entry-level, corporately-attired humans have no idea what is really happening here. Before the doors of the subway car close, Reed is by my side, pulling me against him and backing away from the doors as they shut. Fog clouds the glass panel of the train door as an Inikwi presses his face to it. He is wearing a filthy, navy blue suit jacket with a moldy red tie over a dingy white shirt. His skin is deathly pale and black mold crusts around his hairline. His dark hair is matted and clumped. *Did the Inikwi dig up that body?* I wonder. As I gaze beyond the snarling monster on the platform, I see that there are now three, inert Inikwi bodies on the ground, dead.

The train moves away from the station, slowly gaining speed. My eyes follow the one remaining Inikwi as he keeps pace with our train car. Aching fear squeezes my chest as he weaves between columns along the underground platform and analyzes the attributes of our car. The humanoid body of the Inikwi drops down on all fours when the train gains momentum, then he leaps to the roof of the car behind ours.

Shivering, I glance at Reed, seeing the blank expression on his face. "Remind me to explain to Buns and Brownie exactly what I mean when I say, 'leave the portal open in a safe place,'" he murmurs in a rueful tone, before gazing around at the contents of the train, gauging its defensibility.

"OY, ANGELS! Where's the bloody costume party?" one drunken human calls from the other end of the car. He looks like he started drinking during happy hour and had to stop when they closed the place. His comment elicits laughter from his buddies who begin to discuss us from their seats.

"Reapers," Reed mutters under his breath. "I'll be right back, love," Reed says in a concerned tone, looking towards the back of the train. Through the glass panel at the back of our car, the Inikwi climbs through the window of the car attached to this one. "Sit here," Reed says, gently pushing me into a seat that faces the exit on the side of the train where we entered. "Oh," Reed says as an after-thought, "Buns said to give you this after you came through the portal.

He hands me an envelope from inside his armor before he turns and strides towards the car attached to ours. I open the envelope and a pack of breath strips tumbles out of it. In a daze, I pop a couple of the minty strips into my mouth and sit numbly in the seat, trying to shake the sense of unreality that I'm experiencing. I have been living in Faerie-land for months now where everything is Gancanagh, fallen angels, magic, and terrifying creatures. I am the queen of the wild things. But, in an instant, I have been thrown back into the "real world," only to find that this now feels like a fantasyland—unreal.

As I peer into the next car, I see Reed lift the Inikwi off his feet and hurl him into a row of plastic seats. I shift my gaze the other way and listen to the humans continue to discuss me, never noticing the Inikwi in the car next to ours getting his head beaten in. *Will I always be caught in the middle between two worlds?* I wonder in a detached way.

When the train pulls away from the next station, Reed walks in front of me. Crouching down, he gently touches my face, assessing the cuts on my head. His hands slip over my body next, checking for broken bones and contusions. When his hands move over my gunshot wounds, I flinch, sucking in my breath sharply.

Reed's eyes narrow. "You've been shot," he states as his jaw clenches tight, making him look lethal.

I nod. "You already avenged me," I whisper, seeing the fury in his eyes. "Casimir…" I trail off as flashes of his dismemberment at Reed's hands flicker in my mind.

Reed rises up from his crouched position and walks towards the humans in our car. Using his voice that has the power of persuasion, he instructs them to exit the train at the next station. He also tells them to forget everything they saw on this train. He walks back to me and begins to take his body armor off, exposing his beautiful, bare chest beneath it.

When the train pulls into another underground station, everyone exits the car, leaving us alone. Reed moves to the doors, pulling the wiring so that the doors malfunction and won't open again automatically. He pulls a couple of handrails off the wall and uses them to lock the doors at either end of the car. Then he strips the rest of his armor off so he is left in just his tracksuit bottoms. He kneels down in front of me, tearing the bottom of my pant legs up and exposing the healing gunshot wounds in my thighs. Ripping the fabric lining out of his body armor, Reed makes strips, wrapping them securely around each thigh. When he finishes, he hangs his head, looking down at the floor.

"I'm sorry. Please forgive me," Reed says in a voice filled with contrition, letting his forehead rest lightly on my knees.

"What?" I ask, while tears I have been trying really hard to hold back, fall from my eyes. The tips of his fingers gently smooth over his soft hair, just as my heart contracts painfully in my chest.

"I swore to you that I would protect you," Reed says with bitterness. He lifts his head and looks at my face with torment in his beautiful green eyes.

"You did. Casimir didn't drag me down into the abyss because you were there. You did everything right—everything, and I'm so grateful that you still want to fight for me after what I did," I whisper, crying now.

"Evie, you are my *aspire*...my only love. Don't you understand? It's just you," Reed says solemnly, reaching out and holding my cheek, while wiping my tears with his thumb. "I am no longer whole without you." His other hand goes to the mark of my wings branded on his chest above his heart. "I will never love anyone but you," Reed promises with the certainty of billions of years.

"I love you…I'm sorry…" I can't continue because my throat burns with emotion.

"Evie," he whispers, seeing my anguish and regret for what he has gone through to be with me. Rising from his knees, Reed reaches down and picks me up off the seat before sitting down in it and placing me in his lap. He holds me to his chest, stroking my wings hypnotically as he speaks to me in Angel. The dark tunnels of the subway flicker by, illuminated by florescent lighting where advertisers have placed their latest ads.

Listening to Reed's voice, I calm down as the sway of the train lulls me in a different way. "What did you say?" I ask him, feeling better.

"I was thanking God for giving you back to me," he replies, tightening his grip on me.

Laying my cheek against Reed's heart, I decide that being near him is an assault on my senses. His voice is like hearing the first incredible notes of my favorite song; the way it excites my mind while my body yearns to move closer to the source of its soft timbre. The solid muscle of his chest beneath my fingers has my face flushing with heat. "Breathe," Reed whispers near my ear, his warm breath sending shivers through my body as he does things to me with one word that no one else can do.

Inhaling shallowly, I raise my head from his chest and see desire in his eyes. His cheek tilts softly towards mine, brushing the plane of my face with the sensual scruff of his male skin. I exhale at the caress while my fingers curl involuntarily against his chest, wanting to hold onto him as tight as I can. My cheek moves against his again until I turn my lips slowly to his skin. Kissing him softly, I close my eyes. Tentatively, Reed turns his face to cover my lips with his own as if afraid that I'm not real. His arms pull me closer to him, like he would keep me here even if I object. But there is no chance that I will object.

I slip my hands up to wrap around the back of his neck and press my body closer to his while deepening our kiss. Reed groans softly. In an instant, my wings unfold, arching out boldly around me with a loud *snap*.

"Evie," Reed groans my name, kissing me feverishly while his lips turn up in the corners, "that's…" he trails off, not completing the thought as his hand reaches back to touch my wing.

"What?" I breathe against his mouth, feeling wildness inside of me growing with each caress from Reed.

"So incredibly hot," he breathes, stroking my wing gently.

"I missed you…" I whisper against his ear. His arms tighten around me painfully. "Ah…" I breathe, and he eases up immediately. Reed reaches for the seat next to us and tears it from the bolts with his bare hand.

"I burned for you," he says in a soft tone, nuzzling my neck.

The train begins to slow down when we enter the next underground station. I continue to kiss Reed until I hear the doors of our car being pried open and a soft, musical voice say, "Uh, sweetie, this is your stop, but we can meet you at the next one if this is a bad time."

CHAPTER 24

The Island

"Is she okay?" Buns directs her question to Reed as he stands up with me in his arms and walks to the doors of the subway car. We exit onto an underground platform where Brownie and Buns stand together looking concerned. "Sweetie, are you hurt?" Buns asks me. She rests her hand gently on my arm, her eyes clouding when I nod my head to her question.

"She has been shot, among other things," Reed says in a low tone, holding me closer to his body.

"She's not 'coma girl!'" Buns says, looking surprised and confused.

"No, she was released from the contract," Reed says, rubbing my wing soothingly.

When my eyes move to Brownie next to Buns, I see her eyes filling up with tears, too. "Thank you, Evie," Brownie says with a tight voice, referring to the deal I made with Brennus to save her from Valentine.

I nod again, not being able to speak about any of that right now. Brownie moves to me, hugging me while I remain in Reed's arms. She smells incredible, like cocoa butter, and both the girls have exotic, hothouse flowers tucked behind their ears. In fact, they are not dressed for the London Underground Transit system in early November. They are hardly dressed at all. Buns is wearing a bold, flower-print, string bikini top with matching sarong skirt and Brownie has on a soft-yellow bikini top with matching sarong skirt and sandals.

"Here," Buns says, touching Reed's arm lightly to move him forward, "we need to leave now. They should have all their surveillance cameras running again soon and we don't want to freak out the humans."

Brownie pulls back from me, wiping her hand against her tears and asking, "Did you have any trouble with the portal?"

"The London Tube, Brownie?" Reed asks skeptically, looking around the platform of the subway station, assessing their choice of destinations critically. "What to you denotes 'safety' here?"

"No Fallen?" Brownie asks, like it has to be a trick question. "Buns and I thought it was brilliant because no angels seem to use it. It's not very 'playa' squeezing into a train with humans when we can fly faster than the trains. Plus, you don't know how hard it was to shake the Dominion Powers following us," Brownie continues. "We had to go lingerie shopping with some other Reaper friends to distract them. Our friends modeled the new holiday line by the storefront window while we slipped out the back."

"And that worked?" Reed asks, like he is having a hard time believing it.

"Let's just say that some of those Powers like it more naughty than nice," Brownie replies.

Buns chimes in, "And, we had to create a diversion near the turnstiles above the stop where you came through so there wouldn't be anyone on the platform when you arrived."

"What did you do?" Reed asks with curiosity in his tone.

"Well, it was kind of like belly dancing, wouldn't you say, Brownie?" Buns asks, looking for help from Brownie.

"More or less," Brownie agrees with a shrug.

"Our Reaper friends are still working this terminal's entrances, but we can't hang here all night," Buns continues. Buns ushers Reed forward and we move to the end of the platform. She steps ahead of us, opening the door to the woman's bathroom and holding it for us to enter.

Confused, I wrinkle my brow. I want to get out of here and get to somewhere warm, preferably with a bed where I can crash for as long as it takes not to feel terrible. As I glance at the florescent-lighted ceiling and rows of stall doors, I say, "I'm good, Buns, we don't have to stop here for me." I indicate the stalls with a weak flick of my wrist.

Buns and Brownie both grin. "Sweetie, we hadn't even thought about that. This will take us to Zee's island," Buns smiles, pulling out an onyx compact inlaid with mother-of-pearl so that it looks like the night sky. My stomach does a flip inside of me as I pale, remembering how it felt to go through the last portal to get here. I shift in Reed's arms as I look around for a way out of this.

My eyebrows draw together in a concerned expression. "Uhh, that's okay, Buns," I say as my mouth goes dry. "I can probably walk now. We can catch a cab—or they have those red, double-decker buses here, right? I've never been to London. It must be pretty in the winter—magical."

"London is too dangerous right now, love," Reed says near my ear. "Everyone will be looking for you. We just needed a stop before heading to the island to make sure we are not followed."

Everyone is looking for me, and if Brennus escaped, he'll be the most determined to find me. If he survived, my mind whispers and the air suddenly becomes very thin. The Fallen could've gotten him after I left. I feel cold inside, thinking of the Fallen torturing a member of my family...a member of my...Confusion grips me, making me feel tired, sad, and drained. I drop my head against Reed's chest and I can't seem to sort it all out. A part of me is still lost in their Faerie world—still fighting for air.

How do I rescue that part of me that they still own? I wonder.

"Sweetie?" Buns says with concern.

Reed turns my chin so that he can look into my eyes. "I'm here, Evie," Reed says, using his sexy voice. "The current is shifting—can you feel it? It's bringing you back to me. Hold on to the thread, love. Don't let go," he says with sultry tone that makes me want to do anything for him.

I nod, gazing at his perfect face as Buns opens the portal.

I distort and twist into forms that no one should ever have to take as I rocket through the portal. It spews me out on the other side, feeling like I have been half digested by an enormous earthworm.

Daylight hits me like an anvil, shining so brightly on my face that I'm almost grateful for the need to turn over and vomit again. The softest, whitest sand cushions my hands and knees, and with the warm, fragrant breeze blowing, it helps to ebb my nausea.

"You get used to it, sweetie," Buns says while Reed rubs my back as I heave.

"No, thanks," I mutter when I can speak. "Let's not do that again."

I open my eyes, getting my first glimpse of Zephyr's island. Off in the distance on a hill, there is a sweeping plantation estate, spanning a large area of the plateau. It faces the beach, overlooking the bluest water I have ever seen. Beautiful, teak bungalows built off the ground on stilts with thatched roofs are scattered along the beach, nestling among the lush palm trees. Reed scoops me up off the sand and moves supernaturally fast towards the nearest bungalow, which has a little veranda with teak furniture.

Reed traverses the wooden veranda and opens the shuttered, folding doors, so that the breeze from off the ocean sweeps in with us. He turns immediately to the left. We enter a bedroom containing a large bed covered in snowy white linens and fat pillows beneath whimsical, mosquito netting. Reed places me in the bed before moving to close the shutters on the windows, dimming the room. As I look up at the ceiling, a lazy, teak fan turns tranquilly amid the pitched roofline.

Buns enters the room with a pitcher of ice water and some soft rolls on a primitive wooden tray. She sets it on the bedside table, pouring some water into a delicate glass and holding it out to me. "Drink this. You look like you're getting dehydrated," she says in a soothing voice, sitting on the side of the bed and waiting for me as I push myself up on the pillows. "Do you think you can hold down some aspirin?" Buns asks, and I shake my head slowly, trying to swallow the water.

"Where are we?" I ask as Brownie sits on the foot of my bed.

"South Pacific, sort of near Tahiti," Brownie answers, watching as Reed comes up on my other side, sitting near me and gently unwrapping the bandage on one of my thighs. I don't look at it when he takes it off, but I see Brownie pale a little before she glances up at my face.

"It looks like its noon here," I say, trying to think of something else while Reed starts examining my legs again. My body is still shaking from trauma, making me appear cold.

"I think it's something like a ten hour time difference from where you were, sweetie," Buns says, trying her best to help keep me focused on something else. "It's protected…safe," she adds. I keep my face blank, trying not to give away the fact that this world is too small to ever be safe for me.

I attempt to hide my sense of unreality as I ask with a smile that is not reaching my eyes, "What do you call this kind of jet lag?"

"Jump fatigue," Reed answers. "You have surge sickness, too," he adds gently.

"That sounds serious," I murmur, giving him a real smile that seems to spark something in his eyes.

"It's minor," he says, pausing for a second and then looking down, like he forgot what he is doing.

Buns takes the glass from my hand and she and Brownie keep up a steady stream of conversation. They outline all the things that the island has to offer: sailing, snorkeling, scuba diving, surfing, hiking, horseback riding—like we are just on vacation and not hiding out from the Fallen and the Gancanagh, Werree and Ifrits, Inikwi and Kevev.

I nod mutely, not asking any questions or commenting on what they are saying. As I lean back against the pillows, Reed finishes rewrapping my wounds with gauze, securing the ends with clips.

"Do you think you can eat something," Reed asks me hopefully, but I shake my head, feeling my eyelids droop.

"Sweetie, Brownie and I are going out to wait by the other portal now," she pauses, looking at Reed. There seems to be some kind of silent communication going on between them. I quirk my eyebrow in question, looking between their two faces.

"Full disclosure on everything, Buns, like we all agreed. We are a team. No one gets shut out," Reed says gravely and I watch Buns nod.

Buns smiles. "We're waiting for Zee and Russell to return from Operation Armpit," Buns says.

"I thought we were calling it Operation I-HOS, the International House of Stink," Brownie says, rolling her eyes.

"No, I'm pretty sure it's Armpit," Buns replies. "Anyway, they should be here soon. The plan has been executed. Do they know that you have Evie?" Buns asks. Reed nods, watching my reaction to what they're saying. "Good, then they'll be here."

"Russell was there, too?" I ask, feeling sweaty all of a sudden.

"Yeah," Buns says, "he took his lucky Louisville Slugger with him. He said he would see if he could improve his RBI." I give her a frown thinking that they promised me that they would protect Russell for me, not let him go out to a fierce battle like it's batting practice.

"Russell is really freaking strong," Brownie says, seeing my expression. "He's gaining strength like we have never seen before, Evie. Russell is like—super evolving and some of the things he can do are amazing. He's stronger than Buns and me put together and then some, and he can shapeshift into just about anything you can imagine," she says with awe.

"He has the ability to adapt like a chameleon, too, and his complete understanding of the human realm makes him confusing to the Powers. They all want to be around him—study him, because to them he's unpredictable–unfathomable," Buns adds.

"It's total bromance, Evie," Brownie smiles. "The Powers want to hang with him, like he's completely killa and they want to try to emulate him."

"Yeah, he's a balla," Buns agrees, nodding adamantly.

"What language are you speaking?" Reed asks sourly.

"Balla means someone who has skills—athletic ability," I explain absently. "You're a balla, Reed."

Brownie nods. "Preben keeps trailing him everywhere, like he wants to figure him out or something," Brownie says.

"Sweetie, Preben follows him because you're with Russell most of the time and Preben can't seem to take his eyes off you," Buns says, smiling.

Brownie blushes, rolling her eyes, "Shut up, Buns, you're being ridiculous."

"Oh, please, he *so* wants you," Buns teases her. "I wonder what will upset him more: the fact that we're giving Dominion the slip or the fact that he won't know where you are, Brownie."

"We're giving Dominion the slip?" I ask.

"For now, Evie," Reed says. "We trust a few of them, Preben, Sorin, Elan, but Dominion really wants Russell. We have been able to stall them, mainly due to Preben's help, but we need some leverage. We can gain that if they don't know where he is. We can make them negotiate with us and agree to terms, so they don't just seize him as their weapon."

I begin to shake my head slowly, trying to process this new information. "Dominion wants to make sure the Fallen don't get their hands on Russell and he doesn't have anyone to bind to him to stop them," I murmur, seeing that both Brownie and Buns don't have the rank to stand up to Dominion. Reapers don't have the clout to trump a legion of Powers.

"Sorry, love, I'm already bound to someone, so we have to protect him this way instead," Reed replies, giving me a cheeky smile.

Leaning over, Buns kisses my forehead before getting up from the bed. "We have so much to tell you, but you need to get some sleep first."

"I don't want to sleep, Buns," I reply, holding on to her hand.

"You need to heal and you can't do that if you don't rest. Plus, the Powers will try to wring every last detail out of you about the Gancanagh and the Fallen. They want to know how your plan went with Casimir," Buns says, not knowing that it failed miserably as the bullet holes in my thighs signify. "Its all Zee could talk about…" she trails off when I feel myself grow paler.

"Great," I murmur, not looking forward to briefing them on anything that has happened in the last few months. *Anything*.

"We will let you know as soon as they get here," Buns says, moving to the bedroom door.

"Thank you," Reed says, but I'm still numb from what they just said.

"We will talk later, Evie," Brownie says in a low voice, squeezing my foot gently before following Buns out of the room towards the beach.

The breeze that enters as they leave feels so light. It lacks the kind of sweetness that, although not offensive to me anymore, was definitely a hallmark of living with the Gancanagh. I close my eyes and inhale deeply. The bed moves as Reed leans against the pillows next to mine. I turn towards him and rest my head on his shoulder, snuggling into his side. His scent is even better than the scent of the tropical plants carried on the wind.

"I've spent so many days wanting this, Reed," I murmur, staring at his eyes that are trained on my face. "To be in the same bed with you and able to respond…but I'm almost afraid that this isn't real."

"It has to be real because I can finally breathe," Reed says in a soft tone, reaching out and touching my hair.

"How did you find me?" I ask, searching his face.

"You mean today? In the car?" he asks. Seeing me nod, he says, "I felt you. The butterflies led me to you. You didn't feel them?" he asks, his green eyes looking concerned.

"I…" I pause, not wanting to tell Reed anything about what happened at Brennus' estate because I don't want to see the dark pain in his eyes when he hears it. I shake my head no and look away.

"Don't do that," Reed says with a grimace, lifting my chin gently and looking in my eyes again. "Don't hide things from me. There has been so much that has happened to you that I don't know about. There are broken pieces of you that I can't see and I need to know." Reluctantly I look into his eyes again. "Why didn't you feel me?" he asks gently.

"He…hit me," I admit in a low tone, biting my lip so I won't cry and willing the tears not to come to my eyes.

I try to look down again, feeling all of these fierce emotions swirling around in me: guilt, rage, pain, fear, and intense hurt. Reed leans his face near mine trying to keep eye contact with me.

"Who hit you? Casimir?" he asks, his voice is calm enough, but his eyes can't hide his pain from me.

I nod again.

"Where did he hit you?" he asks, scanning my body.

My throat feels tight, so I take his hand and place it on my abdomen.

"Here?" he breathes, his hand lightly skimming my middle. "Does it still hurt?" he asks as his brows rise a little in question.

He inches my shirt up gently, exposing a large, yellowish bruise left behind by Casimir's fist. I shrug, not knowing how to answer because it isn't like getting shot or magically stabbed—it hurts a lot less, but it's more…personal. Being hit with a fist is…intimate.

"Can you teach me how to protect myself on the inside when it's impossible to protect myself on the outside?" I whisper, trying to keep the tightness from my tone.

"Evie," Reed groans in pain. He leans over, his perfect lips kissing my bruised abdomen gently. "I don't want you to have to learn how to feel nothing when someone is hurting you. I will show no mercy to anyone who tries to hurt you again."

"I'm sorry, Reed," I whisper, feeling sorrow for causing him so much pain.

I thread my fingers through his hair, feeling the poignancy within the sensual kisses he's raining gently on my sensitive skin.

His body stills and I can feel his breath tickling my skin and causing a shiver of pleasure to rush through me. "For what?' he asks in a low tone.

"I'm sorry for…for not telling you what I was going to do…" I trail off. I can't apologize for going. I had to go, but I should've told him everything before I went. He shouldn't have had to hear it from Phaedrus.

His hands tighten again as he rests his cheek against my abdomen. "I would never have let you do it," he says honestly.

"I know," I whisper, my voice straining.

"I have never had to…" he trails off.

"You have never had to what?" I ask, looking up at the ceiling fan slowly turning above us.

"I have never had to fight so hard to take a breath. When I found out what happened…that Brennus had you and the circumstances of the contract…" he trails off again, sounding hollow.

I close my eyes, feeling tears slip from the corner of them. "I'm sorry," I say again, feeling the misery of that moment through his eyes.

"I did not intend for you to conclude that the only option open to save Brownie and Russell was for you to go in there alone," his tone is tight, filled with self-accusation. "Not only did you feel you could not tell me, I made it so that you had to face a monster with nothing more than your clever mind."

"You act like you stranded me there. It was what I had to do—it was my mission. I had to go before it was too late," I explain with desperation in my voice.

"I nearly lost you…so many times," Reed says with his body tensing. "I had moments when I was sure that there would be no way you could survive what was happening to you."

"You were with me—in my blood. I will always fight to be with you," I whisper.

"I don't know if I can change, Evie. I'll always need to do whatever I think is best to protect you," he admits, lifting his head from my abdomen and looking at me grimly.

"Okay," I say in a low tone, touching his cheek with my fingers. "I can live with that."

"What?" he asks, his expression softening a little.

"I'll take you as you are. All I care about is being with you. I need you," I say, leaning forward and brushing my lips against his cheek. "I want you," I whisper, moving my lips to his other cheek and pressing them to it. "Only you," I breathe, kissing his lips tenderly. "Reed," I whisper, feeling his lips moving over mine, making me want him despite the pain I'm in.

"Evie," he says my name like a prayer, pulling me closer to him. He lies back against the pillows, letting my head rest on his shoulder.

"I don't want to close my eyes," I admit, snuggling against Reed's side, trying hard not to let the warmth of his body lull me.

"Shh, I've got you, my angel," he whispers, gently stroking my hair as he speaks in Angel, lulling me to sleep with his soft voice that is like a caress.

❦

When I awaken, my eyes adjust to the almost total darkness of the room. Lying on my stomach, I grasp my neck and rub it because it's sore from sleeping in one position for hours. As I sit up in bed, the sheet slips down and I realize that I'm no longer dressed in the clothes I had on before. I'm wearing a large, white t-shirt that definitely belongs to Reed because it smells like him.

Looking around, everything is so quiet. The only sound is the water lapping gently against the beach outside. I rise from the bed and cautiously move to the hallway. There is a glow from the dim lighting in the small kitchen of the bungalow, but it's empty.

A shiver passes through me because it feels very strange to be alone here. Bodyguards and fellas have surrounded me for months. Even when I was in my room at Brennus' estate, I never truly felt alone.

Something must be wrong, I think, moving stealthily to the front of the villa.

The front doors are wide open, allowing me to scan the beach for threats. I don't find any, but I find Reed alone on the sandy edge of the water. He looks completely human, lying on his back in the sand and gazing up at the night sky with his arms crossed behind his head. I smile seeing his sexy body only covered by a pair of loose fitting, cargo shorts.

I move soundlessly towards him and he doesn't make a sound either as I near him. I drop to my hands and knees and crawl the last few feet to him, obscuring his view of the sky by covering his lips with mine. I feel him tense for a moment before he relaxes, kissing me deeply.

In a second, I am flat on my back, looking up at Reed's eyes that smolder with a dark passion I haven't seen for months.

"Hi," I breathe, seeing the predatory glint as his eyes rove over my t-shirt clad body as it hitches up daringly on my thighs.

"You're awake," he says against my neck while he nuzzles my ear.

In the next second, I hear a tearing sound as my wings shoot out of my back causing my eyes to grow wider, knowing that if I move, I will be completely naked. My wings stretch out beneath me, like they have a mind of their own.

Reed lifts his head from me, watching my wings move and stretch. In the next instant, his wings answer mine, shooting from his back, blocking out the night sky as they elegantly flank him.

"My wings just told you something, didn't they?" I ask, seeing his satisfied expression.

"Yes," Reed answers, looking elated.

"What did they say?" I inquire, feeling my cheeks flush with color, knowing this is going to be a little embarrassing.

"You find me sexy," Reed says, and it's painfully obvious he is enjoying every second of this.

"Is that all?" I ask, feeling my face flush more as he shakes his head slowly, a sultry heat building in his eyes. His eyes skim my body slowly, causing the flush from my face to run the length of me.

"They also said, 'I will fight anyone who keeps me from having you,'" he breathes, his finger tracing the collar of my t-shirt.

"Oh," I exhale as Reed's finger moves the torn collar lower, trailing a line to my heart. "Is that it?" I ask.

"Not exactly," he smiles possessively, when he sees the mark of his wings on my heart.

"There's more?" I wonder aloud, captivated by his sweet expression.

"Uh huh," he murmurs, pressing his lips to my flushed skin above my heart, kissing the symbol of our union.

My back arches a little, responding to his touch. "They are chatty tonight," I whisper back, biting my bottom lip in pleasure and hearing him give a low laugh.

"They *are*," Reed agrees, nodding and looking into my eyes again. "They are also very possessive because they told me that I belong to them. They said, 'mine.'"

"Well, they are very smart, you see?" I reply, smiling back at him, feeling the satisfaction coming from him.

"They are…brilliant," he replies, lowering his head and kissing me deeply.

When his lips slip to my neck, I ask, "What did your wings say just now?"

"They said, 'I love you, Evie. Just you…only you,'" he answers me in a soft tone.

"They said that?" I ask, feeling completely happy in this moment as a warm glow rushes through me.

"Yes," he replies with a heated smile, his voice holding a note of humor at my reaction to his words.

"I'll have to learn their language, too," I reply as my t-shirt slips a little further down. "I love you, too, Reed," I whisper, frowning. "I wish…" I trail off as the scruff from his chin grazes my sensitive skin. I exhale, my eyes becoming hooded as I watch him kiss me.

"You wish?" he murmurs as his hands slip lower on my body.

"I wish I had other words… 'I love you' is so inadequate to describe what I feel for you," I whisper.

Instantly, Reed picks me up off the sand and holds me securely to his chest. He begins striding purposefully towards the bungalow with me in his arms.

"Then show me, Evie," Reed says near my ear, and my arms wrap around his neck as my shirt falls to the ground and is left behind on the beach.

CHAPTER 25

Persephone No More

*Thwick…thwick…*the unmistakable sound of a club hitting golf balls wakes me up from the disturbing nightmare I am having. I roll over in bed, staring up at the slowly turning ceiling fan, feeling disoriented.

Sensual lips brush over the curve of my shoulder, causing me to glance to my side. Reed lifts his head from me, his dark green eyes changing from satisfaction to concern as he gazes into my eyes. "Were you having a nightmare?" Reed asks me in a low tone, his brown hair falling over his brow in an elegant mess.

Reaching out, I sweep his hair back, feeling the silkiness of it. Then, I glance around the room, disoriented by the tranquility of it after being immersed in…dread.

"What is it, Evie?" Reed asks, reaching out and touching my forehead with his hand. It feels warm and dry against my damp skin. He trails his fingers over my cheek, inhaling softly the scent from my hair.

"I thought that I wouldn't be having any more nightmares," I say, rubbing my eyes. "I haven't had one since China."

Reed frowns, like this is new information to him. "Do you remember the nightmare you just had?" he asks, stroking my arm gently.

"A little...it was really cold...icy and there was a storm blowing up on the horizon...out there," I explain, pointing weakly in the direction of the sea outside.

"It doesn't get cold here, love," Reed says, sounding puzzled.

Thwick. Another golf ball being hit sounds outside.

Russell laughs while he says, "Ahhh, Zee, yer gonna kill someone with that wicked slice. SORRY, BUNS! HE'LL GET YA A NEW ONE! Look what ya did, Zee—ya broke that thing she likes so much."

"What was that thing anyway?" Zee mumbles.

"I don't know and don't ask her...just say yer sorry and that yer gonna get her another one just like it," Russell replies, cracking up.

"How am I supposed to do that when I do not even know what it is?" Zephyr asks, sounding exasperated by Russell's advice.

"Ya ask her to take ya where she got it," Russell advises, his voice full of humor.

"Why can't I just give her some money for it?" Zee inquires, like he is questioning Russell's logic.

"Ya could, but then ya might get caught if she asks what the money is for and ya don't know the answer to that, do ya?" he asks rhetorically.

Smiling, I turn to Reed, seeing that he still looks concerned. "Do you remember anything else about your dream?" Reed asks. I lean back against the pillows, thinking before I shake my head.

As Reed tucks a piece of hair behind my ear, I blurt out, "It's coming closer."

"What's coming closer?" he asks in a calm tone.

"The storm..." I trail off.

"Does the storm know where we are?" he asks, gently twisting his finger in a strand of my hair.

"I don't know," I whisper. "I haven't dreamed—it didn't work when I was with them," I admit, glancing up at Reed.

"It works now," he says neutrally.

"Brennus thought that I didn't dream because I was safe with them," I say, playing with the corner of my blanket.

"That is an interesting theory," Reed replies, remaining neutral. "What do you think?" he asks, his green eyes studying mine.

"I think that Heaven doesn't tip it's hand to the wrong players," I reply, feeling ashamed, but for what I'm not exactly sure.

His eyes soften in the corner as he says, "You are never the wrong player, Evie. Are you hungry? Everyone has been waiting for you to wake up. We have breakfast ready out by the water."

I nod, knowing that I should eat something.

"Buns and Brownie bought you some new clothes. Do you want to take a shower and meet us out by the water?" he asks, his fingers trailing through my hair, gently.

"Yes," I smile, trying to pull myself together.

I want to see my friends again, but I don't know if I'm up for talking about my fam…the Gancanagh. My heart sinks. *Are they all dead?* I wonder grimly. *Did Zephyr and his Dominion army kill them after I left? Or were they all taken out by the Fallen?* I lose the smile I am trying to hold on to for Reed's benefit.

"The shower is in here," Reed says, getting up from the bed and holding out a linen robe to me. I wrap myself in it before taking his hand and walking to the adjoining bathroom. "I'll be just outside, if you need anything," Reed says, before kissing my lips lightly.

Showering quickly, I brush out my hair and put it up in a quick ponytail. I walk to the bedroom and find mostly bikinis with matching wrap skirts. There are some dresses in the closet, but they are more formal. I select a black bikini with matching wrap skirt that will probably end up being sheer in the sunlight. I slip on a pair of strappy sandals and walk out of the bedroom towards the beach.

A snowy-white pavilion has been erected on the sand. Within it, a large, wooden, dining table has been set up with comfortable rattan chairs placed around it. As I walk towards the pavilion, Russell turns around and watches me make my way to them. He is wearing a pair of board shorts and it looks like they have been here, on the island, for a while now because his skin is tan and his tawny hair is lighter.

"Good Lord," Russell murmurs, leaning his arm against the pavilion's post, watching my every move. I blush, feeling awkward as they all stare at me like I'm a stranger.

Buns and Brownie immediately walk towards me from the shade of the tent, engulfing me in a group hug. "Sweetie, how do you feel?" Buns asks, scanning my legs. They can't see the bruises under my wrap skirt that are now the only indication that I had ever been shot.

"Much better," I reply honestly, continuing to walk with them to the tent.

When we reach the wooden planks that lead to the arching pavilion, I pause in front of Zephyr who has been watching my approach.

"Is it okay to have my wings out?" I ask Zephyr, trying to find something to say so I don't feel so weird with him.

He is wearing board shorts similar to Russell's and his hair is getting longer than I remember him wearing it, making him look a little older but just as attractive.

"Yes," he replies, smiling at me. "It is just us here during the week. I have a human staff that comes by boat to the other side of the island. They bring supplies and a cleaning crew. I will advise you when they arrive in a few days."

I nod, staring into his blue eyes that are the color of the sky above us. Zephyr reaches out and hugs me, lifting me off my feet. "From now on," Zephyr says, "when one of us says, 'stay behind me,' I want you to do it…and don't you know that you're too young to go off alone to face an Ifrit?" His voice is strained. I have never heard him sound like that before.

"I'm sorry, Zee," I whisper, hugging him back just as tight.

"You should be," he scolds me in a stern tone. "I nearly killed Phaedrus—"

"What?" I choke, my fingers curling on his back.

"He left you there alone," Zephyr says with a menacing tone. "You are so little—when I think of you walking up to that church alone…" he trails off.

"He had to, Zee." I say, feeling sad that I caused them to be at odds with each other. "It was my mission."

"I didn't hurt him," Zephyr says gruffly. "He led us back to the church. When we found Russell and Brownie—we understood—if you had not gone when you did, they would not be here now. But, I would have gone with you," he adds, leaning down and setting me on my feet so that he can look into my eyes again.

"It was a solo mission, Zee," I reply, not wanting to argue with him, but wanting him to see that I did what I thought was best for everyone.

He grunts. "That doesn't mean I have to like it," he replies. "I want details on everything from the moment we were frozen by Safira to the moment Reed found you in Casimir's car."

I put a shaky hand to my forehead and I can feel myself growing paler. Russell must see it, because he steps forward and puts his arm under my arm and around my waist.

"Shoot, Zee, wait a second," Russell says, leading me to the table and pulling out the chair for me. I sit on the soft cushion, feeling grateful to Russell for rescuing me from the interrogation I know is coming. "When was the last time ya ate, Red?" Russell asks me and I shrug.

"She ate some bread and a little bit of cheese last night," Reed recalls helpfully, placing a plate in front of me laden with pancakes, French toast, biscuits with gravy, and fruit. I look at it, wondering how anyone could possibly eat all of that food.

"Ya best get started, 'cuz we're not lettin' ya leave 'til it's gone," Russell says, handing me a fork and looking completely serious as he sits in the chair next to mine, engulfing it with his large frame. Reed takes the seat on the other side of me, pouring water into my glass.

I eat steadily for a while as Zephyr and Russell fill Reed in regarding the number of Fallen they were able to take out and their last known positions.

"Are you still committed to the plan?" Zephyr asks Reed with a blank expression.

"Yes, we should try to find the one angel that might know everything about Evie," Reed says in a serious tone.

I stop chewing and swallow hard. "Who knows more about me than you guys?" I ask, my brows drawing together in thought.

"Tau," Reed replies in a gentle tone. "If he is your father—"

"That's a waste of time," I reply. "If he cared at all, he would have found me—helped or at least dropped by to say, 'Hi,'" I reply as casually as I can, but my mouth feels dry.

"He could be helpful now," Reed says, his hand shifting to cover mine as it rests on the table.

"I spoke to Casimir," I say, trying to deter them from trying to find the angel that has treated me with complete indifference. "He told me things—I don't know how much of it we can believe, but it may be more informative than anything Tau could tell us." I quickly recount my conversation with Casimir before he had escaped back into the portal.

Reed and Zephyr make eye contact when I tell them about Casimir calling me a "warning" to all angels. They don't seem to like Casimir's take on the fact that I'm a new species and a threat to replace both humans and angels alike. I pause when I see their faces go blank to ask, "Do you think he's right?"

"No," Reed replies instantly. "I think he is completely wrong, but others may not. If the Fallen could convince angels to believe that it is your purpose here, then we have some problems. It makes finding out your true purpose much more important," he states, looking at me with a reassuring smile.

"Your trap was very enticing," Zephyr compliments me with admiration in his tone. "I had doubts that Casimir would ever risk himself like that, but he probably could not help himself, thinking you were alone and vulnerable."

"It was Eion's idea," I say, deflecting his praise. "I made a rooky mistake by not closing the portal."

"Which is why ya should've let us take ya outta there in the first place," Russell chimes in next to me, looking a little pale after hearing how I messed up the trap to kill Casimir. "The Fallen were fixin' to kill ya, Red. Yer lucky Casimir seemed to change his mind after talkin' to ya. If he would have come in with guns a blazin', ya would be dead now."

"Are you going to keep playing that role, Russell?" I ask him quietly, picking up my fork again and using it to spear a piece of mango, popping it into my mouth.

Russell's eyes narrow. "What role is that?" Russell asks.

"Bad cop," I reply, chewing and watching him lean back, assessing me.

"Well, Reed already took the role of 'good cop.' Someone had to tell it to ya straight," he says, picking up a glass of orange juice and taking a sip of it. "We were losin' ya to them. They're very clever creatures...seductive. I bet they didn't show ya half that place, did they?" he challenges me.

"No, I bet they didn't," I agree softly, feeling humbled by his assessment of me and them.

"It took a lot for him to do that, Evie," Brownie says in a quiet voice from her seat across the table. "It would've been easier for Russell to be the nice guy, but that wouldn't have been helpful to you."

Feeling cornered, I reply, "It took a lot for me to be there, too. So cut me some slack about how I performed in captivity."

"No one's gradin' ya," Russell says, frowning, "we're all just tryin' to figure out why yer so protective of them."

"I'm not protective of them," I reply, not looking up from my plate.

"Okay, then tell us how they operate. Who is their second in command? Name yer personal guard..." he trails off when I won't look at him. "Naw, they still got ya, don't they?" he asks in a rhetorical way, sounding bitter.

"Russell, it wasn't like what you went through with Valentine—they didn't torture me or hurt me. They taught me magic and ways to defend myself..." I trail off, looking at his face.

"They indoctrinated ya," he replies. "They did that so that ya would begin to see things through their eyes and not think for yerself, 'cuz if ya were thinkin', ya would have seen that they were killin' women with the efficiency of a factory."

"Did you kill them?" I ask, looking down again and not at his face.

"Why?" he asks me, assessing my question.

"DID YOU?" I shout, not caring what he thinks.

Russell gazes at me with a sad smile and says, "Naw...we don't know what happened to them. They could've been killed by the Fallen. Our focus was killin' Casimir's army and tryin' to rescue ya. Reed was the lead on findin' ya...because of the attraction between ya both. We still had one of the Gancanagh, Leif, here. The plan was to get ya back here and let him bite ya so the contract would be broken."

"Where is Leif?" I ask, feeling sick that they are holding Leif hostage.

"He's dead," Russell replies, watching my reaction. "Well, ended, 'cuz he was already dead before we got him. How did ya get Brennus to break the contract?" he counters.

"We were going to leave through the tunnels under the estate, but Casimir was waiting for us. He shot me and he was going to kill me if Brennus didn't agree to let me go," I explain.

"So, he let you go to save his own life," Russell replies, his brows drawing together in a scowl.

"No," I reply, looking at Russell again. "He would've died to keep me. He let it be my choice. He said he knew he would be ended either way. Casimir would be smart enough not to let him live."

"So Casimir killed Brennus?" Reed asks from his seat on my other side.

"No," I reply numbly, "when Brennus used magic to break the contract, I stole some of his energy and called the ocean to me. Casimir and I were separated from them when the water washed us out the window of the kirk."

Every set of eyes at the table becomes wider. "That was you?" Zephyr breathes.

"Yeah, it was me and a horrible attempt at poerty, Zee," I reply, knowing he has no idea of what I mean by that.

"We saw the current enter the caves below the estate. It was massive," Zephyr says, sounding awed. "What else can you do?"

"I don't know...it all depends on what I need..." I trail off. "I needed to stop Casimir from pulling me back into the portal we opened during our plot to trap him, so I conjured some fire. I think it burned him—his hands were burned when he tried to take me with him. It made me think that maybe my magic would work on him."

"Your magic works on Seraphim—on angels?" Zephyr asks, getting to his feet from his chair at the table and looking around. "Can you show me?" he asks excitedly.

"You want to see if I can affect you with magic?" I ask him, seeing his grin broaden.

"Yes," Zephyr says with an air of expectation.

"I'm not always sure how it will turn out though, Zee. It seems like if I just pull a little energy to me, then I get a different effect than when I use all the energy that I can gather," I explain nervously. "I don't want to hurt you. Here…sit back down in your chair—I'll try something I have been thinking about."

Zephyr sits back down and I rest my fork on the table and push my chair out. As I stand next to Russell, he asks me, "What are ya gonna do?"

"The moon," I reply. His eyebrows shoot up, trying to figure out what I mean as I gather a small amount of energy to me and I whisper, "Catch the moon today, Drift up and float away. Gently rising, in no pain, Soaring softly as you reign."

I flip the switch on the energy and it flows from me, reaching out to the angels around the table. They begin to levitate from their seats: gently rising above the table like they are in zero gravity and floating towards the top of the tent. Buns giggles as her head bumps against the canvas awning.

"Come back easy; goodbye moon. Resting safely—None too soon." I pull the energy back to me slowly and everyone gently floats to his or her seat.

When I sit back down at the table, I see all of their stunned faces. I notice Zephyr stare at Reed with that male telepathy thing. As if answering a silent question, Reed shakes his head "no." Zephyr turns to Russell next and asks, "Can you feel the energy Evie is employing?"

"Heck yeah," Russell responds with a crooked smile. "It's sorta like standing next to a downed power line. I can smell it and feel it ripplin' in the air. Can't y'all feel it?" he asks.

"No…we do not possess magic, so it is difficult for us to detect it," Zephyr admits. "If you can feel it, perhaps Evie can teach you how to manipulate it. You should be able to do it, too. Evie can teach you magic and you can work with her on her clones."

"Sweetie, Russell's clones are so amazing! He worked really hard with Phaedrus to develop them," Buns says, smiling at Russell. "Brownie and I were worried about him. He worked so hard on them that he would get headaches and nose bleeds, but it was the only way to communicate with you so we couldn't convince him to take it easy."

"It wasn't that bad," Russell says, deflecting her concern, not looking at me, but I know that it was. I can remember what it felt like when I tried to control a clone and he did it much, much better than I ever did. Guilt hits me again. He has been killing himself to get me back.

"What was it like, Evie? Living with them?" Brownie asks me, looking sad as she pulls my attention to her. All of their eyes fall on me again as I pick up my fork and push my food around on my plate.

I shrug, looking up. I want to try to evade her question, but I can see that they're all very attuned to my response. "At first it was terrifying," I admit, hearing my voice waver. "I was afraid all the time. I stayed in my room for the first few days. When I did leave my room, everything was so unreal…so completely bizarre—like a plastic version of a wicked fairy tale." My throat is taut, I take a sip of my water. "But, then, I began to get lost in their fairy tale and everything became real to me. Their gravity kept pulling me to them and it became almost impossible to hang on to who I was. I couldn't run from them. I couldn't escape. It became easier to be who they wanted me to be. It was a relief from being afraid all the time—accepting my role in their world. It got so that I didn't have to try to play along anymore—I could just be one of them," I say, feeling like I betrayed everyone at the table.

"I'm so sorry, Evie," Brownie says, getting up from the table. She is gone in an instant.

"Brownie?" I ask, surprised by her reaction to what I just told them.

Russell gets up from his seat and holds his hand up to Buns. "I'll go," he says to Buns who looks like she is getting up, too.

Russell leans down and whispers in my ear. "We need to talk, Red." When I nod numbly, he kisses the top of my head and then he is gone in a fraction of a second, too.

"It's okay, sweetie," Buns assures me as I look at her face in confusion. "Brownie feels responsible for what happened. She thinks that there must have been a way that she and Russell could have avoided being captured by Valentine."

"How could she have seen him coming?" I ask. "He was... brutal and resourceful."

"Just like Brennus," Buns says, staring into my eyes. "You survived, Evie. We're amazed by you and proud of you. We just want to help you come back to us. Let us know how we can do that and we'll do it."

"You already did it," I say in a soft tone. "You never let me forget why I needed to come back...you never let me forget that you're my family."

Buns gets up from her seat and comes around the table to hug me. "You're home. That's what matters. We'll be okay now. I'm going to go see if I can talk to Brownie."

Buns walks away from the table and I gaze at Reed next to me. "Do you want to see the island?" Reed asks me.

"Yes," I reply, smiling in relief that I won't have to answer any more questions now.

Reed gets up from his seat and then pulls my chair out for me. After he helps me up, he says, "We'll take the Jeep. I want to show you something."

"Will you be back for lunch?" Zephyr asks Reed, while rising from his seat and picking up his golf clubs.

"Don't count on it," Reed replies, smiling at Zephyr. Reed picks up a couple of muffins and wraps them in a napkin.

"Then we will not wait for you," Zephyr smiles. "Evie, I am glad you are home."

"Me too," I say as he reaches out to touch my cheek lightly. "Call if you plan to miss dinner," Zephyr says to Reed, dropping his hand from me.

"Okay," Reed agrees. Zephyr turns and heads in the direction of the large, white plantation house on the hill.

"Why aren't we staying with them at the plantation house?" I ask Reed as he leads me along a path behind our bungalow where a 4-door Jeep is parked.

Reed opens my door for me and helps me into the car before moving supernaturally fast to the driver's side. "I wanted to be alone with you for a while," Reed replies, starting the car and driving between the dense trees and over the jungle-like path that is posing as a road. I smile as I hold on to the door handle and glance at Reed's beautiful profile.

"How did that go over with the rest of the crew?" I ask, watching the scenery whip by faster than necessary.

"Not well, but since you are my *aspire*, they had to deal with it," he replies, his eyes shiny with satisfaction.

"Pulling rank again?" I ask, watching his hand reach out and cover mine as it rests on the console between us.

"I will do whatever it takes to be alone with you, Evie," he says, taking my hand and bringing it to his lips.

"I never thanked you, Reed," I breathe, feeling my heart contract.

"Thanked me? For what?" he asks.

"For avenging me…and my uncle," I say, watching his eyes change from question to understanding. "For what you did to Casimir."

"It was over too fast, Evie," Reed says, his lips turning down a little as his eyebrows draw together. "He was shown too much mercy. He did not suffer enough."

"He intended to make me his slave," I say, feeling chilled by the fact that if Reed hadn't been there, I would probably be in Sheol right now.

"That is not going to happen. I will fight to see that no one ever makes you their slave again," he says with his jaw tense.

I let go of his hand and reach up to touch his cheek. He closes his eyes for a moment, savoring the contact. "Thank you," I say, feeling like my words are still so inadequate for what I mean by them.

"You never have to thank me, Evie," Reed says with a sultry look. "It's my mission—you are my mission."

The car emerges from the lush jungle into a clearing. I hear the roar of a waterfall before I see it. When we drive around the bend of an outcropping of stone, I almost lose my breath at the majesty and power of the cascading water above us. Parking the car near the edge of the water, Reed climbs out. He comes around to my door and opens it for me.

"I want to show you something," he says, picking up a backpack from the back seat of the car, he hands it to me as he pulls me into his arms. His wings sweep out of his back, causing me to feel a little thrill at seeing them. As we lift off the ground and into the air, Reed whispers in my ear, "Prepare to get wet."

I cringe as we fly directly towards the waterfall. I close my eyes, thinking that we will crash right into the cliff face behind the falling water, but instead, we pass under the pounding deluge right into a cavern hidden behind it. Smooth rock lines the space, a clear indication that water had spewed from this opening until it had been redirected elsewhere at some point. Light shining through the cascading water is reflecting on the rock walls that have crystallized quartz embedded in them. Sparkling points of light shine on both Reed and me, making us look like we rolled in glitter.

"How did you find this place?" I ask, gazing around in wonder.

"I had a hard time sleeping without you," he says, taking the backpack from my hand. "I wanted to work all the time, but Buns insisted that I come to the island to rest every once in a while. Russell and Phaedrus were working on trying to find you. We didn't know where they had taken you for so long."

He frowns, pulling a blanket that is still mostly dry from the bag and spreading it out on the ground. "For such a little thing, Buns manages to get her way." Reed looks up, smiling at me and my heart contracts at how lovely he is when he smiles. "But, when I arrived here—I rarely slept longer than a few minutes at a time, so I wandered around. I knew you weren't here, but I kept searching for you anyway," he says with pain in his tone.

I move to him then, reaching up to cup his face and bring it to me. I cover his lips with mine, feeling his arms wrap around me. "I couldn't find you, Evie," he whispers against my lips.

"I'm right here," I whisper back, feeling my clothes falling away from me as he unties the strings. My body covers his as we lie on the blanket together, the sound of the rushing water echoing around us. We fit together perfectly, as I show him everything that is in my heart. All the pain and regret melts away and it is just the two of us.

Lying in Reed's arms afterward, I rest my cheek against his chest, tracing shapes with my finger on his perfect abdomen. Reed's fingers trace a path over my back. His fingers pause for a moment, and then continue slower than before. In a hollow voice, he asks, "Did he...did he hurt you?"

My fingertip halts on his skin as I close my eyes, realizing what Reed is asking me. "No," I say, before lifting my head and looking in his eyes that are dark from the passion we just shared. "He...he kissed me a lot...and I kissed him," I admit, choking on the last words. "I had a plan. I collected my own blood when I was in the shower. I would cut myself and store it in perfume bottles. Then, when I had enough, I tried to see if I could make him bite me. Lust and bloodlust are entwined in them. I thought that he might lose control if I pushed him a little." My cheeks fill up with color as a flush of shame passes over me.

Reed remains silent so I go on, "He wanted me. He was getting to a point where he began to press me to respond to him. But, what he really wanted was for me to come to him. To ask him to love me," I explain, watching Reed struggle to keep his features blank. "I think that to someone who has always had women throwing themselves at him, it was repulsive to him to force himself on me...he would rather try to seduce me into it."

"So...you two never..." he says, his hands tightening around me.

"No, I was his queen in name only," I reply to his unspoken question, watching Reed close his eyes.

"Evie, when I told you to do anything to survive...I truly meant *anything*," he says, staring into my eyes. "If you had to lie, cheat, steal, and seduce him to get away—to retain your soul, then I could have lived with that, just to have you back."

"Well, I did do most of those things...I just wouldn't sleep with him," I reply, watching his face change from tense to euphoric.

"But, he bit you...you must have felt something for him," Reed says, looking blissfully confused.

"I felt something for him," I admit, trying to explain my attraction to Brennus. "He is...compelling and complicated. He makes it difficult to see anything clearly when he's around. But, what I felt for him...it pales in comparison to having you in my blood," I reply, leaning down to nibble on his earlobe. "You're *my* angel. I need you like I have never needed anyone."

"I thought I was losing you when you wanted to stay," Reed says, sitting up with me in his arms and shifting me so we can face each other.

"You can never lose me," I say, pressing my chest to his and hugging him. "I didn't want any of you to be in danger. I thought if I could have the Gancanagh defend me from the Fallen, then I could protect you." I hear a growl escape him and I pull away, looking at his sullen face.

"Evie, we have to talk about your need to protect me," he begins, but I cover his mouth with mine, kissing him seductively as my arms snake behind his neck.

"Let's not talk now," I whisper, moving against him and feeling him respond instantly.

We stay there for most of the day and lose all sense of time. As the light in the cave begins to grow dim, my stomach rumbles loudly, causing Reed to smile with his lips against mine.

"Hungry?" he murmurs.

"Starving," I admit, "do you have any more of those muffins left?" I ask.

"No. You ate all of them an hour ago," Reed says with a smile that almost stops my heart. Reed rises from our blanket and gathers up my clothes, handing them to me. "We have to go back anyway. Buns is planning a barbeque on the beach for dinner tonight. I think she will be hurt if I don't bring you back." He watches me slip into the black bikini and wrap skirt. Then he groans and wraps his arms around me, pulling me to his chest. "Evie, you are so beautiful."

A blush of pleasure rushes over me. "I only really ever feel beautiful when you look at me," I reply honestly, resting my cheek against his chest and hearing his heart beat to the rhythm of mine. "You're going to have to help me out of here. I can't fly very well yet."

"Phaedrus told me you flew," he says, picking me up off my feet and holding me in his arms. "I wanted to be with you when you did that," he says in a disappointed tone.

"It's probably better that you missed that," I reply, remembering jumping from the gazebo and being pursued by Declan. "It's a lot harder than it looks."

"When your wings grow larger, it will be easier," Reed replies with a grin. "You ready?" he asks, and when I nod, he launches us through the wall of water in front of us. His wings snap out around us as we glide steadily to the ground.

"Where is Phaedrus?" I ask Reed when he sets me back on my feet by the car. I climb into the passenger seat and Reed closes the door for me.

"He is still with Dominion," Reed says, starting the car and wheeling it around back towards the beach.

"You didn't tell him your plan?" I ask, watching his face.

"No," Reed says, his hand tightening on the steering wheel.

"Why not?" I ask.

"He didn't tell us of the plans he made with you, so we reciprocated," Reed replies.

"REED!" I say in exasperation, "That's not fair! I made him do things my way. He had a mission and he fulfilled it. How can you shut him out like that?"

"How could *you* shut *me* out like that?" he asks quietly, slamming his foot on the brake and bringing the car to a screeching halt. "You promised me that you would never leave again, but you did."

"Technically I didn't leave you—I just didn't come straight back when I escaped," I reason, watching his face grow darker at my flimsy argument.

"No, you're right. Technically you just pretended that I didn't exist," he agrees, and I have to hold on to the door handle as the car shoots forward again at a dizzying speed.

"I…I had to make a choice—what I could live with," I say, watching the trees whip past the window as the wheels dig up the earth, spattering it loudly against the wheel well. "Valentine wanted me, not them—the time to play it safe was over," I explain, wanting to close my eyes as the car fishtails a little.

"*I* wanted *you*," Reed retorts, looking hostile.

"I was desperate. They were dying, Reed. Valentine kept telling me how he would kill them—and then he promised me that he'd let them go if I came to him," I say, my heart racing with panic. "Valentine wasn't going to stop. He was going to kill them and then he was going to find me…and you. I couldn't live with that. I couldn't live knowing I could've done something!"

Reed lets his foot ease off the accelerator. The car begins to slow down and I say in a low voice that wavers with emotion, "I know I hurt you, Reed. Please forgive me."

"I've never felt this way about anyone, Evie," Reed says, not looking at me. "I didn't know that I'd have this ache within me, but I do and I thought it would go away when I got you back," he says, looking confused as he looks over at me. "I know that what you did was necessary…you don't need to ask for my forgiveness," he says grimly.

"Reed, sometimes it's impossible to make your heart believe what your head knows to be true," I say, crawling from my seat to sit on his lap as he drives the car slowly over the tree-lined path. "Where is this ache?" I ask him, feeling my own heart responding with an ache of its own.

He takes my hand and places it on his chest, above his heart. My eyes fill with tears as I gently touch the spot where my wings are etched. I place my lips against his chest and kiss his skin, before whispering to his heart, "I'm sorry. I love you and I will show no mercy to anyone who tries to keep us apart again. No mercy…I swear it."

Stopping the car, Reed feverously presses his lips to mine. He lifts me out of my seat and carries me towards our bungalow. My arms go behind his neck as I kiss him back, unaware of anything but him. As we round the corner to the entrance, Zephyr calls out, "You are back!"

Wrenching his lips from mine, Reed answers, "No."

Reed kicks the door of our villa in and heads to the bedroom with me still in his arms. Using his foot, Reed closes the bedroom door behind us as he strides purposefully to our bed.

CHAPTER 26

No Sunshine

A knock on the bedroom door wakes me from the dream I'm having. As I open my eyes, I look around the room of our bungalow and see the almost complete destruction of it. A blush stains my cheeks instantly. Reed and I had not been very careful when we returned from our visit to the waterfall yesterday. Our room resembles something close to a rockstar makeover. I sit up against the pillows and notice that I'm alone in the bed. I glance around me and realize I'm alone in the room, unless Reed is somewhere under the destroyed dresser, which I highly doubt.

Another knock sounds. "Uh, just a second," I call out, wrapping a sheet around me and stumbling out of bed. Gingerly stepping around the debris on the floor, I pause at the door. "Who is it?"

"It's me," I hear Russell say. I bite my lip, looking over my shoulder at the carnage of the room and then looking up in embarrassment.

After whispering a few choice words under my breath, I say, "Uh…yeah?" through the door, wrapping the sheet around me tighter and running my fingers through my tangled bedhead.

I crack the door a few inches, peeking at him timidly, I mumble, "Hi."

"Hi," Russell grins, pushing the door open and forcing me to step back from it as he walks into the room.

"By all means, come in," I say with irritation in my tone, feeling my face grow beet-red.

"Good Lord, woman...what happened in here?" Russell asks, his face growing almost as red as mine.

"Nothing...uh, what's up?" I ask quickly.

"Strategy meeting—ya might want to be there—we're gonna discuss security..." he trails off, picking up my black bikini top that was flung over the lamp.

I pluck what's left of the top out of his hand and hide it behind my back with one hand while the other hand grasps Russell by the bicep. "Thanks, Russ," I say, trying to lead him back to the door, but Brownie is right, he is really freaking strong and I can't move him an inch now.

"You know what this room reminds me of?" he asks, looking around and then at my face. I shrug, wanting to crawl under a rock. "Athens. We totally destroyed our rooms when I came back from the campaign in—"

I interrupt him, "Was I the girl or the boy in that life?" I ask, trying to throw him off the story.

"Definitely the girl, Red," he grins. "Ya used to make this little squeak when I—"

"Okay! Where's the meeting, Russell?" I ask, feeling like I can't be any redder than I am right now.

Russell sees my distress and his grin becomes broader. He seems to look right through the sheet I'm wearing. "It's at the big house," he answers, pointing over his shoulder in the direction of Zephyr's plantation house. "We're havin' breakfast there. I bet yer hungry, since y'all missed the barbeque last night. Oh yeah, Zee told me to tell ya that his staff came in early to prepare the food and clean, so ya should try to look human."

"Okay—when?" I ask, trying to smooth my hair down a little more as his eyes go to it.

"Yer hair is longer," he says, watching me try to pull the tangles from it.

"Yeah, I should cut it," I reply absently.

"Naw, don't do that...I like it," he says softly, his smile wavers and begins to slip. I catch a glimpse of his true, raw emotion before he brings the mask back up and smiles again.

"Oh, okay," I say, feeling my heart pick up a little as he looks at me. Then I glance away and say, "I should probably take a shower."

"I thought we could get together after breakfast…just us. I need to learn all they taught ya 'bout…magic." He makes a face. "Damn, sayin' the word, 'magic,' makes me sound *so* stupid!" Russell says, looking at me for understanding.

I grin, "I know, right!" I agree. "It makes you feel like a complete tool to say it, doesn't it!"

"Yeah, I swear, I was in that fight with all those freaks and they're all like, 'I will destroy yer soul!'" Russell says, emulating the deep voice of a Kevev as he hunches his back and shakes his fist like an ogre. "And I'm like, 'do all y'all know what total goofs all y'all sound like?'" he says, shaking his head.

I can't contain the laughter that bursts from me. I have to cover my face with my hands as it keeps coming so that I can't see his face because it just makes me laugh harder to look at him.

Finally getting myself under control, I wipe away the tears of laughter with the back of my hand, "Yeah, it's a trip sometimes."

"It's definitely that, Red," he agrees with a small smile. "So you'll teach me…yer magic?" he asks, looking up at the ceiling and then down at me.

"Of course. I want you to be stronger than anything out there," I reply.

"I'll work with ya on yer clones. Have ya practiced them at all while you were gone?" he asks.

"No," I admit, looking down. "They didn't work…I couldn't send them to you guys and…it was…they're very sort of intimate when I send them, so I didn't send them to the Gancanagh. I used some to get away from Brennus when he first took me, but after the contract I…" I trail off, feeling awkward again.

"Yeah," Russell says, and I realize that he is the only person that can completely relate to what I'm saying. He and I are the same. The only.

I fidget, not knowing what to say because there is so much we haven't said to each other and it's just sitting like a wall between us.

"Ahh, Red, ya can't do that," Russell groans.

"What?" I ask, looking at his face.

"Ya look so lost—so fragile," he says, looking confused himself.

"I'm okay," I say with a nervous smile. "It's just that I'm used to living in a minefield. I don't know how to be around someone who knows exactly how weird this all is. It's hard to fake anything with you."

"Impossible for ya," he replies. "Ya never have to fake anythin' with me."

"Shoot the moon?" I ask him softly.

"And if ya miss completely, I'll still love ya," he says, before walking towards the door.

My throat gets really tight. "Thank you, Russell," I say before he can make it to the door.

Pausing, he asks, "For what?" not turning around.

"For finding me," I answer.

"I think I was a little late," he replies.

"You weren't," I say, not sure that we're talking about the same thing.

"I hope not," he says in a strained voice before he leaves the bungalow.

I pick up the overturned chair from the floor and put it back by the crushed table. Then, I clear a path to the shower and close the door. Turning on the water and unwrapping the sheet from me, I step in, letting the water flow over my hair. I wash and rinse it quickly before stepping out of the shower.

Drying myself off, a cold current of icy air drifts around me. Goose bumps rise on my arms as I sniff the air, trying to recognize the scent, but there isn't anything unusual about it.

I wrap a towel around me and follow the current of air, feeling it like an icy path. It leads me to the closet. My hand trembles a little as I open the door, expecting to see some scary creature inside. There is nothing in there but my clothes.

I search for something to wear and choose a red swimsuit with matching sarong. As I select sandals to match the outfit, my hand touches the boots that I wore here. One boot feels colder than the other. After I pick it up, I reach inside the boot and pull out the knife that Brennus gave me when we were escaping at the estate. The eerie metal begins to lose its frigid chill the minute I touch it, warming in my hand like it's happy to be with me again.

I take the knife with me to the bathroom and place it near the sink before I put my clothes on. Then, I search through the black duffle bag that Reed keeps under the sink. It has weapons of various kinds in it. I find a black, thigh sheath and secure it to my leg, slipping the knife into it. I had promised myself that I would carry a weapon with me if I ever made it out of the caves in Houghton. It's only fitting that it be Brennus' weapon that I carry, since he was the one that made me need a weapon in the first place.

Walking out of the bathroom, I gasp when arms materialize on either side of me, caging me against the wall of the bedroom. A shiver of excitement runs the length of me as Reed presses his body to mine, inhaling the scent of my hair spilling over my shoulders.

"You scared me," I say, my heartbeat increasing even faster as his cheek brushes mine.

"I shouldn't be able to sneak up on you," Reed says in a serious tone. "If I can do it, with our attraction, then that means you are not paying attention to your environment."

"My environment is a bit of a mess right now," I reply, smiling as I lean against his bare torso.

"I will take care of this mess, then we are going to work on improving all of your skills," he says, his mouth inches from mine.

"Are you saying that you're going to start training me?" I ask, trailing my hands over his shoulders.

"Yes," he smiles.

"But, you rarely did that before…" I trail off as his lips meet mine.

"You are tougher now," he says, his mouth teasing mine.

"When do you want to start?" I ask, letting my hands explore his broad back.

"After breakfast?" he asks.

I groan, pulling back and looking into his eyes. "Can't. I promised Russell I'd work with him. He needs to learn how to do what I can do—magic," I explain. "How about after lunch?"

"Is he planning to work with you on your clones?" he asks, his hand pressing to my lower back, causing heat to ripple through me.

"Uh, I think that was the plan," I breathe, feeling a little distracted from the conversation.

"Good," he replies, lifting me up and carrying me to the bed behind us.

"Isn't there a strategy meeting?" I ask, staring up at his dark green eyes and watching his dark brown hair fall over his perfect brow.

"They'll wait for us," he replies, following me down onto the bed.

∽

After finishing breakfast, my eyes keep drifting to Reed's profile as he sits next to me, listening to Zephyr outline all of the security measures that they have in place. There are several islands within miles of this one. Humans inhabit many of them and among those humans are scores of Reaper angels. Buns and Brownie have been cultivating contacts among these angels, setting up networks that will alert them to any suspicious activity from Fallen or any other evil creature that may stumble around in our vicinity.

"Reapers are helping?" I inquire, looking from Reed to Zephyr.

"They are a previously untapped resource, Evie," Zephyr grins. "Reapers are literally everywhere and the Divine ones have expressed vehemence in their wish to aid us."

"Sweetie, now that the word is out about you, you're kinda like a rockstar," Buns says, her cornflower blue eyes shining with amusement. "I just had to mention you and the enthusiasm to help was overwhelming."

"Buns handles that end," Zephyr says with a small smile. "I do not have her patience."

"C'mon, Zee, most of them are very sweet," Buns says cajolingly.

Zephyr grimaces. "Too sweet and too happy. It is disturbing," Zephyr replies in a serious tone.

"But they can spot evil a mile away," she counters, not trying to deny anything he just said.

"Next to them, a kitten can be seen as evil," Zephyr replies. "We also have trusted Powers around as sentries on this island and the outlying islands. These are proven Powers that Reed and I know personally. You will not see them. If you do, there is a problem," he says, watching my reaction.

I try to keep my features blank so that he doesn't know that his words just sent ice through me. It reminds me that I'm still being hunted. I've been having trouble accepting any of this as reality. It's all been a sort of fantastic dream from which I don't want to awaken.

"So, we're staying here?" I ask.

"It is as good a place as any, for now," Zephyr says. "Only trusted angels know our exact location…even the Reapers only know our general vicinity.

"I want you to wear this, Evie," Reed says, pulling an oval, black onyx necklace from his pocket. It is a pendant attached to a platinum chain. The onyx pendant has an opal crescent moon in the center of it.

"It's beautiful," I murmur, lifting it up. It is very much like a cameo and it opens like a locket.

"Don't open it, Evie" Reed says, covering my hands with his so I won't release the latch. "It's a portal, love." Reed gives me a reassuring smile.

I turn white, letting the pendant rest against my chest, as I look back at his face. "Where does it lead?" I ask him.

"Somewhere safe," he replies. "I would rather not say where it goes. Then, no one here, but me, can be tortured into telling where you went. You are finally strong enough to withstand a portal. I couldn't let you have one before because you would never have survived it."

"What about you?" I ask, panicking a little that he expects me to jet when trouble comes, leaving him behind.

He holds up his wrist, showing me his wristwatch. "It is hard for me to wear this portal," he admits with a grin. "But, if it gets me to you, then I will have to deal with it."

I understand him. He never wants to run from a fight, but he will use the portal on his wrist for me. "Does yours go to the same place as mine?" I ask, examining his watch that looks exactly like a Blancpain.

"Yes. Ours are together—just as Zee's and Buns's are together and Brownie and Russell are together," Reed explains.

I glance at Buns who has a pendant much like mine, except hers is a golden sun. Brownie has a copper star, while Russell and Zephyr have watches similar to Reed's. Looking at Russell, I ask, "Where do their portals lead?"

"They're not supposed to tell you. If we need to use them, we will have to find each other," Reed says.

"How?" I ask.

"We are all very resourceful. There is always Facebook," Reed says with a smile.

My eyes shoot to Russell's. He winks at me, letting me know he still has his profile going under Leander Duncan. He can post something for me to follow so that I can find him if we ever get separated from each other again.

"Training," Zephyr says, looking at me with an evil grin. "Are you ready?" he asks.

"Uh…" I hesitate, looking around at all their grinning faces. "Sure."

Zephyr nods, "Good. Russell and you will train together in the mornings, then, you will both train with Reed and me in the afternoon."

"Flying lessons with Brownie and me after dinner," Buns says. "It will be just like field hockey, only no sticks."

"And no Kappas," Brownie chimes in.

"That sounds like a full day," I say, glancing at Reed to get his take on it.

"Yes," Reed says, looking a little sour, seeing that our time alone together will be curtailed.

"We have to try to catch her up to Russell," Zephyr says, hearing the reluctance in Reed's tone.

I glance at Russell and see him kiss each of his biceps for my benefit then grin at me, mouthing, "I'm the man," under his breath. I wrinkle my nose at him before smiling.

"Well, no time like the present. Ya ready to pull a rabbit outta a hat, Red?" Russell asks me, while rising from his seat at the ornate dining table.

"Yes. We should do this on the beach or at least away from the house," I say, rising from my seat at the table and looking around at all the beautiful furniture in Zephyr's house. "I nearly burned down Brennus' estate the first time I did a spell."

"Nice." Russell replies, nodding his head and looking amused.

As Reed rises from his seat, he catches my hand. "When you're finished, find me," he says, giving my hand a gentle squeeze.

"Okay," I agree, leaning over and giving him a quick kiss. I follow Russell out of the enormous house and ask him, "Do you know your way around here?"

"Yeah," he smiles, gesturing to our right, "this path leads to my beach."

"You have your own beach?" I ask, looking amazed as we begin to take a sandy path through lush foliage.

"Zee lets me stay in one of the villas on the north end of the island. I have a suite of rooms in the big house when I want to hang with them, but sometimes I have to be alone," Russell says, losing his smile.

"Why do you need to be alone?" I ask, hearing something in his tone.

"'Cuz sometimes it completely blows bein' part angel," he replies stiffly.

"Yeah," I nod, "especially when you start thinking about where this is all leading—wondering what is just waiting for you around the next curve in the road."

Russell glances at me and a reluctant smile touches his lips. "Or when ya flash back to where you've been," he adds.

"Do you go there often…to the church?" I ask, feeling the color drain a little from my face.

"Yeah, it seems like my mind likes to revisit it a lot," he admits, looking ill.

"Me, too," I say, reaching out and grasping his hand. His warm fingers curve around mine. "What happened after I left?" I ask.

"Reed and Zee showed up with Phaedrus by mornin'. I don't know how they got there that fast. They took care of Brownie and me for a while, but I was done. I couldn't handle anythin' anymore...so I went home," he mumbles, looking away from me.

"To North Carolina?" I ask, knowing that he considers that home, even though his parents had to be moved away when Alfred was trying to kill us.

"Yep and I started drinkin' the minute I got there, too. I don't remember much 'bout bein' there," he says with a wry smile. "Reed came and found me a couple of weeks later. He said...he said ya needed me...they couldn't find ya and if I could work on my clones, maybe we could locate ya."

Russell leads me to a long dock that is connected to a bungalow built right in the water on stilts.

"Wow," I say, checking out his bachelor pad that is similar to the one I share with Reed. Russell's has a huge flat screen, a state of the art sound system in it, and furniture that has not been abused.

"Here," Russell says, handing me a surfboard.

"What's this for?" I ask, holding the board in my hand as he chooses another one for himself.

"Nothin' to burn down out on the water," he says.

"Handy," I reply, carrying the board to the beach.

"Do you want to work on clones or magic first?" Russell asks, and then groans because saying that out loud is so bizarre.

"Uh...I don't...what do you think?" I ask, feeling awkward all of a sudden.

"Oh, definitely magic," he says with a broad grin.

Russell peels off his shirt and throws it in the sand. He grabs his surfboard and runs into the water. Lying on the board, he paddles out into the surf.

"This isn't normal," I mumble, taking off my wrap skirt and exposing my red swimsuit before picking up my board. I paddle out into the clear blue swells while Russell waits for me in the water. I pull my board up next to his and sit up on it with my feet drifting on either side of the board.

"All right, so…how does this work?" he asks, running his hands through his wet hair as water drips onto his enormous chest.

"Can you get closer?" I ask him, blushing a little as the tide gently moves beneath me, bumping our boards together on a gentle swell.

"I can hop on yer board with ya," he replies. Shifting, he manages to sit behind me on my board, leaving his to float beside us. As he holds on to my waist, he says in my ear, "How's this?"

"Okay," I reply, thinking that it should feel awkward to have him holding me like this, but it doesn't…it feels natural. "I'm going to start pulling energy that is all around us to me. I don't really know how to explain exactly how to do it. I'm hoping that you will be able to feel it passing through you to me."

He nods silently, as a signal for me to start. I begin pulling energy to me like a magnet. I can feel it collecting within me, tingling and oscillating like the current of water beneath us.

"I can feel it," Russell breathes in my ear. "Shoot, that burns a little."

I smile, "Good. Try to hold on to some of it—try to block some of it from getting to me. Brennus said that you should try to picture what it is that you want to do—like creating fire. Then he said to say the words to make it so. It can be anything, but I found that something lyrical makes it stronger. When you know what you want, say the words and then try to release the energy and let it flow from you."

I flip the switch on the energy I had gathered and reverse it. I control the flow of it, while singing softly, "I am caged by your desire, Surrounded by it's fire. Love burns as you conspire, It burns like fire…" Guiding the fire with my outstretched hand, I direct the comet of fire to circle around us in a spiraling display of pyrotechnics as we float on the surfboard.

"Wicked!" Russell breathes.

"Yeah," I half-smile. I direct the flame around us, making it dance before finally plunging it into the ocean, seeing the water steam and sizzle as it extinguishes the fireball within its depths. "Do you want to try something?" I ask, trying to see his face as he sits behind me.

His arms wrap tighter around my waist, pulling me back against his chest. "Yeah…shoot, I have to make up a poem?" he asks, peeking at me with one eye, the other closed in a grimace.

"You mean you weren't a poet in one of your past lives?" I ask as I nudge him softly with my elbow.

"Does a bard count?" he asks with a spreading smile.

"Yeah, that counts," I nod.

"Then this should be nothin' at all," he replies.

"Okay," I say, putting my hands on his where they rest against my hips. "I'll help you pull some energy to us and then you can try your spell." I feel him nod behind me so I begin pulling energy to us. When it is burning me I say, "Okay, try it now."

Russell's voice is low and sad as he sings, "Losin' ya is like the death of the sun And I'm crawlin' all alone in the dark. If I can't say a word, not any, not one, Then how do I hold onto yer heart?"

I lose my grasp on the energy I once held as the emotion of what he just said hits me. I release all of the energy in a rush. Dark, storm clouds immediately turn the sky gray as they boil up over us, blotting out the sun that had shone so brightly only seconds ago; it is almost as if the sun is being eclipsed.

"Uhh…Red…" Russell breathes in fear and wonder as darkness falls around us, "did we just do that?" he asks.

"Uh huh," I breathe, feeling goose bumps forming on my arms and legs.

"We're in trouble, aren't we?" he asks.

"Uh huh," I agree.

"We're gonna scare the crap out of everyone…even the good angels," he surmises, beginning to see our problem more clearly.

"Yes, we are," I nod. "I'm sorry, Russell…for all of it—everything. We're so completely toast! I don't even know what to—who lives like this—why…" I say in a raspy voice as I begin to tremble, looking up at the total darkness overtaking us.

"Shh…" Russell says, holding me closer. "We'll figure it out—we'll stay low for now, and then we'll figure it out, " he hushes me in my ear and I nod, willing myself to remain calm as fear creeps over me.

This is no parlor trick. We are a huge threat, Russell and me, and when other beings realize just what we can do…we will have to fight so that they don't use us like weapons or destroy us because of the fear we will inspire. We just went from "dangerous" to "lethal."

"We are really powerful together," I say, looking up at the sky that is as dark as twilight. "I don't think I could've done this alone."

"We've always been stronger together," he says, rubbing my arms and looking around him. "Can ya fix this before we have every evil freak here trying to figure out what's up?" Russell asks.

"I don't know…" I trail off, thinking. "Help me, Russell! Pull as much energy to you as you can." I say, closing my eyes and concentrating on amassing energy. When it's burning me inside, I whisper, "Sun, sun, sun, let it come…" Releasing energy, it works instantly, dispelling the dark, ominous clouds, and melting them as points of light shine through.

Russell's arms relax a little as he says, "Well, that feels a little bit like stealin' yer parent's car keys for a joy ride and endin' up crashin' it, huh?"

I glance over my shoulder at him like he is completely crazy. "We kind of hijacked the sun, Russell," I say.

"Yeah, the scale of things is a little harder to deal with than I expected," he replies.

"You think?" I ask, looking over my shoulder again.

"It's a good thing, Red," Russell says with assurance. "It's gonna help us survive. If I could've done somethin' like this when I was with Valentine, then he wouldn't have…I could've— it's good. We're gonna keep workin' on this every day. We're gonna make it so no one can hurt us again."

"There will always be something stronger than me," I say.

"Yeah, but maybe not us…maybe together we'll put the hurt on anythin' that comes for us," he says. "We've gotta stick together, no matter what."

"Yeah," I whisper, knowing he's right.

"Don't let yer love for him tear us apart," Russell whispers in my ear. "I need ya."

"Russell—" I whisper in anguish.

"I know what ya feel for him. I felt it…when I was talkin' with ya…when my clone entered yer body," he admits as I look straight ahead at the almost infinite expanse of water in front of us. "But…I could hear yer soul, too. Ya love me, too. Just… don't go away. We need each other—for survival, if nothin' else."

"We have to stick together. I've always felt that," I assure him. "This world is going to try to crush us, Russ."

"Well, then…it's time for us to get defiant, now isn't it?" he asks me softly, and his words have a magic of their own. I feel reassured, knowing he'll fight with me.

Reed's masculine voice interrupts my thoughts. "Are you finished playing with the lights?" Reed asks in a calm tone, while hovering next to Zephyr above us on the water, their wings causing a breeze to blow on Russell and me.

"For now," Russell replies, letting go of me and slipping from my surfboard to his.

"Which one of you did that?" Zephyr asks with awe in his tone that he can't hide.

"It was Russell's spell, but we did it together. I couldn't have done that by myself," I reply, looking at their stunned faces.

"What do you call that spell, Russell?" Zephyr asks.

"I call that one a whole can of whoop ass," Russell replies.

"Pandora's box," Reed says in a gentle tone, looking at us with a serious expression that makes a shiver run through me again.

"That, too," I whisper back, my eyes connecting with Reed's.

"I think we have got a shot now, Reed," Zephyr says with a broad smile.

"I think we are going to win," Reed counters, like he's relieved.

Did he believe it was just a matter of time before something annihilated us? I wonder. *It would be just like him to stay to the bitter end of a fight…for me.*

Reed reaches down and plucks me off my surfboard. He hugs me to him and the sky above us begins to lighten.

Glossary

A ghra – beloved
Aingeal – angel
Aontaigh – unite
Ceann - head
Dún do chlab – shut your gob (mouth)
Gob – mouth
Ifrit – shapeshifting demons who hunt divine angels
Iniqui – demons who reside in a the corpses of other beings, especially humans
Kevev – ogre-like creatures who are incredibly strong and wear flesh-like skin over their own gray skin
Laoch - warrior
Máistir – master
Mo chroí – my heart
Mo shíorghrá – my eternal love
Nevarache - lizard-like creature with black scales, yellow eyes, and long talon-like claws
Na – not
Póg mo thóin – kiss my ass
Rua – red-haired
Sclábhaí - slave
Sin é – That's it
Síorghrá – eternal love
Wans – human women
Werree – demons who steal body parts of other creatures to wear over their own shadowy figures

Acknowledgements

Chapter 22 – Quotes from Joe Lewis

COMING SOON

INCENDIARY

THE PREMONITION SERIES VOLUME 4

CHAPTER 1

The Moon

Opening my eyes in the darkness of the bedroom, the sheer canopy surrounding the bed sparkles with frost. I sit up against the pillows, allowing the silken sheet to slip from me. Reed, sleeping soundly next to me, looks so peaceful…angelic. His dark brown hair is falling over his brow in messy wisps. Reaching out, I smooth his hair lightly away from his face, feeling his warm skin beneath my fingertips. His charcoal-colored angel wing slips forward a little, brushing against my thigh. It, too, is warm against my frigid skin.

Something's wrong, I shiver, exhaling a breath and seeing it curl into a white current in front of me, as wintery air will do. *It's too cold…*Goose bumps rise on my arms as dread runs like icy water through me. Zephyr's island is located in the South Pacific; it never gets this cold here.

I toss my long, auburn hair over my shoulder and wrap the white sheet securely around my body. I put my bare feet on the teak floorboards, feeling them crackle with cold beneath me. Frosty condensation covers everything in the room, causing surfaces to sparkle eerily in the hazy moonlight from the half-shuttered windows.

Walking slowly to the bedroom door, I turn and go to the front door of our small, beach bungalow. As I open it, black clouds roll and boil towards the cove of Zephyr's island paradise. My hand clutches the doorframe, watching the ominous storm blowing in. The wind whistles against the feathers of my crimson wings, causing them to ruffle. The palm trees that line the beach are swaying in the breeze as the water churns against the white sand.

I hear cracking sounds, like someone is walking on ice too thin to sustain weight. A dark figure strides beneath the storm clouds towards me out on the open water. A thin layer of ice forms beneath his feet with each step he takes. Coming closer, the wind carries his sweet, sticky scent to me, covering me like it's marking me as his. A terrible kind of love swells in my heart—painful and raw—enslaving and cruel.

With slow, obedient steps, I walk towards the water's edge, feeling powdery, icy sand between my toes. Frigid water laps against my feet, wetting the bottom of my sheet, as I wait for Brennus to come to me. Wearing a dark, perfectly tailored suit, he appears outwardly calm. His steps are unmeasured, strolling over the ice as it continually branches out ahead of each of his strides beneath the wicked sky.

Stopping in front of me, only a breath away, Brennus smiles. He scans every inch of me with his assessing gaze. His black hair, which contrasts starkly with his pale, white skin in the moonlight, doesn't hide his eyes as they darken with pleasure. "*Mo chroí*," he breathes, calling me "my heart." "Ye seem ta have escaped da fallen *aingeals* quite well."

I nod numbly, whispering, "You survived, too, I see." There is fear and relief in my tone, betraying my feelings for him. Looking into his light green eyes, they're registering his relief at finding me.

Brennus shrugs. "I'm a good swimmer, so I survived da spell ye cast ta scatter da fallen *aingeals* and wi'out Casimir ta lead dem, da Fallen lost deir focus and began ta recognize dat dey were losing da battle," Brennus replies with an angelic expression on his beautiful face.

Seeing him smiling, it's hard for me to remember that he's truly a killer—a lethal predator. It's difficult for me to think of Brennus as evil now because he protected me. But, he had also enslaved me, keeping me from everyone that I love.

Brennus adds, "I tought dat ye were taken by da fallen *aingeals*. Dat's where we've been looking for ye."

His words evoke images of the last time I saw him a few weeks ago. Casimir and his army of fallen angels had cornered us at Brennus' estate in Ireland. I had used magic to save us by summoning the sea and drenching us all in a churning, swirl of ocean water. It had separated me from Brennus, washing me away from him and into Casimir's control.

"How's Molly? Finn? Declan?" I ask, not able to stop myself from inquiring about Brennus' brother, Finn, and my Gancanagh bodyguard, Declan…my prison guards.

"Molly is grand. Finn is better. 'Twas Declan dat we were all worried about. He took losing ye very hard. He improved a wee bit when we found Casimir's corpse in pieces on the lawn of da estate. Was dat ye who killed him?" he asks with approval.

I shake my head, "No. Reed killed him," I reply, seeing a flicker of jealousy enter Brennus' eyes at the mention of Reed's name. He warned me never to speak my angel's name in his presence, so I try to cover my slip by asking, "How did you find me?"

"Ye took me blade wi' ye. 'Tis moin…it calls for me, jus as ye do, but ye do na know dat, do ye?" he replies. I close my eyes, feeling my heart begin to race as I think of the knife I'd taken and shoved into my boot. "Come, we'll find a way for ye ta leave dis island now. Yer family misses ye. I miss ye," Brennus says softly. "'Tis time we had ye home."

Opening my eyes and staring into his, they reflect absolute certainty that I'll follow his orders and return with him. As his captive for the last few months, I had done my best to act like I was one of them, a Gancanagh, in order to survive. But now, I'm no longer his hostage. Now, I have a chance of staying with Reed. Moistening my lips that have become very dry, I say, "I can't come with you, Brennus. I'm sorry."

"Why na?" he asks me patiently, like he has all the time in the world to sort this out.

"Because my family needs me and I need them," I reply, seeing his brows turn down as his mouth slants into a frown.

"We are yer family, *mo chroí.* Ye're our queen," he says calmly enough, but his pale face looks stern. "I am yer king."

I shake my head at him, taking a step back from the edge of the water and from his outstretched hand. My heart is beating so fast now that it's pounding in my ears. "I belong here, with them...with him," I say quietly, watching Brennus' frown turn into the darkest anger. A *click* sounds from Brennus as his retractable fangs shoot forward in his mouth and he bares their razor-sharp points menacingly.

"Ye would leave me alone wi' whah I feel for ye? I would die for ye. Is dat na enough for ye ta see dat I love ye?" he asks, sounding wounded and hurt.

"I know that you love me, Brennus. I even know that you would protect me with your life if I'd let you, but I can't let you. I can't be with you," I say, feeling tears coming to my eyes.

"Ye can and ye will," he retorts, reaching out to take my arm. His fingers pass right through me, leaving a frigid gust of air where his hand had been. Amazed, I look at his face, seeing his frustration.

"You're a clone...a spell," I breathe, looking at him. "You're not really here!"

"Ye're surprised?" he asks, losing a little of his anger as he sees my astonished expression. "Ye live wi' an extraordinary *craitur*, such as yerself, for long enough, ye learn a ting or two. 'Tis a spell, Genevieve. I liked whah ye can do wi' yer clones... da images of yerself dat ye create. I tought I would try it meself. Do ye want ta see more?" he asks, but he doesn't wait for me to answer as he casts his hands in waves about us.

A rippling echo of energy billows out around us. Murky forms of Gancanagh begin emerging from the depths of the sea and striking out in legions onto the beach. These undead Faeries swarm around us, looking very real beneath the light of the moon. Fear and anger sweep through me, seeing the army he would bring down upon me, but I try to hide it as I say, "They're not here either."

"Na yet," he replies darkly. "Do na make me bring dem ta fetch ye back ta me. I tought we had gotten past dis. Chasing ye is beginning ta take a toll on me, *mo chroí*. I do na know how ta make ye understand dat ye are me heart. Wi'out ye I do na exist...and wi'out me, ye will na exist."

"So you're saying that if I don't come back to you, you'll kill me?" I ask him, feeling cold inside.

"I will bleed ye dry," he threatens, showing me his gleaming, white fangs. His image leans closer to my neck, allowing icy air to radiate near me. Remembering the gut-wrenching pain of being bitten by him, I cringe.

"If you bite me, you'll have nothing," I retort, feeling betrayed by him. "I won't drink your blood and become one of you."

"I have nuting now! When I bite ye, ye'll be Gancanagh," he counters. "Me true queen. Ye'll be unable to resist me blood."

"No," I reply, shaking my head. "I'll refuse," I say bravely, trying to mean every word.

Anger makes him sneer, "Ye may, and ye may na. I'm willing ta take dat chance."

"Are you?" I ask, feeling like every word he ever spoke to me was a lie.

"I am," he affirms, staring back at me with a predatory gaze.

"You'd give my soul to Sheol? To those monsters for eternity?" I ask him, feeling crushed. If I do drink his blood, then my soul will be surrendered to Sheol, to the fallen angels for eternity. I'll die and be reborn an evil, undead creature…like him.

"If ye make me, I will," he replies without a hint of doubt.

Russell's voice interrupts us as he nears. "Brrrr, ya feel that, Red? Now that's cold," Russell says, swinging his five-iron to dispel the imaginary Gancanagh that Brennus has conjured on the beach.

As their sinister images ripple and fade away, Russell rests the golf club on his shoulder. When his tall frame towers over me, he doesn't hesitate, but drops his club and engulfs me in his arms. Picking me up off my feet, he gives me a bone-crushing hug that takes my breath away.

"Russell," his name escapes me like a prayer as I look into his chocolate-brown eyes. His tawny hair looks almost golden in the moonlight.

Russell grins broadly at me. "Ah, ya know I've been wantin' to do that for so long, it hurts," he admits, loosening his grip on me, but not putting me back on my feet. "Am I interruptin' somethin'?" he asks, looking at Brennus' livid face. "Ah, it's the stalker again. I should've known, but yer stink is not so bad out here…maybe all y'all should move somewhere tropical," he suggests in a smart-ass tone. Seeing Brennus' eyebrows draw together, he adds, "I'm just sayin'."

"Da other, I—" Brennus begins, using the name he has attached to Russell.

Russell holds up his hand. "Just one second, Brennus, ya *total* freak," Russell says insultingly. "I just gotta get a little smackerel from my girl."

Russell's hand snakes up to weave in my hair at the base of my neck, while his lips press firmly to mine, kissing me with an intensity and longing that I'm not expecting. A low growl comes from Brennus, and an instant later, another growl answers his from Reed. Reed directed it at Brennus, I'm sure, but I push against Russell anyway, trying to make him stop kissing me. However, Russell is really freaking strong now, stronger than me, so I can't budge him an inch.

When Russell ends the kiss, he looks into my eyes, like we're alone and says, "I missed ya, Red."

I touch my fingertips to my lips, feeling confused and overwhelmed. "I missed you, too," I respond softly. We haven't had much time alone together since I'd been rescued from Brennus' estate in Ireland. Most of my time has been spent with Reed. There is still a lot left unsaid between my soul mate and me.

"Ya still here, Brennus?" Russell asks, not looking at him, but just at me. "Why don't ya give up now? Go on and find someone else to haunt, ye creepy, dead bastard."

"I will enjoy killing ye," Brennus says intently.

"Well, that's really easy to say, when yer not really here, isn't it?" Russell replies, smiling into my eyes, like it's a private joke between us. "Next time, ya should come in person…ya get more respect that way."

"What are you doing," I whisper to Russell, feeling fear wash over me at his provoking words.

"I'm pickin' a fight I know I *can* win," he replies with a cocky grin.

Looking at Brennus' face and smiling unabashedly, Russell's crimson, Seraphim wings stretch out menacingly from his body. They remind me of the fierce strength that Casimir showed with his.

Brennus turns his eyes to mine. "Do na hide from me, *mo chroí*, and do na make me come ta ye. I do na want ta make ye beg," he says, ignoring both Reed and Russell as they growl at him.

My skin pales, feeling like my whole world is caving in on me. I feel as bad as I did in the cell in Houghton—when Brennus first tried to turn me into an undead monster like himself. No, I feel worse. I hated Brennus then. He was never my friend then. Now…it's like Freddie all over again. I let him into my heart and he's tearing it apart.

"Why are ya such a major tool, Brennus?" Russell asks, scowling as he puts me back on my feet.

"He can't help himself, Russell," Reed replies, holding his hand out for me to take. Taking it and holding it tight, I feel Russell reach out and take my other hand.

"Red," Russell says, "just tell him that things weren't working out, that he's a *really* bad boyfriend. Tell him that it's definitely not ya—it's him," Russell says, smirking at Brennus' image.

The air around us is growing colder. I can feel it and see it as my breath makes smoky plumes.

"Open up yer eyes, *mo shíorghrá*," Brennus warns me. "I'm coming closer and ye know whah I can do. When I find ye, ye had better be ready ta submit ta yer true family. Do ye need more tellin'?"

My hands are shaking, like he's really here. Both Reed and Russell tighten their grip, feeling my fear.

"Come and die, Brennus," Reed says, stepping between Brennus and me.

Brennus sizes up Reed, saying "I have one ting ta say ta ye. *Cogadh.*"

I pale at the word. It means "war."

"*Tuigim*, Brennus," Reed replies casually, saying "I understand."

"*Póg mo thóin*," Russell grins, telling Brennus to kiss his ass. "Now run along. I wanna talk to my girl."

"Carnage. I like it," Zephyr says from behind us, making me jump. "When will you get here? I grow tired of waiting." Zephyr asks as the light-brown feathers of his angel wings ruffle in the ocean breeze.

"Soon," Brennus replies coolly to Zephyr, not taking his light green eyes from mine.

"Don't do this. Please," I whisper to Brennus.

Brennus' image nears me and it feels just like he's here. "Ye're such pretty pain, Genevieve. Beautiful poison." he says as his eyes fill with the bitterest regret.

"Then let me go," I beg him as a pain in my chest begins to ache.

"Why would I do dat when I enjoy pain...all types of pain?" he asks as his eyebrow rises in question. "Ye'll be my lover and ye'll learn all about pain, I promise ye."

Russell growls. "Look at the dead guy trippin', Zee," Russell says with an undercurrent of menace in his tone "He must not know that we have more game than Mattel."

"I was going to crash your party as soon as I found you, Brennus. Consider yourself invited to ours, if it's more convenient," Reed says lightly. "Just make it soon."

"I will, *aingeal,*" Brennus replies to Reed, trying to keep his cool.

Gazing at me, the light from the moon causes Brennus' black hair to shine with a silvery glow. "Ye were right...ye did end up doing me wrong. I gave ye everyting. Ye'll spend eternity making dis up ta me," Brennus whispers in my ear with the harshness of betrayal.

Turning, Brennus' image begins walking away, back over the sea and into the frightening, black-cloud horizon. As he retreats across the frozen waves, one thing is clear to me: I believe him. Touching the onyx locket hanging from my neck with trembling fingers, I whisper, "He's coming. We have to leave."

Reed's gentle voice interrupts my panicked thoughts as he says softly, "I will never let him have you again."

The murky clouds roil back, receding and uncovering the night sky speckled with pinpoints of fire. Russell and Zephyr come nearer to us, lending me their support with their presence. Shivering in Reed's arms, I drop Russell's hand and huddle nearer to Reed, while the moon casts its light upon us.

"Still…we should go," I reply with my hands shaking.

"We expected him to find us," Reed remarks softly, stroking my wings. "You have his knife—"

"You knew he'd find me!" I frown, pulling back from him so that I can see his eyes.

"Yes," Reed answers honestly. "The only thing I regret is that he didn't really come here tonight. I would've felt him if he had, but since I'm not affected by his magic, I did not sense his shadowy presence. We put Russell on point to detect Brennus' magic.

"I felt that cold freak all the way over on the other side of the island," Russell says grimly.

"Why didn't you tell me that his knife would lead him to me?" I ask Reed, feeling like I have just attended my own funeral.

Reed's eyebrows draw together over his lovely green eyes. "I didn't want to worry you, Evie," Reed says with concern in his tone. "You have been through so much—"

"Yeah," Russell chimes in. "We'll take it from here." He points his chin towards Reed and Zephyr.

"You don't know Brennus, Russell," I warn. "He'll destroy himself to get me back."

"Good!" Russell shoots back. "It'll be his funeral—we're ready for him and his army to come. I like the way ya stood up to him, though, tellin' him ya weren't goin' with him. I thought maybe he still had ya wrapped 'round his finger—"

"I'm not his slave," I interject defensively.

"The last few weeks you were with him, ya acted like one of them," Russell counters quietly. "I was afraid they might own ya now."

"I had to act like one of them," I reply, truly beginning to shake now. The breeze is becoming gentle with only the scent of salt and tropical flowers woven within the balmy heat. "But I always wanted to come home."

"Shh," Reed hushes me in a soothing tone. "Of course you did," he agrees as he shoots Russell a look full of censure.

"You have a plan and you haven't told me about it?" I ask, before piercing each one of them with my narrowing eyes.

Zephyr's light-brown wings twitch as he replies, "We were waiting until you fully recovered from your captivity."

"When did you think that was going to happen?" I counter, annoyed that they're keeping things from me again.

Zephyr's eyebrow arches over his ice blue eye as he smiles, "I believe that you just proved that you are ready," he replies.

"Okay," I breathe, trying hard to slow the pounding of my heart. "So, what's the plan?" I ask, needing something to concentrate on other than Brennus' inevitable arrival here.

Reed's shoulders cave in around me protectively. "Zephyr, would you please go and wake Buns and Brownie? We will meet at the big house to discuss the plan with Evie." I look towards the huge, plantation-style house on the ridge above the beach.

Zephyr nods to Reed before he steps forward, placing a gentle kiss on the top of my head. "I am glad you are back," he says, treating me like a little sister.

"Me, too," I reply. Zephyr nods towards Russell before he leaves in the direction of the big house. Russell looks reluctant to leave me, knowing that I'm still scared. "I'm fine, Russell," I assure him.

"Naw, yer not," he replies in a discerning way, "but you will be after we kill Brennus."

"Brennus is already dead, Russell," I frown, thinking of Brennus' beautiful, cold skin against mine. I shiver.

"Semantics, Red. He's not dead if he's walkin' 'round," he replies.

"No, he's undead with magical powers that can crush you and me," I counter hollowly.

Reed smiles. "His magic can't hurt me, therefore, I'll take down Brennus and his fake empire," Reed says quietly.

My heart beats harder in my chest at Reed's words. I can't lose him now, when I only just got him back. "Let's run," I whisper in Reed's ear. "We can hide again," I plead.

"You haven't even heard our plan, Evie," Reed says softly, hugging me tighter to him.

"If it involves you getting close to Brennus, then I'm against it." I say as my stomach twists at the thought of Brennus using his thrall to control Reed.

"Shh, Evie," Reed says, smoothing back my hair as he listens to the pounding of my heart. "Now that your life is no longer bound to Brennus' life, I can kill him without any repercussions. The magical contract he made with you that tied you to him is the only reason he's still alive. Without it, he would already cease to be. I have had so many opportunities to kill him, but I couldn't do it without killing you, too. But, Brennus broke the contract, so he's as good as dead when I see him."

I pale. "Reed, he has an army," I argue.

"You'll never be his slave again. I promise you," Reed breathes in my ear, and I want so badly to believe him. "Let me explain our plan to you. You'll see."

Gently, Reed leads me towards our bungalow on the beach. Hesitantly, I look over at Russell who's watching me walking away with Reed. Pain is in his eyes, seeing me with Reed. I've always been Russell's love in every one of our lifetimes together...except for this one. Now, he's my best friend.

"Are you coming, Russ?" I ask him over my shoulder.

"Naw," he says, softly swinging his golf club against the sand at his feet. "I already know the plan. We can talk on the beach tomorrow when we train together."

"Okay," I agree, not knowing what else to say. I know that my love for Reed is torturing Russell, but I don't know how to fix it. If there's a solution, I don't know what it is. I watch as Russell walks away from me, back towards the other end of the island... as far away from Reed and me as possible.